MARIA J. HART

Bound By Ancient Blood

The author of this work is a staunch supporter of human rights and freedom for all oppressed peoples. If you have at any point in time found yourself on the side of the aisle that supports, enables, or turns a blind eye to humanitarian crises, up to and including genocide and ethnic cleansing, and have been comfortable staying on that side of the aisle, place this book back on the shelf. This book is not for you, and neither is this author - and she doesn't want you as a reader. If, however, you have raised your voice - in whatever capacity you may have - to oppose oppression, then please do stay and enjoy.

First edition

This book was professionally typeset on Reedsy.
Find out more at reedsy.com

To my band of thieves in ripped up jeans,
I had the time of my life fighting dragons with you.

Contents

Pronunciation Guide

Arkenvale: ARK-en-veil

Amhar*: AM-har*

Andred: AN-dread

Auberon Danodraic: OH-ber-on DAN-oh-drake

Azaeroria: az-uh-ROAR-ee-uh

Bastet: BAS-tet

Bleddyn: BLEV-in

Cuhloch: KOO-lock

Dhabiha: va-BEE-ha

Diego Vidales: dee-AY-go vee-DAL-ays

Eilidh Shaw: AY-lee SHAW

Esclados: es-CLAD-os

Himesh: hih-MAISH

Imane: ee-MON-ee

Jang Hyun-Joo: JAHNG HYUN-joo

Kianga Nabil: kee-AHN-gah na-BEEL

Lycysius: lie-SIS-ee-us

Mallory Smith: MAL-or-ree SMITH

Martín Peña: mar-TEEN PEN-yuh

Mòrag: MORE-ack

Mordrenian: more-DRAIN-ee-uhn

Nabeyha: na-BAY-ha

New Camlann: New CAM-lin

Ousmane: oos-MAH-nee

Saif Rahim: sigh-EEF ra-HEEM
Sassarinth: SASS-uh-rinth
Tenazeryth: ten-AZ-uh-rith
Valentina Peña: val-en-TEEN-uh PEN-yuh
Yazgash: YAZ-gash
Zaehora: za-HOR-uh

Content Warnings

Alcohol consumption (on page), alcoholism (discussed), anxiety, BDSM, bigotry (in a fantasy context), blood (no, really — a lot), body image issues, child abuse (past events mentioned), daddy issues, death, depression, drugging (consensual), explicit language, implied sexual assault (while discussing the past; doesn't happen on page), injuries/wound care, knives/cuts/cutting, mommy issues, morning people, murder, primal play, PTSD, self harm (ranging from digging nails into own palm, to injuries caused by intentionally foolish choices, to self sacrifice), sexual encounters (all consensual and *very* explicit; 18+ only!), social commentary, suicidal ideations (discussed; call 988 in the US, or visit 988lifeline.org for help), vegans, vehicle accident (mentioned), and war.

Author's Note

In Born Anew in Blood, Eilidh was the main POV, though Saif and Diego also had brief chapters of their own. There were no designations on who the voices of those chapters were, in part to keep the fact that Diego was writing the poetry about Eilidh a secret from you, dear reader.

In this book, a fourth POV has been added, and for clarity's sake, most of the chapters that are not from Eilidh's POV are labeled. There are a handful of exceptions, but, again, there's an element of mystery to those chapters. Figuring out the POV is part of the fun.

I hope you enjoy.

Recap of Born Anew in Blood

SPOILERS!

(But honestly, if you haven't read the first book, what the fuck are you doing here? Go read that one! I'll wait.)

Ready? Okay.

Eilidh Shaw is a loner.

At least, she was. But then the reclusive librarian was attacked by a fucking werewolf, and found herself in a new dimension surrounded by people who became her chosen family.

The first face she saw in the new dimension was Saif Rahim, a caring (and handsome) man with the power to control plants. Saif grew up in Iraq, and was living in America to get his nursing degree until his magic awakened.

He fell first, but she wasn't too far behind.

She now also has Martín and Valentina Peña, siblings with fire and water powers (respectively) from Miami whose father had been the first of many people to ostracize them for what - and who - they were. But despite the cruelty of the world, they are two of the fiercest and most loving people Eilidh has ever met.

Speaking of fierce, there's also Jang Hyun-Joo. She can turn invisible and creep up behind you silently to slip a knife in your back — or cut your bonds if you find yourself as a sacrifice to a fairy tale monster. She can also create force fields, and won't hesitate to whip them like saw blades if the need arises.

Hyun-Joo's platonic other half is a murderous six-foot-nine vampire who seemed to hate Eilidh from her first day at Arkenvale Castle. It turned out, though, that Diego Vidales pushed her away because he didn't want to repeat past mistakes — and because Eilidh already had Saif by the time Diego admitted his feelings to himself.

She was happy, and that was enough for him.

That is, until Saif poisoned Eilidh with wolfsbane, and was only narrowly thwarted in his attempt to kidnap her, though no one knows why. It could have been to get revenge on Diego, who got the woman Saif had loved a decade ago killed.

Or maybe, it had something to do with King Auberon, who Saif said would be removed from the throne — whatever *that* means. He's got immense power and a short temper according to Diego, but Eilidh has only ever seen him be kind and generous.

Oh, and he's Eilidh's father.

Eilidh trained under Diego's tutelage for five months to become a warrior and hone her newfound werewolf powers, and when her training was complete, she, Diego, and Valentina managed to bring down the monster that ruined her life.

Except . . . *had* he ruined her life?

Despite the last-minute realization that Bleddyn had inadvertently given her a family and the father she had always wanted, Eilidh killed him, and got her justice.

That *is* justice — right?

She didn't have much time to consider whether it was or not. As soon as she and Diego traveled back through the portal to the dimension of Tenazeryth, a rebel leader captured them. But, since the Universe has such a twisted sense of humor, that leader just so happens to be the woman that Diego and Saif had loved and lost all those years ago.

And, it turns out, that woman has quite the habit of rising from the grave. Because she's also Eilidh's dead best friend.

And now, for the rest of the story . . .

BOUND BY ANCIENT BLOOD

One Month Before Born Anew in Blood (Bastet)

"What do you mean, you're leaving?" Lycysius clips one hoof against the floor in agitation.

Bleddyn looks back at the centaur evenly, his glowing eyes unblinking. *Exactly that.*

Azaeroria flicks her tail back and forth, examining her claws with a bored expression.

"You want to walk away from us now, when we're so close? I hadn't pegged you for a coward." Yazgash minces no words, but then, she never does.

There is something that I must attend to. Bleddyn's harsh telepathic voice scrapes at the inside of my skull, and I suppress a grimace.

It's Mòrag's turn to express her annoyance. "You're turning tail like a frightened house cat."

I'll try not to take that personally. I glance at her sideways, but the wulver is too busy glaring at the werewolf to notice.

The succubus and I have done our part. We've kept Auberon and his Order busy for a year now. Surely you can complete this last phase without us?

I look toward the wall ahead of me, wondering, not for the first time, why Bleddyn refers to his mate as "the succubus." She doesn't seem to mind, but it prickles me on her behalf all the same. Perhaps it's an inside joke, or maybe it's because they're a product of another time. Bleddyn and Azaeroria have been together for at least a century, if the rumors are true. I've never actually asked.

I realize there has been a lull in the conversation, and I look to my left at Zaehora, who is uncharacteristically silent. Her black eyes are focused on the other succubus, her mouth twisted in a disapproving frown. They had been childhood rivals, some thousand years ago.

Even I can't hold a grudge that long. Probably. I guess I'll never know.

"Zaehora," I prompt, and her eyes flick to me. "Have you no opinion on this?"

Zaehora has never *not* had an opinion on something.

She takes a deep breath and sighs, slumping back in her chair. "I'm loathe to admit it, but he's right," she finally says.

I cock a brow at her.

"We've basically won already. What does it matter what they do now?" She gestures dismissively across the bench at them.

I tap my foot, contemplating. While I appreciate her confidence, I haven't made it this far by being cocky.

Being cocky is what nearly got me killed — twice.

"It matters because the mission isn't complete," Mòrag snaps beside me.

Bleddyn sighs through his nose, clearly done with this conversation.

I clear my throat, and the retort dies on Zaehora's tongue. "Bleddyn," I say firmly. "Your work with this Council has been critical in our success thus far. I can't force you to stay with us and see it through to the end, but I ask you, as a friend, why are you giving up now, when we're so close to bringing Auberon down? You agreed to help us because you wanted revenge. What could possibly be more important to you than this?"

The werewolf's ears flatten, and he glances at Azaeroria. He must be asking her a question the rest of us aren't privy to, because she shakes her head.

I'm sorry, Bastet, Bleddyn says. *I will not tell you. But just know that I do hope to rejoin you in the future, should my plan come to fruition.*

Mòrag growls and opens her mouth, but I hold out a palm, and the other Council members settle themselves.

"Then I suppose we must part ways." I rise, and he and Azaeroria do the same. "Good luck with whatever it is you're planning to do. I hope we meet again."

As do I, Bastet. As do I. The two turn and exit the courtroom without another word.

I sit down once more, and the Council waits for me to speak. I drum my fingers against the bench for a moment, deep in contemplation.

Zaehora finally breaks the silence. "So. Next order of business. Who are we sending to New Camlann?"

I lean back in my chair and cross my arms. "Well, Himesh and Ousmane said that Balin has a weakness for redheads."

A pair of emerald green eyes flash through my mind, and I shake them away. *I guess Balin and I have something in common,* I think ruefully.

"And we'll need someone clever. Really clever. But Balin's a prick. She'll need to have . . . tough skin."

No one else speaks for a moment, but then Zaehora claps her hands together and cackles. "Oh, she's perfect."

Lycysius whickers in annoyance. "Surely you don't mean . . ."

"She'll snap someone's neck on the first day and ruin everything," Yazgash remarks.

Her concern is not unfounded. That woman is as wild as her name suggests.

"It's not like we're sending her to flounder alone. She'll be with

Liz. She'll balance her out." I press a button under the bench, and a centaur enters the room.

"Rhenilla, could you please do me a favor?"

She salutes. "Of course, Bastet. What do you need?"

I prop my elbows on the bench and steeple my fingers in front of me.

"We need Tempest."

~ Waning Crescent ~

A Ghost From the Past

I wake up in a cell.

It's not the one in the greenhouse at Arkenvale, but rather a dark, damp, stone cell. The only light comes from a small window, maybe a foot wide, at least six feet above me.

I groan and roll over, my eyes still fluttering open slowly.

Saif is sitting on the floor, wearing a rumpled cream tunic over black slacks and black loafers, staring at me through the thick bars. He looks like he hasn't slept in days.

I push myself up and crawl toward him. "Saif, thank god, get me out of —" But then my memories hit me all at once, and my blood freezes.

This man is no longer mine.

I throw myself back and hiss through my teeth.

He grimaces, his eyes glistening as if he's in pain.

I stand in fury and stalk to the bars as he stands and dusts the dirt off his pants. I don't bother to swipe at the dirt all over myself.

"Where the hell am I?" I growl.

"Tal Basta," he says calmly, adjusting his glasses.

"And where the fuck is that?" I bite through my teeth.

"All in time, my love." He turns away from me, and I look around frantically. All I can see are sandy stone walls to my sides, and another row of cells across from me. They're all empty.

"Where is Diego?" I hiss, trying to keep the desperation out of my voice, but it creeps in, nonetheless.

He freezes and turns halfway around, clenching his jaw. "Don't worry about him."

If I could get to him through the bars, I would strangle him with my bare hands. "Don't walk away from me!" I yell.

He ignores me, and walks down a hallway to the right, out of my view.

I curse and throw myself against the bars, but they don't budge. I try pulling on them, pushing them, lifting them up out of the ground, and yanking them down from the ceiling.

Nothing works.

I scream and punch one of the stone walls, scraping my knuckles. I put my fist to my mouth and try to take deep breaths. Freaking out isn't going to save Diego, wherever he is. Unless he's already . . .

No, I won't let myself even consider that.

After a few minutes, my knuckles have healed themselves. I look around the cell walls for any spot that may be weak, or that I can dig into. Nails or claws, I don't care. I have got to get out of here.

There's nothing. The absence of my dagger on my thigh is like a missing limb.

I back up against the bars of the cell, then take a running jump at the tiny window high up in the wall. All I can see is midday sun shining on a rolling field of dead grass. I pull on these bars as well, even though I'd never fit through the window, but they don't budge anyway.

I circle the cell like a feral animal for what feels like an eternity. Finally, I hear footsteps approaching. Thinking it's Saif, I press myself against the stone wall, prepared to grab him through the bars as soon as I see him. A figure walks into my view, and I snatch at them as fast as I can.

They're faster.

They grab my wrist and pull me hard against the bars. My head slams into the metal, and then they shove me back onto the ground. I hold my head and look up, wincing.

My dead best friend stares back at me coldly.

Her frigid eyes are vibrant brown, shot through with streaks of honey and apricot. I've had the pattern of her eyes memorized since I was five.

She used to wear a small stud in her nose, but now it's a gold ring. Her left brow is pierced too now, and small gold spikes protrude through the skin above and below it. Her rich mahogany skin is flawless.

She's wearing a simple gold tunic over tight black pants and knee-high black leather boots. Her crochet braids are still adorned with various gold beads and coils.

She's, well, a goddess.

I choke out a sob. "Kianga."

Her expression tightens even further. "What the hell are you doing here, Lee?"

I wince; the old nickname that only she could get away with calling me stings like an old scar being ripped open. "I have no idea; I woke up here."

"No. What are you doing *here*?" She gestures wide. "In this nightmare fucking fairy-tale land?"

"I." My mouth works silently as I try to come up with a succinct answer. "I'm a werewolf," I say, shrugging helplessly.

Her mouth is a thin line. "Yeah, I gathered that."

My eyes sting, but I'm afraid if I blink, she'll disappear. "What are *you* doing here, posing as an Egyptian goddess?"

She doesn't smile. I had always been able to make her smile so easily.

"Trying to kill your father."

My blood turns to ice.

She pulls a key from between her breasts. As she swings the door open, her hand moves toward me, just an inch, before it curls into a fist, and she brings it to her side. "Follow me."

I climb to my feet and trudge behind her with leaden steps, between two rows of cells, up stone stairs. I gasp when she opens the door at the top.

"Are we in a fucking *pyramid?*"

Civilization

Kianga simply makes an affirmative noise and keeps walking. I gaze around in awe as I follow.

It's like I've stepped into an alternate dimension - or rather, *another* alternate dimension - where Ancient Egypt has merged with a sci-fi movie.

There are three floors above us; sunshine radiates into the glass pyramid, illuminating the entire space. Sleek escalators zig-zag between the floors, which are ringed with waist-high glass panels topped with glimmering gold. Glass bridges arch between the upper floors, saving people from having to walk all the way around like we do at Arkenvale.

Throngs of people walk between the rooms around us, separated by walls made of yet more marble, as well as glass with intricate designs sand-blasted into it.

Something rubs against my calf and I jump. Wide yellow eyes meet mine when I look down; the tabby's ears lay back flat, and it emits a low growl as it puffs up as big as it can.

I step away from the cat, strangely wounded. "What's your problem?" *Cats usually love me.*

It turns and bolts into the crowd. It takes me several seconds to realize that the crowd isn't just made of people, but also . . . creatures.

Centaurs, minotaurs, wulvers, and various otherworldly beings that can only be Fae walk around and mingle with one another. Some have shimmery skin and jagged teeth, others look like dryads, their skin blending seamlessly with bark and leaves. All the Fae have glittering black eyes which narrow when they meet mine, but that's where the similarities end. Wings that evoke both bats and butterflies, curling horns, antler racks large and small, and bodies of all shapes and sizes mill about.

A lavender lizard the size of an elephant sits in a corner watching me, and after I blink hard and rub my eyes, I realize that it's a wyvern. I stop in my tracks.

Kianga doesn't wait for me. "Staring is rude. Let's go, *habibti*," she snips.

I wince at the sarcastic term of endearment, but follow her as my eyes continue to rove through the crowd. "What . . . how?" I'm dumbstruck. "Have you tamed all these Mongrels?"

I feel the burning pain in my cheek before I even register what happened. I stumble back and rub the side of my face, staring at Kianga, open-mouthed. Hot tears spring to my eyes, though not as a result of the physical pain.

She lowers the hand she had struck me with and curls it into a fist at her side. "Don't *ever* say that word again. And they didn't need to be *tamed*. They're as sentient and civilized as you and I." She looks me up and down once, one corner of her mouth twisted in disgust. "Or more." She turns and prowls away from me. I follow her, trembling.

A mural on one wall catches my eye, and my breath catches as I do a double-take. The outline of a black cat sitting on a silver crescent moon stares back at me; the interior of the moon is full of twisting Celtic knots. The very center of the crescent is a green circle, like an emerald. My hand moves involuntarily to the empty space where my pendant had once hung. I fight back more tears and continue following Kianga.

Numerous creatures turn to stare at us as she leads me through the crowd. At first I think they're watching her, but then I realize almost all of them are glaring at me. I wrap my arms around myself. "Why are they all looking at me?"

"You're the daughter of the man who wants to eradicate them. They're wondering why we let you live."

That sends a brief chill through me, but anger burns it away in a flash. "That's not what he wants," I hiss between my teeth.

Kianga stops and looks up at the pointed ceiling high above, her shoulders rising as she inhales deeply. She turns to look at me as she exhales. "You have *no idea* who he really is."

"Then enlighten me!" I snap. "And while you're at it, how about telling me how the fuck you're *alive*? Your parents and I *buried* you, Kianga!"

She glances around furtively and motions for me to quiet down. I do, but only a fraction. "They got divorced because they couldn't look at each other without seeing you! I've spent almost as much time with your headstone as I did with *you*!" I hiss the last few words at her.

Her eyes and voice are icy. "It's a long story."

I scoff. "What, you don't have time for me?"

"No, I actually don't," she snaps back. "You aren't supposed to be here. It wasn't supposed to be *you*."

She might as well have slapped me again. I rake my hands through my hair, then clutch at my temples, taking deep breaths as I squeeze my eyes shut. If she won't talk about herself, then maybe I can get something else out of her.

"Where is Diego?" I rasp at the floor.

She bounces twice on the balls of her feet, like she's preparing to run. *Or kick me.*

"Why were you alone with him?" She asks, instead of answering me. "We watched the others come through the portal and head back to Arkenvale at least twenty minutes before you two showed up. He said —" She clamps her mouth shut and narrows her eyes.

"What did he say?" I can't stop my voice from shaking.

She clicks her tongue. "He said he loves you. But I know you're smart enough not to fall for a monster, so what's the real story?"

I stare at her for three long heartbeats. *"He's* not the monster," I whisper.

Her expression closes off completely. "Oh. I see." She turns to walk away, but I grab her arm.

"Goddammit, at least tell me he's alive!" My voice breaks, and tears burn my eyes.

She doesn't turn back to face me. "He's alive," she finally bites out, then rips her arm from my grasp and walks on.

I exhale shakily and follow.

Trial

Finally, we make it to a pair of large frosted glass doors. She opens one and gestures for me to go first. I glare at her, and walk through into the massive courtroom. I take in my new surroundings with wide eyes.

Sunlight streams in through the glass of the slanted wall straight ahead of us, bright and cheery, as if the world isn't falling down around me.

Rows and rows of wooden benches fill most of the room, and Kianga leads me down the aisle between them. In front of us, two podiums sit in front of a high bench. Four creatures are behind the bench, along with one empty chair in the center of them. From across the room, they're backlit, casting them into ominous shadows. But as we approach, I see them clearly, and my pulse quickens.

Two of the creatures I've only seen as illustrations in the Guide my father had given me, but the other two, I've already gotten up close and personal with.

The creature on my far left is an ogre, judging by her green skin, muscular build, and the long tusks protruding from her bottom jaw. Thick braids frame her face and fall past her chest; her hair appears black at first, but as she moves her head, strands of it appear blue in the sunlight. The wulver that had nearly choked me to death sits between the ogre and the empty chair, glaring daggers at me, and I rub my neck faintly as I look away.

On the other side of the empty chair sits a shirtless white man with flowing, cinnamon-colored hair. He stretches as I look at him, and I see that the lower half of his abdomen is covered in fur the color of cocoa. A satyr maybe, though he seems tall. I can't see his legs to tell for sure.

The fifth seat, all the way to my right, is occupied by a strikingly gorgeous woman with cinnabar skin. Two small horns poke through a silky black bob, and her black irises gleam like fresh ink. Leathery bat wings are tucked tightly against her back, the taloned tips poking up above her head, glittering in the sunlight.

My heart hammers at the sight of her — probably because the last of her kind I had seen up close had tied me to a freezing stone slab and prepared to sacrifice me to a monster. The succubus peers back at me and licks her matte black lips hungrily. I shiver and quickly avert my gaze back to Kianga.

She points to the podium on my right, then walks up behind the bench and makes a shooing gesture at something in her seat. As she sits, a fuzzy orange cat jumps onto the bench, flits its tail in the wulver's face, and curls up on Kianga's other side.

My stomach twists. This woman sitting in front of me is a complete stranger. My lip quivers as I stare up at the person who had been my other half, a lifetime ago.

The door behind me opens again, and I turn to see Saif striding down the aisle toward me. He doesn't look at me; his eyes are fixed straight ahead.

My lip curls. *Coward.* I take a step toward him when he's a few yards away, fully intending on strangling him, or ripping him to shreds, but he simply tosses seeds at my feet. Vines shoot up , wrap around my wrist and ankles, and bind me to the podium.

"No!" I yank on them uselessly, and glare at him as he comes to stand on my right. He looks at Kianga expectantly, his hands clasped calmly behind his back.

"Just relax, my love." It takes me a moment to realize that Saif had murmured this between his lips, which are parted only a few centimeters. He knew I'd be able to hear him, and that the creatures on the bench wouldn't.

Relax? I hang my head so they can't see my mouth. "You don't get to call me that anymore," I hiss at the podium.

The corners of his eyes tighten, and he takes a shaky breath, as if filling his lungs with oxygen is painful. "We'll see," he whispers.

I open my mouth to say more, unconcerned now with who can and can't hear us, but Kianga's ringing voice cuts me off.

"Bring him in!" As she scratches the cat under its chin, the frosted glass doors open. Two ogres enter the room carrying a haggard Diego between them. My heart stops beating entirely at the sight of him.

Thick chains are wrapped around his ankles and wrists, which are pulled tight behind his back. A steel muzzle covers his mouth. His arms are covered with bruises and cuts in various stages of healing. His filthy black jeans are ripped in more places than they had been previously, and his blue muscle shirt is caked in dirt and dust. He grunts in pain as the ogres drop him unceremoniously to the ground next to the left podium, and exit once more.

"Diego?" My voice crackles with panic.

He turns his dull eyes to me, and, despite the dire situation we have found ourselves in, he smiles faintly. *"Lobita,"* he rasps, and I take a ragged breath.

He's in desperate need of blood.

I redouble my efforts to pull free from Saif's vines, but to no avail. "What did they do to you? Get up, we have to get home and —"

Saif grabs my chin and turns my head back toward him sharply.

His warm eyes are wide with a panic that nearly matches my own. "Eilidh don't—"

He doesn't get the chance to say anything more before I bite down on his pointer finger as hard as I can. He yelps and rips his hand free, staring at me in shock as he clutches it to his chest.

"Touch me again, and see how many fingers you come away with," I hiss between bared teeth.

He has no response.

Diego barks a weak laugh. He's grinning at me languidly from the floor when I look back at him. "Vengeful harpy."

I smile tightly back at him.

The wulver makes a disapproving noise from the bench. "Perhaps we've muzzled the wrong one."

You're goddamn right you did.

A beat passes, and my brain finally processes who just spoke. I look up at the wulver slowly, my eyes widening in horror. "It talks," I breathe to no one in particular.

The wulver crosses its arms and glares at me vehemently. "It does indeed, you insolent *pup*," it - she? - spits at me in her thick Highland accent.

My blood runs cold. The Mongrel is *talking*. My father had said they were hardly capable of communicating with one another, but this wulver is speaking just as well as I am. Better, in fact, in this moment.

"That's enough." Kianga's dangerous growl snaps the room to attention. Saif, Diego, and I turn to her in sync. "Eilidh, Saif just threw his life away for you, and he's here to argue your case before this Council. I suggest you play nice with him."

I squint at her, my mind still reeling from the wulver reprimanding me. "What case? Am I on trial or something?"

She makes a bored gesture at Diego. "Yes, you both are."

I snort. "For what? Getting kidnapped and thrown in a fucking cell? Guilty as charged!" *This is madness.*

"For the murder of Bleddyn, a friend of this Council."

If the vines weren't holding me against the podium, I would have collapsed to the floor just like Diego. "What?" I rasp.

She doesn't repeat herself.

A velvety voice breaks the silence, and I turn to the succubus, whose eyes are twinkling with more than a hint of amusement. "You and your delectable little friend are here because we have reason - given your actions, and *your* lineage - to believe that you are enemies of this Council. That you are working with King Auberon to eradicate The Fabled. Why should you go unpunished?"

My head spins, but I'm saved from having to find a reply. Saif takes a deep breath and lays a hand on the small of my back, where I can't reach him with my teeth. My skin crawls through my shirt and I try to pull away, but he twists his fingers into the fabric.

I clench my jaw.

Diego lets out a low growl from the floor.

"Council, I am here as a witness for these two, who were lied to, deceived, and ultimately coerced into the murder of Bleddyn. It is unfortunate that a Shifter has met his end, but let me assure you all that the blame should not be laid at their feet, but rather King Auberon's, who has manipulated them into fulfilling his evils machinations."

I glance at him from the corner of my eye. *You could have been a lawyer* and *a nurse*, I think, before I remember that I hate him.

The Council members look at one another briefly. "Explain," says the man to Kianga's left. Her eyes are boring into me, as are the cat's. I swallow hard.

Saif recounts my story, from the night I was attacked, through my months of training. How my father put Diego in charge of me, and how he always had stressed that Bleddyn was an irredeemable monster. How he had to die for the good of everyone, not just me.

I do nothing but stare at the podium and flick my gaze occasionally to Diego, who is breathing more heavily by the minute.

Saif ends his tale by recounting how he had made me drink the wolfsbane in order to incapacitate me and have me brought here, but that he was thwarted by the Order.

I can keep silent no longer. "You got Martín killed." I inject as much venom into the words as I can.

He winces, and I could almost believe that there is real pain and regret in his voice, if I didn't know better. "No one was supposed to get hurt."

"No one except me, you mean."

He flinches, but says nothing. I don't bother saying that Martín is going to be fine. Let him sit with that guilt. I hope it eats him alive.

The ogre speaks, her voice grinding through the room like a blade being dragged through gravel. "What say you, daughter of the Mad King? Do you have any regret for what you have done?"

"My father isn't mad," I spit back. "This Council is, if you all think I regret the fact that the monster that ruined my life is dead."

The Council members say nothing aloud, but their pinched expressions say plenty.

"She didn't kill Bleddyn." Diego suddenly rasps form the floor. "I did. It was *my* blade that slew him, so let her go."

I snap my gaze to him in horror. Kianga would never actually hurt me, but she had already almost killed him once, back in that clearing. I am not about to let him fight my battle for me *again*.

"Diego just wounded Bleddyn." I raise my chin at the Council. "*I* dealt the killing blow." Saif has finally removed his hand from my back, but now he's got his fingertips pushed to his temple, as if I'm giving him a migraine.

Good.

Kianga's eyes narrow. "Tell me the truth. Did you kill Bleddyn?"

I set my jaw. "Yes."

"Do you regret it?"

I swallow. "No."

The wulver sucks in a scandalized breath.

I ignore her. "Diego is just lying to protect me. So let him go, and you can do whatever you want with me."

I can feel Diego's eyes on me, and I know he's thinking of what I had said after the battle. *I wasn't even sure I wanted to kill him.* Yet here I am, declaring it proudly.

The ogre twists her mouth in distaste. "I think we have our deci—"

"Yazgash," Kianga warns sharply. The ogre clamps her mouth shut. Kianga's glacial gaze sweeps to Diego, then back to me.

"So you just wanted revenge?" Her tone is hard as diamonds, but though no one else can probably tell, I hear dubiousness as well. "Wanted to dole out some vigilante justice?"

I huff air through my nose. "I learned it from the best."

Her eyes flash dangerously before she turns to the cat to scratch behind its ears.

Saif glances between the two of us with a bewildered expression. "If I may —" But she cuts him off.

"You may not." As she stands, the cat jumps onto her shoulder and perches there like a fuzzy orange owl. "Keep an eye on them while we confer. Yell if either of them makes a move." The rest of the Council members stand as one, follow her down the steps, and over to a door on the left wall that I hadn't noticed previously.

As they walk into the room, I see that the shirtless man is a centaur, not a satyr, and that the succubus has a long, thin tail that ends in a triangular point. She uses it to shut the door behind her, but not

before giving me a quick wink.
 I shiver.

Impossible

As soon as the door closes behind the Council, Saif rounds on me. "I know you don't have any sense of self-preservation, but are you *trying* to get yourself killed?" He hisses.

I roll my eyes. "She's not going to kill me."

He gapes at me like I've lost my mind. "Eilidh, you have no idea what Imane is like. She's been through so much since *he* left her to die in the werecat's cave." He makes a dismissive gesture at Diego, and I yank sharply at the vines, wishing desperately that I could slap him.

"And now she's the leader of this entire rebellion. I've heard from others here that she's not known for her leniency. She could have you executed in a thousand different ways if she wanted to."

By the time he's done with his little monologue, a vicious smile has spread across my face. *He has no idea.*

He glares at me, fuming. "*What* is so funny?"

The entire situation is so convoluted and unbelievable even with the full picture, and he's trying to finish the puzzle with only half the pieces.

"*You're* the one who doesn't know her." I giggle madly. Maybe I *have* lost my mind. "Imane is her *middle* name."

I hadn't thought much of it; why would I? It's a pretty common name, after all. I had thought it was just a cruel irony that the woman

Diego and Saif had loved and lost had a name in common with the woman I was only able to hold in my memories. A fun little chuckle the Universe was having at my expense, just like it always does.

"I don't know why she chose to go by it when she came to Tenazeryth. Maybe it made it easier to leave us all behind. But *that* is Kianga Nabil."

Saif's mouth hangs open for several long moments as he processes my words, then he shakes his head, blinking rapidly. "No, that's impossible."

I laugh derisively, glancing around at the pyramid's walls. "All of this shit is impossible, *habibi*," I sneer, and he stills. "I'm a librarian who got turned into a werewolf. Those creatures in that room are all supposed to be nightmares and fairy tales. You control *plants*, for fuck's sake. Take 'impossible' out of your goddamn vocabulary."

He's silent for a long, tense moment as I glare up at him. "What . . . did you call me?" He finally asks quietly.

I raise an eyebrow at him, uncomprehending at first, but then I realize what he means. *Oh.*

He stares at me like he's never seen me before. I see the realization dawn in his eyes. "Immigrated from Egypt." He runs his hands through his hair, and my stomach twists. "Six months, Eilidh," he says tightly.

I frown. "What *about* six months?"

He shakes his head slowly. "We've known each other for six. Months. We've shared a bed for most of that. And you never *once* mentioned that you know Arabic."

I blink rapidly, trying desperately to quell the spark in my center at his mention of us sharing a bed. *He poisoned you, remember?*

"I *don't* know Arabic," I say petulantly. "I just know a few random words." I shift uncomfortably. "Or how to tell you to clean your room and do your homework."

"It still would have been nice to know. To *hear* it. I could have taught you more." His voice wavers, and it takes me several seconds to quash the guilt that threatens to freeze me in place.

"I haven't . . ." I trail off, and cast my gaze to the ground. "I haven't used it since I lost her."

Until Saif, hearing Arabic had always reminded me of weekends spent at her house - *my* house, eventually - and filled my mind with her father's boisterous cries at whatever soccer game he was watching, or her mother's singing while she prepared the *koshari* that she made every Saturday night, because it was my favorite. I lick my lips, tasting the *baharat* spice blend as if I were sitting at their dining room table.

I can even hear Kianga herself speaking in rapid Arabic with her parents for the first few years after we met, though she had steadily lost her control of it, like trying to hold a wave as it rushes back out to the ocean; it had slipped away from her when she was no longer surrounded by it.

The sight of her, here, *alive*, has shaken something loose within me. Doors that had long been locked and forgotten in the darkest recesses of my mind are being forcibly blown open with every passing moment.

The memory of her father sitting down heavily on the couch one night, two years after he had buried his daughter, and explaining that he would be moving out, but that I was welcome to visit him anytime. "My door is always open to you, *habibti.*"

My mind had locked a piece of me behind a door after that. *Click.*

I feel her mother holding me tightly, her soft hijab pressing against my frizzy hair as she hugged me goodbye the last time I left her house, when I got my own apartment. "I'll see you next Saturday, *Qamar.*" Her voice had wavered, and I had just nodded silently.

I had made an excuse that weekend, and for many weekends after that. Eventually, she stopped asking.

Click. Another piece preserved in a forgotten corner of my mind.

Saif's sharp voice yanks me from my reverie. "So what *do* you know? How much have you had to *pretend*?"

I blink for a moment, still wrapped in my shroud of nostalgic grief, before I process his words. Anger flares, replacing the grief in a flash. "I'm sorry, are you *angry* with me?" I ask indignantly.

He throws his hands in the air. "Of *course* I'm angry with you!"

I sputter, furious. "You don't get to be angry with me after you *poisoned* me!"

His voice rises sharply. "This has nothing to do with that!"

I match his volume. "It has *everything* to do with that!"

He opens his mouth, but Diego suddenly makes a disgusted noise. I start and turn toward him. He's more haggard than ever, his head hanging; his voice is weak and strangled when he speaks.

"Can you two please . . . finish this lover's quarrel . . . *after* they kill me?" He finishes in a whisper, swaying on his knees, as though he's going to topple over at any moment.

I shake myself, fighting the flush that is threatening to color my cheeks. "I - this isn't - how long do you have?" I can't keep the tremble out of my voice.

He doesn't even look at me, he just shakes his head faintly, his limp hair swinging.

Fear clutches me, and I turn back to Saif, who is still glaring at me, his arms now crossed. "Let me go. He needs blood."

His mouth twists as he glances around me to Diego's folded form. "I can't," he says tightly, eyeing the closed door the Council had gone through.

I pull at the vines uselessly and hiss through my teeth. "Goddammit, will you put aside your feud for one minute? You hated him because you thought he got Imane killed, right? But here she is, perfectly fine, undead twice over, so let me go so I can fucking help him."

Saif's anger dims as I speak, and he looks at me hesitantly for several moments, searching my gaze, though for what, I don't know.

I grind my teeth. *We don't have fucking time for this.* "Please," I whisper beseechingly.

He must have found what he was looking for; he lets out a mirthless chuckle as he waves his hand, shaking his head at the glass wall ahead of us.

By the time the vines reach the floor, I've crashed to my knees at Diego's side.

I cup his cheek awkwardly around the muzzle and tilt his face gently toward me. I brush my fingers through his hair, pushing it out of his eyes. I've never seen their color this muted. It sends a needle of fear into my heart.

"Hey, hey," I whisper, running my thumb over his sharp cheekbone through the steel. "Stay with me, Diego. Here." I stick my fingers through muzzle, trying to get his fangs to pop out so I can at least drip blood down his throat.

Finally, his eyes focus on me for a moment. "Eilidh." His voice is nothing more than a reedy whisper.

I don't waste time. "Fangs."

He complies with my command immediately. His razor-sharp fangs elongate from his gums, and I scrape three fingers against them, gritting my teeth through the pain.

I tilt his head back as beads of blood drip from my fingers. As soon as the first drops hit his tongue, his pupils dilate, and then he bites down and begins sucking my fingers like they're straws.

I wince, gasping quietly. His bite hurts much more against the bones of my fingers than it did in the fleshy areas he sank his fangs into that night behind the cabin. My heart races at the memory.

Soon though, his venom rushes up through my fingertips and into my arm. I close my eyes and take a shaky breath as the pleasure from his venom fogs my brain. I lean into him until my forehead rests on his shoulder.

When he stops, I lift my eyes to his dizzily. They're somewhat brighter, though I can tell he still hasn't had enough.

"Don't stop," I say huskily, my eyes half-lidded.

But he shakes his head gently, then leans into my touch on his cheek. "That's enough for now."

I nod faintly and sit back hard, the room swirling slightly around me. I turn back to Saif, but instead of anger or disgust like I had expected to see, he just looks sad.

I extinguish the spark of pain his expression elicits deep within me as I stand shakily, and walk back to the podium. He waves a hand without looking at me, and the vines wrap around me once more.

Just as they finish tightening, the door opens back up and the Council re-enters the room.

"Release her, Saif." Kianga commands once they're all seated.

He does.

I blink hazily up at the Council. Kianga isn't looking at me at all, but at the wall behind me, her mouth in a hard line. The succubus, however, leans forward, chin propped in her hand, gazing at me with a devious grin on her perfectly symmetrical face. When our eyes meet, she winks at me again. My heart skips a beat, and I quickly avert my gaze.

"Enter!" Kianga barks loudly. The ogres who had brought Diego come back through the doors. "Remove him." They approach us, and I scramble between them and Diego.

"No!" I look at Kianga desperately. "Where are you taking him?"

She closes her eyes for a moment, gathering patience. "Relax. He's just going back to his cell."

I stiffen. "Why? I thought we were being released."

"*You* are being released. *He* is going back in a cell. Just because we believe he's been manipulated by Auberon doesn't mean he isn't dangerous."

The venom is fading from my mind, and my anger is rising just as quickly. I shake my head at her fiercely. "I'm not going anywhere without him. If you don't trust him, why do you trust me? Throw me in the cell with him."

Kianga looks at me coolly for a moment. She doesn't answer my question. "Saif, if you please," she says finally.

He sighs, and I tense my muscles to fight him, but he simply sends his vines toward me again, and they twist around my ankles and wrists.

"No!" I yelp, but it's no use. As I'm dragged across the floor, the ogres grab Diego and haul him up and out of the room. I struggle, but the vines just get tighter, then haul me to my feet.

Saif pulls me backward into him, and as I thrash, he hisses into my ear. "If you don't cooperate, they're going to hurt him."

I stop moving instantly, though I can't stop trembling. The feeling of his hard chest against my back used to provide me with such comfort.

Now it just makes my skin crawl.

The Council members rise and file out of the room one by one, save for Kianga, who waits for the room to empty before she jerks her head toward the side door. Saif pushes me gently forward, and I follow her, my hands still bound.

Revelations

We enter the room, at the center of which sits a large rectangular table with a marble top and shiny golden legs. It and the six chairs around it are the only furnishings in the room. Dark sconces line three of the walls; the sun blazes through the glass wall to our right. Though, unlike the glass towers of Arkenvale, this room is pleasantly cool.

The orange cat glares at me from its spot on the tabletop.

Saif leads me to one of the luxurious chairs, and I sit down heavily as Kianga closes and locks the door behind us. "Okay," she says, and Saif releases the vines around my wrists.

I briefly consider throttling him, but decide it's not worth it if it puts Diego in danger. I glare at him instead as he takes the seat opposite me. Kianga sits at the head of the table between us, then props her head in her hands and digs her nails into her scalp.

She had always picked at her skin when she was stressed. My heart twists at the sight. "Kianga —"

"No," she says to the table. I clamp my mouth shut. After a pause, she finally meets my eyes. "That's not who I am anymore."

Saif shakes his head faintly, as if he hadn't truly believed me until now.

Tears well up in my eyes instantly. "What happened to you?" My voice breaks. "How are you here? What the hell is going *on?*"

She takes a long breath. "I don't even know where to start," she says quietly.

My lip trembles. "How did you survive the crash?"

"I almost didn't," she says finally. "It was storming so hard on the way back from the store. It was dark, and I was going way too fast. Stupid. But I just wanted to get home." Our eyes meet for an instant, but then she looks back down at the table.

"I came around a bend and there were two people walking across the road. I hit the woman, then a ditch, and rolled. Then . . . the tree stopped me."

I shudder, remembering the photos of the charred remains of her tiny two-door toaster of a car obliterated against a shattered trunk.

"I crawled out of the wreck, and then blacked out for a minute. When I came to, the man had put the body in the driver's seat, and set the car on fire to cover everything up. I took my pendant off and tossed it, hoping it would let someone know I had made it. To look for me. I blacked out again just as he grabbed me."

My stomach churns.

"The next thing I knew, I was in a cave. It was about a week later, after my Stasis." I think back on my own Stasis; it had taken two weeks for all my mundane human cells to transform into Shifter ones.

I had dreamt of her the entire time.

"He had brought me to Tenazeryth, and bitten me, but I didn't know that yet. The next day when he left, I ran. I don't think he thought I could at that point. I was still in fairly bad shape; it was one hell of a head injury. But I wasn't waiting around to see what he was going to do to me for killing his partner. I stumbled through the woods for hours, and then . . ." She trails off, glancing to Saif.

His voice is tight. "And then Diego and I found you."

Her eyes fill with painful memories. I reach for her hand slowly, and my heart skips a beat when our fingers touch. I had half expected my hand to pass through her, but no. She's solid, and corporeal, and *real*.

I choke back tears and grip her hand tightly. "Kianga, you're alive," I whisper. I have to speak the words aloud to believe them.

She stares at our intertwined fingers silently for a beat. "I'm alive," she murmurs, then her steely eyes lifts to meet my teary ones. "Despite that monster."

I sniff. "But you must have beat him, right? When you went back?"

She pulls her hand from mine and puts it in her lap. A pang echoes through my chest at the loss of it.

"I'm not talking about the werecat," she growls, and my blood runs cold.

I do *not* want to ask the next question, but I have to know. "What happened when you and Diego went back there?" I whisper.

Her eyes harden and she clenches her jaw so hard I fear she may break a tooth. Saif opens his mouth, but she silences him with a fierce look. He casts his eyes downward, his lips pressed tightly together.

"I had no clue what I was in for, and neither did Diego. The werecat seemed twice as big as I remembered. He was so *fast*. He was faster than Diego, and ten times faster than me. I hadn't been adequately prepared."

She grinds her teeth. "He got some good swipes in at me, knocked Diego around, and then pounced on me and sunk his teeth into my shoulder. I was bleeding everywhere. And Diego —" She takes a shuddering breath.

"He ran. He didn't even look back. About a second later, the werecat disarmed me, and I thought I was dead. I curled into a ball on the floor, just hoping it was quick. But then I felt a hand on my shoulder. I looked up, and the he had shifted back into his human form. He helped me stand, then . . . hugged me."

My mouth drops open. "What?"

She shrugs. "He hugged me. Said he remembered me. That he was glad I was still alive."

I shake my head in disbelief. "He — he wanted you alive?"

She nods. "He bit me to save my life, Lee. I would have bled out from the accident if he hadn't. He could have let me die — probably should have. I killed his *wife*. But he said that it had been his fault they were on that road in the first place. He couldn't save her, but he saved me."

"But you just said he bit you and —"

"Well, we attacked him first."

I stare at her, processing. "Holy shit."

A corner of her mouth curls into a microscopic smile. "I know. It's fucking unbelievable."

My head spins. *We attacked him first.*

Just like I had done to Bleddyn.

"He welcomed me into his home, once he realized he could trust me. His real home — not the mouth of the cave. He and a bunch of other Shifters and Fabled lived in that cave system to hide from Mages. He's the one who introduced me to Mòrag."

"The wulver," Saif says quietly, answering my unasked question. The cat had crawled into his lap, and he's rubbing his thumb over its nose and forehead as it nuzzles into his hand.

That word again. "What is a Fabled?"

"That's what the creatures call themselves collectively. Instead of . . . Auberon's word." He grimaces.

I have to admit that I like their word much more than my father's. Or rather, the Guide's. I tap my fingers rapidly against the table, and Saif makes a small movement like he wants to take my other hand, but then stops.

Kianga makes a sound of annoyance. "Speak of the Devil."

My eyes narrow, and I'm immediately tense once more.

She frowns, but continues. "About three years ago, your father started attacking different settlements of Fabled. Capturing the strongest of them, and eliminating the rest."

I open my mouth to retort, but she plows over me.

"Not long after that, we realized that the land itself was starting to wither away. Forests are dying. Fields that were once lush and green are turning brown. Our wildlife populations are plummeting. He's the only one thing that could cause everything all at once. He's poisoning the very world he claims to protect."

I shake my head. "That's not true. He wouldn't." She and Saif exchange a look, and I dig my nails into my palms. "Besides, he's one man. How *could* he?"

She narrows her eyes. "Do you even know what your father's power is?"

"Telekinesis," I spit.

She shakes her head. "But that's not all he can do. Every other Mage is limited to one element or power. Your father has set villages ablaze, has mind-controlled siblings to battle one another to the death. He either moves impossibly fast, or teleports; we aren't positive. There isn't any rationale to his power."

I stare back at her blankly. "No, that doesn't even make sense. Besides, he isn't like that. He may be a bit misguided about the Mon— The Fabled, but I'm sure if you let me explain things to him, he'll see he was wrong. He wouldn't hurt anyone."

Kianga clicks her nails against the table — her patience is running thin. "Eilidh, you're not that fucking stupid. He's the most powerful man in this dimension. He's a fucking *king*. He benefits from the Mages and Shifters thinking they're superior to The Fabled. As long as we're all divided, *he* stays at the top. He's not going to just give that up."

"If you think he's so evil then why bother with this whole fucking trial?" I snap. "Why the suspicion of Diego and I if my father is the source of all misery and woe?" I wiggle my fingers derisively.

Her mouth twists. "I can't make any decisions by myself — the Council decides collectively. And Bleddyn was one of us."

"He was a feral monster!"

She rolls her eyes. "No he wasn't. And with everything Auberon has been doing the past few years, I didn't know how much he had been able to twist you into his way of thinking. How feral *you* had become."

I'm about to become much more feral if she doesn't shut the fuck up about my father.

I change tactics, and jab a finger at Saif. "*You.*"

He winces, and his hand freezes in the middle of petting the cat. "I tried to tell her —"

But I cut him off. "When you poisoned me, you didn't say anything about my father being a mass-murderer. I just assumed you wanted he and Diego to pay for —" I glance at Kianga. "Apparently *nothing*," I finish scathingly.

He looks appropriately chastised. "I know," he murmurs. "I didn't know Bastet was Imane at that point; I had only communicated with her through her envoys. I decided to get you away from Auberon during that meeting when he nearly sent you off to get killed. I told the bartender at the Howling Jackal that I was ready to join, and he filled me in on what's really going on to prepare me. But when I told him I was bringing someone with me, he refused."

"He was under my direct order to bring *only* you when you were ready," Kianga says tightly. "I knew I could trust you, but didn't know about anyone else."

Saif nods, and continues his explanation. "Then I had more reason than ever to get you away from Auberon, and I wasn't going to devote any more of my life to a monster. But I wasn't going to leave you behind. I went back to Arkenvale, wracking my brain to figure out how I could convince him to let me bring you, but I had no bargaining power. Until . . ." He hesitates.

"Until I told you that I'm his daughter," I finish bitterly.

He grimaces and nods. "I went back to the tavern that night after you fell asleep, and he relayed the message."

I look down at the table before he sees me flush at the memory of that night. I shiver at the ghost of his lips on my spine. When I meet his gaze again, I know he's remembering it, too. His eyes dart to my lips before he continues.

Kianga glances shrewdly between us, but says nothing.

"I told her that I would bring her Auberon's daughter so that she could use you as leverage. I was planning on appealing to her humanity once we got here to ensure she wouldn't *actually* send you back to him. But that's all it was. None of it had anything to do with Diego."

I narrow my eyes. "I find it hard to believe it had *nothing* to do with him. You hate him."

Saif sighs, but when he looks at me, his eyes relay nothing but honesty. "I know I did."

An awkward moment passes. I shift uncomfortably. "How did you know you could trust the bartender?"

Kianga answers. "Himesh is a Fae man who works for the Council. I had told him to try to recruit Saif several times over the years. Saif never agreed, but he never gave us up to Auberon, either."

I raise a brow at him. "Why?"

He shrugs. "I don't know. It just didn't feel right, didn't seem necessary, and we had far bigger issues. Bastet's group wasn't a priority until that meeting."

"That's why you were so skittish when we were at the tavern."

He just nods.

"And Ousmane?" I turn back to Kianga.

"Also ours," she says.

"Fae?"

"Mage."

My eyes widen. So they have Mages, too. "Why didn't you just tell Saif years ago about what you think my father is? About yourself? What changed?"

She glares back at me and begins picking at the skin around her thumb nails. "I was scared," she finally spits. "I was scared he wouldn't believe the truth about Auberon. That he would reveal us if he found out I was still alive. I was a coward, and we had other plans into motion. But then, after the latest attack, the Council was done waiting."

I suppress the anxiety gurgling in my core. "When was that?"

Kianga sighs. "During the last full moon. A group of wyverns far to the south were all killed, save for one, who was taken."

"Is that why you started marching on Lisanor?"

Her mouth is tight. "We weren't marching on Lisanor at all. That was just along the way. We were marching on Arkenvale."

Holy shit.

"But nothing came of it anyway; we pulled everyone back here after Saif sent word that he was bringing you to us." She looks me up and down quickly. "We thought that the wisest course of action, given that we have no idea how he'll react, with his little girl gone. He might set the whole damn world on fire."

I grip the edge of the table. "Well it would have been pointless bloodshed anyway," I snap. "You've got the wrong man. My father has been at Arkenvale every day for the past six months. I've seen him with my own eyes, talked with him, studied with him in the library. Someone would have noticed if he had come back that day with a fucking wyvern. There's no way it could be him. Obviously, there's a Mage out there with the power to look like other people or something. Wreaking havoc for their own personal gain."

Kianga inclines her head at me, like she's preparing to explain something to a particularly obstinate toddler.

I bristle.

"Just because you finally got the father you always wanted doesn't make him a good person, Eilidh. He's a *monster*. You'd be better off going back to your drunk of a mother if you want to be with a terrible parent."

I stand abruptly, and my chair clatters to the floor. The cat hisses at me, but I ignore it. I glare down at her, my eyes stinging. I think for a moment that there's a flash of regret in her eyes, but she doesn't apologize.

"Fuck you," I whisper.

"Eilidh." Saif's voice is soft. Placating.

I had never told him about my mother. About her disease. Had never really planned to.

His eyes are flooded with just as much love and concern as they had been the morning after my first transformation.

"Both of you," I hiss. I stalk away from the table and fling the door open, relishing the sound of the handle hitting the marble wall.

Kianga doesn't follow me.

Thunderstorm (Saif)

I mane sits as still as a statue until we hear Eilidh slam the door to the courtroom shut. I wince, expecting to hear glass shatter, but it must be magically reinforced.

Suddenly, she lets out a sob and lays her head in her arms against the cool marble of the table. Her shoulders shake silently as Topaz butts her fuzzy head into her arm, trying to comfort her.

I only hesitate a moment before I reach out and rub her upper back.

"This is all so fucked up," she says quietly, her voice thick and muffled. "Why did it have to be *her?*"

I swallow hard, at a loss for what to say.

"I should go after her." She sniffs as she gives Topaz a quick chin scratch. Her eyes are red and glistening, but she's already composing herself. I've never seen her cry before. It's jarring, and that part of me that always needs to jump into action when I see someone hurting kicks me into motion.

"No," I say gently, laying a hand over hers, suppressing the rush I feel at the touch of her skin. "I'll go."

"But —" She begins to protest, and I cut her off.

"Imane, please." I find myself standing, and placing a firm hand on her shoulder. "You've got enough on your plate."

She searches my gaze briefly. "Okay," she relents. "But be careful.

She's like a fucking thunderstorm when she's mad; she'll fling bolts of lightning at you without even realizing it." The small ghost of a smile curls one corner of her lips, and I find my own mouth twitching up in response.

"Believe me, I know."

I exit the room, and head for the storm.

Lost Treasure

I don't know where I'm going, but I don't care. I won't let Kianga see the tears streaming down my cheeks. As I slam the door and enter the large common area, several Fabled look at me, but most continue on with their business.

I have to find my way back to the cells, but I've no idea where they were, and my head is still spinning with Kianga's words. I register that my breathing is quick and shallow, so I take a few deep breaths through an imaginary straw, extending my stomach with each inhale. I have to talk to Diego. He'll clear everything up.

Won't he?

Yes, I think firmly, pushing away the doubt that creeps into my mind. *He will.* And then I'll free him somehow, and we'll get the fuck out of here.

I turn in the general direction I remember the door to the dungeon to be, but I only manage to make it a few steps before I feel a warm, calloused hand on my bare shoulder. I whirl, and Saif is standing with his hands up placatingly. I wipe furiously at my eyes and look away from him. "What do you want?" I bite.

"Where are you going?" He asks gently.

It doesn't occur to me to lie. "To find Diego and get the fuck out of here."

He sighs. "Well, before you go, will you at least let me give you something? I know you've been missing it."

I squint up at him suspiciously. "If it's a beverage of any kind, heat it to boiling first so I can throw it in your face."

He winces. "That's fair. But no, it's not. It's in my room."

I purse my lips and cock an eyebrow at him. "How dumb do you think I am?"

"Please, Eilidh. Just trust me," he pleads.

Fresh tears sting my eyes at that. "I did," I rasp.

The corners of his eyes tighten with pain. "I know. I'm sorry I fucked that up. I made the hardest choice I've ever made, and it was the wrong one. I knew you might hate me at first, but I thought you would understand once we explained everything. I should have just told you, but I didn't think you'd believe me."

I bite my cheek. *He's right, and you know it.* I wouldn't have. I'm not convinced even now.

He takes my hand, and I inhale shakily. He looks so mournful. A few weeks ago that expression would have melted my heart and made me want to stab whatever made him feel that way. But those two weeks may as well have been a lifetime.

I want to tell him to keep whatever it is he has for me. To fuck off forever and let me break Diego out without interfering. He owes me that at least. But when I open up my mouth, that is not at all what comes out.

"You said you loved me." My voice breaks, and I sag. He pulls me into his chest, and just like always, I fit perfectly under his chin. It shouldn't feel so comforting, but it's familiar, and my body hasn't quite gotten the memo from my mind that this man betrayed me. Whether he thought he was ultimately helping me or not, he had still drugged me and got Martín killed — albeit temporarily.

He doesn't shush me as I weep against him in the middle of this crowded building. He just runs his hands along my hair and holds me together. When my tears dry up, I step away from him roughly. I don't want to look him in the eye, but he reaches out tentatively and takes my hand.

I look at our intertwined fingers, and wipe angrily at my eyes.

"I wasn't lying when I said that, Eilidh." He rubs his thumb over my hand and rattles something off in Arabic.

"What does that mean?" I ask hoarsely.

"Oh, you don't know?" He asks, and though his tone is light, I can tell he's still annoyed at me.

I sniff, unsure if I'm more sad or angry. "*No.* I told you I only know —" I begin, but he cuts me off.

"I would sacrifice myself for you," he whispers.

I shut my eyes tightly so that I don't cry again. He puts his other arm around my shoulder and guides me off. I walk beside him numbly.

We finally arrive at a small door on the second floor, and he leads me inside to a room that's barely larger than a closet. The glass of the opposite wall allows late afternoon light to shine through, bright and cheery. It blackens my mood further, until I notice the ceiling, and my eyes widen.

He has it covered in some kind of plant that has lush, heart-shaped leaves and large, round flowers. They're a dozen different shades of white, blue, purple, and pink, and they fill the room with a sweet aroma. I gasp and forget for a moment that I hate him.

"What are these?" I ask in awe, reaching up toward a large purple flower to caress its petals.

"Moonflowers," he says quietly. "To remind me of you."

I look at him, stricken. The longing in his eyes is nearly enough to break me. I cross my arms and look away.

A narrow bed sits directly to the right of the door, and a small desk sits in the opposite corner of the space, against the glass wall. He gestures for me to sit on the bed, but the thought makes my stomach twist, so I just lean against the closed door instead.

A skewed frown flashes across his features, but then he takes the two steps to the desk and pulls the drawer open. He pulls out some kind of trinket, then clasps his hand around it before turning back to me.

"Just so you know, I had to find a new chain; the old one was slashed to bits. And I tried to see if there was a way to buff out the scratch marks, but I was told there isn't." He adjusts his glasses nervously as he holds his hand out.

I hold out my palm apprehensively. *What is he babbling about?*

He drops it into my palm, and I gasp sharply. It's the pendant that I had lost when Bleddyn attacked me. The one that was the only thing they had recovered from Kianga's car wreck. The one that I had given her for her eighteenth birthday.

The same as the mural that I saw painted on the wall.

It's scuffed up, and it does indeed have a different chain, but I don't care.

I clutch it to my chest, my fingers shaking as I run them over the Celtic knots and the outline of the cat. "How did you find this?" I whisper.

He takes a step closer, rubbing the back of his neck. "I had a few days to kill. I went back to the clearing to look for it. It really wasn't a big deal, it's easy to look through a lot of grass when you can control it."

But it *is* a big deal to me. "I . . . thank you," I breathe.

He takes it from me gently, slips the chain around my neck, and clasps it together. He moves my hair out of the way, then adjusts the pendant so that it's centered just under my collarbone. This chain certainly is shorter, but I'm too relieved to have the pendant back to mind.

I don't even notice that his fingers linger for a moment too long over my sternum until I look up to see that his face is very close to mine.

"You're welcome," he says roughly. He moves his hand to my cheek, and my heart hammers against my rib cage.

"Saif . . ." I don't know where to begin.

I conjure up the image of him standing over me as the wolfsbane takes control of my limbs. I flinch, but he doesn't move his hand.

Then, unbidden images flood my mind. His face right before he kissed me the morning after my first transformation. The setting sun lighting his bronze skin ablaze as we sat together at Arkenvale. How scared he had looked when he first told me he loved me, as if he would shatter if I didn't feel the same.

He moves closer. "Eilidh," he rumbles.

"I. . ." I cast my gaze downward.

Another step closer. "Yes?"

Diego's face is next to appear in my mind. Laughing after swinging us over the ravine in the woods. The set of his mouth as he tells me that he had been preparing for my failure against Bleddyn and getting his own silver blades. Him staring hungrily at my throat as he pins me to a rough cabin wall.

And then a scene I wasn't there for, but can still see as clear as day: him fleeing the werecat's cave while Kianga screams behind him. Leaving her to die.

"Kianga said you threw your life away for me. Why would you do that?"

He tilts my face up, and I look at him, trembling. "Any life without you isn't one I want to live."

I shake my head jerkily, even as I feel my heart willing me to forgive him. "But the wolfsbane . . ."

"Hurting you was the worst decision I've *ever* made. I am so, so sorry, Eilidh." His voice breaks, and tears fall from his eyes. He kisses my forehead tenderly, then my cheek, which, I realize, is wet with tears just like his.

"I'm still angry at you," I whisper shakily.

One corner of his mouth quirks. "I'm still angry at you, too."

"Then we're both still angry." I can't tear my eyes away from his mouth.

"Furious," he whispers.

"Good," I murmur.

"Good." Then he leans down and kisses me, closes the centimeters between our bodies, and presses me into the door as I kiss him back instinctively. My lips know his by heart.

Kissing Diego had been like playing with those extra-large sparklers that I had been terrified of as a child. Dangerous, crackling, but breathlessly exhilarating. Kissing Saif is like the steady warmth of a fire in a hearth. The heat wraps itself around me, warms me inside and out.

At the thought of Diego, my kisses turn desperate, and Saif doesn't shy away from my intensity; instead, he answers it with his own, and my pulse kicks into overdrive.

I don't want to *think* any longer. I can't. If I think about everything that has happened, everything I've learned, I'm going to shatter into a million fragments. I'll never be able to put the pieces of myself back together.

My hands snake up his back, twisting in the fabric of his tunic. He wraps one hand around the back of my neck, and the other around my waist, pulling me deeper into him.

Then he shifts, and we topple over the foot of the bed and onto the narrow, firm mattress. He lands roughly on top of me, and I let out a small cry against his lips that is significantly more pleasure than pain.

He hauls me up toward the headboard. I cling to him as our legs tangle together and he grinds his hips against mine. The way we fit together, it's like our bodies had been searching for one another.

Heat rushes between my legs, and I arch into him, feel him pulse against me. He exhales heavily against my mouth, and I moan in reply.

He kisses me desperately, and parts my lips quickly with his tongue. I dig my nails into his back, but he doesn't stop or pull away like he would have before. He moans into my mouth as he kisses me, then runs his lips over my jaw, hot and heavy. I'm so drunk with pleasure that I see stars behind my eyelids.

I whimper as he digs his fingers into my thigh. His mouth moves down my neck methodically, and I breathe heavily with each kiss, but when he reaches the crook of my neck where Diego had first bitten me, I freeze and gasp sharply.

He stops kissing me immediately and pushes himself up. "What's wrong?" He asks breathlessly, adjusting his glasses, which had been knocked askew.

My stomach twists. *Me. I'm wrong. What the fuck have I done?*

"I . . . I can't do this." My voice trembles. He pushes himself up farther, and then sits back on his heels.

"No, of course, I'm sorry, I shouldn't have . . ." He trails off as he moves off me completely, running a hand through his dark curls, swallowing hard. I sit up and press myself back into the headboard.

"No, don't be sorry." I can't believe I'm saying those words to him after the number of times I had pictured strangling him in the last day, but the whole world is upside-down right now. "I just. *Fuck.*" I rake my nails through my hair. The words tumble out of my mouth before I can stop them.

"I slept with Diego."

I'm terrified to so much as look at him, but when he says nothing for several long moments, I finally do, expecting to see shock, rage, disgust, anything other than what is there.

A skewed smile tilts his mouth, and his warm eyes are filled with resignation. "I know," he says softly. A jolt runs through me, but he continues quickly. "At least, I suspected, given the way you threw yourself at him in the courtroom."

I wince, and he frowns at the floor. "And the way he's looked at you for months when your back is turned."

I curl in on myself, but he places a firm hand on my knee. "I'm *not* angry with you," he says vehemently, then smirks. "About that, at least. I messed up. I hurt you, and you found comfort where you could. And this." He gestures widely. "This rebellion is about so much more than me and Diego. Besides, like you said, Imane is *alive*."

He stares into the space above my head for a moment, as if he's still processing this information. I suppose he probably is. I know I will be for some time. He also doesn't spit Diego's name like he normally does.

He inhales as if bracing himself before pulling a knife out from between his ribs. "I'm glad he was there to comfort you when I couldn't. And if he really did kill Bleddyn, I'm grateful to him for keeping you safe. For getting you out alive."

I swallow the lump in my throat. "I really *did* deal the killing blow," I say in a small, queasy voice. "But I couldn't have done it without him. He replaced two of his blades with silver. Bleddyn was already close to death anyway."

Saif's eyes are wide by the time I'm through speaking. "I tried to keep you both away from that monster," he says quietly. "I tried to block off the tunnel." He shakes his head faintly. "I should have known nothing would have stopped you two."

He slides closer to me, then wraps an arm around my shoulder to pull me into him.

"I don't know what to do," I whisper.

"I'll respect whatever decision you make," he murmurs into my ear. "I love you, Eilidh. I just want you to be happy. Whatever that means to you, I'll support it."

He slowly guides me to lie down, then pulls me into his chest. Just to comfort me, because I need it. Even though I might decide to break his heart later.

The thought chills me, and then guilt twists heavily in my gut. *I don't want to lose either of them.* But neither of them deserve to be strung along just because I can't make up my mind.

After some time, I finally have the courage to voice the other thing digging into my heart.

"If my father really is a monster, what am I supposed to do about it? I wanted to find him my whole life, and now I have. How am I supposed to just let him go?"

Can he be shown the truth? Or worse — does he already *know* the truth? No, he can't possibly.

Right?

I can't reconcile the two versions of my father in my head. One version of him sits on the arm of my chair in the library, and we bond over the story of King Arthur. The other one slays Fabled in cold blood and topples villages single-handedly.

But they aren't the same man. How can they be? There has to be a way to stop the latter without harming the former. There has to be.

"I *can't* lose him, Saif. There has to be something else I can do. Kianga and the Council want blood, but that can't be the only option . . . can it?" I desperately need him to confirm this for me. I need it more than anything I have ever needed from him.

Saif squeezes me tightly and plants a long kiss on the top of my head before he replies.

"Sometimes, both options are soaked in blood, and the only real choice to make is whose it will be."

A few tears fall silently, dampening the cotton pillowcase beneath me. He laces his fingers through mine and rubs a thumb across my hand soothingly. "I love you, *Lahabi*."

I don't bother lying. "I love you, too."

He holds me until I fall asleep. I don't wake until the next morning.

Worth the Fight

"You have to let me see him."

The ogre raises a burly eyebrow at me. "Bastet says no entry." His gravely voice rakes across my sensitive eardrums, and I grit my teeth.

It's the same thing he has said to me the last three times I've tried to get past him. Saif stands a few steps back from me, but he has no more leverage with the eight-foot Fabled than I do. Kianga - *Bastet* - apparently has the final say as to who gets into the dungeon to see Diego.

"What if I transform and start rampaging through here?" I gesture at the area around us, full of people going about their business. I can't transform at will - I had tried this morning and failed, so what had happened under the willow must have been a fluke - but the ogre doesn't know that. "Then you'd have to throw me in a cell too, right?"

Saif intervenes at that, and steers me away by the shoulders before the ogre either repeats himself again, or possibly hits me with the club strapped to his back out of sheer annoyance.

"Why don't we just try to find Imane and get her to give us clearance?" He tries to appeal to my rational side. Unfortunately for him, that side is *very* small right now.

"Who the fuck does she think she is?" I spit. "Why does she have him caged up like an animal?"

He grimaces, but doesn't answer.

"Does she have an office or something? Where's her room?" I look around as if a blinking sign will be waiting to point the way for me.

"No, she doesn't have an office." Saif says soothingly, like he's approaching a vicious lion to pull a thorn from its paw. "All decisions are made by the Council. And, I don't know where her room is." His tone is suddenly deliberately even.

I glance sidelong at him. *Oh.* I hesitate, then decide to be frank. I owe him that much, especially with the way he has taken everything regarding Diego and me in stride.

I sigh heavily. "Saif, I know you still love her. I can tell by the way you look at her."

His eyes widen in alarm, and opens his mouth as if he's going to deny it, but at my expression, he shuts it again. There will be no denial.

I twist my mouth into a rueful smile. "It's okay." I bite the inside of my lip and look at the floor. "I still love her, too."

Not that she ever loved me, not like that. And sure, I have her back, but now she's leading a rebellion to murder my father because she thinks he's a mad dictator.

Irony is a cruel fucking bitch.

He takes my hand. "I guess we've both got choices to make," he says sadly. I swallow the lump forming in my throat, and squeeze his hand tightly.

Here we are, two people who love each other, despite everything. Shouldn't our love be enough? Shouldn't everything else just fall into place around us?

But of course it isn't enough. Love is never enough on its own to hold the world together. It never has been. At least, not for me.

"You two are just *delicious*."

The velvety voice makes us both jump. We turn, and see that the succubus from the Council is standing no more than a foot behind us. She's at least as tall as Diego, and looks down her strong nose at both of us. We had been too engrossed in one another to notice her approach. Or maybe she's just that silent when she moves.

I try to twist around and take a step back at the same time, but my feet refuse to cooperate, and I just end up tripping over myself. Saif grabs me before I smack unceremoniously onto the cold floor.

"Don't fall for me, Doll, I'll only break your heart." She winks at me as her long, whip-like tail flits back and forth behind her.

I gape at her in reply.

Saif clears his throat. He must be just as affected by her intoxicating presence as I am. "Zaehora," he says tightly.

She glances between the two of us, and somehow I feel like she knows everything we've ever done. *Everything.* I take a step away from him and cross my arms.

"So you're trying to get down to the dungeon to see your other boy toy?" She teases, her eyes locked on my pendant. Her wings flex and flap gently, swirling the air around my feet.

"He's not . . ." I flush, and grab the crescent moon with one hand, squeezing tightly. It makes me feel more complete than I have in the better part of a year.

"Can you get me by the guard?" I ask, cocking an eyebrow behind her at the ogre, who is looking straight ahead at nothing at all. Or perhaps at everything.

She pouts, and I have to look away. "No, but I know where you can find Bastet." She jerks her tail behind her like it's a thumb. "She's outside. Follow me."

Saif and I glance at one another, then follow Zaehora silently. She leads us to the south side of the pyramid, judging by the sunlight blazing through the glass on our left.

I look around at the architecture as we walk.

Kianga is really leaning into her Egyptian roots in her new life. A small piece of me - one of the few pieces that isn't currently filled with rage at her - smiles. She used to speak of Egypt like it was a particularly wonderful dream she had once, and had never forgotten. She had always wanted to go back, take me with her, and show me all the places that I had loved looking at pictures of.

We'll run up the stairs of Hatshepsut's Mortuary, she had joked once, as we laid side by side in her backyard, gazing up at the constellations above us. *We'll dance under these same stars in the Valley of the Queens.*

You were born hundreds of miles away from there, Kiki. I had rolled my eyes, and she had laughed easily.

Then it will be a new adventure for both of us.

The memory stings, and I reach for Saif's hand without thinking. He takes it firmly, without question.

As we approach the exit, I see another mural of my pendant on a wall. I clutch it again. Suddenly, Saif stops walking, and I'm yanked back.

"Ow! What?" Then I realize that only his grip on my hand had prevented me from running straight into Zaehora, who has stopped, and is now leering down at me.

She flashes a pearly white smile as I scramble back next to Saif. "Bastet came up with that symbol for the rebellion all by herself. It's the only thing that isn't Egyptian-themed around here. When I asked her why she wanted to go with that instead of an Eye of Horus or something, she said that it was a symbol of the only thing that was worth the fight."

She glances down at the pendant on my chest again, still smiling. I flush, but she just turns back around and heads toward the exit. I look at the ground in front of me as I walk, still holding Saif's hand.

The only thing that was worth the fight. What on earth does *that* mean? And then it dawns on me. *Friendship.*

I grimace.

Zaehora reaches the exit, and I follow her out into the blazing sunshine. Kianga is nowhere to be seen. "Where is she?" I ask. She points up with her tail. Saif and I lift our gazes to the sky, where I see the underbelly of a golden wyvern making circles, descending near us.

My mouth hangs open in awe as the wyvern lands and Kianga jumps nimbly off their back. She turns and gives them a small bow, and they bows their head in return before taking back off into the sky and disappearing behind the pyramid.

She turns to us, hands on her hips. "What are you doing out here?" She frowns at Zaehora, but the succubus just smiles back at her, utterly unconcerned.

Saif tries to negotiate first. "We were hoping that —"

But I have no patience for diplomacy. Not right now, and certainly not with her. "Let me see Diego." I snap.

She snorts. "Not a chance."

I throw my hands in the air. "Why is he even in a cell? You think my father is an evil mastermind, but you still keep Diego chained up? For what? Your own personal vendetta?"

She narrows her eyes at me dangerously, but I meet her glare for glare.

Zaehora wears the expression of a cat watching two mice as she looks between us, a small, amused smile on her lips. Her tail twitches wildly.

"Just because he's innocent of cold-blooded murder doesn't mean he isn't a liability." Kianga's growl puts Diego's to shame. "How do I know he won't run to Auberon and reveal our location the second he's unchained?"

I set my jaw stubbornly. "He wouldn't leave me here *alone*." Saif adjusts his glasses beside me, and guilt grips my stomach.

It's Kianga's turn to set her jaw. "You'd be surprised what he's capable of running away from," she says, her voice low and dangerous.

I bite my lip. I hadn't meant to throw his abandonment of her in her face like that, but that's how it had sounded nonetheless. Heat creeps into my cheeks.

I had managed to hurt both Saif and Kianga in one single sentence. *That has to be a record.*

A tense moment passes before Saif clears his throat. "I'd be happy to supervise if that would make you feel better about it."

I wince. That would be incredibly awkward, but I suppose it's a preferable alternative to not seeing Diego at all, and him running dangerously low on blood again.

Kianga throws her head back and sighs at the clear sky, her hands still on her hips. "Fine," she finally bites. "Let's go."

As we walk past the moon and cat mural on the wall back inside the building, I desperately want to ask her about it, but I'm afraid that will lead to another spat, and her changing her mind about letting me see Diego. I keep silent instead.

After she informs the ogre guarding the dungeon door that I am to be allowed down only under the condition that Saif is with me, she stalks away without looking back. I give her a long look before heading down the stairs.

Immense Power

I glance back and forth anxiously as I stalk down the damp hall between the cells. I have no idea which one had been mine, nor which one they've chained Diego in. My heart rate increases more with each one I pass that is conspicuously free of vampires — or anyone, for that matter.

What if he isn't here at all? What if they've moved him somewhere else? What if he broke free himself and fled like Kianga feared he would? I'm nearly in a full-blown panic when I reach the final cell on the right, and my heart skips a beat entirely.

Diego is lying prone on the ground, facing away from the cell door. His wrists and ankles are manacled to a chain that is bolted into the back wall, and the straps of the muzzle wrap around the back of his head. His black jeans are covered in dirt from the floor, and his hair sticks up madly in every direction.

My heart twists in horror at the sight of him chained up like an animal, but then my stomach is engulfed in flames of fury.

This is ridiculous.

I grip the bars and slide down to kneel on the ground. There's no way he didn't hear us approaching, but he hasn't turned to look at me yet. He must think I'm a guard. Or Kianga. Saif stops several feet back down the hallway and looks around awkwardly before he crosses his arms and leans against a wall.

"Diego?" I whisper. He turns, and after seeing me in the corner of his eye, rolls over to face me completely. We gaze at one another for a few moments, each making sure the other is real.

"Hey *Lobita*," he says weakly, pushing himself into a sitting position against the wall. "What are you doing here?"

I blink rapidly. "Checking on you, idiot." The shadow of a smile flicks across his face at that.

"Well, frankly, I've been better. The room service here is *terrible*." He leans back against the wall, his hair falling back from his face.

I swallow a lump in my throat. "Yeah, you've looked a lot better, too," I say, trying to tease a real smile out of him.

He snorts. "What, this isn't doing it for you?" He asks coyly, rattling the chains. "I thought you'd say it was rugged."

"Usually when chains are involved, I'm the one in them."

He cocks an eyebrow and gives me a quick once-over. "I thought you said chains weren't your thing?"

I smirk.

"She was lying about that, *believe* me," Saif says tersely, unable to resist needling Diego.

I wince, having already forgotten he was standing there. He's looking pointedly at the wall, his arms still crossed.

I turn back to Diego, my cheeks reddening. The small shadow of mirth I had coaxed out of him has vanished; his eyes are crimson slits.

"Kianga won't let me see you without a chaperone. Afraid I'll incite a prison break, I think," I say awkwardly.

"Tell him he's lucky I'm muzzled and chained after what he did to you." Diego's tone is ice cold.

Saif exhales quickly through his nose. "Noted," he bites out sourly. "Not that she couldn't rip me apart herself if she was so inclined."

I raise an eyebrow at him.

Diego barks a harsh laugh. "Oh, *now* you think she's good enough? Now that she has a reason to put a knife in your back like you did to her?"

I wince at the venom in his voice. "Guys," I say quietly.

Saif finally turns away from the wall, his eyes blazing. He strides into Diego's view.

"I always *have* thought she was good enough," he growls as he wraps his hands around the bars. "It's *you* who isn't."

"Alright!" I yell as Diego opens his mouth to retort. Both of them look at me as if they had forgotten I was here. "I think the three of us need to talk," I say shakily.

I scoot over so that Saif can sit as well. He hesitates a moment, but I raise my brows at him, and he reluctantly lowers himself to the ground.

"Good boy," Diego drawls mockingly. Saif shakes himself slightly, and glares at Diego through the bars.

Diego looks back at me. "So, you two have made up already." It isn't a question. His voice is deceptively even, but I can tell how he really feels. He's pissed, or hurt. Probably both.

"No," I say quickly, at the same time Saif says, "Yes." We look at each other, and Diego snorts.

"I . . ." I groan softly, pressing the heels of my palms into my eyes until I see stars. I take a deep breath to gather my courage and say the words I am dreading before I can get cold feet.

"Saif knows we slept together."

The smallest self-satisfied smile lifts one corner of Diego's mouth as he looks at Saif. I frown at him.

"And I told her I'm not angry with her," Saif says curtly. "I fully expected you to swoop in and take advantage of her while she was hurting. That's what you're best at."

Diego just smirks sardonically at him. "Don't worry, *querido*, I helped her stop hurting three times that night."

If Saif had *Dhabiha* on him, he might have actually tried to impale Diego with it through the bars, but luckily, I'm not the only one missing my weapon.

"Both of you *shut up!*" I yell into my hands. My face must be as red as my hair. Maybe I can get that wyvern Kianga had been riding to burn me to a crisp and put me out of my misery.

"In case neither of you have noticed, I am a grown woman. I'm perfectly capable of making my own decisions when it comes to who I fuck." I glare between them. "*Neither* of you has taken advantage of me."

They both look appropriately chastised.

I close my eyes and take a few deep breaths. "I don't . . . I don't want to hurt either of you." I try to keep the quiver out of my voice, but it creeps in at the end of my sentence all the same. Besides, I know, selfishly, that hurting either of them would hurt *me* immensely.

"I don't know *how* to not hurt either of you. But *this.*" I make a quick circular motion between the three of us. "Is just not my biggest concern right now."

My lip trembles as I address Diego. "Kianga wants to kill my father. She says that he's got all these ridiculous powers, and has been killing and kidnapping The Fabled - these creatures - for a few years now. She's also worried that you're going to run back to Arkenvale the moment you get out of those chains to warn him and lead him here."

Diego's face twists in confusion. "That's ridiculous. Did you tell her what I told you about him?"

I glance at Saif, and for his sake, I say, "That you warned me he's dangerous and unhinged? Of course not. I know you don't like that he sent me on that mission, but she thinks he's a *monster*. I need you two to help me prove her wrong."

I look between them, expecting acquiescence, but instead, they look at one another, apparently deciding who is going to be the one to tell me something first. I'm not sure if Diego wins or loses, but either way, he sighs and speaks, suddenly sounding even more exhausted.

"Eilidh, she's not wrong."

I gape at him, then at Saif, whose mouth is set in a grim line. For what I'm pretty sure is only the second time ever, he doesn't disagree with Diego. "What?"

"I've been looking for a contact for the rebellion ever since you came to Arkenvale." Diego says. "I wanted to get you out of there before he could get you killed. I suspected the bartender at the Howling Jackal, and the bookseller, but neither of them ever gave anything up." He twists his mouth in frustration. "So, I had to take matters into my own hands to keep you safe."

The silver blades.

"Your instincts were right," Saif says begrudgingly. "They're both working for the rebellion. Imane just gave explicit orders not to engage with you."

Diego's eyes narrow, but not out of anger. He just looks wounded — and more so than any physical injury I've ever seen him endure.

I get the conversation back on track. "So, you both believe that my father is some rabid monster that needs to be put down?"

Saif grimaces.

Diego makes a frustrated noise. "I told you, *Lobita,* just because he doesn't wield his power openly doesn't mean it isn't there."

I recall his exact words from that night in his bedroom. *You haven't seen what he's capable of.*

"What did he do?" I whisper. Saif looks at Diego expectantly. Diego puts his head back against the stone wall and swallows hard. For a long moment, I think he's going to refuse to answer me.

"A few months before Imane was - well, *not* - killed, Auberon took me with him on an emergency mission that he said was top secret and vital to the stability of the realm." His head sinks into his hands, the chains rattling and setting my teeth on edge. "It was a bloodbath," he whispers.

"What?" I croak when he doesn't continue. "What does that mean?"

I absolutely do not want to know.

I absolutely *have* to know.

He takes a steadying breath. "It was a settlement of Fae, maybe fifty of them. Families. Auberon said they had encroached upon land that belonged to Mages. To this day, I don't know if that part was true. I never went back to check. When we got there, Auberon commanded the leader of the Fae to vacate the area immediately. She, of course, refused. And he . . ."

Diego looks at me, his narrowed eyes full of sorrow over the past, and apology over what his next words will do to me. "He flayed her alive with a wave of his hand."

I don't realize I've stopped breathing until Saif reaches over and grips my knee. I inhale sharply, and faintly shake my head in horror as a chill shoots down my spine.

"He tore the entire settlement apart in just a few minutes. There were *children.* But he didn't care." Diego's voice breaks, and he has to take a moment to collect himself.

I want to slap him. To tell him to stop talking. I grip the bars of the cell so hard my arms shake.

He doesn't stop talking.

"The entire area was in chaos, and a little girl ran blindly at me in her terror, covered in blood. Her own, or someone else's, I — I don't know. Back then, I didn't have as good a handle on my . . . urges . . . as I do now."

He takes a shuddering breath, and tears begin to fall down his cheeks. "I couldn't — I couldn't stop myself. I . . ."

He doesn't continue. He doesn't need to.

I sit in numb silence.

"Diego," Saif finally says quietly. "It wasn't your fault."

Diego just shakes his head, sniffing harshly. "I should have stopped him. I should have died trying. At the very least, I should have left after he killed the first woman. I should have known I wouldn't be able to resist once the blood started flowing. I think that's why he wanted me there. To see what I could *do*." He twists the last word bitterly.

"Nothing like that ever happened again. There were days when I convinced myself that it hadn't happened at all. That it was just a horrific nightmare. But it wasn't. I was a ticking time bomb, and he knew just when to set me off when it was most convenient for him."

Diego looks at me again, his expression that of a man who is about to fall on his own blade in penance for some unforgivable atrocity. "That's another reason Saif has always been the better choice for you. If I lose control again, I could kill you in no time. My venom may not harm you, but I could still paralyze you and suck you dry without even realizing it. It's why Hyun-Joo is the only one I trust myself to take blood from. I feel drunk just being *near* you, Eilidh. You make all my senses go haywire."

My heart pounds so hard he can probably hear it. Can probably hear the *whoosh* of each pump of blood. Saif's grip tightens on my knee protectively.

"It isn't like that with her; I can control myself, and she'll put me down if she needs to. I've never been able to trust anyone else to do that for me." Diego's maroon eyes blaze with intensity. "I'm a *monster*, and you deserve a partner who's good to you. Who's good *for* you."

He gives Saif a look so thick with reverence that I suddenly feel like I'm intruding on a private moment. "Like him," Diego whispers. "He's the best man I've ever known."

Tears fill my eyes, and I don't bother trying to blink them away. Saif, too, appears stricken as they stare at each other for several beats.

I can't argue with Diego again right now about choices, and who gets to make them. He won't listen anyway, and a much louder question is ringing in my head right now.

"Is that why you left Kianga in that cave?" I whisper, and he looks toward the ceiling and swallows hard. More tears flow down his cheeks as he nods jerkily.

"The werecat was too fast. She was bleeding, and I felt myself starting to lose control. I knew that I couldn't stay there. I didn't realize she was hurt as badly as she was; I thought she could still beat it without me. But if I hadn't left when I did, *I* would have killed her. I left to get a grip on myself, and ended up sucking several deer dry in the process. I went back a few hours later, and they were both gone." He shrugs helplessly. "I thought she was dead."

I curl my nails into my fist hard as I lean my forehead into the bars. *Your father is a monster,* my inner critic berates me.

Diego turns to Saif. "So, I guess the wolfsbane was to get her the hell away from Auberon?"

But I just got him back, I plead.

Saif nods stiffly, then relays everything he had told me yesterday about Himesh's warning and how he knew I wouldn't believe him if he told me outright what was happening.

Cold-blooded slaughter.

When he's done speaking, Diego sighs with deep remorse. "Maybe if you and I had put our shit aside and had one honest conversation we could have gotten her out of there sooner."

Saif makes a pained sound. "Add that to my growing list of regrets," he mumbles.

A little girl.

"Why *didn't* you ever tell me?"

Diego barks a soft chuckle. "Because you're too goddamn righteous."

Saif raises a questioning brow, but Diego clarifies. "If I had told you, you would have drawn your sword on him in an instant. Challenged him. Tried to bring him to justice. And he would have killed you. I couldn't . . . I wasn't going to let you get hurt."

I waited for you my entire life.

Saif scoffs, but his heart isn't in it. "So you took on the weight of the world for *me?*"

Diego gives him a long look. "Do you remember that mission to Lohengrin?" He asks quietly.

How much more innocent blood is on your hands?

Saif blinks, and I swear his cheeks color, just a touch. "Yeah," he mumbles at the floor, before lifting his eyes to Diego's once more.

Someday, I will have to hear about whatever the hell happened in Lohengrin.

Diego searches Saif's eyes. "That's when I knew. I knew that I would have held the weight of the world for you for the rest of your life if I had to."

At that, a tear that has been glistening in Saif's eye for several minutes finally breaks free and streams down his cheek. He doesn't brush it away. "You're an idiot," he whispers.

I should have known the Universe wouldn't let me keep you.

"Yeah, I know." Diego's small smile is heavy with regret.

"Guys." They turn to me, concern on both their faces. I realize too late that hot tears are streaming down my cheeks.

A righteous fury has lodged itself deep in my core while they were talking — far stronger than anything I ever felt for Bleddyn. He may have turned me into a monster, but Auberon had broken Diego irreparably, and manipulated both he and Saif into serving him. He had traumatized one of them into compliance, and made the other feel like he was finally fulfilling his dream of healing the world.

The entire Order, in fact, has been nothing more than pawns to him. He found the loneliest and most broken people he could, and gave them hope for something more. For a purpose. For acceptance. He had convinced them all to maintain the status quo, under the guise of stability for the realm. Had convinced them that they were too broken to belong anywhere else.

And for that, I will never forgive you.

"It doesn't matter now what should have been done before," I growl. "All that matters is what we have to do now."

I glance between them silently, and they look at me expectantly, both their gazes full of love and devotion. To me? To our cause? I can't be sure, but I have my suspicions that it is more the former than the latter.

Fuck. My fury slips for a moment, overshadowed by a crash of panic. I realize suddenly - and absurdly, for this is certainly *not* the time for such concerns - that I'm never going to be able to make a choice between them.

I bite the inside of my cheek to keep from crying. *Focus, Shaw.*

I tamp the panic down, and the fury resurfaces. I take a steadying breath, buoyed by that familiar feeling, as well as the presence of these two men. My voice doesn't waver with my declaration.

"My father has to pay."

Reconciliation

Saif goes to the top of the stairs to tell the ogre that we need Bastet immediately. Within five minutes, I hear her footsteps on the stone stairs, light and quick. She takes in the sight of us with her hands on her hips, her jaw taught, her eyes guarded.

I look up at her from under my eyelashes. "We have something to tell you." There is no longer any anger in my voice, no resentment. There is only pain and resignation.

Her face instantly morphs back into the Kianga I know. For now, at least, Bastet is gone. She drops to my side and takes my hand, holding it firmly.

The three of us relay everything to her. Diego once again recounts the massacre of the Fae settlement, though Saif supplies information when he can't continue.

She puts the pieces together more quickly than I had. "Which is why you left when I was bleeding in the cave." It isn't a question.

The look Diego gives her in that moment, so full of remorse, and honesty, and *love*, would be enough to make any mere mortal break down and weep.

But Kianga Nabil is a goddess.

"I've spent every day since then wishing that I had stayed and died with you, *querida*," Diego rasps.

Her eyes glisten, but she meets his gaze evenly, her chin held high.

Even now, she's as regal as a queen. "I'm glad you didn't."

His eyes glisten as well.

I catch Saif's eye, and he gives me a small smile. I suppose if Diego and Kianga can make up after what they went through, Saif and I can as well.

My heart swells as I find strength in his warm eyes. "Kianga."

She looks me up and down and sighs.

"You were right about my father," I whisper.

Kianga *loves* being right. She relishes it. Boasts about it.

There is no boasting now. "I'm sorry, Eilidh," she says firmly. "I wish I wasn't."

I take a shuddering breath as I try to memorize the way each twist of gold wraps around her braids. "I know. Me too. So what do we do now?"

Her eyes narrow in sympathy. "We?"

I pull my pendant out from under the high neck of my turtleneck tank top, and she inhales sharply at the sight of it.

"The only thing worth the fight?" I ask, the faintest ghost of a smile playing at my lips. "The power of friendship?" My attempt to tease her into smiling doesn't succeed.

Her lips tighten at the corners, and she scoots closer to me. "Not exactly," she says quietly. Our legs press together, and I suppress a shiver. She's not a touchy-feely person, which had always been perfectly fine with me. It was much easier to maintain boundaries that way.

"Then what?"

"I . . . fought for *you*. I fought for you every *day*, Lee," she says haltingly. "The memory of you kept me going." She brings a hand to my cheek, and I lean into her touch and take what feels like my first unobstructed breath since I lost her. "I love you so much," she says, her voice thick and husky with emotion.

I wince. "I love you too, Kiki," I say tightly, trying to smile, and failing miserably.

Diego and Saif glance sidelong at one another.

I attempt to turn to them, but Kianga holds my face firmly and rolls her eyes at me. "No, you *idiot*," she says, exasperated. "I. Love. You."

And then she leans in and kisses me, and the world around me dissolves into insignificant nothingness. The only thing in the entire universe is the two of us, and our lips pressed together.

My eyes stay wide open for several moments in pure shock, trying desperately to get my brain to pick up the signal that they're sending.

Kianga is kissing me.

A tidal wave crashes over my mind, as if every synapse is suddenly bursting with this new information. Ripples of the message cascade throughout my head, down my spinal cord, and roar through my entire nervous system.

Kianga is kissing me.

My body takes over. I close my eyes and drink her in, inhaling her scent — she smells like lilac and gooseberries. The smell of it makes me drunk in a way that no alcohol, nor vampire venom, ever has.

If she ever removes her lips from mine, I may lose my mind entirely. Her kisses are quick, and gentle, but steady as waves crashing against a shoreline. I part her lips softly with my tongue, and suddenly I taste her. She tastes like —

I break away from her and gasp. "You have coffee here?"

She stares at me hazily for a second, breathing heavily, then collapses onto my shoulder, laughing until tears spring to her eyes.

I hold her so tightly to me I fear I may leave marks in her shoulders, but since she doesn't protest, I don't let her go.

I'm never letting her go again.

Drinking

Kianga pulls two keys from between her breasts and unlocks Diego's cell. While she works on his manacles, I carefully remove the muzzle from his face.

"*Mil gracias*," he mutters. I frown, but he's already trying to stand. He lasts for about half a second on his feet before he collapses to the dusty floor once again with a grunt.

I drop beside him and tilt his chin toward me. He winces, trying to pull away, but I hold him fast. A pang echoes through my chest at the dullness of his irises.

"You need blood."

He shakes his head. "I already took some from you yesterday."

As if that settles the matter.

I roll my eyes. "And my healing factor is better than yours, in case you forgot. I'm *fine*. You're not even going to make it out of this dungeon in this condition. You need blood, and more this time. You've been running short for a week."

He tries to frown at me, but his mouth just twists in pain instead. "Did you hear me when I said I might fucking kill you on accident? It doesn't seem you did."

I cross my arms. "Did you hear *me* when I said 'healing factor?' It doesn't seem you did."

Kianga snorts behind me, and I turn to see her smirking at Saif, who is shaking his head at her, a small smile on his face.

I turn back to Diego and jerk my thumb at them. "They're your only other option, and neither of them can heal like I can. So I'm the best you've got. Fangs."

Saif chuckles. "Seeing someone more stubborn than you truly is a gift, Vidales. Finally, there's some justice in the world."

Diego doesn't miss a beat, despite his diminished strength. "Then how lucky we are that she's stuck with us, eh, Rahim?"

The men look at each other, and something passes between them that I can't identify. Their gazes are utterly devoid of the hostility that has been burning between them for years.

My heart flutters, and then I realize Kianga is staring at me, one eyebrow cocked amusedly. I return her gaze as innocently as I can, thinking back over what I had just said, wondering if it had somehow been incriminating. "What?"

She puts a hand on her hip and tilts her head at me. "What does he mean, he took some yesterday? You weren't allowed near him yesterday."

Busted. I bite my lip as my eyes go immediately to Saif.

When Kianga turns to him, he throws his hands up in mock outrage. "*Et tu,* Eilidh?" He marches away down the hall, out of my sight, as I emit a small chuckle.

Kianga smiles after him. "We'll be right down there if you need us." She follows him down the hall.

Once she, too, is out of sight, I turn back to Diego. "Fangs," I repeat.

He purses his lips, but then sighs and does as he's told. His fangs slide out from his gums just as I realize that I don't really know how this works. He's never bitten me when we weren't either fighting or fucking, other than yesterday, and though my fingers are healed, I would rather not feel his fangs scrape against my bones again.

"Which . . . which part do you want?" I ask, suddenly flustered.

His mouth quirks as his eyes glide down my body, and his words slur slightly around his fangs when he speaks. "Well, if I had to narrow it down —"

"Seriously?" I cock my head at him and glare.

He huffs through his nose in amusement. "Thigh or neck is usually best."

I nod, then look down at my moss-green turtleneck tank top. *Not exactly ideal for neck biting.* But I've got long leggings on, and no underwear, so my thigh is definitely out of the question. I take a breath, remove my shirt, and pull down the right strap of my black sports bra.

Diego looks like he's stopped breathing for a moment, but then he clears his throat. "Back up against me," he instructs roughly.

I scoot between his legs, and he pulls me into his chest. My breath catches when we collide. His skin practically burns me through his shirt; my heart begins racing immediately.

He moves my bushy hair off my right shoulder, then tilts my head to the left, cupping my jaw, his pinky finger brushing the corner of my mouth. When he lowers his face toward the base of my throat and breathes against my skin, goosebumps erupt all over me.

"I can be gentle," he rumbles, more to himself than anything, as if I'm not the one who needs convincing.

"Don't be," I whisper.

Without any further hesitation, he sinks his fangs into me, and I cry out softly. Within seconds, the high from his venom reaches my brain, and I let out a long, shuddering sigh and melt against him.

He seems to move against me involuntarily, pressing into me as though gravity has suddenly changed course, and is pushing us together. I arch to curve with him. His claws begin to elongate and dig delectably into my right bicep.

I dig my nails into his left thigh as I bring my right hand up to tangle in his hair, and he moans into my neck. It shoots a violent shiver down my spine, which then ignites desire between my legs.

Holy shit.

"Diego." He tugs my hair in response to my whisper, and I exhale shakily, trying not to lose myself entirely.

He sucks my life force away in long, steady draughts as the venom burns its way into every nook and cranny of my brain. With every pulse of my blood, I feel just a bit weaker, but he moves more firmly, as if he's becoming solid once again, more corporeal, after having been a shade of himself for a week.

But even as a shade, he lights me up like a goddamn firework. Diego is the electricity that shoots through my nerves. Every movement when I'm near him is supercharged, like I've downed a gallon of espresso without eating breakfast first. He makes me feel like there is nothing I can't do. Like I'm invincible.

As he drinks, I become absolutely certain of something: I am hopelessly in love with this man.

I hold him tighter as his drinking slows. *But will I get to keep him?*

I think hazily of Saif, who, for some reason to which only he and the Universe are privy, loves me. Chose me. Fucked up a bit in the execution, but threw his entire life away for me. To keep me safe. To put me first.

And Kianga, who had just kissed me. Whose reemergence into my plane of existence has made the world feel complete once more.

And Diego still loves her.

My head swims.

And so does Saif.

This should feel like an absolute fucking mess. The worst possible scenario. The makings of a daytime reality drama that will end with chairs being thrown and the audience chanting the host's name.

But for some reason - and, granted, perhaps the reason is the venom fogging my brain - I just can't find it in myself to be concerned. My gut instinct is not a voice I can usually listen to, what with the depression, anxiety, and PTSD voices constantly drowning it out, but, somehow, thinking about the four of us, and the intricate web holding us together, just seems . . . right.

Diego stops drinking, exhaling shakily through his nose against my skin.

For what may be the first time in my life, those other voices hold no power over me. *Things are going to be fine.*

Just when I think that I would be okay if Diego left his fangs in me for the rest of the day, he removes them, and then kisses the four puncture wounds, one after the other, as I tremble.

"Just putting some pressure on them to stop the bleeding," he rumbles in my ear between kisses.

"Of course," I breathe dizzily.

I slump back into him, and he gently slides me down until my head is on his thigh. "Just rest a minute, *cariño.*"

My head lolls as I look up at him. "Didja get 'nuff?" I ask. His eyes are tight, but they're glittering again. *They're always so beautiful when they glitter like this.*

He nods stiffly, and I giggle. *He's so stiff all the time.*

"Loosen up, Diego," I say, and his name in my mouth tastes like candy. "Diegoooo." I stretch it out to savor it longer. I reach up and run my finger along his sharp cheekbone, just as I had when I woke to him asleep on the floor of the greenhouse at Arkenvale.

He doesn't flinch away this time; he grabs my hand gently, and plants a long kiss on my wrist, not breaking our eye contact as he does so.

I shiver.

He runs his hand over my hair. "*Sí, amor?*" He asks quietly.

"*Tu es muy caliente.*" It's one of the only full Spanish phrases I know.

Unless I'm looking for a library, this is about as far as my Spanish will get me in life.

He smiles at my attempt, and I point triumphantly. "There it is!" I giggle again.

"Everything okay?" I hear Saif say somewhere nearby.

"Yes," Diego calls, still smiling down at me. "She's just a little drunk."

Kianga comes back around the corner. "If that's the case, I'm not surprised her top is off. That always seems to happen when she's had too many."

I scoff at her in mock indignation. "That was *one* time, and that guy said he'd pay our tab if I let him do a body shot, so, you're welcome for the free booze."

As Kianga sits down beside me and takes my hand, Saif comes into view too, apparently intrigued at this talk of me topless.

"It was definitely *not* just one time, no matter what you don't remember." Kianga laughs, and I smile back at her easily. "Those fake IDs sure did come in handy that summer," she says wistfully.

I look at her mouth. *Those lips were on mine.* Kianga had kissed me, and Diego had just sucked my blood. It had been so intimate that I probably would have orgasmed if he hadn't stopped when he did.

Saif catches my eye as he comes to sit against the wall near the rest of us, and places a firm hand on my shin, grounding me.

Suddenly, my heart is so full, I fear it may explode. Genuine tears of joy threaten to stream out of my eyes and into my ears, or onto Diego's dusty, ripped jeans.

I will never be able to choose. The thought isn't anxious. It's just a fact. How could I? I'd be more capable of choosing whether I want only water, oxygen, or food for the rest of my life than I would be capable of choosing which two of these people to let go.

Kianga shifts one knee just slightly so that it brushes Saif's, and he swallows, looking at the floor. Diego watches this, but doesn't seem angry, nor does he wipe the emotions from his face entirely. A small smirk lifts one side of his lips, and he strokes my hair gently.

The four of us. It could work. If this thought is nothing more than venom-induced whimsy, I don't ever want to come down from this high.

Unfortunately, my healing factor has other plans. The effects of the venom are beginning to dull already, but I still have enough courage to say one more thing.

"I love you," I say to the ceiling, as three pairs of eyes watch me. "*All* of you," I finish quietly, my gaze sweeping between them.

Kianga. *Utterly.*

Saif. *Irrevocably.*

Diego. *Eternally.*

Then I close my eyes, and the silence stretches on for a long moment.

"We love you too, Eilidh," Kianga says as I fall asleep.

Dreaming

I wake up in Diego's lap with only a hazy recollection of what had transpired a few minutes before. He's got me cradled against his chest, and he and Kianga are conversing quietly.

As my eyes flutter open, they land on Saif. He's sitting against the wall, his long legs pulled up to his chest, his arms crossed and propped on his knees. His chin rests on his wrists, and his eyes are volleying back and forth between Diego and Kianga like he's watching the world's most riveting tennis match.

I watch him for a moment silently, and he must feel my eyes on him, because his gaze snaps to me, and he smiles. "Hey there, Sleeping Beauty."

Diego helps me sit up. I give him a grateful smile, then turn back to Saif. "You're supposed to fight a dragon before I wake up, you know."

He exhales quickly through his nose. "If I ever find one, I'll fight it for you."

I smile widely as Kianga snorts. "You'll be looking for a while, since dragons aren't real."

He smirks, and I can't help but pout. I knew that already, but still. *Disappointing.*

Suddenly, I realize that I'm still not wearing a shirt. Diego's body heat had kept me so warm I hadn't noticed, but now that I'm sitting on the floor beside him, I'm very aware that I'm wearing only my sports bra.

I rub my arms quickly and look around, and Kianga hands me my top with a smirk. Our fingers brush when I grab it, and I shiver. I throw it over my head and turn to Diego. "Is that what it's like with Hyun-Joo?" I ask as I throw my hair on top of my head in a bun.

He swallows hard, watching as I twist my hair and try to tame the flyaways — to no avail, of course. "Not at all. With her it's very . . . clinical."

I nod slowly as we all climb to our feet. Saif stands first and reaches a hand out to Kianga, and she grips it tightly as he pulls her up.

Diego steadies me as he rises. "Can you walk?"

I scoff. "Yeah." In truth, I'm feeling like I've just spent way too long on the treadmill; the floor seems to move under me, and my stomach twists. I take a tentative step, and promptly pitch sideways into his chest.

Saif reaches out to me instinctively, but Diego raises a calming hand to him as he cocks an eyebrow at me. "*Lobita,*" he scolds.

I push away from him. "I'm fine."

His pinched mouth conveys just how fine he thinks I really am, but he doesn't argue. I stand as though on a rocking ship, but as Kianga takes my hand and leads me down the hall, my steps steady.

We make our way through the dungeon and up the stairs, our fingers intertwined. As she opens the door, though, she pulls her hand from mine, and I try not to take it personally. I know that Kianga has to stay behind closed doors.

Bastet leads us out into the main concourse with her head held high.

Diego walks beside her easily, as if he hadn't just been chained in a dungeon.

Saif falls into step with me. "I'm pretty sure I'm dreaming," he says idly, and I look up at him in surprise.

"Why?"

He smirks and gestures, palm up, at everything in front of him, shaking his head. "Why *not*? Imane is alive." His eyelids flutter slightly as he looks at her back. "Diego is smiling at me again." He inhales shakily as his eyes rove down Diego's form. "He hasn't smiled at me in *years*," he whispers.

I take Saif's hand and he looks at me, his eyes glistening. "And you . . ."

This could go several different ways. I stiffen as I wait for him to finish the sentence, forcing myself not to clutch his hand too tightly.

The look he gives me is a loaded one. "Eilidh, I . . . I'm sorr—"

"I forgive you," I say quietly, cutting him off. "I understand. You had to make an impossible choice."

"And I made the wro—"

"No, you didn't."

He shakes his head, but I take his other hand and we stop, in the middle of the pyramid. People and magical creatures alike go about their business around us, giving us a wide berth.

"Saif, I'm a stubborn asshole."

He must not have been expecting that; he barks a laugh that he immediately tries to cover up as a cough, but I just smile up at him.

"I *am*, and I know I am, but I'm going to try to be better. I'm sorry that I made you feel like you couldn't just talk to me. That I ever doubted you." I swallow the lump forming in my throat. "I'm sorry you took all that on alone."

He pulls me in tightly against him, tucking me under his chin, and I breathe in his floral scent hungrily. The soap he's been using here must be ivory instead of charcoal, but it doesn't make one bit of difference to me.

"I love you," I say to his chest, feeling his strong heartbeat beneath my ear. "I promise I'll be better. I'll listen more."

He kisses the top of my head. "I love you too, *Lahabi*. But please, don't just listen. I need you to let me in, too."

"I did a little bit," I say, though with little conviction. "I told you about Kianga. And my fear of eternity."

He pulls back and looks me in the eye. "You are more than just the reasons you think you're broken, *hayati*." He smirks, and a small smile creeps onto my face, too.

"Soulmate?" I ask quietly. I remember Kianga's dad calling her mom that sometimes, but I'm not positive what it actually means.

"My life," he responds with a quick kiss to my forehead, and his beard prickles my skin in the best way. "Share your happy secrets with me too, not just the deepest darkest ones. Okay?"

"Okay, I will. I promise."

"Good," he says quietly, his eyes lowering to my lips.

"Good," I repeat, and then I close my eyes and lean up into him.

As soon as his lips are on mine, I hear someone clearing their throat directly beside us. We pull away quickly and turn to see a very amused Kianga, her hip cocked, and her arms crossed. "No making out in the public areas. This is a rebel base, not a Roman bathhouse."

Indeed, several people are looking at us with varied expressions of annoyance on their faces. I flush, and take a step back from Saif, who adjusts his glasses and clears his throat. "Sorry," I mutter, and Kianga just rolls her eyes.

Saif and I follow behind her and Diego toward the west side of the pyramid until suddenly, the smell of food cooking hits me. My stomach roars loud enough that Saif looks at me in concern, and I clutch it tightly. "When did you eat last?"

"I . . ." I comb through my memories.

"She hasn't eaten since we were in the Cuhloch Forest," Diego says over his shoulder.

"*What?*" Saif turns to me indignantly.

"Well, something came up!" I shoot back at him, gesturing at Kianga, and he looks at the ceiling in exasperation. "Snitch!" I hiss at Diego's back. I know he can hear me, but he ignores me.

I think back to the final morning in the woods when Diego, Valentina, and I had woken up in the cabin, then eaten the last of our provisions before making our way back to the portal to meet Hyun-Joo and get Martín from the hospital.

It's a miracle I haven't passed out, or that I'm walking at all. The only explanation is that my healing factor must be able to counteract hunger as well. *That's pretty cool.*

My stomach growls a second time. *But apparently not forever.*

My mouth is watering profusely by the time we walk through the door into a large cafeteria. A few steps in, I grab Saif's hand tightly, and he turns to me in alarm. "What's wrong?" He asks, seeing the expression on my face.

Diego and Kianga turn as well.

"I have *one* more deep dark secret I need to divulge," I say hesitantly.

Saif glances at the others, then back to me, his warm eyes dancing with concern. "What?"

I take a deep breath.

"I'm vegan."

~~~~~~~~~~

The four of us sit outside at a round table, shaded by the ceiling above us that runs parallel with the pyramid. Kianga is picking delicately at her fish, broccoli, and rice, and Diego and Saif had both opted for some kind of dish with chicken and pasta. Both of them are watching me devour my overloaded burrito like they've never seen me eat before.
~~~~~~~~~~

"What?" I ask around a mouthful of rice and black beans.

"Just picturing you with the blood from that steak running down your chin," Diego says idly, and Saif runs his hand through his hair.

"Was it a frog steak?" Kianga asks mildly, popping a broccoli floret into her mouth, and I shudder violently.

"Please don't," I plead.

Diego takes a bite with an amused expression. "Do I want to know?"

"No," I say firmly, poking at a slice of bell pepper that had escaped from my rolled tortilla and landed on the plate.

Kianga snorts. "We had to dissect frogs in seventh grade science, and I thought she was going to wash ours away in a river of tears. She never touched meat or dairy again after that."

Saif smiles at me sympathetically.

I turn slightly green as the smell of formaldehyde fills my nostrils through the years. I had told Kianga that very night that if she ever let them put that vile substance on me when I died, that I would haunt her for eternity.

How ironic.

"It's not my fault lycanthropy has no respect for my principles," I mutter, then, after a moment of hesitation, take another bite of my burrito.

"Is it a bad time to mention that those *empanadas* I made for Val's birthday had cheese in them?" Diego asks.

I grimace, but shake my head. "No, I knew they did. But I wasn't going to pitch a fit about fucking *cheese* when I was already freeloading in a magical castle."

Saif crosses his arms, looking like he wants to argue, but I don't give him the chance.

"Besides, I don't let the perfect be the enemy of the good. A little cheese doesn't negate nearly twenty years of *not* having it."

"How the fuck did you kill a werewolf?" Kianga asks seriously, scrutinizing me. "You're so . . . you."

I scrunch my face at that, but she continues. "V-word aside, I've never even seen you kill a spider. You made your grandparents get humane traps so mice could be let go. You cried every summer when the neighbors bought a pig for their annual roast."

"That's different," I shrug, crumbling a napkin in one hand. "Bleddyn wasn't an innocent animal. He was a monster."

Saif glances sidelong at Kianga, who sighs at the table. "He wasn't, you know," she says after a moment. "Not really."

I rub my left shoulder, drawing her attention to the ragged scars. "Yes, he was," I say firmly.

She grimaces. "Well, maybe he was by the end," she relents. "But he wasn't always."

When she catches the dubious look Diego and I exchange, she stands and jerks her head toward the door that leads back into the cafeteria. "Let me show you."

Invisible Connections

We follow her through the cafeteria, into the main area, and to one of the escalators. As she steps onto it, and the stairs start gliding smoothly upward.

I grip the railing tightly to catch my balance. "How —?"

She chuckles at me. I glance around for buttons, but there are none. "Magic, *habibti.*"

When we get to the fourth floor, she heads to a marble door in the center of the eastern wall. The silhouette of a humanoid black cat is engraved on the door — Bastet.

"Subtle," I say.

Kianga just rolls her eyes and places her palm on the door. After a second, a light blue stream of light ripples out from her hand, and the door swings open.

Magic, I think with awe.

I gasp as I enter the room. It's far bigger than it should be. I step back out and look at the next door over, which is only about ten feet away. A wide grin is plastered on my face when I re-enter the room. "Kianga."

"Don't," she deadpans.

"Your room."

"Eilidh Joann."

"It's bigger on the inside."

She crosses her arms and releases a long-suffering sigh, a small smile on her lips. "I knew you were going to say that."

"Fucking *magic*." I shake my head in wonder as I take in the rest of the room. The cheery afternoon sky is bright through the glass wall, though the room is the perfect temperature. Torches - actual, honest to goodness torches - line the walls in evenly spaced sconces, though none of them are lit yet. "You have escalators but not light switches?"

She pushes a spot on the closest torch, and flames burst to life in every one of them. She grins at me silently.

I cross my arms. "Well now you're just showing off."

Diego snorts.

A white wardrobe is against the wall to our left, and a few feet away from that is a door that I assume leads to the bathroom. A bed so large it could be two king-size mattresses shoved together sits on a dais in the corner to our right, piled high with satin sheets, and a small mountain of pillows.

Against the glass wall opposite us, one side of a sleek desk is buried under what must be a forest's worth of papers, scrolls, folded letters, and books. But on the other side . . .

"You have a *computer*?" I kick my shoes off and set them hastily on the rack beside the door, then cross the expanse of her room and run my fingers over the shiny gold of the monitor. "Why? Playing Solitaire?" Saif and Diego seem just as surprised as I am.

She smirks at the three of us, obviously satisfied with herself. "It's how I communicate with my people throughout the continent."

Diego shakes his head. "That's not possible. There are no satellites in this dimension. No communication lines, or grids, or anything that could —"

"Ley lines, *corazón*." He blinks hard as she presses a button on the underside of the monitor, and the bright screen pops on instantly.

The interface is sleek and clean. An opaque golden bubble with a "42" is attached to an envelope icon, which Kianga frowns at. "Get to those later," she mutters to herself.

Saif is gaping at her. "You used the ley lines like internet cables."

She tries to keep the pride from her voice, but she doesn't succeed — and rightfully so. "I didn't even know if it would work at first, and the Tech Mages put in some serious overtime to figure out how to do it. But we finished it up just over a year ago, and now we can talk to our agents, no matter where they're stationed. Tenazeryth is fucking full of ley lines. It's like this place is held together by them."

Diego whistles. "They don't even have this tech in New Camlann."

Her expression clouds, and she nods solemnly. "They don't have it anywhere that Auberon rules over, because he's keeping this whole dimension in the Dark Ages."

I wince, but only Saif notices. He puts a comforting hand on my shoulder, then points toward the wall to our right. "Look." My eyes light up when I see what he's drawing my attention to.

An elegant golden beverage cart is set up against the wall. The lower shelf is lined with wine and whiskey bottles, but on the top shelf sits a gleaming espresso machine with several cut crystal jars of coffee beans beside it.

I all but float to the cart and open one of the jars, inhaling the heavenly scent of the beans — notes of cherry and chocolate send a chill of delight down my spine. I set the jar back down and lightly caress a French press and a large hourglass-shaped pot for pour-over coffees, just making sure they're real.

"Want some?" Kianga asks from beside me. I had been so engrossed in the treasure trove in front of me, I hadn't heard her approach.

"More than anything," I say, surveying the other jars.

She puts a cool hand on my shoulder, reaching for one. I suppress another shiver at her touch. "You'll want this one." She holds the jar under my nose and I inhale deeply.

"God yes," I breathe.

She brews a pot of the hazelnut coffee in the hourglass pot; Saif is the only one who declines a cup. Finally, it's time to get down to business.

Kianga sits at her desk and brings up a file on her computer. I find myself clutching the back of her chair and leaning in, trying desperately to not get distracted by her lilac and gooseberry scent.

Saif and Diego stand on either side of me as a picture of a lithe, platinum blonde white woman pops up on the screen. They both inhale sharply, and I raise a brow at Saif.

"Bleddyn's last victim," he explains. "Before he attacked you."

Kianga makes a disgruntled noise. "Yeah. Now look at *her* victims." She opens another file folder, and begins clicking through dozens of pictures of people. There seems to be no pattern to them; they're various ages, races, and genders. The only thing they have in common is that their lifeless bodies have all been mutilated.

I flinch away from the screen. "Why are you showing us this?" Saif looks ill. I squeeze his hand. Diego is frowning at the screen, analyzing each photo as quickly as she brings them up.

"Because these are the people that she killed."

"How?" Diego hisses through bared fangs.

Kianga closes the file and spins in her chair to face the three of us. "All the women Bleddyn killed were trafficking humans. Selling them off to the highest bidder for their amusement. And when they were done with them . . ." She gestures at the screen.

Saif sits down hard on the ground just as Diego begins pacing back and forth. I look between them as my heart twists in sympathy.

"Where?" Diego asks, glaring at the floor as he paces.

"Not in New Camlann, if that makes you feel better," Kianga says gently. "Those traffickers were evil, but they weren't stupid. They knew there was always one member of the Order or another out in the city, so they never took their shit there."

"How?"

She doesn't need him to expound upon this. "Azaeroria was the first to catch wind of it. Apparently succubi were some of the first Fabled that they approached when they started, thinking they'd be the most likely to pay top dollar."

She rolls her eyes. "Stupid fucking move. Succubi don't need to pay to have their fun. They can find consenting participants all on their own. But the Mages had their prejudices, and that was ultimately their undoing."

Saif's voice wavers when he speaks. "So she and Bleddyn came to you with the information? Why?"

Kianga glances at me, her eyes tight with sympathy. "It was no secret in the Fabled Underground that I had been searching for help to get to Auberon. A way to bring him down. Azaeroria and Bleddyn came up with the idea to use the deaths of those Mages to keep the Order busy. Keep your focus on them, instead of where our forces were hitting."

Diego stalks past us once again. "And where is that?" I can't tell if he sounds more annoyed or impressed. I for one am definitely more of the latter.

"The Lords."

He stops in his tracks, utterly bewildered. "You killed the —"

"No!" She throws her hands in the air. "We haven't killed anyone!" She pauses, tapping an almond-shaped nail against her chin. "Well, except the traffickers." She takes the final sip of her coffee. "The Lords just work for us, now. Feed us information. Send fake intel to Auberon, when we need them to."

Diego runs a hand over his face, and she watches him closely as she says her next sentence. "We have all of them except Balin."

Diego scoffs and continues his pacing, muttering in Spanish. I specifically catch a *"Pendejo"* in the mix. Clearly, Diego is not a fan.

I dig through a few memories of my library chats with my father. "The Lord of New Camlann?"

She nods. "He's the last nut we have to crack. I've got my best agent on it, and I'm hoping to get good news from her any day now."

Diego stops once more, puts his hands on his hips, and sighs at the ceiling. "You're an evil mastermind."

She smirks. "That's the nicest thing you've ever said to me."

He holds her gaze for a long beat before he blinks and turns away.

"So what's the actual plan?" Saif asks.

Kianga muses on this a moment. "To wait for Balin's defection, then take out Auberon with the support of his Lords. Set up a new government with them that benefits *everyone*. And with you three available to us now, maybe we can develop a backup plan."

She begins pulling documents from the piles around her desk, seemingly at random, but she apparently knows exactly what she's looking for. "Diego." She spreads a map across the desk and leans over it.

He's at her side in an instant. "What do you need?" He places a hand gently on the small of her back, and the tension goes out of her shoulders. She points something out on a document, and they launch into something about personnel and informants until my eyes glaze over.

Saif holds out his hand, gesturing for my coffee mug. "Here, I'll get you a refill. I think you're going to need it."

Kianga glances at him as he walks to the beverage cart. "Actually, I think we're all going to need a drink."

As Saif pours drinks, a thought occurs to me. "Who's Arthur Pendragon?" I ask Kianga.

She glances up at me like she's about to start checking my pupils for concussion symptoms. "You're the one who had a birthday party where you made everyone dress up like knights of the Round Table, Lee, not me."

I roll my eyes. "First of all, you spent hours bedazzling your paper towel roll sword. Don't act like you didn't have fun. Second, I mean *here*. Bleddyn said someone using the code name Arthur Pendragon hired Azaeroria to kill me. So who is it, *Bastet*?"

Her brow furrows, and she looks off into the distance, deep in thought. After a moment, she shakes her head. "I have no idea. I haven't heard of anyone using that code name."

"Damn." I sigh and take my mug from Saif. "Well, I intend to find out who it is at some point."

"That's fine. If what he said is true, we'll find them once we're done with Auberon." Kianga smiles sweetly. "And then I'll rip their throat out."

Plotting

Hours later, we've made no headway with a backup plan.

"Absolutely fucking not." Diego says for the thousandth time as he sits down hard in his chair and tosses back of swig of red wine. Three additional chairs had been brought up by an ogre, and we had pulled the desk away from the wall.

"Seconded." Saif stands and begins pacing the path Diego had just abandoned, swirling his whiskey thoughtfully.

Kianga leans over the desk, bracing herself for a battle.

"You aren't winning this argument boys, trust me." My sing-song statement is punctuated by the sound of the tennis ball I'm tossing hitting the wall with a *thunk* before it bounces back to me.

I had found several of them in a drawer when we moved the desk - *Plantar fasciitis doesn't give a damn what dimension I'm in, Lee* - and have been tossing it against the wall for some twenty minutes.

"She's the most stubborn bitch in this dimension and the next. Why do you think she's in charge of this rebellion? It isn't talent — she just filibustered the competition."

"It's a good plan." Kianga draws herself up with exaggerated bravado. "And this most stubborn bitch is the former debate team captain, thank you very much."

"I'm sorry, can we focus?" Saif begs of the ceiling, with one hand pressed against his cheek.

"No need, it's not happening." Diego is obstinate.

"Shouldn't *I* be the one who gets to decide that?" I ask of the tennis ball. It doesn't reply, but I know it agrees with me. I toss it again, a bit too hard. It zings back at me with surprising alacrity, and I barely manage to snatch it from the air before it hits me in the face.

"No," Saif and Diego say in unison.

I glare down at the ball, wondering if I can hit them both with it at once. "I distinctly remember that just this morning I reminded you both that I can make my own decisions." I look at them pointedly.

Saif cracks under my glare and frowns at the wall, sipping his drink, but Diego holds my gaze.

"And I remember that having nothing to do with you getting to decide to walk into a lion's den *alone*." His tone is light, but his claws are out, scratching against the top of the table.

I wince at the sound it makes. "If I can convince my father that I was captured - which is technically true - and that I escaped to return to him, he won't suspect a thing." I chop my right hand into my open left palm. "I'll get the location of the missing Fabled from him. Then I slit his throat in his sleep. Mission done. Peace restored. Countless lives saved without even needing war and bloodshed." I pause, my hand still hovering in midair from making a slicing motion. "Well, only a little bloodshed."

"I'm not putting you at the mercy of an '*if*,'" Diego bites.

I use both pointer fingers to draw his attention to my mouth. "My. Choice."

"Then we're going with you." Saif has his hands on his hips. His glasses are slipping down his nose, and his hair is rumpled from him running his hands through it so frequently.

I look at him sadly. "*You* definitely can't. Valentina will drop the entire lake on you if you get within a hundred yards of Arkenvale."

Diego snorts. "If Martín doesn't build a pyre and immolate you first."

Saif freezes. "But Martín is dead," he rasps.

I wince. I forgot that I had let him think that. Diego glances sidelong at me.

"Yeah, he was," he says slowly, waiting for me to finish the sentence.

I sigh. "Until I . . . resurrected him?" I end it as a question and look at Kianga and Saif with one eye open, the other wincing shut.

Saif slumps back against the wall, staring at me.

Kianga steeples her fingers and presses them to her mouth for a moment. "You. What?"

I sigh again. "I was still immobilized." I glance at Saif, who looks sick. "So Diego carried me over to Martín's body. I couldn't let it end like that. He —" My voice breaks. "He protected Valentina from their father when they were kids. From the whole world. He had always stepped in for her, and all I could think about was how no one ever stepped in for him. It made me so *angry*."

I swipe my hand over my eyes. "I reached out." I mimic the movement to show them. "Grabbed him, and wished to bring him back. Then there was a buzzing in my navel." I press a hand to my stomach, remembering exactly how it had felt. "It went up through my arm and into Martín. There was a rust-colored glow, his skin stitched itself back together, and he woke up."

Saif and Kianga are both staring at me with their mouths open.

"Holy. Shit." Kianga says finally. "That's . . . *amazing*. You're incredible."

I shake my head. "I'm not. I didn't control it, it just happened. I have no clue how, or how to do it again." I look at my hands, but they're just as normal as ever. "And he was only *mostly* dead."

Kianga rolls her eyes. "Focus, Shaw. Don't reference the greats right now. This is serious."

Saif slides down the wall, puts his head in his hands, and begins sobbing silently.

I stand quickly and make my way over to him. "Hey," I whisper, putting a hand on his arm. "He's okay. It's all okay."

Saif just shakes his head. "I thought I'd live with that guilt for the rest of my life," he says between gasps for air. I pull him into my chest and he shakes against me.

I look up at Kianga, who comes and sits down on Saif's other side, placing a soothing hand on his leg. He reaches toward her blindly, and she clasps his hand tightly.

Diego watches Saif for a moment and begins to rise as if he, too, wants to come hug him, but instead sits back and casts his gaze down at the floor. Saif had let him shed his tears earlier as he recounted the story about the Fae settlement. Now he lets Saif shed his over a brother he thought he lost being returned to him.

Though I don't think even the ever-jovial Martín can forgive him.

Some bridges you just can't rebuild after they burn, even if you had the best of intentions when you lit the match.

After a few minutes, Saif's tears cease, and I kiss his forehead. He just looks at me sadly. "He'll never forgive me. He *shouldn't*," he says quietly.

I say nothing. I may have forgiven Saif, but he hadn't gotten a wulver's ax buried in my chest. I think of Valentina, and the cold fury in her voice as she screamed at Hyun-Joo that she was going to get him justice. She'll never forgive him either.

The Order is broken.

Kianga stands and makes her way back to her desk, shuffling various papers around as she sits. "There have been no reports of any of the other Order members - or Auberon himself - out looking for you two. I know it's only been two days, but I expected some activity by now."

"How is this place kept hidden, anyway?" I ask her. "It's a huge pyramid in an alternate-dimension Illinois. Not exactly subtle."

Saif had pointed out on the map earlier that we are on Esclados, a tiny island to the west of the main continent. The closest portal on Earth is in Chicago.

She exhales sharply through her nose as she looks through some scrolls. "It's glamoured. Anyone who doesn't know this is here just sees trees and an empty island."

I gawk at her. "Your Mages seem to be able to do anything," I say, thinking of Ousmane. Come to think of it, I have no clue what his power is.

"I wish," she says. "But maybe eventually we'll have enough, and they actually can."

Diego doesn't look up from the paper he's reviewing. "How many do you have?"

"Not as many as I'd like. We're always recruiting more, but that's one of the hardest parts about this whole operation." She frowns, lost in thought.

I can only imagine what she has had to deal with the past few years, coordinating all of this. I'm exhausted just thinking about it. *She's a goddamn superhero.*

Saif wipes a hand across his face a final time and stands, then holds a hand out to help me up.

Diego clicks his claws on the desk. "If you both think this is the best plan, then we'll do it." He looks at Kianga as he points at me. "But she's not going back there alone. I'm going too. I can tell Auberon I escaped and broke her out. He'll believe me."

I bite my lip. It's risky, but it *would* make me feel better to have him with me behind enemy lines. I worry, though, about separating him from the rebellion now that he's here. He's a great leader, and a brilliant strategist. He can do so much good here at Kianga's side. He can provide the help she hasn't had all this time.

She doesn't *need* it; she's perfectly capable of running it by herself. She's proven that. But I'm sure she would appreciate some help all the same.

"I won't be alone. Once I'm back at Arkenvale, I can explain to the others what's going on and —"

"No." Kianga cuts me off sharply. "We can't risk one of them revealing our plan to Auberon."

I cross my arms. "None of them would do that."

"Maybe not on purpose, but it's too risky. What if he grows suspicious and tries to get information out of them? I don't know the others, but I know Hyun-Joo would die before she betrayed Diego. Do you want that on your conscience?"

I suppress a shudder. "No," I say quietly.

She looks at Diego. "And I just don't know if you should go. We don't know how long it could take for her to get the information out of him about the missing Fabled, or get close enough to end him. Can you act like things are normal for an indefinite amount of time?"

His mouth twists in annoyance. "I know perfectly well how to play the part of the stoic soldier."

Kianga jerks her head at me, and some of the cuffs around her braids clink. "And can you act like nothing has changed between you two? Auberon has shown you what he really is. If he sees you two have gotten too close, he'll suspect she knows as well, and then the plan goes to hell. It could put her in danger."

He presses his mouth into a line at that, but he doesn't answer.

Kianga sighs. "I didn't think so."

His gaze sweeps briefly to me, then Saif, then back to her. "I've had plenty of practice pretending I don't have any feelings for her. I can do it again."

Saif mumbles something under his breath that sounds an awful lot like, "You're not as subtle as you think," but Diego ignores him.

My stomach clenches. "Valentina already knows about us," I say to the desk. "Which means Martín probably does, too."

Kianga puts her head in her hand. "Fucking hell. Could you for *once* not kiss and tell?"

"It's not my fault!" I say indignantly.

"*How* is it not your fault?" She asks dubiously.

Saif sits down beside me, and I bite my lip.

Diego saves me. "Bleddyn said during the battle that he smelled my scent on her. Valentina heard him clear as day."

Kianga runs her face over her hands and looks up at the ceiling. "Well then, you guys are going to have to really sell that it was a one-time thing, and that you've gone back to hating each other."

"So Diego can come?" I try to keep the pleading note out of my voice.

She sighs. "Fuck it. I'm not going to be able to stop him anyway." I smirk.

He stands, and goes to refill his drink at the beverage cart. "That settles it then."

Just then, there's a soft knock at the door. As Kianga goes to answer it, I walk to the glass wall and gaze over the brown field. Saif joins me, and rubs a hand over my upper back. "Are you sure that this is what you want to do?" He asks quietly.

I cross my arms and lean into him. "I have to, Saif. Who else could? Look at what he's doing." He sighs through his nose as I gesture at the dead grass. "He's killing The Fabled. He's killing the dimension. He has to be stopped."

"I just worry about you," he murmurs.

I put a hand to his cheek and pull him toward me until our foreheads are touching. "I know. But I can do this. I need you to believe in me."

The corners of his eyes tighten. "I've always believed in you. But that won't stop me from worrying."

Kianga closes the door. As we turn back around, I catch Diego's eye. He's watching Saif and I intently over the rim of his glass. The wine has painted his lips a dark red, and I swallow involuntarily as he licks them.

Saif follows my line of sight and, once he realizes Diego is observing us, takes a step back. I reach out to him instinctively, but though he lets me take his hand, he stands up straight and clears his throat. "I should get to bed."

Kianga plops in her chair beside Diego and reaches for her whiskey. "I don't think so."

Saif freezes. "What?" Diego smirks and takes another sip of his wine. My gaze flicks between the three of them.

Kianga takes a quick swig and turns off the monitor. "What what?" She widens her eyes at Saif innocently. "You think you're going to leave me stuck with these two alone? I don't think so."

My mouth twitches upward. "Who said I was staying here?" I ask teasingly.

She chuckles and swirls her drink. "Well you don't have to, I suppose. Where did you stay last night, anyway? You didn't trip any alarms, so I knew you hadn't left the pyramid, but by the time I sent someone to bring you to me, you were nowhere to be found. I thought maybe you had found the library and passed out in the stacks."

My eyes immediately go to Saif, who is suddenly scratching his beard, apparently having found something intriguing on the ceiling. "I was with - you have a li - wait, you wanted me here?" My pulse kick-starts as I register what she had said. "Why?"

She gives me a quick once-over, still smirking. She and Diego exchange a look. Despite their years apart, they seem to be able to communicate with each other silently. "Eilidh, I know you got drunk on venom earlier, but do you remember what I said before that?"

I swallow hard and squeeze Saif's hand. "Yeah." I fight to keep my voice steady. As if I would ever forget her telling me she loved me. As if I won't taste her lips on mine for the rest of my immortal life.

She beckons us with a curl of her finger, and we pull our chairs closer to her and Diego so that the four of us create a circle.

"I meant what I said. I love you. I love you now, and I loved you then, even though I didn't know it yet."

I can practically hear my heart pounding. "You did?"

"Of course I did. You think I would have wasted a perfectly good fish on someone who was just a *friend?*"

I chuckle, but though I try to smile, it quickly dies. My eyes flick between all three of them briefly, then settle on the desk. "What do we do about . . . this?" My leg bounces rapidly.

She makes a thoughtful noise. "Well, we're all adults, and we don't have the luxury of time for bullshit. So let's just be open about it." She looks between Saif and Diego. "You both love her."

They both glance at me, and I swallow hard. But then, Saif places a hand on my bouncing knee and nods. Me knee stills under his calming touch.

Diego watches him for a moment before he answers. "Yes."

Kianga turns to me. "And you love them both." It isn't even a question — by the time I open my mouth to confirm this, she's moved on, back to them. "And I assume you two finally slept together at some point, so we've all got some choices to make."

My jaw drops open audibly. Saif's cheeks instantly flame, and he starts sputtering, but Diego just barks a humorless laugh. "No, we didn't, actually. He was too busy hating me for getting you killed."

One side of her mouth lifts, and she puts a hand to her heart as she looks at Saif. "That's actually very sweet. You held a grudge for me this whole time?"

Diego shakes his head at me and raises his palms to the ceiling. *Can you believe this?*

I bite down hard on my lips to keep from bursting into laughter.

Saif smiles sideways at Kianga. "You knew how I felt about you."

Diego's brows shoot up in surprise. "You did?"

She nods. "He finally told me a few weeks before our last mission. But I had already made my choice."

"I don't —" I clamp my mouth shut, afraid that if I say my wish out loud, it will shatter. As long as I keep it locked away, it's safe, but reality is always so cruel to our most precious desires.

What if they say no?

Diego inclines his head and looks at me through his lashes, and suddenly, I can hear the words he had said to me behind that cabin. *Use your words, and tell me what you want.*

Saif and Kianga are both staring at me, waiting for me to continue. I hold Diego's gaze, and find my strength in the fire of his eyes, just as I had that night. "I don't want to choose."

Diego smirks. "Good girl," he breathes softly, so that only I can hear it. My heart skips a beat. I glance nervously at Kianga and Saif, but they're each wearing a small smile. "I don't want *any* of us to have to choose. Is . . . is that okay?"

Saif tucks a hair behind my ear. "I told you I'd respect whatever decision you made, and I meant it." He casts his gaze to Diego and Kianga briefly. "Besides . . . I don't want to choose either."

Kianga sets her glass down decisively. "Okay then. Fuck choosing. Any objections?"

Diego shakes his head. "No. Just a request."

He leans forward and grabs Saif's chin. Saif inhales sharply, and then in the next instant, Diego's mouth is on his. The air practically ignites when their lips meet, and Saif's rigidity melts away. He kisses Diego back fiercely, grunting against his mouth, and wraps a hand around the back of his neck.

When they pull apart, Saif pants desperately, his eyes still on Diego's lips. Diego grins wickedly.

"Get in the fucking bed."

Quartet

The next thing I know, Diego has dragged Saif onto the bed, and climbed on top of him. Kianga stands and holds a hand out to me with a smile.

I take it in a daze, my eyes on the men as we approach. It takes Diego no time to kiss down Saif's body and remove his pants.

As Kianga lies down and pulls me with her, Diego takes Saif's erection in one gulp. Saif's eyes fly open and he puts a hand into Diego's hair, gasping at the ceiling as Diego moans against him.

It's an unbelievably arousing sight.

I lower myself onto Kianga and begin kissing her feverishly. She moans against my mouth, but just as I'm about to dig my nails into her thigh, Diego grabs my hand.

"She likes it gentle," he says, before he licks Saif from base to tip. Saif, who is clutching the bars of the headboard desperately, mutters something that could either be a curse or a prayer.

I run my fingertips lightly from her hip to her knee, and she shivers. "I can be gentle." I undress her slowly, kissing every inch of her, relishing every second. When I'm done, I position myself above her, and she smiles up at me.

She's as radiant as a goddess.

I gently pinch one of her nipples and suck on the other one. She writhes under me, and I can feel myself getting wetter. I straddle her thigh and chase delicious friction while I kiss every inch of her I can. She moves her thigh with me, and I gasp against her skin, drunk with lust.

"I love you," I say, planting a long kiss on the side of her neck. "I always have. I always will." I kiss her collarbone. She puts a hand into my hair, brings me up to kiss her, and I comply immediately.

She pulls back after a moment and looks at me like she's trying to memorize my face. "I love you too. I'm sorry that I didn't realize I was in love with you until I didn't have you anymore." Tears form in the corner of her eyes. "I wish . . ."

I kiss her quickly, cutting her off. "We're together now. That's what matters."

I look over as Diego crawls back up Saif, who is trembling and panting with lust. I smile as he pulls Diego into a deep kiss.

"We're all together," I say. My heart is so full, I fear it may burst.

I've been going through life with jagged edges that kept everyone at arm's length. Anyone who tried to get too close had gotten sliced, and never tried again. But now, miraculously, I've come upon the people whose cracked borders align with mine perfectly. Instead of pushing them away, my broken pieces hold them more firmly to me.

I kiss Kianga one more time, then go down on her. I moan as I flick my tongue against her. She tastes amazing; better than I had ever imagined.

In my periphery, Diego and Saif are moving against one another; Diego has both their throbbing erections in one hand, and he's slowly jerking them off together as Saif moans and squirms underneath him.

Diego brings his mouth to Saif's jaw and nibbles, his fangs firmly tucked away. "Still hate me, Rahim?" He rumbles.

Saif grunts dizzily, his eyes shut tightly. "Shut the fuck up, Vidales."

Diego chuckles into Saif's neck. "Good boy."

Saif melts down harder into the blankets.

Kianga pushes her head back into the pillow and grinds her hips up into my mouth. I let her move as she needs to, licking up and down until she suddenly cries out and her legs tremble. I don't stop moving my tongue until she stops shaking.

I sit back on my heels for just a moment before Diego grabs me and pulls me roughly into his lap. Saif takes my place, kissing his way up Kianga's body. They move slowly with one another, tender and gentle.

I can tell from the glint in his eye that Diego has no such plan for me. My heart pounds in excitement. He bites the side of my neck, and I moan as he tangles a hand into my hair.

I rake my nails down his back, and he growls into my collarbone before sinking his fangs into my neck. I scream my pleasure just as he clamps his hand over my mouth.

"Don't worry about being loud," Kianga says after my cry dies down. "All bedrooms are warded and soundproof." She goes back to kissing Saif and holding him tightly as he thrusts inside her deliberately.

Diego raises his brows and looks down at me like an entirely new world of possibilities has just been opened to him. His pupils dilate.

"Very interesting," he rumbles. He trails his pointer finger up my neck and scratches the underside of my chin, holding me with his gaze as he decides what to do with me. I shudder in anticipation, and his erection throbs against me.

I grind against his lap and close my eyes while he thinks, but then he digs his claws into my chin sharply, and I gasp as I look back at him. "Eyes on me, darling," he commands through his teeth, his eyes lidded heavily.

Holy fuck.

He kisses me deeply, his tongue pushing as far into my mouth as he can manage.

"Now then," he says when we break apart.

He throws me down onto the mattress, then flips me over. Before I can blink, he wraps an arm around my hips and pulls me back toward him until I'm on all fours, my ass and pussy facing him.

He shoves one thick finger into me as he leans down and kisses down my spine, pricking me with his fangs. I moan slowly as I tremble, trying to steady myself so that I don't collapse into a puddle under his touch.

"If one finger makes you moan like that, I can't wait to hear what my cock does to you," he growls.

I growl back and turn to look at him. "Then put it in me already, and find out."

He bites his lower lip, and crimson blooms around his fang. I wish desperately that I could reach to put my mouth over his.

"I will, but only after you beg for it," he smirks.

He is absolutely evil. But I'm learning how to be, too.

"Make me." I throw back at him.

His eyes widen momentarily, then he closes them and exhales slowly, relishing my words, his fangs glinting as he smiles diabolically.

"I was hoping you would say that," he breathes.

He pushes my head down into the mattress and shoves two fingers deep inside me, rubbing my clit as he does so. I cry out once again as his pace increases, and he scratches down my back.

Then he moves down and bites my thigh while his fingers twist inside me. The venom reaches my head seconds later. Finally, I can't take it anymore. The orgasm crashes over me in wave after delirious wave, and I moan his name loudly.

He pushes his tip into me and holds it there, trailing his nails up and down my back. My pussy clenches around him and he moans. I try to push myself back onto his throbbing erection, but he holds me away.

"So eager, aren't you?" He rubs my clit in steady circles, and it's all I can do to not come again. I grip my hands into the edge of the mattress and whimper into the blankets. "What did I say you had to do if you wanted my cock?" He asks devilishly.

I push my face in the blankets and moan loudly, then rise again. "Please Diego. *Fuck.* Please put your cock in me. I need to feel you inside me. *Please.*" I'm begging, and it feels so *right.*

"That's my good girl." He finally pushes into me, inch by inch, and I moan into the mattress the entire time. When he's fully inside me, he grabs my hair, and pulls my head back.

Once my throat is exposed, he wraps his other hand around it, squeezing as he thrusts inside me, hard and slow. Pleasure explodes throughout my entire body, and I whimper loudly.

Diego's breath comes in gasps as he fucks me. "You have no idea what you do to me, Eilidh."

I have *some* idea, given that his rock-hard cock is sliding in and out of me, hammering my G-spot, but I can't get my mouth to form the words to tell him so, so I just moan wordlessly.

Just when I think I can't take any more pleasure before I explode, he yanks me by my hair up onto my knees, and pulls me against his solid chest. As soon as we collide, he sinks his fangs into the base of my throat, and I moan in ecstasy as his venom hits my brain.

He removes them, then licks up my neck until his lips brush my ear. "How loud can you get for me, darling?"

I intend to find out. I moan as loud as I can as his thrusts become frenzied. He sucks the crook of my neck, and then whimpers against my skin as his cock begins to pulse inside me.

"Come for me, *cariño,*" he pants into my ear, then kisses me roughly on my cheek. He twists his hand into my hair even harder, still holding my throat with the other.

I scream again as I lose all control and gush around his cock. He continues steadily thrusting in and out of me as my entire body shakes.

"That's my girl." He says when my scream subsides. I reach up and wrap my arm around his neck and moan, quieter this time. He plants kisses up and down my neck and shoulders until I stop shuddering.

When he pulls out of me, both of our fluids drip down my legs. Blood pounds in my ears as I collapse to all fours.

I look dizzily over at Saif and Kianga. She's riding him steadily.

Diego lays me down again, gently this time, and when I look at him questioningly, he smiles warmly, his lustful wickedness gone.

"Aftercare," he says simply, then begins kissing me everywhere he had bitten or clawed, applying pressure with his lips and licking away the residual blood. With each kiss he plants, he murmurs lovingly into my skin.

"You're amazing." He kisses the crook of my neck. "Your body is so perfect." He kisses my thigh. "You're gorgeous." He kisses my arm.

He massages my legs and feet, then lies down next to me and curls around me, pulling my head onto his bicep, holding me tightly.

"You didn't do that last time," I murmur, tracing circles over his forearm.

He chuckles and rubs a thumb lightly over my hip. "You didn't give me a chance to do that last time before you were trying to take my head off again," he replies teasingly. I exhale through my nose and he kisses my neck tenderly. It's a fair point, I suppose.

Just then, Kianga moans loudly and starts shaking on top of Saif, who pulls her down into a deep kiss. When they've both stopped coming, she falls off him, lying down beside me, and he rolls onto his side to wrap an arm around her.

The four of us lie together in blissful silence for a few minutes before we take turns getting cleaned up in the bathroom.

After Kianga has got her hair put up in her bonnet, and we've all returned to bed, we fall asleep in a tangle of limbs. Saif passes out first, on his stomach, one leg twisted with Kianga's; she lies on her back between us. Diego is curled around me, and I soon feel him breathing steadily. I take Kianga's hand, and she opens her eyes sleepily. I bring her hand to my lips and plant a gentle kiss. She dozes off still holding my hand.

Finally, sleep claims me, and for once, it's peaceful. No nightmares plague me tonight. I'm the happiest I've ever been.

Training

The four of us spend the next morning around a table outside going over the finer points of the story we plan to tell my father. Diego and I were ambushed by a squad of Mongrels as soon as we traveled through the portal tree. They brought us to Bastet, at a stronghold in the south. It's just a slapdash operation, and their guards were lackadaisical.

Bastet planned to ransom us back to Auberon in exchange for money and more weapons. Diego broke out first, and then saved me. We killed as many Fabled along the way as we could.

"Mongrels," Kianga corrects me as I recite my story.

I grind my teeth.

Diego, of course, gets the story down perfectly after going through it just once.

"You lie too easily. Were you a politician in your previous life?" I bite into an apple.

He chuckles and shakes his head. "I may be a monster now, but I wasn't then. I was an investigative journalist."

I pause mid-bite. "What?"

He blinks. "What?"

I shrug. "I don't know. I just wasn't expecting that."

He puts his chin in his hand and grins. "And what *were* you expecting?"

I ponder as I chew. "President of a biker gang. Fitness cult leader. Stripper."

Saif chokes on his tea.

Diego pats him on the back without breaking our eye contact. "Those were just my weekend hobbies."

I laugh. "I'm serious! What kinds of things did you investigate? Government cover ups?" I wiggle my eyebrows at him. "Sex scandals?"

"Drug lords."

I drop my apple. "Holy *shit*. Wasn't that dangerous?"

He shrugs, utterly nonchalant. "The most dangerous part was the vampire that was the head of the gang I was investigating. Though I thought he was just some kind of sick fuck with a blood fetish at first. Until he bit me, that is."

I gape at him. "How old were you?"

"Twenty-three. Barely out of college, but convinced I would change the world."

I do some quick math. So he's - technically- thirty-five.

"You're going to have to tell me all about that some day."

He smiles. "Some day."

After breakfast, Kianga leads us to the third floor of the pyramid. I admire more of the architecture as we walk. "So. Tal Basta?"

"Appropriate, no?" She smirks, obviously pleased with herself.

"Naming your stronghold after the center of worship for the goddess you resemble isn't exactly original, though," I tease.

She waves a dismissive hand. "I was too busy to be original. Now go make some friends, werewolf." She pushes open the door and waves me ahead of her.

I blink in shock as we enter. The room is the size of a football field. Fabled and Mages of all types are grouped together throughout the space, sparring, chatting, or, to my dismay, staring at me. I bite the inside of my lip and pretend I don't notice.

An Ice Mage creates a jagged wall in one corner, just for a centaur to rear up and smash through it with her front set of legs. Small beings with iridescent wings flit overhead, and as one swoops down, I realize that it's a pixie. She gnashes her pointed teeth at me before she yanks a hair from my bun and zips away.

"Hey!" I take my hair out and bend over to redo my bun. As I stand up again, I am suddenly face to face with Mòrag. I yelp and step back, knocking into Diego.

"Watch yourself, pup. This isn't a playground."

I bristle, but Diego puts a hand on my shoulder. "We're here to observe the troops," he says. "Bastet's orders."

Mòrag's dark eyes narrow at Kianga, who is off with Saif and another Mage. He hands her a seed, and she grows it into a rose with unnaturally long thorns.

Mòrag sighs through her nose. "Fine," she snips. "Your kind are in that corner." She points with her snout toward the back left corner, where a group of about thirty people are standing in a circle.

Diego takes my hand, and we set off toward them, dodging various elements flying through the air haphazardly whenever a Mage's attack gets deflected.

As we approach the Shifters, I realize that they're watching a fight in the center of the circle. Two werewolves are ripping at one another; fur and blood flies around them as they clash. One of them is white as snow, while the other one is the exact same shade of ginger as Kianga's fluffy cat from the courtroom.

The white wolf finally pins the ginger one by the throat, and after a squeal of defeat from the latter, they both transform back into their human selves.

The person on top helps the ginger man under them up, and pats him on the back. "Good round." The man limps off and joins his friends, who rib him over his loss.

The person who won scans the circle of people around them, and their icy blue eyes land on me. Their mouth curls into a devious smile. "Look alive, everyone. We've got royalty in our midst."

My cheeks blaze as all eyes turn toward me. Diego puts a hand on my shoulder. I'm pretty sure it's less to comfort me, and more to keep me in place.

The person saunters over to me, hands in the pockets of their baggy jeans. They swipe a hand through their platinum hair, which is cut in the style of a nineties heartthrob. They smile. "Wanna go a round, Princess?"

Diego's grip on me tightens — he's definitely holding me back. I grind my teeth and glance at the circle of people around us. A woman to my right glares at me with bright red eyes. *Vampire.* I inhale deeply through my nose, and somehow I can smell both canine and feline scents swirling through the air, as well as other scents I can't quite place.

"Sorry," I finally bite out. "Just here to watch."

They click their tongue. "Oh, come on. I promise to be just as gentle with you as your father was with my old pack."

My blood runs cold. "I — I'm sorry." *What the fuck else can I say?*

Their eyes narrow. "'Sorry' doesn't bring anyone back from the dead, Princess. How can you even show your face here?"

My heart pounds against my rib cage. "I'm here to help," I say shakily.

They take a menacing step forward, and Diego releases my shoulder. "If you think we need the help of a Danodraic —"

"I am *not* a Danodraic," I snap.

Their eyes flash dangerously, but before they can say another word, a giant red bat wing flaps open, forming a leathery wall between us. "Now now, Rhae," a sultry voice says.

I look up to see Zaehora smirking down at me before she turns to the person on the other side of her wing. "If we're going to start turning on each over the sins of our fathers, I'd like to know now so I can make myself scarce."

"Sorry, Z," Rhae mutters after a tense moment.

Zaehora lowers her wing, and Rhae turns away from me with one final scowl. She leans down toward me then, and her voice reverberates from my ear to my very core. "I'll talk to them, but for now, you'd be better off with the Mages."

I swallow hard, but nod. "Okay." Diego and I make our way back over toward Saif, who has found at least three more Plant Mages. They either already know each other from the days he was here before us, or he's made friends incredibly fast, judging by his easy smile.

He glances our way and does a double-take when he sees my face. "What's wrong?" His smile fades as I plaster one on my face.

I squeeze Diego's hand in warning. "Nothing. Just overwhelmed. Lot of people."

He takes my free hand and plants a kiss on the back of it. "I've got you." He smiles up at Diego. "We've got you," he corrects himself, and my smile turns genuine.

Diego tucks a hair behind my ear. "Come on, *Lobita*, let's see if we can find someone who knows about resurrection magic. Maybe we can figure out how the fuck you did *that*."

I wince, shaking my head. "It still doesn't make sense. Mages don't keep their magic if they become Shifters."

Diego snorts. "Yeah. Just like werewolves don't turn in broad daylight, or gain control of their telepathy in a few months."

I frown, but he's got a point. Something has always been weird with my supernatural powers. Maybe the Mages here can help me figure out what it is.

The three of us set off in search of Kianga. Saif leads us to a series of perches built into the wall. Several house cats - *pyramid cats?* - are lounging on them. They hiss at me and retreat to a higher perch as I approach. A few of them disappear into the shadows about halfway up the wall.

"Where's Ki— oh my *god.*"

The shadow above us moves. It jumps down and lands in front of me, with barely more than a whisper of noise. The sleek black jaguar winks at me when she straightens to her full height — she's *still* taller than me.

"We don't have any fucking necromancers, if that's what you're asking," Kianga says once she shifts back.

I sigh. "What about Mages who channel electricity, or lightning? That's what it felt like. Maybe that's how his heart restarted."

Diego scoffs. "Does electricity heal bones and knit gaping holes in organs?"

I run a hand over my face in exasperation, and Kianga puts a comforting hand on my shoulder. "It's a place to start, anyway. And there are a couple of Storm Mages, but they work outside. I'll message them and see where they are."

She pulls a phone from her pocket, and it takes me a second to register it as something strange. Only six months ago, phones were as ubiquitous as oxygen, but certainly not here in Tenazeryth.

"Where the fuck did that come from?"

She raises her brows as she types the message. "My pocket, Lee. Keep up."

I roll my eyes. "Can I have one? I'm sure my social media apps have been feeling neglected."

"No can do," she says as her phone buzzes in her hand. "Well, when this is all over, sure. But I can't send you to Arkenvale with a piece of tech that would lead your father straight to us."

I sigh dramatically.

She pockets the phone once more. "The Storm Mages are outside to the south. Go see if they can diagnose you."

A Storm Brews

I leave the Storm Mages without a diagnosis. Saif walks at my side; Diego had stayed inside with Kianga to organize a training exercise for some vampires who had been recruited recently.

I brood silently as we walk. I had completely failed to harness the power from the small storm clouds that the Mages had conjured for me. I couldn't sense the energy of them at all, which, according to them, meant that whatever that rust-colored glow had been, it was not the power of a Storm Mage.

"But I'm a werewolf, too," I had pleaded with them, as if they were kicking me out of their clubhouse. "What if it's different for me than normal Mages?"

"Sorry, Ms. Eilidh," the girl who may have been all of nineteen had said. "But Mages who have been turned into Shifters can still sense their element."

"Maybe it isn't element-based," Saif says gently. "Not all magic is. I mean, look at Hyun-Joo. And Ousmane can talk to animals. So maybe your magic is something else."

"Ousmane talks to animals?"

He nods. "I ran into him in the cafeteria the day before you and Diego got here. He was dining with a rat."

Despite my sour mood, I chuckle. "Maybe," I relent sullenly. "I just don't know what it could be. Or where the hell it came from. Why it never showed up before."

We come to a halt next to a large boulder. He leans back against it and pulls me close, then searches my eyes for a moment, as if weighing his next words.

"What are you thinking?" I reach up and run a hand through his curls, and he sighs through his nose.

"I'm thinking that I'm going to miss you when you leave."

I swallow hard. "I'm going to miss you, too." I stretch up to kiss him, and he runs his hands along my curves before he spins me around and presses me into the boulder.

I lose myself in his touch and his kisses, and by the time we pull apart, we're both panting. "We should — we should get back to work," I whisper.

He rumbles deep in his throat. "The only thing I want to work right now is you."

I whimper as he kisses my neck.

Just as I run my hand down his back and slip a finger under his waistband, a gust of air and a *thwump* beside us causes me to jump.

Zaehora straightens up from her landing and winks at Saif as he adjusts his tunic. He clears his throat.

"You're just everywhere today, aren't you?" I don't succeed in keeping the annoyance out of my tone, but if she notices, she doesn't acknowledge it. In fact, her black eyes might twinkle a bit brighter.

"Just wanted to let you know I spoke with Rhae. They agreed to let you train with the pack."

Saif gives me a confused look.

I give Zaehora a look that I hope she can interpret as a sarcastic, "Thanks a lot," and clarify before he can ask. "The other werewolves don't like me."

"Actually, none of the Shifters like you," Zaehora says brightly.

"Gee, thanks."

She's undeterred. "But Rhae's the alpha, so the werewolves, at least, will accept you as long as they do." She begins ticking off her fingers. "The werecats follow Bastet's lead, so you're fine with them, too. The vampires are all deathly afraid of your other half. Er — " She glances between Saif and I. "Your other fourth, so none of them are going near you, and the weremice said they'd ride with you into battle, no questions squeaked."

I stare at her, trying to process it all.

"I made that last one up, Doll. You can laugh."

I exhale heavily and shake my head instead. "That's . . . Okay." I scratch the back of my neck. "Why are the vampires afraid of Diego?"

She licks her bottom lip, and I blink rapidly. "You've never seen your vamp in action, have you?"

"Of course I have," I say, just as Saif says, "No, she hasn't."

I raise a palm to the sky. "Azaeroria? Bleddyn?"

He briefly tilts his head to one side in concession. "Well, maybe with Bleddyn. But that's still only one opponent, and Azaeroria was child's play for him. We've faced much worse than her over the years. Remind me to tell you about the lava monsters sometime."

I turn and press my forehead to the boulder, desperate for something to ground myself. I do not have the capacity for unpacking lava monsters right now. "Is that not normal for vampires?" I ask of the stone.

Zaehora snorts. "Vampires are mostly focused on hosting blood orgies with paying Mages. They're not typically fighters at all. Yours is the First Paladin of the King's Order for a reason, Doll. He'll be a great example for the few we've wrangled to our cause. Maybe even get us some more."

Guilt twists in my gut. And he'll be leaving with me in a few days to go back to Arkenvale and be my chaperone. What will they do then?

As if reading my thoughts, Saif puts a hand on my shoulder. "And they'll do fine once he's gone. Now let's go back inside."

~~~~~~~~~

That evening, I limp to Kianga's room - *our* room, I suppose - for a shower. Rhae had indeed let me train with the pack, but once they found out I can't shift at will, they had enjoyed making me fight them in their wolf form.

I had tapped out after their last bite to my ankle resulted in a sickening pop that is still healing as I open the second wardrobe. It had materialized in here during the day after Kianga's request to someone that Diego and I be supplied with clothes for our stay. I throw on a green long-sleeved shirt and black athletic shorts, and toss my hair into a bun at the nape of my neck.

By the time I'm done getting dressed, the others have returned to the room as well. "Did you eat?" Kianga asks as Saif goes into the bathroom for his shower. Diego stares at the closed bathroom door for only a moment before he follows.

I shake my head at Kianga's question, and sulk my way over to the beverage cart, pushing the sneers of the other werewolves to the back of my mind.

A calico cat is asleep on my chair when I attempt to sit at the desk, so I lay a hand gently on its back. It chirps as it wakes, then turns and sniffs my hand.

"Ow!" I withdraw my hand from the creature, which had puffed up instantaneously and swiped at me. "Why do all your cats hate me?"

Kianga gets up to let the cat out of the room with a chuckle. "You smell like a wolf to them."

I sniff my wrist, suddenly self-conscious. "Is that . . . bad?"
~~~~~~~~~

She raises an amused eyebrow at me. "If you're a whopping eight pounds, yeah, I imagine it would be."

I sit down with a sigh. "Do you think Ousmane would put in a good word for me?"

Kianga laughs brightly, and my heart fills with warmth at the sound.

Twenty minutes later, she's had spaghetti brought up to us, I've had a cup of coffee, and my mood has improved significantly. Diego and Saif, apparently, had a very satisfying time in the shower, judging by their smiles after they exit. Neither of them bother putting on shirts, and I, for one, am very appreciative of that fact.

"No more coffee." Kianga takes my mug from me and kisses me on the head before she sets it on the cart and heads into the bathroom for her own shower.

I wait until I hear the water running before I get up and refill my mug.

Diego and I recite the story we will tell my father once more, and by the time we've finished, Kianga is done in the shower. She snatches the mug from me once again as she uncoils her crochet braids from the clips on the top of her head.

Diego goes to the beverage cart and brings her and Saif drinks, then returns to it to fetch one for himself.

Just as Kianga takes her first sip of whiskey, someone knocks on the bedroom door. She looks in consternation at the clock hanging on the opposite wall.

Saif goes to open the door, and a centaur steps into the room. "Bastet." She glances at the rest of us. "And . . . others."

Diego snorts as he pours a Merlot.

Kianga smiles. "Yes, Rhenilla?"

"She's back."

Kianga claps her hands together and rises from her chair. "Excellent! Please show her in."

Rhenilla exits the room, and I hear her murmuring to someone else.

"Who is 'she?'" Saif asks.

"The agent who was working on Balin. Hopefully she has good news."

"Cheers to that." Diego spins around with his drink.

A thin Black woman with a long silk press the same shade of auburn as my hair enters, and stops short just as the door shuts behind her. She's strikingly gorgeous. Her eyeliner is sharp enough to kill a man, and her outfit is . . . exciting. She's wearing a black cropped leather halter top, a tight snakeskin skirt that shows off plenty of her muscular thighs, and strappy brown shoes that wind up to her knees and have a five inch heel that puts her at my height.

Kianga begins introductions. "Everyone, this is —"

The piercing crash of glass shattering makes me wince. We all turn to the source of the noise. Diego is standing as still as a statue, staring at the woman with abject horror across his face. His wine has splattered everywhere, coating the clean marble in what looks sickeningly like a small tidal wave of blood.

None of us move for several heartbeats.

"Tempest?" Diego's disbelieving whisper sets off all the alarm bells in my head. Something is wrong. Is this woman dangerous? Is this a trap?

Saif senses it too. He reaches into his pocket for a seed, eyeing Diego for some kind of signal.

Kianga's brow furrows. "Wait, how do you . . . ?" And then she puts her head in her hand. "Are you fucking kidding me?" She hisses.

Tempest ignores her entirely — she only has eyes for Diego. I tense my jaw harder the lower her eyes rove over him. Her gaze is haughty and entitled, like she has a right to the sight of his bare skin.

"Hey there, big guy. Long time no see."

Tempest

Kianga runs a hand over her face. When she speaks to the ceiling, her voice is deliberately even. She is *pissed.* "Tempest, when I assigned you this mission, what was the first rule I gave you?"

Tempest bats her eyelashes innocently. "Stay away from the Order," she intones.

"And what did you do?"

Tempest's lip curls up in a smirk. "Forgot."

The look of cold fury on Kianga's face is enough to make me lean away from her.

Tempest wipes her expression blank.

Diego has been standing so still, I wonder if her power is freezing blood. But finally, blinking as though he's waking from a dream, he shakes his head. "You were *working* with the rebellion? The whole time?"

She tilts her head and pouts in sympathy at him, then flicks her eyes to me. Her irises are the deep gray of a thundercloud. She lifts her chin at Diego. "Wow. Liz was right."

Diego flinches like she slapped him.

"Who the fuck are you?" It comes out more rude than I had intended.

"Fired," Kianga spits before she downs the whiskey in one gulp.

"She's fired." She slams the cup down, and I wince.

Tempest shrugs, utterly unconcerned. "Fine, but don't you want my report first?"

Kianga's mouth twists, and while she decides what to say, Tempest turns back to me. She chuckles and flips her straight red ponytail over her shoulder. "I've heard so much about you, Eilidh." She stretches my name out, tastes it on her tongue. "Should I tell her exactly what I've heard?" She asks Diego, still looking at me.

"Enough." Diego's chest is rising and falling rapidly. "Keep her out of it."

Her eyes blaze. "I didn't bring her *into* it! *You* did."

Kianga prowls over to Tempest wordlessly and glares down at her. They stare at one another for several beats, and Tempest finally turns away, quelled, at least a fraction.

"Balin's a lost cause." Unshed tears are in her voice as she walks to the door. "He said he'd die before he saw anyone but a Danodraic on the throne. So unless you want me to go back and oblige him, there's nothing else I can do."

She hesitates for just a split second at the door. "I'm sorry," she whispers over her shoulder, then strides out the door. It shuts gently behind her.

None of us speak for a long moment.

Saif steps lightly to his chair as if he's inching his way through a minefield. "So."

Kianga glares at Diego. He tries to hold her gaze, but fails. "So," she says, tight-lipped.

I wait one more beat to see if Diego will speak, but he just stares at the floor. "What the fuck was that?" I finally ask.

Diego sinks into the closest chair and puts his head in his hands.

"How long?" Kianga asks.

"Since the night before Eilidh's first full moon," he mumbles to the desk.

Saif's brow furrows, then his eyes widen. "'It was too stormy.'"

"What?" *It doesn't even storm here.*

But Diego sighs heavily, so the sentence means something to him, at least.

My patience is gone. "Is anyone gonna tell me who she is and why she looked at me like I kicked a puppy?"

Kianga crosses her arms. "She's the one I had trying to turn Balin to our side. And apparently, she's also Diego's latest *distraction.*"

"But —"

Diego growls in frustration. "Eilidh." He finally meets my gaze. "I've been sleeping with Tempest for five months. It started out as a drunken fling, but then . . ."

He trails off, and his eyes flood with memories. "Then things got . . . complicated. And she got attached. She looked at you like that because." He sighs. "Because I chose you."

My head spins. "But when we left Arkenvale, we weren't —"

He barks a humorless laugh. "I know, believe me. But that didn't stop me from loving you. And for her resentment to build."

Saif huffs a breath through his nose. I drum my fingers on the desk. Kianga pours herself another drink.

"Are you actually going to fire her?" I ask.

Kianga sighs. "No. She's one our greatest assets. But she needs to understand that what she did was too risky. She could have ruined our whole operation by exposing herself."

She grimaces and takes a swig. "No pun intended."

Diego runs a hand over his face.

"Well, so much for that plan." Kianga joins us around the desk. "So I guess you better do a good fucking job murdering your dad."

My stomach roils. "But you have the rest of the lords, right? That's twelve powerful people and their armies —"

"*They* are the army." She jerks a thumb at Saif and Diego. "There is no standing military force in Tenazeryth. It's never needed one. That's what the Order is for."

"I'm starting to think your father didn't actually teach you anything useful during those sessions in his library," Diego mutters.

I cross my arms. "I just assumed Lords came with some kind of task force or something," I say sullenly.

She scoffs. "That would give someone else too much power, which is the one thing your father doesn't give away freely."

Bur then I remember that my father *had* actually mentioned local authorities before. "What about the Enforcers?"

All three of them grimace.

Yikes. "That helpful?"

She rolls her eyes. "The Enforcers are useless for anything other than paperwork and taking bribes. They keep the ones in the capital on their best behavior —" She nods toward Diego and Saif. "But in other cities they're nothing but uniformed gangs."

I bite the inside of my lip as Diego rises. "I should go talk to her," he mumbles.

"Are you sure that's a good idea?" Saif asks.

Diego huffs a breath through his nose. "Not in the slightest. She might rip me limb from limb."

Kianga swirls her drink. "She could do it, too. She's one of the strongest Fae we have."

Diego's eyes widen. "She's Fae?"

She gives him a withering look. "Maybe she wasn't as close to revealing us as I thought. Her glamour must be pretty fucking powerful if you never noticed."

Diego rakes a hand through his hair and clears his throat. "I'll be back. Hopefully."

We watch him go silently, but as soon as the door closes behind him, Kianga hisses, "Idiot."

I try to suppress a smile, but don't fully succeed. "Him or her?"

She muses for a moment, then tilts her glass toward me emphatically. "Both of them."

Worship

A few days later, the night before Diego and I are due to leave, the four of us lie around Kianga's room drinking while Diego and I recite the story countless more times. Luckily, he had survived his encounter with Tempest, though I had seen her casting longing glances at him in the training room several times since then.

I set an empty coffee mug on the bedside table and suppress a yawn, then lie with my head hanging upside down over the edge of the bed to look at Kianga. She's wrapped in a fluffy golden robe, seated at her desk, her second whiskey half finished.

Diego and Saif are sitting against the glass wall opposite the bed, nursing their drinks, and the more Saif drinks, the closer he shifts to Diego. Eventually, Diego pulls him between his legs so that his back is against Diego's chest.

Saif blinks rapidly, as if unsure how he ended up there. Diego wraps an arm around him and rubs a thumb idly over his chest as he goes over the vampires' training schedules with Kianga.

I smile and wink at Saif when I catch his eye, and he takes a quick sip of his drink, trying to hide his smile.

"Do you remember the week we crammed for our junior year AP exams?" I ask Kianga as the blood rushes to my head. "This isn't nearly as bad as that."

Kianga throws her head back and cackles at the memory. "I distinctly remember you saying you were going to jump off Veterans Bridge if you had to make another flash card." She turns to me with a radiant smile. "Do you remember that?"

I roll over, and my hair drapes around my face. I keep my tone as light as I can. "Oh, uh no, I don't." I chuckle hollowly.

I peek through my hair, and they're all staring at me. Kianga and Diego look confused at my tone, but Saif is gazing at me sadly as he runs a thumb back and forth over Diego's thigh. "You need to tell her, Eilidh."

Kianga glances between us. "Tell me what?"

I sigh and swing myself off the bed, then walk over, remove my sock, and put my foot up on her desk so she can see my ankle and the semicolon tattoo. She looks at me, stricken.

I tell her everything. About how I hadn't thought I could live without her. About the bridge, and that fluffy black cat that had saved my life. Tears fill her eyes, and by the time I'm done speaking, my cheeks are wet.

"And now I'm going to lose you some day all over again, because I've been cursed with *fucking* immortality," I finish bitterly. I look between the three of them sadly. Diego's arm tightens slightly around Saif, and he meets my gaze, his eyes full of understanding. One day, he and I will be all that's left of *us*. I don't think I will ever be prepared for that.

Kianga pulls me down onto her lap and kisses me; I kiss her back like this is my last chance to do so. Like some day she will only be a memory.

"Then let's make the most of the time we have," she says when we break apart. I take her hand and lead her to bed. I offer myself to her, body and soul, and she accepts. I lose myself in her, kiss every inch of her, worship her — she is a goddess, after all.

Just not an immortal one.

I rub two fingers over her clit, then lick her juices off them as she watches, biting her lip. I slide those fingers inside her and curl them to reach her G-spot. She moans as I find it. I go slow for her, just how she likes.

I kiss her wrists, her thighs, and her ankles as I move inside her gently. I climb back up her body and kiss her deeply, our bodies moving in sync as she comes.

When her orgasm finally subsides, she looks over to Saif and Diego, who are stroking each other as they watch, and motions for them to join us. Then she pats my thigh and twirls her finger in a circle. "Turn around."

I follow her direction as they climb into bed with us, Saif behind me and Diego in front.

Kianga pulls my hips down until I'm sitting on her face, and she runs her tongue all around me. Diego pulls me into a deep kiss and Saif runs his nails down my spine before he pushes himself into me slowly.

I moan loudly and look down to see Diego gradually enter Kianga's pussy before he grabs my chin and holds me tightly, kissing me again so hard his fangs sink into my lips. She moans up into me, and the vibrations rush up from my center to spread through every nerve in my body.

The four of us move in sync. We are one mind, one heart, and one body. Kianga and I both come quickly. Saif follows shortly after, leaning his forehead into my back and moaning against me desperately.

When he's done shaking. I collapse on the bed next to Kianga, but Diego grabs Saif gently and pushes him over, face first into the mattress. He gets behind him, and Saif spreads himself open. Diego enters him slowly, inch by inch, his cock still slick from being inside

Kianga.

He showers Saif with praise, and fucks him gently, his entire length thrusting in and out as Saif moans into the blankets. I can't resist the urge to touch myself as I watch them.

Kianga, sits at her desk, sipping water, watching them intently.

Within minutes, Saif is hard again, and Diego looks at me, licking his lips. "You need more, don't you darling?"

My brain is far too occupied with the sight of them to try to be coy. "Yeah."

He flashes a fang at me. "Then get under him so he can fuck you. He feels like he needs more, too."

To illustrate, he pulls Saif up by the shoulder and reaches around to stroke his hard cock. Saif grunts and curses in Arabic, then reaches around to pull on Diego's hair to hold himself upright while I situate myself under him.

Once I'm on my back underneath Saif, Diego guides him into me. My legs are pinned between theirs, and the heat radiating between them sets me ablaze.

Saif lowers himself onto me, and I immediately pull him into a rough kiss. Diego picks up his pace, and Saif moans loudly against my mouth.

I run my hands through his thick curls and tug just gently enough so that I can hold him steady and nibble at his jaw like Diego had done to him before. He grunts heavily, and I chuckle as his cock throbs inside me. All at once, I push my hips up hard, he slams deeper into my pussy, and Diego strokes farther into him.

Diego whimpers, and Saif lets out a loud moan the likes of which I have never heard before. My brain snaps, and all I can think is that I need to hear that sound again.

Then I try something I've never done with him before, have always been to nervous to attempt. But watching him melt under Diego the other night had ignited something deep within me that I want to explore, and I think we'll both like it.

"Wait a second." I motion for Diego to halt, and he pulls out of Saif gently. Before Saif can question my next move, I flip him over onto his back. His expression is a mixture of surprise and pleasure.

I mount him quickly, and Diego enters him again; his scorching chest burns my back as Saif writhes and moans under us. I tug his hair just a fraction harder; his eyes are half-closed in drunken delight.

Diego grabs one of my breasts and kisses my neck. "Do you like the show, *Tesoro?*"

Kianga licks her lips, leans back in her chair, and puts a hand between her legs. "Very much. Keep going."

I do as I'm told. "You feel so fucking amazing, Saif. You're being such a good boy."

His pupils dilate slightly, and he emits a grunt so full of pleasure and lust that I feel like I'm going to explode.

I chuckle, my voice low. "You like being fucked by both of us, don't you?" As I tease Saif, Diego claws down my back.

It takes Saif three tries to respond through his moans. "Yes," he gasps, and it turns to a grunt immediately as I tangle my fingers in his hair. "Fuck yes."

"You're taking him so well," I praise him, and pull him into another rough kiss. "I can feel the way he makes you throb inside me. Do you want him to fill you up?"

Diego growls, and Saif and I both exhale heavily. He's losing his composure, and the sound of it has the same effect on us both. "Better decide quick," he rumbles, then mutters more curses in Spanish.

I run my fingers through Saif's curls. "Please," he gasps, and I chuckle again.

"Good boy," I whisper in his ear, and then he kisses me, hot and rough, as Diego's strokes quicken.

"You heard him," Kianga purrs.

Diego whimpers, and Saif moans loudly against my lips. "Come for me," Diego growls. Saif gasps, then begins pulsing inside me, filling me up just as Diego is filling him.

Diego wraps one hand around my throat and pulls me against him. "You too, *cariño*. Be a good girl." Saif cups my breasts, and Kianga appears at the bedside to pull me into a kiss.

I'm tipped over the edge in an instant.

~ New Moon ~

Departure

The morning of our departure comes far too early. Diego and I get dressed in the clothes we had worn when we were captured. I pull on the dirty leggings and moss-colored shirt with a grimace.

Diego puts on his black jeans, blue muscle shirt under a red hoodie, and jean jacket. How he can look so hot in such ratty clothes is beyond me.

"I'm ready," I say as I secure my dagger to my right thigh.

Diego walks over to examine me, and points to my pendant. "Can't take that with you, *Lobita*."

I clutch it tightly; I hadn't even thought of it. "But . . ." I look at Saif, and he sighs resignedly. He walks over and holds out a palm.

"I'll keep it safe for you," he murmurs.

I undo the clasp slowly and place it into his outstretched palm. He puts his other hand over mine as it hovers, and squeezes it tightly. "You'll get it back soon. I promise." He smiles reassuringly, but it doesn't reach his eyes.

I just nod, and look at Diego. "Anything else?"

He walks around me in a circle like a lion examining a gazelle, looking for any weakness in me that will give us away.

"You're good to go," he says finally.

The four of us head to the cafeteria, and Diego and I eat a hearty breakfast. We're going to be dropped about a day's walk to the south of Arkenvale without any food or water in order to preserve the appearance of having been on the run. This will be the last meal we get for a day or more.

Finally, it's time for us to leave. We walk outside, and the other members of the Council are already there, conversing in a cluster around the midnight blue wyvern who is to take us to our destination.

"Council members." Kianga nods to the group. She looks to the wyvern and bows deeply. "Sassarinth."

The wyvern, who is about the size of a school bus, inclines her head. Her piercing gaze turns from Kianga to me, and I have the distinct feeling that she is looking into my soul and weighing what she sees. I don't blink until she looks at Diego.

After she's done with him, she looks back at Kianga. Her voice booms in my head, not unlike Bleddyn's had. But where his telepathic voice had sounded like hammers on sheets of metal, Sassarinth's is like the crashing of a waterfall, powerful and cool.

It's, well, magical.

I will carry your precious cargo with great care, Bastet. You have my word.

Kianga nods gratefully, and places a hand over her heart. "Thank you, my friend."

Saif grips my hand, and I turn to him, looking at the ground. If I look in his eyes, I'm going to cry. He kisses my forehead and holds me tightly. I inhale deeply, trying to fill my nostrils with his scent. He had just finished making charcoal soap for himself yesterday, and now he smells like home. I don't want to let him go. "I'm sorry I ever believed you were trying to hurt me," I whisper into his chest.

He swallows hard. "I'm sorry I put you in a position where you had to think that." He pulls a seed from his pocket, and it sprouts in his hand into a gorgeous green dahlia, the same color as my eyes.

Just like the one he had grown for me when we met upon my waking in Arkenvale.

Tears fill my eyes now despite my best efforts as he tucks the flower into my hair behind my ear.

"We'll be together again soon, my love. Be careful." He tilts my chin up to look him in the eyes. They're just as rich and warm as they ever are, shot through with rays of caramel and copper, but they're glistening with unshed tears.

"You can do this, *Lahabi*. I believe in you. I always have." He kisses me again, and I wrap my arms around his neck, wishing desperately for time to stop so I never have to let him go.

When we break apart, he wipes a hand across his eyes and turns away quickly. Diego pulls him into an embrace, murmuring promises to keep me safe.

Kianga puts a hand on my shoulder, and I turn to look at her, wiping my eyes. Hers are dry, but she gives me a tight smile, which I return. She pulls me into a hug strong enough to crack my ribs. I clutch her back, trembling.

All I can see in my mind's eye is her, eleven years ago, grabbing her keys on a gloomy summer night, telling me she would be right back.

"Come back to me, Lee" she says quietly.

I sniffle and try to laugh, though it comes out more like a sob. "You aren't getting rid of me again so soon, Kiki."

She releases me and cups my cheek. "And figure out who 'Arthur Pendragon' is while you're there. I want to know who I have to kill once we're done with your dad."

I laugh in earnest at that. "You can never just let a grudge go, can you?"

She grins, but it's shadowed with sorrow. "For you? Never." She leans in and gives me a long kiss.

I grip her hand tightly and turn to Sassarinth when we break apart.

Diego kisses Saif one last time and steps to my side. We both bow to the wyvern, and she inclines her dark blue head at us before crouching down so we can climb up into the saddle that is strapped onto her back.

Diego lifts me up so I can get seated first, then he climbs nimbly up behind me and wraps his arms around me protectively.

Hold on tight, Sassarinth booms, then leaps into the air.

Into the Woods

My stomach flips and I wholeheartedly regret eating a big meal as Sassarinth ascends into the clouds. I press my forehead down into the pommel of the saddle and grit my teeth until she levels out and begins gliding along in the sky, occasionally flapping her leathery wings.

My eyes sting in the wind, and my hair flies wildly behind me, whipping around Diego's neck and chest. He still has an iron grip around me, and his chin rests tightly against the top of my head. I look at his hands gripping the saddle in front of me; his claws are out and digging deep into the material.

I can't move my head, so I just shout. "Are you okay?"

He doesn't answer, but he moves his head to the side and nods against me. I turn to him and realize his eyes are squeezed shut.

"Is my hair getting in your eyes?" I yell, and he shakes his head.

"Don't. Like. Heights." He bites each word out and buries his forehead into my neck.

And here we are, probably three miles off the ground, traveling at dizzying speeds in nothing but a fucking saddle on the back of a not-so-mythical creature.

"Why did you agree to *fly*?" I screech at him.

"Fastest," he yells.

At least we aren't on the back of a giant bird.

I plant a kiss on his head, then face forward and shut my eyes against the wind.

My thoughts drift idly as we fly. I practice how I'm going to deliver each line to my father, and the others. I wonder what has become of the solarium with Saif gone all this time, and Martín injured. Perhaps Hyun-Joo or Valentina had stepped in.

I certainly can't picture my father attending to the plants in his absence. An absurd image of him pruning a tomato plant, then ripping the flesh off a Fae elder flashes through my mind, and I shiver, feeling sick to my stomach.

I think of Arkenvale itself, and how strange it's going to be being there without Saif, and with the knowledge I've gained since I was last there. *I could write an entirely different book for your library, Dad,* I think bitterly.

After two hours, Sassarinth speaks for the first time. *We are halfway there.* My leg muscles have long since gone numb, and I'm not sure Diego has opened his eyes once since we took off.

"Okay!" I yell through my teeth.

The next two hours are a blur of stinging wind and aching muscles. When we finally land in a small clearing in the woods, Diego removes his claws from the saddle, and it takes considerable effort to dislodge myself from it, too.

Sassarinth leans down so that the two of us tumble off her back and land in a heap on the ground. It's the first time I've seen Diego land on anything other than his feet. He rolls over and presses his face into the grass, breathing deeply. He digs his claws into the dirt as though to remind himself what solid ground feels like.

I crawl over to him and put an arm around him until his breath steadies. Sassarinth waits with us in silence as we get our bearings. Once he sits up, she nods to us. *Good luck. We're all counting on you.* With that, she jumps back into the air and takes off into the afternoon sunlight.

I look at Diego. "But no pressure," I croak.

He huffs a laugh, falls onto his back, and throws one hand over his eyes. I lie down at his side, and he reaches blindly for my hand, squeezing it tightly when I lace my fingers through his.

"You're a hypocrite," I say a few minutes later.

He looks sidelong at me. "What?"

I smirk at him. "The day you had me jumping on the tall balance beam, you made a snarky remark to Martín that I was afraid of heights. Projecting much?"

He rolls to his side and shoves me playfully, then slowly sits back up and looks around. "We should try to get a couple miles in today and then find somewhere to sleep."

I groan, but slowly push myself off the ground. My legs tremble under me as I stand. We both do some stretching, then head north through the woods. It's eerily quiet with just the two of us after being at Tal Basta.

We walk for two hours and finally slow as the sun starts to dip below the trees and dusk sets in. We come across a creek where we decide to stop for the night. We don't have any food, so we just take long drinks from the creek.

I look around the area after I've quenched my thirst. It's a beautiful, peaceful spot. River rocks make up this side of the creek's bank, and the other side slopes up dramatically, thick with trees. The creek babbles brightly, heedless to the danger that awaits the world it occupies should I fail this mission.

I grimace and start undressing myself.

"Uh, what are you doing?"

I turn to see Diego's eyes on my ass. I smirk.

"Taking a bath. And washing these gross clothes." I wade into the creek until the water reaches my waist, and dunk the shirt and sports bra underwater, scrubbing them together vigorously to get the dirt out. By the time I take them to the bank and grab my leggings, Diego has stripped down as well, but he tosses his clothes far back from the water as he wades in.

"What, you don't want to do laundry?" I ask as I try to get a particularly large dirt stain out of the leggings.

He grabs the leggings from me and tosses them back to the rocks on the bank.

"No. I have something better in mind to do." He pulls me into a kiss, the water of the creek sloshing between us as our torsos collide.

I kiss him back, breathless. He pulls us out farther into the water until my feet can no longer touch. I wrap my legs around his waist as he kisses down my neck, and licks the water off my chest. I run my fingers through his hair, and he smiles up at me dazzlingly.

"We should probably go get dry," I say as I tuck a strand of his hair behind his ear.

He sighs, still smiling at me. "I know."

He gives me one more long, deep kiss, then carries me to shore.

I throw my clothes over a log to dry, and he gives me his hoodie to wear. "Before you put that on," he says hesitantly, brushing my hair off my shoulder. "Do you mind if I . . . drink?"

I furrow my brow in confusion, then realize what he means. "Oh. No, I don't mind. I guess you would have gotten a lot of blood killing all those Fabled, huh?"

He makes a thoughtful noise, but his expression is pinched.

"Hey." I put a hand to his cheek, and he looks at me. His last feeding had lasted longer than what he normally gets, but his irises are definitely a bit dull. "It doesn't hurt me like it does Hyun-Joo. It actually feels amazing. It's okay."

He grunts. "It still weakens you though."

I pull him down into a firm kiss. When we pull apart, I smirk. "You know I don't break that easily."

That elicits a smile from him. "Fine. But since this is the last I'll be able to drink from you for awhile, we're making this one count."

"What does that m— ah!" He sweeps my legs out from under me and holds me by the back of my knees and my shoulders as he carries me toward the treeline.

We find a bed of needles under a tall pine tree and he lays me down gently. He kisses down my body as I exhale shakily. When he's settled between my thighs, he looks up at me with heavily-lidded eyes. "Ready?"

"Yeah," I breathe, though I'm not exactly sure what to be ready for.

He kisses my thigh, then sinks his fangs into the skin. I inhale sharply, in portion due to the pain, but mostly from the blood rushing between my legs, and the venom burning its way back through my bloodstream.

"Oh, fuck." With each pull as he drinks, blood and heat rush between my legs, and tension rapidly mounts. "Diego," I moan, and he digs his claws into my thigh. "I think - oh - I'm going to —"

He presses a thumb to my clit and begins circling it rapidly. I emit an animalistic cry as my orgasm crests and crashes over me like a thunderclap. I yank sharply on his hair, and grind against his thumb, chasing the friction.

He removes his fangs from my thigh, and in the next instant, his mouth is on mine. I moan as the taste of copper fills my mouth. "Fuck me," I pant desperately when at last we part. "Now."

He nibbles on my ear and chuckles wickedly. "What do you say, *cariño?*"

I bark a dizzy laugh. "*Please* fuck me now, you asshole."

"As you wish." He enters me, and I arch against him with a sharp whimper. His long, steady strokes quickly bring my pleasure to a head once more.

I scratch down his back, and he growls his own pleasure in my ear. "You're taking me like such a good girl."

I come undone in an instant. I gush around his cock as he hammers my G-spot. Blood pounds in my ears surprisingly loud for having just lost a good bit of it. Finally, he pulls out, panting. "Did you finish?" I ask.

He kisses my forehead. "You rest. I can —" Surprise crosses his face as I push him to the side and rise to all fours. "Eilidh, you shouldn't — *¡Coño!*" He writhes as I take his cock into my mouth as far as I can.

I suck vigorously, working his base with one hand, and holding myself upright with the other on his hip.

"Eilidh." I will never tire of hearing this man moan my name. He tangles a hand in my hair and props himself up on one elbow. I look up at him through my lashes, and he exhales shakily. "Fuck. You're so beautiful."

His words set me ablaze. I moan around his cock, moving in steady strokes. It doesn't take long for his grip to tighten in my hair. "Harder," I moan, and he does just that.

A few rapid heartbeats later, he moans loudly. "I'm coming."

I hold my mouth steady around his tip and work him with my hands as his cum shoots to the back of my throat. His whimpers nearly set me off again.

Once he's done, and I swallow, I lie down heavily on my side, suddenly acutely aware of how dizzy I am.

He tosses his hoodie over me and curls around me. "Now will you rest, *obstinada?*"

"Mm-hmm." I snuggle into him, and he holds me tightly as I fade.

When I wake, the watercolor sky tells me the sun is setting. He stirs as I try to shift out from under his arm, and we take a quick swim in the creek to clean up before finding another pine bed to sleep for the night.

Diego lays his jacket down before throwing himself down. He tucks an arm behind his head as I lie down beside him, exhausted, but he pulls me in so my head is resting on his arm as he wraps it around me.

The darkness of true night has not yet blanketed the world when both of us fall asleep.

~ Waxing Crescent ~

Homecoming

We don't wake until late the following morning.

After I pull on my clothes, we walk along the creek for several minutes until we find a spot where it narrows. Diego gets a running start and jumps it, landing nimbly on the other bank.

I cock an eyebrow at him. "Thanks for the help."

He grins. "I wouldn't want to rob you of the chance to overcome another obstacle."

"And they say chivalry is dead," I quip as I judge how far across the water I will make it before I plunge in.

"Chivalry was made up by men so they could pretend women needed them," he calls.

I put my hands on my hips. "We're allowed to be strong and still want to be pampered, you know."

He chuckles. "I thought you said Imane was the master debater." He winks at me, and I shiver.

Maybe some cold creek water would be good for me right now, actually.

"Yeah yeah, save your comedy special for open mic night at the Howling Jackal. And I was on the team, too!" I shake myself, ready to plunge into the water. "Maybe I wasn't a *Master*, but I was definitely at least a Pada—"

"Try four legs instead of two." He cuts me off, apparently not in the mood for my space opera jokes. *His loss.*

I scoff at him. "The only time I've transformed on purpose was when I thought Mòrag was going to chop your head off, and I couldn't even hold it long."

He spreads his arms wide. "No time to practice like the present."

I toss my head back and make an exasperated noise. "I thought my training was done!"

"Training is never done, *Lobita.* Now jump!"

I groan, then take as many steps backward as I can before I hit the treeline. I flex my arms and legs, trying to get paws to appear. *Change.* I gnash my teeth, trying to get them to elongate. *Please?*

Nothing happens.

Diego jumps back over the water. He strides over to me, his hands in his jacket pockets.

"This isn't going to work," I huff.

"Try."

I glare at him. "What a great idea. Hadn't thought of that."

He doesn't indulge me. "Use your head. Put the pieces together like you're solving a math equation."

I squint at him. "You brought the wrong woman with you if you want to talk about *math.* I once drove Kianga's dad to tears with my inability to grasp whatever the hell the quadratic equation is supposed to be, and I'm pretty sure I'm the reason my undergrad trig professor retired a year early."

He blinks at me slowly throughout my rambling. "You're stalling."

I bite my lip. "I know," I grumble.

"Get on your knees," he says.

I tilt my head and give him a look.

"*And* your hands. It will put you in a more wolfy position." He grins mischievously. "Which, incidentally, is what I think we should start calling it when —"

"Okay, okay!" I drop to the ground and dig my knees and fingers into the dirt. Still nothing. "How did you learn to control your shifting?" I ask, sitting back on my heels.

He frowns in thought and looks at his hands, sliding his claws out. "It was mostly out of necessity. I kept cutting into sheets in my sleep. And people when I was awake. I caught Saif pretty good the night I got bitten. He was trying to stop me from hemorrhaging out in the entrance hall, and I slashed him across the chest." He grimaces, ashamed.

I think of the set of scars that runs from just under Saif's right collarbone to his sternum. Saif, I'm sure, forgave him instantly.

Diego shakes himself slightly. "Anyway, I just had to clear my mind, and focus. That took some practice, a lot of meditation and grounding exercises. But eventually, it clicked. I was able to just think the change into existence when I needed it, and now it's second nature, and I don't really think about it at all. So try that. Just think."

I don't *think* that helps me at all, but he's trying, which I appreciate. Unfortunately, thinking about it was what I had been doing, and that had gotten me nowhere. And I certainly hadn't been thinking when Diego was in danger under the willow. I had just *felt*. I had felt helpless, terrified, and full of rage.

Maybe that's it.

I take a deep breath and try to remember what it feels like to be in my wolf form. I can see my red fur, the white sword-like mark on my snout that plunges into my tawny nose. I try to focus on the transformation itself, remembering how it feels when my fur sprouts and my muscles ripple with power when I take the first steps on four paws.

I try to remember the primal rage that fills my body every full moon. I've been able to tamp it down, but it's still there, every time I transform. An insatiable hunger, like a wildfire consuming a forest.

I need something to make me angry. I close my eyes, and think of the one thing I know will do so — my mother.

For several agonizing moments, nothing happens. Then, my vision flashes red, and I slip into my wolf form like I'm slipping into my favorite pair of jeans, perfectly formed to me.

I open my eyes and see my paws. My senses are sharpened; I can smell the damp mud at the edge of the creek, and Diego, who smells like earth and pine needles. I inhale deeply and turn to him, my gleaming green irises reflected in his pupils.

"You okay?" His voice is so . . . soft.

For a split-second, I feel like I might lose my hold on the form, but then I shake myself, and hold that fiery anger in my belly. I can focus on him, but I still feel the anger faintly in the background, like the radio in my apartment that I always kept turned on, the volume down low, just to have some external noise to drown out the always-present commotion in my brain.

I take a deep breath and nod.

"That's my girl." Diego smiles. "Now let's go."

He runs and jumps over the creek again, and I follow suit, landing even farther away than he does on the opposite bank.

"You're spectacular," he says as he approaches me.

I've had a good teacher. I close my eyes and concentrate for a moment, breathing deep, and try to release the anger. My therapist had told me once to visualize holding my mother's hand, and then letting it go. That way, I could be the one in control. I would be the one to walk away from her, if only in my head. I picture myself letting her go and stepping back.

When I open my eyes again, my wolf form is gone. *Thanks, Susan.*

We walk for the rest of the day, but we don't come across anyone, Mage, Fabled, or otherwise. At nightfall, we are still several hours away from Arkenvale, and utterly exhausted. Though both of us can see perfectly fine in the darkness of night, we decide to rest and finish our journey tomorrow.

We come across a natural lean-to formed by a fallen tree. I lie down under it and make room for Diego, but he doesn't join me. When I look at him questioningly, he sighs.

"We probably should sleep separately tonight, just in case anyone comes across us. Since you hate me again, and all."

"Oh," I say, casting my gaze to the ground. "Right. Of course." I know it's for the best, but it still stings.

My heart aches as he walks to a tree several yards away and lies down with his back to me.

I toss and turn all night, plagued by nightmares of my father. I watch him sip wine from his chalice before calmly flinging a dagger into my heart. I watch him throw a giant silver net over me, zapping me of my energy, and tearing the flesh from Diego's bones with a wave of his hand. I watch him hold Saif and Kianga aloft with his telekinesis while red mist swirls around their heads and suffocates them.

I finally wake with a start as the first rays of dawn peek through the trees. I groan and sit up, then realize Diego is not where he had been when I fell asleep.

I twist frantically, then catch sight of him, walking back toward me from the north; he must have scouted ahead. I put a hand over my heart to calm its furious beating.

As he gets closer, his expression grows concerned. "I was going to let you sleep longer. Are you okay?"

I wince. "Yeah, just nightmares. Not that a guy who hates me should care." I look at him pointedly.

His lips press together tightly. "You're right."

I stand and stretch as he watches me. I take a look around, just in case, then wrap my arms around him tightly. He hesitates for a moment, his hands frozen in midair, but then he squeezes me back. "This is going to suck," I whisper.

He sighs. "Yeah, it will." He pushes against me gently, taking a step back, and I try not to let it hurt. "*Vamos.*"

I follow him, hugging myself closely.

Finally, a few hours later, I hear waves crashing, and we crest the hill to see Arkenvale. The light from the midday sun gleams brilliantly off the glass of the two towers on the south side of the castle.

It's as beautiful as ever, but a heavy, unseen darkness hangs over the place now. I shiver.

"You can do this." I glance up at Diego, who is eyeing me gravely.

"How do you know?" I whisper.

He squares his shoulder. "Because you're you."

I swallow hard.

As we walk down the hill toward the main entrance, the door slams open, and Valentina runs out, straight toward us. She flings herself into my arms, but I'm too exhausted to catch her, so we just end up tumbling to the ground in a tangle of limbs. She squeezes me so hard I think she might legitimately crack one of my ribs.

"Val," I choke out. "Too tight!"

She releases me and scrambles off, but grabs my face and turns me side to side, examining me. There are worry lines at the corners of her eyes that weren't there a few weeks ago. She's taken out her locs; her hair curls around her face in a soft twist-out style that brushes her shoulders.

"Are you hurt? Where the fuck did you two *go*? What happened?"

Just then, something hits Diego, and I realize Hyun-Joo has jumped into his arms like Valentina tried to do with me. Diego, of course, catches her easily, and holds her close. I just manage to stop myself before I smile.

You hate him, I scold myself. I look back at Valentina, and put as

much venom into my tone as I can muster.
"Bastet happened."

Belly of the Beast

After Diego and I have gotten cleaned up, we all meet at the circular table in the east tower. My father sits at the head of the table grimly as I enter. Everyone else is already there, save for Valentina, who has quite literally not left my side since we returned.

Martín sits in his chair stiffly, but he still manages to smile as I sit next to him. He looks exhausted. His braids are disheveled, and he has dark circles under his eyes.

I pull the skirt to my flowy sundress under me as I sit, and resist the urge to look at Diego. My eyes end up landing on Saif's empty chair across from me instead, and a very real look of pain and sadness crosses my face.

"Eilidh," my father says finally, and I look at him, managing - just barely - not to gulp as I do so. He looks the same as he always has. Salt and pepper hair and beard, eye patch, his face hard but not unkind. His chalice sits in front of him, and his simple golden crown adorns his head.

"Your Majesty," I rasp. We had decided that until we know whether or not the others had told the King that they know of our familial connection, that we would pretend everything was the same as it had been.

His eye tightens momentarily, but then his gaze is as soft as ever.

How is this man a sadistic mass-murderer? It doesn't make any sense.

"What happened? Where have you two been?" His tone is neutral.

It takes everything in me not to glance at Diego. I don't want to give any impression that we have coordinated our stories in any way. I make my lower lip tremble.

"We were captured the moment we came through the gateway. They ambushed us and took us south. There's a small encampment in the woods, probably thirty Fa—" I gasp a fake sob to cover my near mistake and put my head in my hands. "Ferocious Mongrels." I feel ridiculous, putting on this histrionic performance, but it seems to be working.

My father breathes out heavily. "Oh, dear girl. You're safe now." I peek through my fingers and see him turn to Diego.

"How did you escape?"

Diego had to have been lying about being a journalist — he obviously went to a prominent acting academy. He perfectly recites a tale about how he was able to overpower two moronic ogre guards, then found me locked in a cage, kept weakened by wolfsbane, but that he managed to break me out, grab our weapons, and carry me until I could walk myself.

We had all agreed it would be best to make me sound as incapable as possible, so that my father wouldn't think to have his guard up around me in the coming weeks. But hearing him call me 'utterly useless for several hours' still stings.

Diego growls in anger at all the right moments in his story, and glares at me when he tells my father how I had forced him to return the SUV rather than leaving it as he had wanted, which resulted in our ambush.

He's a little too convincing when he spits those words at me. I don't have to pretend to wince. "She nearly got us all killed by Bleddyn, and then she immediately got us captured by Bastet. I'm sorry Your

Majesty, but I was wrong. She has a long way to go yet before she can be a member of this Order."

I hang my head and try not to think of the argument we had while waiting outside the hospital for Martín and the others. We hadn't exactly apologized to each other for that, and his words, as rehearsed as they are, are not entirely untrue. I try not to let it get to me.

The room is silent for several long moments. I look up to see my father staring at me, and for the first time, his golden eye holds disappointment. Real tears burn at the back of my throat before I remember what this man truly is.

I had spent my whole life wishing for a father, had spent the last six months doing my best to learn everything I can from him and gain his approval, and now it has all been destroyed in a matter of minutes.

But of course, it shouldn't matter what he thinks of me now. He's a monster. Still, a small part of me wishes that I could have the approval of my father just one more time.

Keeping the full picture in my head of what he truly is might be more difficult than I had thought it would be. I worry for a moment that I won't be able to. But then I remember Diego's face when he told us about the Fae child who had run at him, covered in blood, and my heart hardens.

He has to pay.

After an excruciatingly awkward pause, the King sighs. "You did well, Diego." He looks around the table to the other Order members. "Today, we will let these two rest. Tomorrow, we begin planning. If Bastet wants a war, then she shall have one."

Disappointment

My father isn't in the library that evening, so I make my way to the east tower, past the circular table, and up the small spiral staircase to his living quarters.

I take a deep breath and knock on the door, which swings open on its own. Every alarm bell in my head is ringing, but I tune them out as best as I can. *I have a mission to complete.* I enter the room and huff an amused breath through my nose.

This room is *huge.* It's not even just one room; it's a suite. The area that I've stepped into is a Medieval-style living room; several heavy wooden doors lead off into the unknown.

Though one wall of the room is glass, the rest of the walls are all layered gray stones that look like they've been worn down over a thousand years. The furniture is all dark, lacquered wood. More bookcases line one wall, stuffed full of weathered tomes.

A blood-red couch sits near a hearth that's at least ten feet wide, but the room is just comfortably warm, instead of sweltering as I would have expected, between the flames and the bright sun pouring in from the glass wall.

A sword hangs over the mantle on a stone plaque, gleaming in the sunlight. I stare at it for a long moment, then take a few steps toward it, as if entranced. I hear whispers, small and distant. I can't make out the words, but the tone is urgent. Pleading.

"What?" I breathe, not taking my eyes off the sword.

"Eilidh." His voice pierces through my hazy thoughts. I shake my head, snapping my eyes to my father, who is seated at a small table tucked into the far corner of the room.

"I . . . sorry." *Why the fuck had he been whispering?*

He just blinks his golden eye at me. "It's enchanted. The room."

I nod slowly. "It's bigger on the inside," I say, suppressing a smile.

He pulls a thoughtful expression, and nods. "I suppose it is." He gestures toward the seat opposite him. "Sit."

I swallow my apprehension and approach the desk, where he is pouring over maps of Tenazeryth by the light of a table lamp. I sit and wait silently as he dips a quill into an ancient-looking inkwell, marks a spot on the map, then flips through a book full of the same cramped handwriting that fills nearly every other book in the library.

Finally, I can take it no longer. My heart hammers against my chest as I clear my throat. "Father," I say timidly. His quill pauses in mid-air, but doesn't look at me.

"I'm sorry. For messing everything up. For nearly getting your best paladin killed. Twice. For . . . not being good enough." The last few words come out as a whisper. I don't have to pretend that they hurt to say.

Finally, he sighs and puts the quill tip-down into a pewter holder that looks like it could be from the Renaissance. His gleaming gold eye pierces me. I can't even blink. "I had higher hopes for you."

Ouch. I swallow a lump in my throat and picture Diego's face to harden my resolve. *It doesn't matter what he thinks of you,* I remind myself fiercely.

Only part of me accepts this.

"I know," I say quietly, wrapping my arms around my chest to keep from shivering. "I'm sorry."

He leans back, steepling his fingers on his chest. I get the same feeling I did when I was thirteen and had been caught trying to sneak out of the house with Kianga to go to a school dance. My grandparents had lectured both of us for some time before they called her parents, who then also showed up to lecture us.

"Eilidh," he says, snapping me from my reverie. "I want to hear exactly what happened with Bleddyn. I have heard Valentina's version of the events, but I want to hear it from you."

I swallow. I hadn't had the chance to talk with Valentina to see what all she had told him.

Did she tell him what Bleddyn said about me and Diego? I decide to leave that part out and feign embarrassment if he brings it up. Otherwise, I tell the truth. How I had lost my dagger, and if not for Diego's own silver blades, that we'd both be dead.

He listens attentively. I also don't know if Valentina had mentioned this so-called Arthur Pendragon, but I decide that it's worth it to reveal. If anyone knows who the code name is for, my father will.

"Bleddyn said that the succubus had actually been hired by someone *else* to kill me. They apparently go by the name Arthur Pendragon. I don't know if that's some Mongrel, or what he meant — if he was telling the truth at all. It just seemed to track, since we've already got an Egyptian cat goddess running around. Why not a legendary king, too?" I try to chuckle, but it just sounds like a grunt of pain.

My father's brow furrows at Arthur's name. He's silent for several moments. "It sounds like he was trying to confuse and distract you to stall for time," he rebukes. "You shouldn't believe everything a foe says in the midst of battle, particularly a desperate one."

I look at the table, scolded. He's right, of course. Kianga doesn't know who this "Arthur" could be, and if he doesn't either, it's highly unlikely that they even really exist.

"I understand," I say quietly.

My father folds up the map he had been marking. "I think you should get some rest now, Daughter. You have a lot of work ahead of you." He motions for me to leave.

I begin to rise, but hesitate. "There's something else."

His frown deepens.

I just manage not to gulp. "I . . . I have magic."

I expect him to be surprised, but instead, his lips curl into a smirk for a moment, and then he gives me a long look, his golden eye burning into me. "What kind of magic?"

Great fucking question. I sit once more. "I healed Martín."

He stares.

"Well, actually . . . I resurrected him. He was dead. And I brought him back." I shrug helplessly. "I have no idea how."

The King leans back and steeples his fingers, deep in thought. "Has your magic ever shown itself before?"

I shake my head vigorously. "Never."

He taps a finger against his table. "Tell me what happened."

I do. He doesn't interrupt. "Can you show me?" He asks when I finish.

I shake my head. "I haven't gotten it to work since then."

He watches me for a long moment, and I resist the urge to fidget. Finally, he smiles. "You've inherited the Danodraic magic, dear girl."

My eyes widen. "But I thought Mages didn't pass on their magic?"

Martín had told me once, not long after I got here, that a Mage's child has a higher chance of developing their own magic, but it isn't a guarantee. The recessive gene allows non-magical children to stay in Tenazeryth, and use the portals, but many leave as adults, simply because they can't stand staying in a magical world without gifts of their own.

Either that, or they pay Shifters to change them. There is apparently a rather lucrative underground market for just such services. When I had shuddered and questioned why anyone would choose that, Martín had just shrugged. *Human nature, roja. The need to feel included. The fear of being* other.

My father nods. "We don't. Mostly. But the Danodraic magic that runs in our veins is different than that of a typical Mage. And now it has awoken in you. When you have children, it is very likely that they will inherit it as well."

My head spins. I don't have the bandwidth right now to tell him I will never be passing on these magical genes. "Danodraics have . . . special magic?"

He nods. "It feels like electricity, doesn't it?"

I gape at him a moment. "Yeah, that's exactly it. Like I was holding lightning."

He smiles. "Indeed. Tell me what you were feeling when it started."

I cross my arms. "I was scared. Terrified that we were going to lose Martín. And I felt so useless. I thought there was nothing I could do. And Val was sobbing, and Martín is such a force of *good*, and . . ." I trail off, blinking back tears.

"And you were furious," he says quietly.

My eyes widen, but I nod shakily. "And I was so. Fucking. Furious. About being helpless. About Martín being hurt. He's . . . he's been hurt enough."

My father nods solemnly. "Yes, I'm familiar with their history. It's quite unfortunate."

I dig my nails into my palms, wondering if he sees the irony. "I just couldn't do *nothing*."

My father smiles. "I think there's hope for you after all, Daughter. You'll master your magic soon, I'm sure of it."

"How? How do I even start?"

"The key to your magic is your rage. Harness it. Feel it. Your rage makes you powerful."

I suppress a shiver. "But how do you know?" I ask timidly. "How do you know I can do it?"

He smiles warmly. "You're my daughter, Eilidh. I know what you're capable of, because I see myself in you."

I fight to keep my face neutral.

"The magic sparked to life in your center." He points to his own abdomen. "In the same spot that twists when you're angry. Right?"

I nod silently, liking less and less how accurately he describes the things I feel.

"What makes you angry? What's something you can always think about to spark your rage?"

I chuckle mirthlessly. "Plenty of things. Dog-eared pages. People who don't yield to pedestrians. The Dewey Decimal system."

He raises a brow at that.

"It's problematic. I refused to use it in my library."

He opens his mouth, then shakes his head. "What about . . . your mother?"

I freeze.

He gives me a once-over and tilts his head thoughtfully. "I just know that when I found out she abandoned you, my magic did not take kindly to the news."

And yet, in the library that evening, he hadn't shown any sign of his magic being out of control. He was able to keep it reigned in. *That's what I need.*

I stare into the flames in the hearth. "What do you think about to activate your magic?" I ask quietly, watching him from the corner of my eye.

He looks toward the sword on the wall. We both brood silently for a moment.

"Destiny," he finally says.

My brow furrows. "What about destiny?"

The flames reflect in his golden stare. "The cost of it. And the people who have tried to keep me from mine."

I barely manage to keep from shivering. I flick my gaze to the sword instead. The sunlight glints off the golden pommel, and my father whispers something that I can't interpret.

"What?" I tear my eyes from the sword with great effort.

He's watching me intently, with a small smile on his face.

I do not like the look of that smile.

He rises, and I follow suit. "I have some things to attend to before I turn in for the night, Eilidh. And you should go get some rest, too. We'll talk more in the coming days."

I nod as he gestures toward the door. I rise and cast one last look to the sword above the mantel. "Okay. Goodnight."

He guides me out the door with a gentle hand on my shoulder, and closes it softly behind me.

I walk numbly down the stairs, then stare for a moment at the circular table. After a moment, I walk to Saif's chair and run my hand lightly over the arm. I amble over to a giant pothos that is bathed in the light of the sunset, and rub a leaf tenderly between my fingers. "I miss you," I whisper, gazing toward the western sky.

With a final look around the tower, I sigh, and exit.

Useful (Kianga)

I find Saif in our bedroom, staring out the glass wall at the darkening eastern sky. He's got my - well, *Eilidh's* - pendant in his hand, rubbing his thumb absently over the emerald.

"Hey there." I lay a hand on his shoulder, and some of the tension goes out of him.

He gives me a small smile, and tucks the pendant into his pocket. "Hey, *habibti*." He plants a tender kiss on my forehead, and my heart skips a beat.

"Missing them?" I ask.

He looks forlornly out the wall again and gives a small nod. "Diego should have been the one to stay. He's of much more use to you than I am. He's the leader. I'm just a soldier. But now I can never go back there, and it's all my fault."

"Hey." I put a firm hand on his cheek to make him look at me. "You're not *just* anything. You're as important to this rebellion as he is. Besides." I pull him into a slow kiss.

When we part, I lick my bottom lip, and his eyelids flutter. "I can think of plenty of ways you can be of use to me."

He exhales a small laugh. "Is that an order?"

I smirk. "Only if you want it to be. I don't want to get called into HR tomorrow."

He quirks a brow. "In that case . . ."

Just as he begins to pull up the hem of my top, my phone rings. I growl through my teeth, but he just smiles. I make my way to my desk, on which, I realize, a snake plant has been placed. I smile inwardly, glad that he's making himself at home.

Mòrag's name lights up the phone screen when I pick it up. "What?"

"Bastet, we need you. Ground Floor, Sector Three."

I suppress a sigh. "Fine. I'll be there in a minute."

"Want help?" Saif asks, putting a hand on my shoulder as I end the call.

For a moment, I consider telling him no, but he *had* just expressed that he was feeling useless. I lace my fingers through his, and answer honestly. "I would love some. But first." I pull him into a kiss.

"You just told her you'd be there in a minute," he says with a smile when we pull apart.

I reach into his pants and begin stroking him steadily. "Then we'll just have to be quick, won't we?"

He pulls down the thin straps of my tank top, quickly unclasps my bra, and sets it on the ground beside us before removing my pants.

I cling to him as he sets me on the edge of my desk, and moan into his mouth when he begins circling my clit with two fingers. I've been wound tightly all day, and he knows the exact pace to make me melt.

He plants kisses across my jaw and down my neck, then drops to his knees. I scratch his head lightly as he eats me out. In no time, pleasure has coiled tightly in my core. "Stop," I pant.

He stops immediately, and looks up at me through his long, dark lashes. "What's wrong?"

I chuckle. "Nothing. Stand up."

As he stands, I open the top drawer of my desk and pull out the small metal device that provides protection for just such occasions. Understanding dawns in his warm eyes only a split second before fear does. "Wait, we haven't been using that. What if — "

"It's fine, *habibi*. I have silphium tea. I'm just ovulating this week. Better safe than sorry."

His eyes widen. "You have silphium here? But that went extinct!"

"On Earth, maybe; The Fabled have plenty, though." I smirk. "But can we talk about that later?"

He shakes himself, and nods. "Right. Sorry. Here." He reaches for the applicator, but I pull it back.

"Uh uh. I've got it." I sink to my knees and pull his pants down.

As I take him into my mouth and moan around him, he leans against the desk, exhaling shakily. *"Ya rab."*

I hit the button on the side of the applicator, and it buzzes to life. As I run the smooth, vibrating end up and down his length, the magical barrier forms, though it's undetectable, as it's only a few atoms thick. The device itself is only about the size of a container of mints, but it holds enough magic to last most people for six months or so before it needs refilled.

Fucking magic, as Eilidh would say. *No pun intended.*

I run the vibrating end around his tip a few extra times just to watch him tremble, then stand. "Come here." I pull him into another deep kiss, and he pulses against me.

I lean over the desk wordlessly. With one hand, he holds my hip, then lifts my other leg and props my foot up. He circles my clit with his tip, then pushes himself into me slowly. We moan in unison as he fills me.

His deliberate movements quickly bring my desire to a fever pitch. I moan his name, and he leans over and plants hot kisses along my shoulder. "You're so beautiful," he gasps. "I love you." Still holding my hip with one hand, he grabs my shoulder with the other, and begins to speed up.

I reach back and squeeze his thigh. "I love you too. Stay with me. *Fuck.* Stay right here."

"*Rohi,*" he gasps, slowing once more, hitting the exact rhythm I need.

"Right there, *albi*. Right there. Yes. *Yes. Fuck!*" I collapse, gasping, as he continues fucking me slowly through my orgasm. I moan against the desk, taking full advantage of the magical soundproofing of my room. Just as it begins to subside, he grunts, and begins pulsing inside me. Even in the throes of pleasure, his touch remains firm, but gentle.

Once he's done, he pulls out slowly, kissing my neck once more. "*Ana uhibbuki,*" he whispers, and I shiver with delight.

"I love you, too." I give him one more kiss. "Now let's clean up quick before Mòrag starts banging on the door."

His adoring smile energizes me for the rest of the evening.

~ New Moon ~

Laboratory

Most of the following day is spent around the circular table, Diego spinning an intricate web of lies regarding the route we supposedly took back to Arkenvale so that we can trace our steps back to the fake camp for retaliation.

My thoughts drift throughout the day, landing mostly on Saif and Kianga. I picture the two of them together, something that Saif had wished for since they first met years ago, and how fate brought them back together.

This elicits a small smile at what is apparently an inappropriate time, because my father clears his throat and gives me an agitated frown. I wipe it from my face and focus back on Diego, who is pointing out a clearing in the woods far in the south. "I believe this is the clearing where we were held." I pretend to examine the map closely and silently nod my agreement.

By the late afternoon, my father has dictated letters to his Lords.

Your Lords already know, I think - a bit smugly - as Valentina rolls up the last scroll and hands it to my father. He stands then, and simply says, "Dismissed" before striding quickly to the staircase to ascend to his quarters.

I deliberately avoid Diego's gaze as I exit the room and wander to the kitchen to find some food. After the sun has set, I make my way to the solarium. I am utterly alone in the darkness of the New Moon.

I examine some of the plants, grateful for my enhanced night vision. None of them have withered and died in the past two weeks, so Valentina must have been watering them since she returned. I pluck a few berries and pop them into my mouth as I meander through the jungle, wishing desperately that Saif was here with me.

I hope Kianga gives him a new space in Tal Basta to nurture and grow new plants. He needs to be able to care for something. Regret pangs in my stomach. I should have asked her to do that before I left.

As I chew on a raspberry, my eyes land on the bamboo divider that keeps the 'unfriendly plants' separate from the rest of the solarium. My eyes narrow, and I walk toward it.

Saif had never let me near this area, but he isn't here to fret anymore. I step behind the divider and gasp in awe. It looks like the lab of a mad scientist back here. Beakers, Bunsen burners, and a rack holding multi-colored vials of liquid are laid out on a metal work bench.

Small plants in labeled pots ring the entire area on shelves that are more than six feet tall. I read some of the names written on the clay pots in Saif's neat, looping hand.

Atropa belladonna (Deadly Nightshade). Nerium oleander (Oleander). Datura stramonium (Jimsonweed). Aconitum (Wolfsbane).

I grimace at the last pot. The flowers that sprout up from the dirt are a beautiful, vibrant purple. If I were to see them in a field, I'd probably go over and smell them.

Note to self, don't sniff random plants anymore.

A stack of thick, hardcover journals sits on the work bench. I open one, and Saif's handwriting fills the page; there's a mixture of English and Arabic. I flip through it, reading what I can.

He has several journals filled with notes on plants, their uses, and the results of various experiments of dosages and effects of mixtures. I let out a low whistle.

Ricinus communis — Vomiting, diarrhea, seizures. Eight seeds to kill an adult.

Cicuta maculata — <u>Caution!</u> Similar to Queen Anne's lace, parsnips, and celery. Convulsions, abdominal cramps, nausea, death. Non-fatal effects: amnesia and lasting tremors.

I close the first journal and snatch up a second. More of the same fills its pages. The third journal, however, is different. When I open the first page, the a date at the top is a few days before I was bitten by Bleddyn. My heart drops to my stomach.

This is a diary. I close it, and slide it toward the back of the table where it had been, then set the other two notebooks on top of it. I can't violate Saif's privacy like that.

Can I?

I bite my lip and look around the makeshift lab, tapping my foot. His notes on the plants may come in handy. Maybe I can slip some poison into my father's chalice that he's always sipping from. Far less messy than slitting his throat.

And less violent.

I decide that learning everything I can about these plants and their uses will become my secondary goal while I'm here. Get the info on the missing Fabled, dispatch my father, and perhaps learn how to whip up a poison in my spare time.

As one does.

I drum my fingers on the metal workbench, then nod to myself. *That settles it.* I turn and walk away, fully preparing to go to my room, get in bed, and go to sleep. But as I put my hand on the knob of the door to exit the solarium, I stop. I argue with myself silently for what is probably longer than what a sane person would.

Then, I turn on my heel, hurry back to the lab, snatch the diary from the bottom of the pile of books, and scurry to my room. I flip the light on, kick off my shoes, and jump into my bed, the diary held tight to my chest.

Just one page.

I read the date at the top again, and try to remember what I had been doing that day. It was the last week of June, so I wasn't working. It seems like it was eons ago, in another life.

I read the entry.

The full moon is in a few days, and we still have no idea where Bleddyn's next attack will be. None of us have had any luck with our usual contacts. No one knows where he is. If we can't find him and put an end to this . . .

I can't look upon another corpse of a woman who's been mutilated by this monster. The last one was too much. I can't do it again. What is the point of this Order if we can't stop one single werewolf?

I shut the book and lean back against the wall. I had never stopped to think how awful it must have been for all of them to see their failure every month in the form of a corpse, torn apart by Bleddyn, or else foaming at the mouth as their body succumbs to the sickness that claims the lives of so many would-be werewolves.

I open the diary back up, and flip to the second page.

It's from the day before I was bitten.

Auberon told us today that one of his scouts up north saw Bleddyn. He's in the Amhar Forest. We're leaving tonight. Please let us save her this time.

My stomach twists itself into knots. *You tried. I know you tried.* I brush away a tear.

The next entry is from two days after I was bitten.

We didn't save her in time, but she's alive. It will have to be enough. Auberon's report was wrong. Bleddyn wasn't in the Amhar Forest at all; he was in the Andred Forest. We made it just before he bit her, and I thought we were going to succeed this time, but then it all went wrong. It went wrong so quickly.

Hyun-Joo was supposed to free her while Diego took care of the succubus and the rest of us distracted Bleddyn. But then, right when I thought we were going to win, Bleddyn got to her. She had been flying across the clearing, running like the wind.

Hyun-Joo says that she tried to get her into the trees, but she froze like a deer in headlights when she spotted Diego, then took off. Diego says she looked like she thought he was going to eat her next.

Of course that's what she fucking thought. It's what any sane person would think, seeing a giant vampire covered in blood.

So she ran.

She must be smarter than the rest of us. We should have all run the moment we saw him.

Then Bleddyn broke free from my vines. I wasn't strong enough, and she paid the price.

But she's alive.

I just hope she can break this fever and make it to the New Moon. Her wounds are bad, but I'm doing everything I can. Valentina is watching her when I need to sleep. But otherwise, I'm not leaving her side.

I can't lose this one.

Tears sting my eyes again, and I wipe at them with the back of my hand, before flipping to the next entry.

She woke up today. Her name is Eilidh. Eilidh Shaw.

She's so incredibly strong. I was worried about her seeing the claw marks, but she barely even cried. I would have been a wreck.

She's beautiful. Her eyes are like emeralds that I could drown in. Her hair is like the sun. Like a blazing fire. And she's funny. I haven't laughed in weeks — months? But she's already made me laugh twice.

She took everything today in stride. She even managed to not faint at the sight of Diego, who, of course, was as menacing as he could be. I told him yesterday that he needed to watch himself, so as not to repeat his past mistakes. I didn't mean he should be awful. But I guess that's a hard ask when that's your default setting.

Auberon told her his plan for her to kill Bleddyn and join the Order. She didn't even flinch. Now, she's sleeping again. Every time I glance at her, she's frowning. I put some extra chamomile in her tea, hoping it would keep any nightmares away, but I don't think it worked.

I'm sorry for not saving you in time, Eilidh. I'm sorry I couldn't keep the nightmares at bay. But I promise, I'll protect you from here on out.

I close the diary and curl around it.

Level Up

The next day, I wake to a knock on my door, and Valentina enters, wearing a pink workout tank and gray athletic leggings. I shove the diary under my pillow hastily, hoping she doesn't notice.

"Hey there, sunshine," she says brightly.

I press my face into the pillow briefly, suppressing a groan, bracing myself for her onslaught of energy.

Saif is a morning person too, but he had quickly realized that I need time in the morning before I become a functioning being.

"I made breakfast. Diego wants us in the training yard in fifteen minutes." She bounces on her toes, her soft twist-outs bobbing.

I roll over and sigh at the ceiling, thinking of spending the day training with Diego while being forced to act like I hate him.

She nods sympathetically. "I know. I'm sure it's awkward for you two after . . . what happened. But it will get better." The compassion in her eyes makes my stomach twist guiltily into knots.

Another secret.

She had already forgiven me once for keeping my past from her. I don't think she'll be able to forgive me again if she finds out everything that I'm keeping from her now.

Saif. Kianga. My father.

I grimace.

"Don't worry," she says. "I'll be there for you."

I rise from my bed and pull her into a hug. "Thank you," I whisper. It isn't enough, but it's all I can say right now.

She squeezes me back tightly. "Of course. Now, get dressed, and let's eat. I'm starving."

She exits the room, and I quickly get changed into a navy workout tank and black capri leggings. I look at my pillow as I throw my hair into a high ponytail, debating what to do with the diary. I decide it's best to hide it in plain sight. I stuff it into the middle of the pile of books on my floor, then exit my room and walk with Valentina to the dining hall.

After we eat, we head to the training yard. Diego and Hyun-Joo are already there, but Martín isn't anywhere to be seen.

"Where's —" I start, but she cuts me off.

"Resting," she says tightly. "He'll be out of commission for a while. Doesn't help that we're down a healer." Her mouth twists bitterly.

I bite my lip. "You know, I uh, found Saif's notes on his herbs and everything last night in the solarium. I could . . . see if I can figure something out that might help Martín."

She narrows her eyes for a moment in thought, as if she unsure she wants anything regarding Saif to get near her brother again, but then she nods. "Sure. I'd appreciate that."

I give her a small smile, then walk to the monkey bars and start stretching. I expect Diego's shadow to loom over me at any moment, but when I'm done stretching, he's at the complete opposite side of the training yard, sparring with Hyun-Joo. I suppress the feeling of rejection that threatens to chill my blood.

When I've gone back and forth across them a few times, I climb on top of the horizontal bars, standing high off the ground. I do my best to walk across the bars without looking down, trying to trust my instincts.

I make it halfway across before my foot slips through, and I crash down onto the metal bars. Pain shoots up my forearms where they slam into the steel, but though it hurts, it also feels . . . good.

This is pain I can control. Pain I will heal from shortly. I grit my teeth and stand, shaking my arms out. I walk to the end of the bars, then turn around. I fall several more times before I move on to my next activity.

Diego has moved on to the wooden dummy with sections that all spin independently. He's slicing at it with his vambraces, moving faster than the wind. He still isn't looking at me.

I look around for what to do next, and my eyes land on the tall balance beam.

Perfect.

I climb to the top of the beam and stand, keeping my center of gravity low. I do a few lunges, then work on moving my feet in grapevine patterns, switching my feet back and forth as I shuffle sideways across the beam.

Holy shit, I can actually do this. I puff my chest out, and let out a triumphant laugh.

Then I promptly stumble, and pitch myself off the beam.

It's amazing how quickly my body hurtles toward the ground, twelve feet below me. It's more amazing how quickly Valentina is at my side, rolling me off my right shoulder, which had just snapped loudly when I hit the earth.

"Eilidh, what the *fuck*? Are you okay?" She asks frantically.

I groan against the grass and just nod. It takes me another minute or so to regain my breath. "I'm good. Just fell." I push myself up onto my left arm, wincing.

"No shit," she says incredulously. "What the hell are you doing?"

I try to move my right arm, but pain lances across my clavicle. I hiss air in between my teeth. "Just . . . clumsy. As usual."

She blinks at me like I've lost my mind.

Maybe I have.

"I'll heal soon. It's fine." I sound convincing, I think. I'm getting better at lying already.

I glance behind her. Hyun-Joo is looking at me with one eyebrow cocked so high it's about to disappear into her hairline. Diego is doing upside down crunches on an uneven bar. Not looking at me. Utterly unconcerned.

I wave Valentina off. "I'm fine, Val, really. I'll just work on my legs while this sets itself." I gesture at my right shoulder.

She purses her lips, then looks side to side conspiratorially. "What if you . . . you know." She wiggles her fingers at me, and I raise a brow at her, uncomprehending.

"Magic." She says simply, dropping her hand. "What if you try to use your magic again?"

I hadn't gotten the chance to talk with her about my magic yet, but now is as good a time as ever. "What do you think it is? Why hasn't it shown itself before?"

She tilts her head to one side in contemplation. "Well, you must not have needed to unlock it before."

"I don't think magic powers work like leveling up in a video game."

She snorts. "Actually, that's kind of *exactly* what it's like."

I clamp my mouth shut. She's the Mage, after all. I furrow my brow. In fact, now that I think about it, she, Martín, and Saif all activated their magic in moments of desperation, like it was just waiting to be unlocked. Like they just had to level up to gain the new abilities.

I sigh. "Okay, let me try." I place my left hand to my right shoulder and take a deep breath, concentrating hard.

Your rage makes you powerful.

I think about my mother. Picture her turning and stumbling away from me once when I had fallen on the playground down the street and cried all the way home to show her my skinned knee. She had just winced at the blood and waved me away. *You're tough. Walk it off.*

The nurse had cleaned the rocks out of my wound for me at school the next day. When she called to ask my mother about it, she didn't even remember me showing her.

The buzzing kick-starts in my navel, and Valentina gasps. I open my eyes to the rust-colored glow, and a warm sensation in my shoulder. There's a tingling as well, like a limb that has fallen asleep. When the buzzing stops, I can move my shoulder again.

"Holy shit," I breathe.

Valentina grabs my cheeks, grinning broadly. "You. Are. Amazing." She stands and pulls me to my feet. "You good to keep going?"

I nod, doing the visualizing exercise of letting my mother go again. It takes a moment longer than it had in the woods when I was shifting. "Yeah. Yeah, I'm fine."

We train for several more hours, then, after we eat and shower, I pad to the solarium, intent on finding something that might help speed up Martín's healing.

As soon as I round the partition, a hand wraps around my mouth. I yelp against it and kick backward.

"*Ow!* Stop, it's me!"

I shoot another kick his way, and Diego sweeps my legs out from under me. I reach up to clutch his shoulder, and he catches me as I fall backward.

He smirks down at me. "Didn't know you could dance," he whispers.

"What the fuck?" I hiss.

He sets me on my feet and shrugs. "I heard you tell Val you'd be in here later. Quick question. What the *fuck* are you doing?" He's keeping his volume so low that no one else would be able to hear him even if they were in here with us.

I shoulder past him and snatch one of the journals, opening it to a random page. "Trying to be of some use to Martín," I say at the same volume.

"Not in here. Out there." He appears at my side, and points to the northern wall that faces the training yard. "Are you trying to ki—" He snaps his mouth shut, and I cross my arms.

His tone is softer when he speaks again. "Are you trying to hurt yourself to get my attention?"

I glare up at him. "No. I'm trying to push against my limits, like some asshole told me to do once. And even if I *had* been trying to get your attention, it sure didn't work, did it?"

His frown deepens, and he takes a step toward me, backing me into the work bench. I grip it with both hands. "You can't self-destruct just because I ignore you for a few hours, Eilidh. We're supposed to hate each other, remember?"

I tilt my head to one side, exposing his favorite spot on my neck. "I'm not self-destructing," I say innocently as his eyes slide across my skin down to my collarbone. "I'm just toughening up."

I hook my pointer fingers through the belt loops of his jeans and slowly pull him against me. He exhales shakily as he puts one hand on the bench, and tangles the other into my hair. "I can't exactly rip your clothes off and ravage you in the training yard if we —"

I yank him down by the front of his shirt and moan into his mouth. He presses his body against mine as if unable to stop himself as I scratch down his back and slip my hand under his waistband.

He breaks our kiss with a growl. "Stop," he pants desperately, his lips barely an inch from mine. He shakes his head as if trying to clear a fog from his mind. "We can't," he growls into my ear. "Not here. It isn't safe."

I lean into his collarbone. "Can't we just say we're hate fucking if we get caught?" I plead.

"Eilidh." He whispers my name like a benediction as he digs his claws into my thighs. "You're going to be the fucking death of me."

With every ounce of strength I have, I pull my hand out of his pants. He steps back, and I wrap my arms around myself, desperate for warmth after the loss of his burning skin. "You should go," I whisper, more harshly than I mean to.

He winces, and makes a motion like he's going to put a hand into my hair again. My heart skips a beat, but he just reaches past me and grabs a journal from a shelf on the wall beside the bench. "Try this one."

He flips it to a page near the middle. This book is clearly older than the ones I had been reading — the pages are worn, and there are several distinctive tea stains on the pages, like Saif was still trying to get into the rhythm of writing and experimenting at the same time, to the detriment of his beverages. "I've seen him make this elixir a million times. If anything can make Martín feel better, this can."

I tear my eyes from his face and read the ingredient list. "Seems simple enough," I mutter. "No eyes of newt. Shame. I was hoping I'd have to ask you for wool of bat."

He snorts, a small smile creeping onto his lips. "Well you've already got the tongue of a dog."

I shove him gently. "Dick."

He smiles again, then looks around, as if he's expecting my father to emerge from the corpse flower in the corner that I very much hope isn't due to bloom anytime soon. Once he's satisfied that we're alone, he leans down and kisses me on the forehead. "I love you," he whispers.

I reach up and brush his sharp cheekbone. "I love you too."

As he exits the solarium, I sigh and start gathering ingredients for the elixir.

~ First Quarter ~

Like Father

I find myself back in my father's tower a few days later.

"So you were able to heal yourself just like that?" The King sips his red wine from his golden chalice as I shrug.

"Yeah. Once I ignited the anger in my stomach, the magic followed. And yesterday I was able to levitate a book to myself."

I'm particularly proud of myself for that one — it's something that I had always dreamt of being able to do.

He leans back into the couch with a smile. "You're a fast learner."

I tug on the end of a long curl, and find myself glancing at the sword over the fireplace again. "I guess," I murmur.

My father whispers something that sounds like, "Claim."

"Hmm?"

"Eilidh."

I snap my attention back to him. "What? Sorry."

"I said, I'm proud of you." He takes another sip of wine.

His words hit me like a freight train. *Fuck.* I duck my head. "Thank you." I bite my lip, debating for a moment. But he's in a good mood, and I don't know how long that will last. I look up at him through my eyelashes. "You said that you believe in destiny."

His expression turns serious. "Absolutely. Everyone has a destiny, and it's their duty to find theirs, and fulfill it."

"What if . . . what if mine isn't to be an Order member?" His eye

181

narrows, and I hurry to continue. "What if my destiny is something else? I'm not . . . a warrior," I say in a small voice. "But I'm smart. And, like you said, I'm a fast learner. Maybe I could . . . be a general or something? I could be in charge of . . ." I trail off and shrug, trying to appear like I have just come up with it on the spot. "I don't know. Maintaining peace with Mongrels. Keeping them contained." I swallow. "Where they belong."

For a moment, I fear I have crossed a line and given myself away, but he takes a long drink from his chalice and stares at the sword, deep in contemplation. "Perhaps." He exhales a soft chuckle. "If nothing else, you've certainly proven yourself resilient. You survived Bleddyn *twice*, after all." He drums his fingers on his knee, and if I didn't know better, I would almost think it's in agitation.

I lick my lips, which are suddenly very dry. "Right. But I suppose I should become acquainted with some first, before you decide. Learn how they behave. I've never even met a Mongrel who wasn't trying to imprison me."

His golden gaze slowly slides to me. "Indeed," he says, before he takes another sip.

A log pops in the fireplace, and I flinch.

"Do you think I can't see what you really want?"

I freeze, but my heart begins pounding so loud, he can probably hear it. "I —"

"You want your justice against Bastet."

I exhale as steadily as I can. "Well." I clear my throat. "Yes. I do want justice." I force myself not to blink.

His smile is almost . . . wolf-like. "And we shall have it."

I clutch the pillow in my lap tightly.

He rises and begins pacing slowly between the couch and the fireplace, swirling his wine. "We'll wait until after the full moon. In the meantime, I'll make the arrangements."

I watch him closely. "For me to observe Mongrels?"

He looks at the sword above the mantel and grins. "For you to fulfill your destiny." His tone turns wistful. "Do you believe one person can change the world, Eilidh?"

One person can certainly fuck it up. But that's probably not what he wants to hear.

I think of Kianga, leading an entire rebellion by herself for so long. Sure, there's a Council, but she leads the Council itself. Even as kids, she was a natural leader. Had our lives turned out more normal, she would have been the president, I'm sure of it.

Or perhaps a cult leader.

I think of Saif and Diego, and how they had been forces to be reckoned with long before they came to Tenazeryth. Saif had scraped by as a teenager in a literal war zone while still managing to look out for the younger kids. He had crossed the world to get an education so that he could go home and help right the wrongs of men far older and more powerful than he.

Diego had taken on crime lords, and shrugged at the idea of the danger. He became the leader of a powerful group of Mages, despite not having any magic of his own. He has moved mountains and bled over and over for the man in front of me.

Flames of anger lick at the inside of my stomach, and I do my best to quell them before my magic activates. "One person can be the most powerful force in the world," I say quietly.

He turns to me, his eye gleaming brilliantly. "Exactly. All it takes to change the world is one person with the talent and determination to do so. Someone willing to do what others are not."

My pulse quickens. *Is he about to start an evil monologue?* I hadn't expected to get this close to my goal so quickly.

Don't give anything away. It could be a trap.

My voice of reason sounds an awful lot like Kianga.

I feign ignorance. "What others are not?" I twist my mouth in innocent confusion. "You mean like, leading?"

He shakes his head, staring at me intently. "How do you like New Camlann?"

I make a face before I can stop myself. *What does that have to do with anything?* "Um . . . I love it," I say simply.

He starts pacing again. "What did you notice about it?"

I stare into the fire. "It's beautiful. Clean. The people are friendly. The architecture is amazing. I like that everything was built with sustainability in mind."

"All of Tenazeryth was designed with sustainability in mind," he says, with a fierce conviction. "It has been that way for generations."

His speed increases.

"This dimension has limited space, and more Mages discover their powers every day. When my scouts find them, they bring them here, and many choose to stay, rather than return to Earth. And why shouldn't they? It's a paradise."

He growls, then continues. "Not to mention, the Mongrels reproduce at extraordinary rates." I wince, but he's not looking at me. "If we didn't do everything in our power to keep things organized and sustainable, then Tenazeryth would have become a wasteland decades ago."

You call killing The Fabled organization? I clamp my tongue between my teeth.

He finally looks at me once more. "Do you remember when you asked me if Tenazeryth suffers from a changing climate? And I said it does not?"

"I — yes?"

His mouth twists. "That isn't entirely true. It's dying, and it's all because of humans." His voice is ice.

How the fuck could that be? They can't even get here.

But he doesn't explain. "Earth is going to go up in flames soon, and Tenazeryth with it, yet they continue to ravage their world for their own personal gain. For *profit*." He snarls the final word like a curse and begins pacing again.

I stare at him, unsure what the hell to say to that. "Yeah, it's . . . sad," I finish lamely.

"It's more than sad. It's unacceptable. But one person can make a difference." He looks at the sword again as he stalks around the couch. "Or perhaps two," he finishes quietly. "Perhaps two people who are destined for greatness. Who are bound by ancient blood."

I frown. I suppose the Danodraic bloodline could be considered ancient, though I don't know how he would know, given that the records of our ancestors only go back a handful of generations. No one even seems to know who the patriarch of the line even was. I stare at him wordlessly.

"Perhaps more than two people," he mutters to himself, so low that he probably doesn't realize I can hear him. "Perhaps it's time for the bloodline to expand after all. Acted too soon, you fool."

I swallow hard. I don't like the sound of that at all.

He gives me a measured look, and sits down once more on the couch, leaning toward me conspiratorially. "What would you be willing do, Daughter, to save the world?"

I gaze at the only father I have ever known with deep, genuine remorse.

"Whatever it takes."

Succession (Diego)

As I drive into the city the night before the full moon, just as I have for the last five months, my mind wanders, and for once, I let it.

Ever since the night before Eilidh's first transformation, I had been escaping to New Camlann once a month to blow off steam — and that had come in the form of my nights with Tempest. Memories surface and then flit away just as quickly: dewy skin pressed together, flashes of her auburn hair, and the scent of raspberries.

One night, even, of the two of us with blood on our hands, surrounded by corpses in a dark alley. She hadn't even required my help dispatching the men after they attacked her, but I had needed blood anyway, and it had been too easy. Fun, even.

That was the night she fell in love with me.

I sigh, and push away the past.

Tonight is going to be very different than those nights. I don't need to find release before a night in close proximity to a woman I can't have anymore. I plan to find it with her tomorrow night when we'll finally get the chance to be alone again, away from the cold walls of Arkenvale.

I also plan to help her find her release — many times. But if I start thinking about that now, I'll never make it through the next twenty-four hours. I shake the image of my fangs sinking into her thigh from my mind firmly.

I park in the King's spot in the center of the city as I always do, but instead of heading toward Colby's tavern like I have since July, I turn instead toward the Howling Jackal to give my status report to Himesh, so that he can pass it on to Imane.

The place is just as packed as it had been when I brought Saif and Eilidh here in October. The only difference is that now, when I enter, instead of trying to blend in and keep up appearances, The Fabled around me don't activate their glamours. Dozens of black eyes follow me as I make my way to the bar, Himesh's included.

"Vampire," he drawls as he wipes a glass with a dish towel.

I smile tightly. "Himesh. I'll take a Cabernet Sauvignon." I sit on the stool at the end of the bar, and he frowns, but grabs a bottle for me all the same.

"Status?" He asks as he pours the wine for me.

I glance at the magical creatures in our immediate vicinity, but there's no need for secrecy anymore. "Everything went off without a hitch. Auberon bought it. And it took awhile, but he and Eilidh are having regular evening meetings again. We seem to have reached equilibrium."

He's tapping the message into his phone, nodding as I speak. As he slides it back into his pocket, I tap a nail on the wine glass. "Can I borrow that?"

He raises a severe brow at me.

"I'd like to talk to her."

Himesh has never liked me, but he must have a soft spot for Imane. "Fine." He sets the unlocked phone on the bar in front of me and points toward the door that leads to the back room. "But no phone sex."

I feign a heavy sigh. "Alright, but I hope you know that there are people who would pay good money to have me hot and bothered in their kitchen."

I know this for certain - I had been propositioned for that exact scenario in the past. Twice.

He makes a disgusted face. "You wish. Now *shoo!*"

I chuckle and tap "Bastet" on the screen once I'm in the back room. She picks up on the second ring, and her face fills the screen. "Just saw your message Him— Diego?" Warmth washes over me as she breaks into a smile.

I lean back on a prep counter. "How are you, *Tesoro?*"

"Better now. Did you steal Himesh's phone?" Her eyes light up mischievously. *God, how I had missed that glimmer.* My world had been so dark without it — until Eilidh, at least, but her fire lights me in a different way.

"No, he let me borrow it. I wanted to talk to you. How's Saif? Worked himself into a tizzy because he isn't here to hover over Eilidh?"

"He knows I'm right here, right?" Saif's annoyed voice crackles from the speaker.

Imane looks up over the camera, still grinning. "I think he was counting on it, *habibi.*"

I decide against relaying the story of Eilidh breaking her own arm by taking unnecessary risks in the training yard. "She's *fine.* Everything's going according to plan."

"Speaking of plans," Imane says. "Have you seen Tempest tonight?"

I freeze. "No. Why would I see Tempest?"

"Good." She frowns at the screen in thought, and taps on it, as if responding to a message. "She went back to her post the other day. Just wanted to make sure she wasn't causing you any grief."

"So you're still trying to sway Balin?" I glance at the door to the tavern, as if Tempest will come storming through it if we say her name enough times. "Mr. Willing to Die for the Throne?"

"Yeah, see the thing is." Imane gestures widely with her free hand as she speaks, and I can't help but smile that I get to re-learn all her idiosyncrasies. "Auberon doesn't even *have* a throne, the unorthodox motherfucker, so Tempest went back to give it one more go while Eilidh works her magic."

I sip my wine and grin at her. "What could she possibly say now that she couldn't have said months ago?"

Guilt flashes across Imane's eyes, just for a moment. "Nothing new. Just trying again." She tucks her free hand to her chest now instead of waving it about.

"Imane," Saif and I say at the same time. She's a good liar, but I know her tells, and he must already know whatever she's trying to hide from me now.

"Ugh, fine. Are you alone?" I nod. "Balin said he was willing to die, right?"

"Yes, unless Auberon's on the throne. So how —"

"No. Not *Auberon.*" She props her phone up against her computer, and folds her arms on her desk. "Unless a *Danodraic* is on the throne."

My eyes widen. "You can't be serious. She'll never agree to that."

"That's what I told her." Saif comes into view and crouches beside her, running a hand through his hair. He's shirtless, and wearing gray sweatpants.

Fucking hell. What I wouldn't give to be there to take those sweatpants off him. We've got so much lost time to make up for.

Imane's jaw hardens. "Look, it doesn't have to be true. If he helps us overthrow Auberon, he can die all he fucking wants after. But if there's any way to get his support, we need to try. We could set up a stronghold in Auberon's back yard!"

I take a long drink of wine. "Okay, fine, you're in charge. I'm just saying, I'm not going to be the one to tell Eilidh why an old man tries to put a crown on her head when this is all over."

Saif raises both hands in the air silently and walks away, washing his hands of the task as well.

Imane rolls her eyes. "Some fearless paladins you both are."

"Fearless, not stupid," I deadpan.

Her smile finally returns. "Fine. If it comes to it, *I'll* be the one to tell her. What else are nine lives good for?"

"You're down to seven, I think, *mi diosa.*"

She flaps a hand dismissively. "Whatever."

A few minutes later, as I walk back to the car, I find myself thinking about my immortality. I had always considered it a blessing, though one with incredibly harsh strings attached. I have so many people that I care about who will one day be gone. It's something I had made peace with years ago, but now that I've finally got Saif and Imane, time suddenly feels like it's slipping through my fingers like a rushing wave. One day, Eilidh and I will be the only ones left of our polycule.

Tears slide silently down my cheeks all the way back to Arkenvale.

~ Full Moon ~

Hidden Talents

I wake on the morning of the full moon to heavy blankets covering me and a steaming mug of hibiscus tea on my desk. Despite the intense drowsiness I feel, my heart soars. This small act was Diego's first way of telling me that he loved me, long before I knew it was him. He had let Saif take the credit for months — not that Saif *knew* he was taking credit for anything.

I sigh and sip the tea, missing Saif. It's my first full moon as a werewolf without him. I wish I could talk to him. I wish I could tell him and Kianga how my mission is going. Let them know that I'm making progress getting closer to my father. I like to think that she'd be proud.

I grab Saif's diary and flip to the entry from my first day of training.

This woman will be the death of me. Eilidh's first day of training was today, and Diego pushed her far too hard. Watching her try to make her way across the bars with her bad shoulder hurt me in a way I didn't know was possible. If this is how he's going to treat her, I'm going to snap. He never pushed Imane this hard, ever. Does he think hurting Eilidh now will bring Imane back?

I brought her into the solarium after training, and she seemed to love it. I hope she did, anyway. I could have spent the rest of the day in here, just watching her. The way the setting sun shone on her hair . . . it was like a fire blazing in the middle of a jungle. She's like a living flame.

I run my finger over the final word, then flip to another entry. It's from July 13th.

Today is Eilidh's birthday, but it's also the anniversary of her friend's death. Her name was Kianga. I can tell by the way Eilidh says her name that she loved her deeply. Maybe even as more than friends. It almost made me feel . . . envious. What would it be like for her to say my name like that?

I set my empty mug down and close the diary, just taking a moment to let myself feel the sorrow that's flooding my chest.

A knock at my door makes me jump, and I slide the diary into the stack of books on my floor hastily. "Come in!"

Valentina enters with an energetic wave. "Hey, you're awake!"

"Yep! I'll be down in a minute!" I say, too brightly.

She smiles sympathetically. "Are you nervous for your first full moon without Saif?"

I grimace, and she takes it as confirmation.

"I get it. I was planning on trying to distract you today. The first big days after a bad breakup always suck." She twists her mouth ruefully.

I turn away, unable to hide the myriad emotions crossing my face. Guilt wins out as I open my wardrobe and dig inside for something to wear. I try to keep my tone even. "What did you have planned for today?" I ask.

"Beach day, or the city. Take your pick." She wanders to my window with her hands in her pockets and gazes out over the rolling hills while I dress.

When I close the door of the wardrobe, she takes in my outfit with a grin. I've put on a cream, long-sleeved tunic with green stitching around the neckline and wrists, a brown corset, gray linen pants, and tall, brown boots. She laughs as I tighten my dagger around my thigh.

"City it is, then." Her eyes sparkle.

I twirl in a circle. "Have I mentioned how much I *love* your fashion sense?" I ask her, smiling.

"Yeah, but feel free to tell me again." She winks mischievously.

I laugh, and it's easy, and sincere. "Now if only I could do my hair so it looked nice enough to match the outfits you got for me."

She clasps her hands together. "I thought you'd never ask."

~~~~~~~~~

We spend the morning wandering around the city, eating street food, and strolling through the parks. When we pass a city pool, she creates a wave, and peals of laughter from the children follow us down the street.

The citizens of New Camlann salute Valentina just as they had Diego and Saif when they brought me here in October. She waves and inclines her head politely at each person who does.

My hairstyle is still immaculate as I return to my room that afternoon and hang my cloak in the wardrobe. I check both sides of my head in the mirror, trying to find so much as a loose end, but there's not a hair out of place.

The numerous small braids mixed in with several larger ones at the back of my head are still completely secure. I had walked tall all morning, my head held high.

It's amazing what a killer hairstyle and high boots can do for one's confidence.

I make my way back downstairs and into the dining hall. I sniff a
~~~~~~~~~

few times, and my mouth begins to water. Something smells *delicious*.

Martín is sitting at the table, and I plop onto the bench across from him. He's looking better than he had when we first returned.

"Hey there," I say. "How are you feeling?"

He gives a small smile, though his eyes hold no mirth. "I've been better. But I think that elixir you made is helping. This is the first time in weeks I've actually been hungry for dinner."

I reach across the table and clutch his hand. "Good. I'm glad I could actually do something for you."

He drops his smile, and lays his other hand over mine. "You've done plenty for me, *roja*. I wouldn't be here without you."

A lump forms in my throat. I look above his head to the three large stained-glass windows, and take in the designs. A sword on a blue background, a simple gold chalice, and a red rock, swirled with black and gray. The windows are like old friends at this point, and I absorb the warm colors while I think of what to say to that.

"I still wish there was more I could do," I say quietly. "I wish I could make everything better."

He squeezes my hand tightly. "No one can make *everything* better," he says fiercely. "But everyone can make *something* better. And you did."

I smile at him warmly and pat his hand. "So who's cooking?"

"Hyun-Joo." My eyes widen involuntarily. He laughs. "It's not often she cooks, but when she does." He kisses his fingers. "*Exquisito*."

Just then, Val opens the door from the kitchen to the dining hall and holds it open. Hyun-Joo walks into the dining hall carrying a large bowl, which she sets down in front of Martín. She lays a hand gently on his shoulder. "Your favorite. Dig in."

My stomach rumbles loudly. Long noodles covered in a thick, black sauce, cubes of tofu, and julienned cucumbers fill the bowl to the brim.

"That looks amazing. What is it?" I ask her.

The animosity she would have once shot at me is gone. *"Jja-jangmyun.* Noodles in a black bean sauce."

Just then, I realize Diego has materialized at my side, carrying a large tray laden with more bowls. "Eat up, *Lobita,* we have a long night of training ahead of us." It's the most he's spoken to me since our encounter in Saif's lab. My heart flutters.

He sets a bowl in front of me, then sets the tray on the table. Hyun-Joo grabs a pair of chopsticks off the tray for Martín, and I pick up a pair for myself.

I dig into the food, and I have to suppress a pleasured moan. "This is fucking amazing," I say in between bites.

One corner of Hyun-Joo's mouth lifts, just a fraction. "Thanks."

Primal

As Diego and I walk into the forest that night, he on two legs, and me on four, a million thoughts swirl in my head, but I don't direct any of them at him. I don't want to have even a one-sided conversation too close to the castle.

Where to even begin? The moon muses above me.

Indeed.

When we make it to the edge of the training grounds, Diego turns to me abruptly. "Shift back."

What?

"Into your human form. I want to see if you can control the transformation the other way."

Why?

He doesn't answer me; he just stares.

Testing, testing?

"I hear you."

A low growl escapes my throat. *Then answer me.*

"I just want to see if you can." He crosses his arms.

I huff air through my tawny nose. *Great explanation.*

I focus for a few moments on the feeling of transforming, of letting go of the anger inside me. It takes longer than shifting into the form had during our travels; the compulsion of the full moon above me is strong. But eventually, my wolf form slips away.

I open my eyes and gasp, still on all fours. I stand quickly. "I did
—"

In one motion, Diego grabs me harshly by the front of my tunic,
slams me into the closest tree, and kisses me fiercely. I yelp against
his mouth in surprise, but my fingers are already tangling into his
hair instinctively.

He pulls me into him, then cups my ass as he lifts me into the
air. I wrap my legs around his waist, and he moans into my mouth,
running his claws down my neck as far as the shirt will allow. I arch
into him, and he kisses my throat, his fangs pricking me.

I gasp as he puts a hand into my hair, twists his fingers under the
largest braid, and pulls at my scalp. "You look gorgeous, *querida*," he
growls in my ear, sending a delightful shudder down my spine. "I
don't know how it's possible, but every day you get more beautiful."

I dig my nails into the sides of his neck and kiss him desperately,
tasting copper. I pull away, and his fangs are tipped with blood. I
lick my lips and glare down at him, my eyes lidded heavily. "How
would you know? You've barely looked at me in two weeks."

My voice is a bit sharper than I had intended, and I expect him
to get defensive, but instead, he grins at me devilishly. "You can't
stand it, can you, not having me inside you every day? Have you been
thinking about me while you lie in your bed at night?" He cups a
hand over my pussy.

I flush and wrack my brain for something clever to say in response.
My brain is absolutely no help.

"I . . ." I moan as he drops me back to the ground, then pushes one
knee between my legs. He moves his leg back and forth steadily, and
I writhe with pleasure.

He puts a claw under my chin and tilts my head back to look up at
him. "I have an idea for a game tonight, *Lobita.*"

I brace myself on his leg, and he pushes into me harder. He runs a thumb over my lips, and I lick the tip of it. His eyes close for a moment as he drinks in the sensation.

"What game?" I whisper.

"You have to run from me. Every time I catch you, I get to take a piece of your clothing off. Once all your clothes are gone, I get to fuck you until the sun comes up."

I smirk. "Who says you'll catch me at all? I'm faster than you in my wolf form."

He moves his hand from my chin to my throat, and pushes against my pressure points until my eyelids flutter. Then he leans in, and licks up the side of my throat. "I've got good motivation tonight," he breathes, and releases my neck. "I'll catch you."

He removes his knee. I inhale sharply at the loss of the sensation, and slump down the tree a few inches. He steps away from me and holds up all ten of his long fingers. He's dropped three by the time I realize he's counting down.

I don't have time to try to shift. I take off, flying across the clearing, and crash through the other side of the ring of trees. I make it maybe five strides into the forest before I hear Diego right behind me.

I veer to the right, but he snatches my hair by one of the braids, and pulls me back into his solid chest. We collide with a *thwump*, and I thrash instinctively for a moment while he bites into the side of my neck. The faintest buzz from his venom hits my brain.

"No fair, you're sober," I say as he rips at the ties on my corset.

"I'm drunk as hell right now, *cariño*; I'm just drunk on *you*," he rumbles in my ear as he drops the corset to the ground.

He releases me, and I turn to see his fingers up once again. His eyes are dark with hunger. Some prey instinct buried deep within my DNA rings like an alarm bell.

I run.

When he catches me about twenty seconds later, he bites me again, and then takes my shirt off. He digs his fingers into my soft waist and kisses my bare shoulder before he releases me again.

This time, I'm ready; I've already ignited the anger in my core. I shift as soon as he lets go, and fly deeper into the woods. I have no idea where I'm going, but I make it significantly farther this time before he suddenly jumps onto my back, and I shift back into a human. It's even easier this time.

He pins me to the ground, one knee digging into my back, as he pulls my boots and socks off. He pushes up the hem of one pant leg and bites into my calf.

I moan into the earth.

I shift again as soon as his fangs release me, but he must not even be counting down any longer, because he snatches me by the scruff of my neck within ten seconds. I shift as he shoves me onto my back. I squirm underneath him, but he holds me down easily.

He presses his full weight into my torso and kisses my neck as he unbuttons my pants, then once they're down around my ankles, bites into my thigh. He's injecting me with his venom in earnest now, and my head swims delightfully.

I can't focus enough to shift into a wolf again, so I try to run, but only make it about fifteen yards before he appears in front of me, crashing heavily into a tree, his claws digging into the bark. Bits and pieces of the tree fly through the air around us.

He looks feral.

I'm already wet when he grabs me. My heart pounds as I struggle against him. He digs his fangs into my shoulder as he unclasps my bra, then he fondles my breasts before releasing me.

I stumble away from him, giggling, but I don't make it half a dozen steps before I trip over a tree root, and he saunters over to me, licking his lips.

"I told you I would catch you." I can see his erection pressing hard against the thick fabric of his suit.

He lowers himself onto me, and I try to fight him off as my pussy throbs with desire. He smirks, pins my arms above my head with one hand, and covers my mouth with the other. "A deal's a deal, *Lobita*," he teases me.

He kisses his way roughly down my body as I shiver and moan. When he makes it to my hips, he rips my underwear away viciously, then buries his face into my soaking wet lips.

I cry out in pleasure. He doesn't shush me; we're deep in the forest by now. I tangle my fingers into his shaggy hair as he eats me out.

Just as I think I'm going to explode, he pulls away from me, a teasing grin spread across his face. "No need to rush you," he mocks. He pulls the zipper of his suit down and pulls out his throbbing cock, glistening with pre-cum.

He shoves it into me all at once, hitting my G-spot sharply. "It feels like you liked our little game," he drawls. I moan at him wordlessly as his considerable length thrusts in and out of me, scattering all rational thought.

He lifts one of my legs up and presses it against his chest, kissing my ankle, continuing to fuck me hard and fast. My moans rise to a desperate pitch.

"Do I make you feel *too* good, darling?" He taunts.

I can only whimper. He runs his claws up and down both my thighs.

"Can you even remember your name?" He questions, thrusting harder still. I try to speak, but all I can do is gasp and moan. His thrusting slows, and he begins moving deliberately in and out of me, still hitting my G-spot with incredible force.

He chuckles as I whimper up at him. "The only thing you know right now is *me*," he says, his voice low and rumbling as he presses his chest against my leg, stretching me out. "You know the feeling of me inside you, the feel of me pressed against you. And you know my name."

He shoves my leg to the side, tangles a hand in my hair, and kisses my neck. When he pulls away, his timbre rumbles directly in my ear. "Say my name," he commands through his teeth.

"*Diego*," I moan desperately.

"Good girl," he gasps in my ear.

I come undone instantly. I am nothing more right now than the pleasure he is giving me. The sole object of his desire in this moment.

He kisses me roughly, and I kiss him back, wishing for this moment to never end. I feel him begin to pulse inside me, and I rake my nails down his back. He whimpers, muttering in Spanish, as his claws dig into me.

He thrusts into me frantically for several more seconds before he slows, and his ragged breathing in my ear nearly sets me off again.

"Fuck," I breathe.

He chuckles, laying his forehead against mine. "She speaks once more."

I pull him into a deep kiss, feeling him twitch inside me a final time before he pulls out. He lies down next to me, breathless, and pulls me close, propping my head on his shoulder.

I curl into him and breathe in his scent. After a few minutes of silence, he shifts slightly, and I raise my head. "Let's go get cleaned up in the stream. Then after that . . ." He flashes a single fang at me, and I lick my lips. "I did say until dawn, after all."

Selfish

He strips his suit off and leads us to the stream at the bottom of the ravine we had swung over together the last time we were in these woods. I wade to the center, careful not to slip on a rock; the water rises to my thighs.

He follows me into the water, which barely reaches the bulge of his calf muscle. Once he sits down, he pulls me into his lap, facing away from him, and brushes my hair over one shoulder, planting kisses on the various marks he had just given me. He cups water into his hand and wipes down my sweaty limbs, massaging as he does.

I'm reminded of when he drank my blood at Tal Basta, and I shiver at the pleasure of the memory. "If you need blood, you can take some," I say quietly.

"I'm fine, *amor*." He moves my hair to my right shoulder, then kisses the four scars on my left. "You're so beautiful," he whispers against my skin. I lean back into him, the flowing water rocking us gently.

He reaches his right hand around to trace the scars with his fingers, diagonally down my torso, and I breathe shakily. "And strong." After he's done, we sit still for a moment, just listening to the creatures of the night, the rushing of the water, and the beat of our hearts. His is fast as always, his vampire cells burning through him like wildfire, consuming him to satiate their hunger.

Finally, I break the silence. "I think I'm getting a handle on my magic."

He rubs my upper arm. "I knew you would."

I can't help but smile as I turn and recount my meetings with my father. How we've been discussing how the Danodraic magic is unique, and how I'll be leaving with him soon to observe the Fabled. *Whatever that means.*

His expression becomes increasingly concerned as I speak. By the time I finish, he's shaking his head. "He wants to leave with you? Take you who fucking knows where? Why the fuck didn't you tell me sooner? We have to figure out a way for you to back out. It could be sui—" He winces.

"Stop doing that," I snap.

He doesn't meet my eye. "Doing what?"

"Stop treating me like I'm made of glass. I get that enough from Saif. I didn't tell you about the bridge just so you can tiptoe around me for the rest of eternity."

His jaw tenses. "I'm not —"

"I *have* to do this, Diego. What if he's taking me to the captured Fabled? And how was I supposed to tell you when you've been ignoring me?"

He throws his hands in the air. "I *have* to!"

"*I know that!*" I jump to my feet. Water cascades down my hips, and though he tries to hold my gaze, his eyes dart down my body. His Adam's apple bobs.

"I *know* he can't know we've gotten close. But I don't have to *like* it, Diego."

He tears his gaze back up to meet my eyes, stands, and takes my hand. I purse my lips and glare at the water running around our feet.

"Look at me." His voice isn't commanding like it normally is; it's soft, and tender.

I look up at him from under my eyelashes.

He breathes heavily through his nose. "I don't like it either, *mi sol*. I don't like it at *all*. Every time I find myself downwind of you I want to rip your clothes off and do unspeakable things to you. But I'm not going to risk your safety, or the success of this mission, just because I can't touch you whenever I want." He brings a hand to my face, and rubs his thumb over my cheekbone.

I lean into his bare chest, breathe in his scent, and sigh. "I'm sorry. I guess I'm just being selfish."

He runs a hand up and down my back reassuringly. "We can be selfish tonight." He plants a kiss on top of my head. "But then we have to get back to the mission."

I run my hands behind his back, and down to his ass. "Then let's go be selfish."

He picks me up easily, his fingers digging delectably into my thick thighs. I wrap my arms around his neck and kiss him as he walks. He finds a soft bed of pine needles under a large tree, and deposits me onto the ground.

He climbs on top of me, and I lose myself in him for several minutes. He hardens as he grinds between my legs, and I moan softly as he plants kisses down my neck and across my chest. His tongue circles each of my nipples in turn, and I shudder as he sucks on them.

He rubs his cock up and down across my clit, presses his tip to my entrance, but doesn't push himself into me. *Tease.*

Desire explodes in my stomach, and I press up against his chest. His eyes widen slightly at first, but then he allows himself to be shoved over onto the ground.

I climb on top of him, and he smirks at me. "*Impaciente,*" he chuckles.

"I'm being selfish." I bring myself down onto his throbbing erection, moaning as he fills me. I throw my head back as I ride him, and he digs his fingers into my hips, not controlling my pace, but just holding me firmly. I savor every sensation, and lose track of time.

Eventually, he sits up as I continue to move my hips against him, and kisses me deeply. He tangles his fingers into my hair, moaning, and I hold him tightly as we move together.

Soon, he begins writhing beneath me, and brings me down harder onto himself, forcing his cock up into me so far that my breath hitches with every thrust. He squeezes his eyes shut, and his breathing grows ragged. "Oh, fuck," he whimpers.

My stomach twists in delight.

He gasps, and his body begins spasming. "*Fuck.*" He sinks his fangs into the crook of my neck, just briefly, then throws his head back.

"I love you, *mi sol*," he breathes.

I reach up to grab his temples, and make him look at me. His eyes snap open, and his pupils are wide and dark with lust.

I come undone instantly, gasping. "I love you, too."

He doesn't break our eye contact again. We look into each other's eyes as our pleasure crashes over us, blocking out everything else in the world. After, he pulls me into another kiss. Blood pounds in my ears as my heart fights to return to its normal rate.

My legs shake as I dislodge myself from Diego's lap, and I lie on the ground, exhausted. He curls around me and pulls me close.

A couple of hours later, I wake with a start. Dawn is just starting to break, and the earliest birds are singing their songs, ready to go get their worms. I shiver and realize Diego is gone. I sit up, crossing my arms over my chest, and look around.

A twig snaps behind me in the trees. I jump, but as I turn, I see Diego walking toward me, holding my clothing. He quirks a smile when he sees me awake, and tosses my clothes at my side. "Good morning, sunshine."

I groan, stretch, and pull my clothes on slowly.

Once I'm dressed, I throw myself back down onto the bed of pine needles, and curl up.

"You can do that in your bed," he chides. "Come on, let's get back so we can shower. You need to get all those needles and leaves out of your hair. You look like you were attacked by a wild beast."

I don't open my eyes. "I *was*. He was huge, and terrifying. He chased me all over the woods."

He snorts. "Sounds like a rough night."

I nod against the ground. "It was *very* rough. But I liked it."

He nudges me with his foot. "Come on, *Lobita*, I can't carry you across the threshold. You've got to walk yourself."

My stomach flutters. I picture him carrying me into Tal Basta, and us staying there, with Kianga and Saif, forever. The four of us, together, just living in simple domesticity.

He must see something in my expression. "Have you ever thought about it?"

"About what?"

He weighs his next words. "Well . . . Marriage. Once we save the world and get our happily ever after, I mean. The four of us. Is that something you would want?"

I cross my arms and shrug. "Honestly, marriage was never on my radar. My grandparents only got married for my Pop-Pop to be able to stay in New York. I mean, yeah, they were together for sixty years after that, but they would have been either way. And I've never had a relationship that lasted longer than a night. So I guess . . . I don't know."

He nods slowly, deep in thought.

"What about you?" I ask.

He sighs through his nose. "I've pictured my wedding day since I was a little boy."

My brows shoot up in surprise. "Really?"

One corner of his mouth curls up. "Shocking, I know. But it's something I've always wanted. The marriages I saw growing up were . . . not good ones. I always wanted to have one that was better than that. Solid. With a partner I really loved. That one special person I could build a life with." He tilts his head to one side with a grin. "Or three."

I smile up at him. "Well, we can talk about it more after we get our happily ever after."

But happily ever after can never happen if my father eradicates all The Fabled. So, I stand. He gives me one last kiss, and we head back to Arkenvale, leaving our selfishness with the trees.

We've got a mission to complete.

Happily Ever After (Saif)

I'm plucking a dead leaf from my trailing inch plant when Imane inhales sharply. I turn to see her pressing a hand to her stomach, still typing at the computer with the other. I stride to her in alarm.

"What's wrong, *habibti?*"

She tilts her face in my direction without removing her eyes from the screen. "Hmm? Nothing, why?"

I lay a hand gently over her typing one. "Are you hurt?"

She blinks at me in confusion, then looks at her hand, still clutching her center, as if she had just realized she was doing it. "Oh. Just cramps. I'm fine."

Relief floods me for several reasons. We've been using protection, and - to my amazement - she does in fact have silphium on hand, but part of me had been nervous nonetheless. More, though, I'm relieved she isn't injured.

I plant a quick kiss to the back of her hand. "I'll be back in a little while."

She gives me a small smile that lights up the room. "Okay."

~~~~~~~~~

When I return from the room on the second floor that acts as an
~~~~~~~~~

indoor greenhouse twenty minutes later, she's lying in bed, wearing her bonnet, and tapping away on her phone.

"How are you feeling?" I ask, making my way to the beverage cart.

"Like shit," she moans, and I can't help but be reminded of the first time I walked into Eilidh's room to find her awake, and she had said the same thing.

I smile even as my chest aches. I fill a metal tea ball with the mix of herbs I had brought back from the greenhouse, and pour hot water from the kettle that has been magicked to automatically refill, and keep the water hot.

Fae magic, she had explained the other day when she brought the kettle to the room for me. Less straightforward, apparently, then the elemental magic that most of us Mages have, but no less useful. More so, in some ways.

As the tea steeps, Imane takes a call from someone in Eigyr. The city is small and isolated, sitting on the northernmost tip of the continent, on a narrow peninsula. By the sound of things, a few Bear Shifters that are stationed in the city tangled with some creature at the base of the nearby Marchog Du Mountains.

"What do you mean, it *flew* away? What the fuck was it?" She asks, exasperated.

I don't hear the reply, but whatever it is causes her to roll her eyes. "Well, don't waste any resources chasing after whatever it is. We've got bigger issues. Just tell your sleuth to stay the fuck away from the mountains from now on, okay? One casualty is enough. We can't afford any more."

"Sleuth?" I ask as I bring her the mug of tea.

She tosses her phone in disgust and takes the mug from me. She sips without question at first, but then makes a face and swallows. "A group of bears is called a sleuth. *Habibi*, I thought this would be coffee." She sticks her bottom lip out in an exaggerated pout, and it's all I can do to not pull her into a kiss and run my tongue over it.

"It's almost bedtime," I admonish. "Drink. It will help."

She smirks before taking another sip. "If it's a love potion, I must inform you that it's a bit redundant."

I smile at that. "It's for your cramps. It's the same blend I make for Hyun-Joo when hers get bad." My smile falters. "Well . . . made."

She gazes into the mug with a smile. "Thank you." She drains the mug, sets it on the bedside table before I have the chance to take it for her, and pulls me down onto the bed next to her. I tuck her head under my chin and pull her close.

"You'll see her again. Eilidh and Diego are going to complete their mission, and we're all going to live happily ever after."

I sigh, but plant a kiss on the top of her bonnet. "I hope so, *hayati*."

~ Waning Gibbous ~

Solstice

Two days later, on the evening of the winter solstice - not that it *feels* like the winter solstice, in the heat of Tenazeryth's eternal fucking summer - I make my way back to my father's living quarters and knock on the door.

I wait for ten full seconds before I knock a second time.

He doesn't answer.

I hesitate, terrified of opening the door, in case it's booby trapped, or cursed. But I'm more terrified at the thought of turning around and letting Kianga down.

I open the door slowly. "Hello?" I peer around as I enter, and shut the door slowly behind me. Flames dance in the hearth just as they always do, but there is no other movement. "Father?"

A log pops in the fireplace. I jump, then growl at myself in annoyance. *Easy, Shaw.*

I tap my foot, looking around the room. There is nothing that jumps out at me immediately as a matter of interest. Nothing labeled 'Evil Plot' or 'Location of Kidnapped Mongrels.' I sigh, preparing to head to one of the other doors and see what's behind it, when the light from the setting sun bounces off something, and I'm momentarily blinded. I raise a hand and squint at the offending reflective surface.

It's the sword. As soon as my eyes land on it, it's like I've been snared in a trap. The sunlight glints off it like a siren's song. I drift toward it in a trance. As I get closer, I hear its metallic whisper more clearly than ever before. *Come.*

I do.

"It wasn't Auberon whispering at all. It was you," I breathe.

The whispers whip into a frenzy, as if confirming my statement, then die down. *Claim.*

I put a single finger on the tip of the blade, the only part I can reach. An absurd vision flashes through my mind of a petite blonde princess pricking her finger on a spinning wheel.

But this is a very different story.

A drop of my blood beads up where the blade slices into my skin with almost no resistance; it's sharper than should be possible. As soon as my blood touches the blade, the sword begins to *glow.* A reddish aura surrounds the sword and I both, crackling around us like flames.

No, not flames.

My ears ring piercingly.

Like *lightning.*

It's like touching a plasma ball; electricity shoots up my arm into the blade, and the blade sends it back; it spreads throughout my body instantaneously. My hair floats up around me as if I'm underwater, and sparks shoot around me in a kaleidoscopic explosion.

Suddenly, memories begin flashing through my head, as if the sword is drawing them out.

I'm five, and the quiet boy in my kindergarten class is shoved to the ground. I charge the bully, and we collide in a tangle of limbs before a teacher pulls us apart.

I'm ten, and someone on an electric scooter hits a cat as I'm walking to Kianga's house. I cradle it in my arms all the way there, and her dad drives us to the emergency vet. It spends its last few years living a pampered life full of wet food and endless snuggles.

I'm fifteen, and walking into the school for the first time after losing my grandparents. Kianga squeezes my hand tightly, and I hold my chin high, blocking out the whispers, and ignoring the pitiful glances of the teachers for the rest of the year.

I'm twenty, and kneeling at her grave. I cry, and scream, and shatter into pieces. Later that night, I'm standing on the side of a bridge, looking down at the stars reflected in the water below me. And then a fluffy black cat butts its head against my shin, and jumps up beside me. The next morning, I walk away from the bridge, and carry on.

I'm thirty-one, and facing down a charging werewolf intent on killing me and the people I love. I don't run away.

Worthy.

The aura around me blinks out, and I stumble back, gasping as the bond between the sword and I shatters.

And so does the stone plaque that the sword was displayed on; it simply crumbles into dust, and falls to the floor in a swirl. I catch the sword by its hilt at the last second before it clatters to the ground.

The hilt vibrates in my hand, like the sword itself is humming with excitement.

I look at the closed doors throughout the room, but my father doesn't storm in and flay me alive, so I'll take that as a win for now.

My arm buzzes, and my energy begins to drain into the blade just as it did when I first held my dagger. This sword must be pure silver, and there's a lot more of it. I grit my teeth and set it gently on the ground.

What the fuck is happening?

I stick the bleeding tip of my finger in my mouth and poke at the sword, inspecting it. It looks perfectly normal. Why had it called to me? *How* had it called to me? What the fuck was with the light show? And why had my father looked at it like it was going to tell him the answers to all his questions?

The hilt is a simple burnished gold. A dragon rears on its hind legs on the pommel, fire emanating from its mouth. There's writing around the pommel's circumference, but the blocky, twisting font makes it difficult to read at first.

I pick the sword up gingerly and hold the pommel close to my face so I can see the letters better. I tilt it toward the hearth, more out of habit than actual need for my supernatural vision to see the letters, and the flames illuminate it instantly.

When I finally realize what it says, I set it down hard as if scalded, and scramble backward, desperate to get away from it.

It can't be.

There's no way it's real. It's not possible.

You've lost your mind, Shaw.

It's just a fairy tale.

I take several deep breaths, then crawl back over to the sword, shaking, and look at the pommel again. The name glows back at me, the flames glinting off it horrifically. I read and re-read it several times to make sure my eyes aren't playing tricks on me.

But no, I hadn't been mistaken. The sword's name is as clear as day, stamped into the gold of the pommel.

Panic begins to claw its way up my throat, and I clamp a hand over my mouth to keep from crying out as I look at its name.

~~~~~~~~~

I careen down the small spiral staircase that leads to the first floor of the tower, holding the sword out from me like a venomous snake. I don't have any kind of scabbard that I can put it into, nor a belt, for that matter. I should probably not be running with a fucking sword at all, but I'm not thinking clearly, and I have no choice.

I stop in my tracks at the bottom of the stairs and stare at the table.
~~~~~~~~~

The last gasps of daylight glint off the lacquered wood as it's slowly devoured by shadows. *Took you long enough*, the circular table sneers at me.

But "circular" isn't the adjective that comes to mind just now. I take off at a sprint toward the second floor.

Diego.

I rush up the large spiral staircase to the balcony, cursing the entire way. *Why is every set of stairs in this place a fucking spiral?* It takes so much longer to go up and down them. It's like the castle itself is a whirlpool, just waiting to drag its latest victim into the depths.

I reach Diego's door and fling it open. "Diego!"

The empty room snickers back at me in answer.

"Fuck."

I think for a moment about trying to stash the sword in my room, but there's no way I want to be anywhere near Arkenvale when my father realizes it's gone. I have no idea what he'll do. Maybe he'll drive it through my heart and be done with it. *Or maybe it won't be so painless.*

I sprint down the stairs and burst through the dining hall door. Diego isn't here either. Luckily, neither is anyone else; the others typically spend the evenings in their rooms, in the city, or down by the lake. Valentina is probably with Martín somewhere, hovering over him like a mother hen, just like he had always done for her.

I consider, for a split second, finding them too, but that would just put them in harm's way. As long as they're in the dark, they're safe.

Stepping into the light is what's dangerous.

I dash to the kitchen just in case Diego is in there, but it too is as still as death.

"Fuck, fuck, *fuck!*"

I lean into the corner of the dining hall and pant for a moment, thinking of where to try next. I look at the stained glass windows, desperate for their familiar comfort, and nearly gag at the sight of them.

A sword, a chalice, and a stone.

A sword. I feel the blade humming in my hand, and try not to vomit.

A chalice. But, no. It isn't, is it? It's a grail. A grail that suddenly looks exactly like the vessel my father always has on hand to sip his wine.

Holy shit.

The stone. I don't know what the stone means, or what it could be. What power it could hold.

Better figure it out soon, the patchwork stone sings to me as I run across the dining hall and back out the door.

Diego. Find Diego.

I sprint into the library, and the shelves of books gaze back at me sadly, unmoving, like immobile spirits of the towering trees they had once been.

It strikes me, for the first time ever, after spending the majority of my thirty-one years alive in rooms much like this one, that libraries are actually just . . . graveyards.

I had always felt the most alive in a room full of books. Books hold answers, and thought-provoking questions. Books hold worlds, and universes, and adventure. Books hold friends, and family, and love, and laughter. A room full of books is a room simply *bursting* with life.

Until you realize that it isn't. Until you find yourself surrounded by austere corpses, and you're just as alone as you always have been.

I press my back into the door and slide to the floor. Panic surges as I gaze around helplessly. The towering shelves loom over me like cloaked specters of death, closing in on me; their gnarled hands are reaching for me, and wrapping around my throat, and I'm suffocating.

I'm going to die here in this castle, and I'll never see Kianga and Saif again, and I'll never find Diego, and —

I slap myself across the face, and the terror gripping my mind removes its claws.

The specters stand straight up once more.

I clutch my chest and the side of my stinging face; I pant and my eyes dart around the room as the specters turn back into bookshelves.

"You're fucking losing it, Shaw." *Spiraling just like those goddamn staircases.* "Focus." *Find Diego.* "I'm trying!" *But where?*

"I don't know!" I rake my nails through my hair and bite my tongue, suppressing a scream of frustration. How does one lose a six-foot-nine vampire? Shouldn't he be easy to find in a relatively small building?

"Of course." *You idiot.*

He isn't in the building.

I bolt to my feet, then halt for several seconds, my hand still on the doorknob.

"Wait." *All the stories are true.*

I run to the bookcase jammed pack with fairy tales and rip a well-worn tome off the shelf. The same book that I was reading the night my father told me who he really was.

Except he didn't, did he?

I run back up the spiral staircase and crash into my room, dropping the sword and the book unceremoniously on the floor. I dive to the wardrobe and find a crossbody bag in the bottom.

I stuff a few pieces of clothing in it at random, then throw my cloak over myself. I grab the notebook off my bedside table that contains all the flowers Saif had given me since my arrival here, and his diary, and stuff them into the bag. I shove the book from the library on top, and clasp the bag shut.

I run to Diego's room, and grab a few pieces of his clothing at random in a bag that I find in his wardrobe as well. I throw it over my shoulders, then grab the sword, sprint down the stairs three at a time, and dash out the front door. I turn east immediately, and fly toward the training area in the forest.

My legs and lungs are on fire, and I don't know how I've managed not to cut myself in half with the sword, but I'm not going to question any ounce of luck I can get. When I'm close to the clearing, I scream.

"Diego!"

There's silence for a long, agonizing moment, and I'm convinced that he isn't here either. But then, mercifully, I hear his voice.

It's the best sound in the world.

"Eilidh?" He emerges from between the trees at a run, and we nearly collide with one another. He steps to the side at the last second, and I screech to a halt, then fall to my knees, gasping for air.

"Pen . . . Pen . . ." I try to tell him, but the word won't come out. It lodges itself in my throat, refusing to be uttered. Once it's spoken aloud, then it will be real.

Diego drops beside me. "Eilidh, what's going on? I thought you were aslee— is that a *sword*?"

I nod, still gasping for air. I grab his hand and put his fingers over the pommel. "Pen . . . Drag . . ."

I lean over and vomit into the dirt.

"What's wrong with her?"

Oh, no. Hyun-Joo approaches slowly, coming out of the trees.

"I don't know." Diego takes the sword and sets it aside, focused wholly on me. He holds my hair back as my stomach empties, and rubs my back tenderly.

When I have nothing left to come up, I crawl a few feet away and press my forehead to the ground. It isn't until I begin to smell petrichor that I realize I'm crying; my tears drip into the dirt, watering it for what very well may be the first time ever.

Diego crawls toward me and grabs my face gently. "Violet," he says firmly.

"What?" I gasp, and it's only then that I realize I'm hyperventilating.

He brushes my hair away from my face, then sits back and draws me into his lap. He wraps his arms around me tightly, and tucks my head under his chin. "Violet," he says again, and I can feel his voice reverberate throughout his chest.

I look around dizzily. "Hyun-Joo's ring."

She glances at the stone on her right middle finger, and he nods against me.

"Indigo," he says.

I grip him tightly. "Your shirt."

"Blue?"

My eyes are drawn to a bush nearby. "Berries."

"Green?"

I rip at the ground blindly and hold up what comes away. "Clovers." My heart rate finally begins to slow.

He strokes my hair steadily. "Yellow?"

"Buttercups."

"Orange?"

There's nothing even remotely orange around us. "My hair," I say quietly.

"That's your one cheat." He kisses the top of my head. "Red?"

I lift my face to his and cup his cheek with a shaky hand. "Your eyes," I whisper.

He kisses my forehead. "That's my girl. Now what's wrong?" He sounds *nervous*. I don't think I've ever heard him sound nervous.

I take a deep breath as he wipes my face with a long thumb, and it comes away covered in tears mixed with dirt.

"We have to get the fuck out of here." I gesture at our bags, which I dropped a few steps away.

"*Mi sol.*" His voice is that of a commander once more. "What. Happened?"

"Pendragon," I breathe, and he furrows his brow, uncomprehending. He glances at Hyun-Joo, but she just shrugs.

I reach for the sword and pull it toward us, showing him the name around the pommel.

He reads it, confusion marring his features, and shakes his head. "It's fake. It has to be."

"All the stories are true," I rasp. "It *called* to me, Diego. It sang with my blood." His eyes widen in alarm and he opens his mouth, but I don't give him the opportunity to ask questions. "It was hanging in my father's quarters in the east tower. Above the room with the round table."

Diego stares at me, realization and horror spreading across his face.

"It was him. It was him all along. He hired Azaeroria." My voice is distant, like I'm not the one speaking these words. I drone on, unable to keep my mouth shut. So much is falling into place.

Like I'm finally solving the equation.

Hyun-Joo walks over as I ramble and looks down at the sword. When she sees its name, she sinks to the ground, ghostly pale.

"Saif said my father trained him in sword fighting when he started the Order. He said that he was like something out of a legend. Like Achilles." A mad cackle bubbles from my throat. I sound utterly deranged.

Diego stares at me silently like he's seen a ghost.

I wipe a tear of mirth from my eye. "He said it was like Auberon and his sword had known each other for a millennium."

Because they had.

The humor of the situation flits away like a will-o-the-wisp. Suddenly, I can no longer laugh. I can only tremble. I look down at the name on the sword once more before I kick it away viciously. Even as I close my eyes, the name burns into my vision, as if branded on the back of my eyelids.

EXCALIBUR.

Diego wraps his arms around me and pulls me close, squeezing tightly, holding me together.

My stomach lurches again, and I sob against him. I have to take another deep breath before I utter the next sentence. Before I make it real.

"My father is Arthur Pendragon."

Old Friend

"We have to get out of here," Hyun-Joo echoes me. "I don't know where we'll go, but we can find somewhere. Not in Tenazeryth. I have some distant relatives in Queens. Or Toronto. We'll start there and —"

"No." Diego cuts her off. "We have somewhere to go."

"*Jeogiyo?*" Hyun-Joo asks in disbelief. Her tone is clear. *Excuse me?*

A beat passes. Diego sighs heavily into my hair.

"You two weren't captured, were you?"

"Well, we were. At first," he says vaguely. "It's a *very* long story, *mi vida.*"

She's not having it. "Give me the highlights. I'll catch the full replay later."

I should probably help him explain, but I simply don't have the bandwidth right now. My mind is covered in a blanket of fog.

"Imane is alive. She's Bastet. And she's got more than a gang; she's leading a rebellion against Auberon."

Hyun-Joo says nothing. I can only imagine what her face looks like right now.

Diego finally unwraps his arms from around me, and I look up at him numbly. He puts a hand on my cheek. "*Mi amor.* We have to go. Can you walk?"

I blink at him, then tilt my head at Hyun-Joo. "Imane is actually my dead best friend." I look back at Diego as she puts her head in her hands.

"How do we get to them?"

"Them?" Hyun-Joo asks from behind her hands.

Diego winces. "Saif is there, too."

"Oh," she says. "Naturally."

He's going to have a lot of explaining to do. He looks at Hyun-Joo for another beat, then back to me. "We have to get to the Howling Jackal."

"Car's gone," Hyun-Joo says.

Diego growls. "Fuck."

"We can run."

Diego raises a brow at me. "Are you sure?"

I nod and rise shakily to my feet. I hold the sword out to Hyun-Joo. "I don't have a sheath. Can you . . .?" I gesture vaguely at the sword, and she takes it wordlessly.

As she runs her hand along the blade, encasing it in one of her force fields, Diego picks up our packs and puts them over his shoulders.

Hyun-Joo finishes the makeshift sheath and hands the sword to Diego, who takes it gingerly, staring at the pommel, as if he's willing it to change its name and erase the past few minutes from his memory.

He sticks it through his belt, memory still intact.

"What about Val and Martín?" She asks.

"No," I say immediately. "We can't drag them into this."

Diego puts a hand on my shoulder. "If he thinks they know something, they'll be in danger."

I rake my nails through my hair. "*Fuck.* But I don't even know where they are."

"Martín's feeling better. They're in the city," Hyun-Joo says. "But I don't know where. They just said they were going for the solstice celebration."

I look to Diego, but he shakes his head. "It's a giant outdoor festival on the west side of the city. We'll never find them without drawing attention to ourselves."

"*Fuck.*" I pound a nearby tree with the sides of my fists, and lightning explodes from where my skin makes contact with the bark. I yelp and jump back.

Hyun-Joo approaches the tree and pokes at one of the blackened craters. "Oh, for fuck's sake," she whispers to herself.

"I'm sorry." I don't know if I'm apologizing to her or the tree, but either way, I turn and drop to my knees, trying to calm myself.

Diego lays a hand on my upper back. "I'll leave a message with my friend in the city. She knows everyone. She'll be able to get word to them."

"And tell them what?" I choke. "Don't go home, stop. Homicidal legend there, stop?"

He sighs. "No. I'll tell them to stay in my room at the hotel near her tavern until further notice. That it's top secret. They'll just think it's for a mission."

I let him pull me to my feet. "Do I want to know why you have a hotel room in the city to yourself?" I swipe my hands at my knees, but there's no helping the amount of dirt clinging to my athletic pants.

He runs a hand through his chestnut hair, staring up at the sky. "Maybe not right now."

I shake my head. "Alright, let's go." I shift without even having to try — there's more than enough rage boiling just under the surface of my psyche right now.

Hyun-Joo looks between us. "I don't exactly have Super Shifter Speed."

Diego begins adjusting the packs on his back, but I nudge him with my snout to get his attention.

I can carry you if you can hold on.

Her face scrunches dubiously, but she approaches me anyway. I crouch down so she can climb on my back, and, once she's in position, stand up. She grips my fur tightly, and I wince at first, but then we adjust, and she grabs big enough clumps that it doesn't hurt.

"*Vamos,*" Diego says, then takes off.

I glance up at Hyun-Joo, who nods, her mouth set firmly with determination. I begin at a trot, then speed up as she hunkers down.

About ten minutes later, we approach the portcullis that serves as the gate to New Camlann. Diego and I are both covered in sweat, so we let Hyun-Joo approach the guard to wave us through.

I take my pack from him, and the three of us walk through the bustling city streets. Diego leads us to a tavern, and if my capacity for shock wasn't entirely expended tonight, I'd have gasped when we enter.

It's like we walked into a snow globe. Giant flakes drift down from some indeterminable source, winking into existence close to the ceiling, then disappearing just above the heads of the patrons. Garland wraps around every surface imaginable. Centerpieces made of candy canes, cinnamon sticks, and bright red berries sit on every table.

"This is Colby's favorite time of year," Hyun-Joo murmurs to me. She and I stay by the door as Diego approaches the bar. The white woman behind it has her back turned to him as she shakes a cocktail and strains it into a glass, humming to herself, though I only catch a few notes over the noise of the tavern. Her long, pecan-colored hair is pulled back into a high ponytail that somehow looks messy but perfect at the same time.

When she turns, my eyes widen — her pregnant belly nearly knocks a bottle off her counter. She puts one hand on it protectively, then sets the glass on the far side of the bar, in front of a man wearing a green cap with a bell on the end.

She finally notices Diego standing there, and her bright blue eyes light up. "Hey there, handsome." But her smile dies instantly when she gets a better look at him. "What's wrong, sugar?" She asks with twang.

He casts a glance back at us. "Colbs, I need a favor."

"Anythin.'" She looks over to us, waves to Hyun-Joo, and gives me a wary once-over. She leans in closer to Diego. "Is she the —"

"Yeah," he says quickly. "Can we talk?"

She nods. "Meet me upstairs. Just give me two minutes to make sure these knuckleheads are topped off." She pats his hand, and he makes his way back over to us quickly.

"Let's go."

He ushers us out the front door, around to the back of the building, and up a steep metal staircase. When we reach the door, he extends his claws, and sticks two of them into the lock. It clicks open a few moments later, and the door to the small apartment swings open.

I lean against one wall, glancing around. She's either moving in or out; boxes are piled high along one wall, and the bed frame is in pieces, propped against another.

Diego goes to the small sink, grabs a mug from the cupboard, and fills it with water. He downs it in one gulp, then refills the mug, and brings it to me. I stare at it blankly for a moment. "Come on, *Lobita.*" I finally take it and sip at the water.

Colby comes up just as he takes the empty mug back to the sink to wash it.

She locks the door behind her. "What's goin' on?" Her drawl gets thicker the more concerned she gets. She gives me a nervous glance and rubs her round stomach. "Hey sugar. I'm Colby."

My eyes dart to her stomach, then to Diego, and I clear my throat. "Yeah. Hi. I, uh. I'm Eilidh." I stare at Diego's back as he dries the mug and sets it back in the cupboard.

She raises a perfect brow at me, and then breaks into a wide smile. "Oh darlin', don't you worry that pretty head 'a yours. I promise it's not what you think."

I shake my head, barely suppressing tears. Too much is happening right now. I already feel like I'm splintering to pieces. "It doesn't matter," I mutter.

"Diego, what did you do?" She turns her blazing blue eyes to him and advances menacingly, even though she's barely taller than Hyun-Joo, who is sitting on the floor, leaning against the opposite wall.

He puts his hands up in defense. "Nothing! Look Colbs, we don't have time. Have you seen the Peñas tonight?"

She squints at him another moment as sits on the edge of her bed. "Nope, sorry. Why?"

He gestures at Hyun-Joo and I. "We're headed out of town on a mission, and I need to get a message to them. We think they're at the solstice festival, but we don't have time to look, and you're the only one I can trust."

"Okay. I'll send someone over. What's the message?"

Diego pulls a key card from one of his pockets. "Tell them they need to go to my room at the hotel. They know the one. Tell them they need to stay there until we come get them. I don't know when that will be, but hopefully no more than a few days."

She nods. "Okay. Anything else?" Her drawl is less pronounced now.

Diego hesitates, and glances at me. "Just . . . tell them not to trust *anyone*. Okay?"

Colby frowns, looking between the three of us. "Y'all are in some deep shit, huh?"

"A legendary amount," I mutter.

Hyun-Joo snorts through her nose, and Diego sighs.

Fairy Tales

"It isn't his," Hyun-Joo says to me. Diego stalks ahead of us, his head on a swivel, leading the way to the Howling Jackal. "You know that, right? He and Colby aren't a thing. I mean." She bobs her head to one side. "Not anymore."

I'm pretty sure I'm too numb to feel anything other than exhaustion. "Okay," I say distantly. "Doesn't really make a difference if it was. That's his business."

She frowns at me. "You wouldn't care if he had a *child*?"

I just shrug. "My father is a walking talking fairy tale who tried to have me killed, Hyun-Joo. I honestly don't think I give a fuck about anything else right now."

She makes a thoughtful noise and flips her bangs out of her face. "That's fair, I guess. So Imane is *really* alive?"

I nod as we round a corner.

"And she's the friend whose grave we visited."

I nod again.

"I'm going to kill him," she mutters glaring at Diego's back, then raises a brow at me. "And you four . . ."

I glance down at her. "How detailed an answer would you like?" I ask flatly.

She snorts. "Never mind."

A thought occurs to me. "Do *you* know what happened in

Lohengrin?"

She blinks and clears her throat. "I think *that* is for them to tell you."

We finally make it to the Howling Jackal, and Diego flings the door open unceremoniously. It's completely empty. The patrons must be at the solstice celebration.

Himesh sits behind the bar, and flips the page in his book without even looking up at us. "What'll it be?"

"Himesh." Diego sets his pack on the bar, and the Fae man frowns at it, as if personally affronted at its presence. "We need to speak with her. Please."

Himesh's eyebrows shoot up, and he pulls a phone from his pocket. "Lock the door, love, if you please."

I do as he asks, and return to the bar just as the call goes through, and Kianga appears on the screen. "Status," she says immediately.

I scrunch my face. *What happened to 'Hello?'*

"Critical," Diego replies, as if this is a perfectly normal phone call. "We need an extraction."

"Is Eil —" Kianga's eyes widen, but he swings the phone to Hyun-Joo and I, and she relaxes immediately. "Oh, shit. Okay. Hi, Hyun-Joo. Okay. We've got — here hold this."

She hands the phone off to someone and begins riffling through papers on her desk. The screen fills with Saif's face.

"Eilidh? What's happening?"

I swipe at my eyes, which are suddenly wet. "A lot," I choke out.

Hyun-Joo sits heavily on a bar stool, and Himesh hands her a glass of water.

Kianga appears on the screen, holding whatever paper she had been looking for. "The closest wyvern is just across the lake. I'll send a message to the Fae that are stationed with him. Can you meet him at the water's edge in ten minutes?"

Diego nods. Kianga grabs the phone from Saif, and types out a rapid message. "Okay. Done. Did you get the location of The Fabled?" Her hopeful tone chills my blood. I failed at the one fucking mission I had.

Again.

Diego, as if sensing my thoughts, grabs my hand and squeezes hard as he places the phone down on the bar. "We'll find them another way."

He picks the phone back up. "No, but we found out who tried to kill Eilidh."

"What?" She and Saif say in unison, and she holds the phone farther away so we can see both of them. "Who?"

"Arthur Pendragon."

Saif's eyes narrow, as if he thinks Diego is playing a very ill-timed prank. "We knew that."

"No. I mean." Diego pulls the sword from his belt, lays it on the bar, and tilts the phone toward the pommel. "Arthur. Fucking. Pendragon."

Himesh reads the name and hisses, taking a step back. Hyun-Joo tips her glass at him. "Cheers to that."

There is silence over the line. Diego tilts the phone back toward us, and both Saif and Kianga are staring with their lips parted in disbelief.

"Where . . . Who?" Saif shakes himself. "Zoom out."

Diego puts his arm high into the air so Saif can see the whole thing. "But that's Auberon's sword."

"Now you've got it." Diego rolls his eyes.

"Eilidh," Kianga breathes. Diego tilts the phone my way, and we stare at one another.

Finally, she swallows, and her eyes turn to steel. "Get on that fucking wyvern and come back to me. Now."

PART TWO

Flight

The emerald green wyvern drops to the ground outside Tal Basta with the first rays of dawn. Kianga, Saif, and Zaehora are waiting for us.

The three of us slide off and crash to the ground. Saif rushes to my side, pushing a metal water bottle into my hands. Kianga does the same to Hyun-Joo, then rounds on Diego. "Show me the sword."

He pulls it from his belt wordlessly. She examines it briefly, then hands it to Zaehora, who runs her finger along the flat side of the blade. Her expression is serious, focused, the exact opposite of her usual aloof self. She sticks the tip of her tongue to the pommel, as if tasting it. "It's certainly old enough," she says after a moment.

"Fuck," Kianga mutters. "Eilidh, tell us what happened. Everything you remember."

I hand my water bottle to Diego and do so as succinctly as I can, recounting how the sword had whispered to me each time I was in the tower, how it had called me to it, and told me I was worthy once it had sampled my blood. By the time I'm done, every eye around me is wide.

I open my pack and spill its contents over the ground. "Here." I hand Kianga the book on King Arthur, and she flips through it, brow furrowed.

Saif picks up his diary. "What —?"

"I'm sorry," I say quickly. "I shouldn't have been reading it. I just . . . missed you."

He sets it on the ground and pulls me into a firm hug. "I missed you too, *Lahabi*. Keep it. I don't mind. It's all about you anyway."

I nod and exhale shakily against him. The weight of last night is starting to creep into my mind. "Okay," I whisper.

Kianga snaps the book shut and turns to Zaehora. "We need to call a Council meeting. Now."

Zaehora nods, pulling a phone from her pocket. "I'll let the others know. See you in five."

Kianga nods as she walks off, then turns to us once more. "You all get cleaned up. We'll need to have a full assembly at some point today. Hyun-Joo, you can take Saif's old room. I'll have —"

Saif puts a hand on her shoulder, and she takes a deep breath. "I've got it handled, *habibti*. You go do what you need to."

She gives him a grateful smile, then grabs my left hand and Diego's right. "I'm glad you're back." She gives us each a tender kiss, then takes off at a jog back into the pyramid.

A goddamn superhero.

<div align="center">~~~~~~~~~~</div>

An hour later, Diego and I have eaten and showered. As I'm pulling on an emerald tunic over black linen pants, Saif enters the bedroom holding a black scabbard and belt.

"What's that for?" I ask warily.

He blinks at me. "Excalibur."

I flinch. "That still doesn't sound real," I mutter. "It'll look good on you, though."

I flip my hair over and throw it into a hasty ponytail. When I straighten back up, he's staring at me with one brow raised.

"What?"

"Eilidh, it isn't for me. It's *your* sword."

I scoff a laugh, but he doesn't smile. "You aren't serious."

"You know him. Always cracking jokes," Diego drawls from where he's lying on the bed, apparently not asleep like I had thought.

I rolls my eyes. "I don't know how to wield a sword."

Saif shrugs, undeterred. "I'll teach you. But Excalibur is yours."

I shake my head, but he continues stepping toward me warily, not unlike Diego had with the silver collar months ago.

He shows me how to wrap the belt around myself and secure Excalibur to my hip. It isn't particularly heavy, but it weighs me down in an entirely different way. I look up at him, eyes wide. "I can't do this."

He doesn't ask what it is I think I can't do. He just puts his hands on my cheeks and gives me a warm kiss on my forehead. "I'm right here, *Lahabi*. You aren't doing it alone. I believe in you."

I clutch the front of his shirt, and he pulls me into a tight hug.

"Sounds like she needs to relax," Diego calls from the bed. "I think I know how we can help her with that."

"Seriously?" I ask, turning my head, but not letting go of Saif. "How can you think about sex right now?"

Diego sits up, frowning. He looks genuinely offended. "I just found out one of my partners is worthy of a *legendary* sword. Pardon me for thinking that's one of the hottest things I've ever heard."

"Oh my god." I lay my forehead against Saif in exasperation, and he chuckles. When I look up at him, he's peering down at me intently.

"Actually, he's got a point."

My brows shoot up. "Really? That's what does it for you?" I can't suppress my smirk. "Women with big swords?"

He shrugs. "Apparently."

"Well, in that case." I unbuckle the belt and set Excalibur on the desk. "Help me relax."

Saif pulls off the tunic I had just put on and drops it to the floor, then buries his lips in my neck. I cling to him as he picks me up and carries me to the bed. Diego unhooks my bra and runs a claw lightly down my bare back, sending a shiver down my spine.

Saif hauls me toward the center of the bed and kisses me as Diego pulls my pants off. As he puts his mouth on my pussy, I reach into Saif's pants and begin stroking him. He moans against my mouth.

After a minute, Diego crawls back up and tilts my chin toward him. His eyes are bright with mischief. "If you really want to relax, I have an idea."

"That can't be good." Saif circles my clit with two fingers, eyeing Diego with a small smile.

"And what's that?" I wriggle under Saif's touch.

Diego reaches across me and begins stroking Saif, who hums his pleasure. "You surrender."

Saif leans in and kisses my neck, and I run my hand through his hair. "How do I do that?"

He circles one of his fangs with his tongue. "Venom."

I quirk an eyebrow at him and smirk. "You want to paralyze me?"

"Is that a good idea?" Saif asks. "*Fuck,*" he gasps, as Diego circles his tip.

"She'll be fine," Diego reassures him. He turns to me. "But it's up to you."

My stomach twists in delight. I kiss him hard and scratch my nails through his hair. His growl reverberates against my teeth. Finally, I pull back. "Yes, Diego. I want to surrender to you."

I reach over and run a thumb over Saif's beard. "But we should get him off first, don't you think?"

Saif's eyes widen, and Diego chuckles. "I was just thinking the same thing." He shoves Saif over, crawls over me, and takes Saif's cock into his mouth all at once.

Saif moans a curse in Arabic, then I kiss him, running my nails lightly over his scalp and down his neck. "You're going to be a good boy for us, aren't you?"

He exhales shakily. "Yes."

He's true to his word. I take Diego's spot between Saif's legs, and as I take him into my mouth, he takes Diego into his.

"Turn around," Diego instructs me with a twirl of his fingers a few minutes later. I comply, and he eats me out from behind. I moan around Saif, who squeezes my thigh. Soon, he begins writhing under me in earnest, and his cum shoots into my mouth as he grunts.

Once I've swallowed, and we've all untangled from one another, he pushes himself up shakily and sits back against the headboard, panting for breath.

Diego gives him one last kiss, then turns his glittering gaze to me. "Ready?"

I lick my lips and nod. "How —"

But Diego's already on me, having moved faster than the wind. He sinks his fangs into the base of my throat, and I moan loudly in his ear. His venom fogs my brain, but he doesn't remove his fangs at the point he usually does. My movements slow as the venom burns through me.

"It's working." My words slur together. "Feelsgood."

He finally removes his fangs as I slump against him. He lays me down gently onto the mattress. "Are you okay?" He asks, searching my eyes.

I feel positively euphoric, but I can't wrap my heavy tongue around all those words right now. "Hell yes," I breathe.

He licks his lips and nods. "Okay."

He disappears from my view, and I try to move my head to follow him before I remember I can't. My head swims with the attempt.

"Where'dya go?"

Suddenly, I feel his mouth against my clit, and I moan loudly as he pushes my thighs apart. He echoes me, and the vibration from his voice shoots up my center. "Just wanted to make sure you're ready for me," he says. He pushes my legs apart farther and rises to his knees.

He rubs the tip of his cock up and down against my entrance, and I exhale slowly in anticipation. Then he thrusts his full length into me all at once, and I cry out in pleasure. I want to dig my nails into him, and the fact that I can't only heightens my desire.

Diego moves his hips slowly back and forth, his abs rippling with his undulating motion. "Fuck, Eilidh, you feel so good," he gasps.

I get wetter as he fucks me. I've never done something like this before, and there's something incredibly hot about him getting off on my body without me even having to do anything. Like my mere existence is enough to make him come undone. Like . . . *I* am enough.

Suddenly, Saif reappears, hovering above me, and plants steady kisses across my skin. He kisses the four scars on my shoulder, and follows them down my body. Finally, he makes his way back up, and holds my head gently, running his thumbs over my cheeks, then moving to massage my shoulders.

I moan wordlessly. Every nerve in my body is going haywire under their touch.

Diego licks his lips and looks down at me hungrily. "You look so fucking pretty when you're taking my cock." I release a high-pitched whimper. He chuckles and lowers himself onto me. His bare chest burns against my skin. Saif trails his fingers over Diego's back, and they exchange a rough kiss.

When they part, Diego sucks on my neck. "You like me using you like this, don't you, *querida*?" He teases. "You like being at my mercy."

His grin is absolutely wicked.

"Yes, sir." I have just a bit more control of my mouth, though my head is still delightfully foggy.

He makes a noise halfway between a moan and a growl, and his thrusting intensifies. He twists one hand into my hair again, and I gasp at the sensation. He grabs my jaw with his other hand. "Don't even think about coming yet," he growls. "I'm not done with you."

I grin at him. "I can't fucking stand you."

He flashes a glittering fang at me. "Yeah, keep telling yourself that, Eilidh."

I melt against the sheets.

He releases my jaw, grabs my wrists, then pins them to the firm mattress. "Kiss her," he commands Saif, and he does. My moan is high-pitched against his mouth. They switch tasks; Saif holds my wrists to the mattress while Diego kisses me, and parts my lips with no effort at all. His growl reverberates against my teeth.

He whimpers, and starts to lose his composure. "Eilidh," he gasps. His dominant masks cracks, and soon he's a shuddering mess, his motions jerky and uneven. He tangles his fingers tightly into my hair, and Saif's grip tightens on my wrists.

"I love you," he mutters, then he groans loudly as he starts pulsing inside me. "Oh my *god*, I love you so much, Eilidh." He mutters and gasps over and over, switching between English, Spanish, and utter gibberish.

Finally, once he has filled me up, he regains some composure. "Now," he pants. "Be a good girl and come for me," he commands.

He pulls his thick cock out of me and grinds his hips so that it slicks up and down over my clit. It's soaked in his cum and my juices, and it's warm, and heavy, dragging the pleasure out of me. He's tugging on my hair, and he's kissing along my throat, and Saif's grip on my wrists is like iron, and my head is swimming with venom, and oh my *god.*

I shatter into a million different fragments. Diego doesn't stop moving; he prolongs my pleasure long after his has subsided. Saif leans into my neck and whispers in my ear, telling me I'm beautiful, and that he loves me, and I have no idea how long my orgasm lasts, but it has to be record-breaking.

Finally, after what feels like an hour, or a month, or perhaps the rest of my infinite lifespan, I'm able to stop moaning, and catch my breath as blood pounds in my ears.

Diego rises to his knees, panting hard. "Now. You rest. We're going to get cleaned up." They each give me a kiss before they head into the bathroom for a shower.

"I love you," I whisper to the closed door as I fall asleep.

Make an Impression

Later, as I emerge from the bathroom, toweling off my hair, someone knocks on the bedroom door.

Saif opens it and stiffens. I frown, but as I round the door, it's just Zaehora, her arms laden with clothing, and a pair of black thigh-high boots dangling from one hand.

She steps into the room without an invitation, drops the boots by the shoe rack, and strides to the bed. Diego, who is sitting at Kianga's desk, narrows his eyes at her, but stays silent.

"Here you go, Doll." She dumps the pile of clothing on the foot of the bed, and turns to me with a hand on her waist.

I blink at her. "What's that?"

She gestures vaguely. "Clothes."

"I have clothes," I say, raising my chin at the second wardrobe.

She grins. "And aren't we all sorry about that."

I flush.

"Anyway, now you have more. You two." Her gaze darts between Saif and Diego. "Bastet wants you in the courtroom, ten minutes ago, preferably, but now, I suppose, will also suffice."

One corner of Diego's mouth pinches in annoyance. He's not used to being the one taking the orders. "She's ready to present the news to everyone?"

Zaehora nods. "Yes, so I've got to get this one ready. Go."

Saif eyes me cautiously.

I frown. "Get me ready for what?"

She grins devilishly. "To make an impression."

~~~~~~~~~

Five minutes later, I stomp out of the bathroom. "What are you trying to do to me?" I ask, exasperated. "I look ridiculous."

She chuckles. "You *look* like a badass. You're the newest figurehead of this rebellion, Princess. You need to wow the crowd."

Thinking back on how Rhae and the other Shifters had treated me a few weeks ago, I scowl. "Don't call me that. And I doubt they will be wowed by me no matter what I wear."

She shrugs, unperturbed. "Bastet thought it was worth a shot."

"This is all from her?"

She nods.

I look down at myself again. I'm in a thick, high necked, black bodysuit. It's sleeveless, but small swatches of chain mail rest coolly on my shoulders. The shorts hug me tightly, and rise alarmingly high on my thigh. The gray corset is covered in chains made of interlocking suns and moons, and the matching fingerless elbow-length gloves each has a wolf's head stitched into the material on the backs of my hands.

The black thigh-high boots are surprisingly comfortable, though they look stiff and severe. They also add about three inches to my height, putting me just north of six feet. An emerald cloak billows behind me as I stride to the bed and strap my blades around myself once more.

I had run my hands over the silver and gold stitching on the cloak in awe before I had put it on. In the center of the back, a large crescent moon intertwines with a blazing golden sun. Silver and gold thread
~~~~~~~~~

runs along the outside of the cloak, and around the opening of the thick hood.

"One more thing. Close your eyes."

I stare back at her apprehensively.

"You can trust me." She grins.

I have my doubts about that, but I close my eyes.

She approaches me and puts her hands behind my neck. I stiffen, but then she steps away as a familiar weight lands just under my collarbone.

My eyes snap open and I look down at my pendant.

Zaehora winks at me. "Your Mage told me to give it to you before he left. Now let's go."

I follow her to the courtroom, finding the colors of the rainbow all around me, and breathing in four-second intervals.

When we finally make it to the door, she pauses. "Deep breath, Doll."

I take a steadying breath, and she nods at me, satisfied.

She opens the door and strides inside. I follow her woodenly.

"Ladies, gentleman, those in between, and those outside of the binary. May I present to you, Eilidh Pendragon."

Assembly

My blood runs cold as the room erupts in whispers and muffled gasps.

I stare wide-eyed at Zaehora. *That's not who I am.* But it is. My stomach churns.

I gulp and look around the room. The rest of the Council members, Kianga included, are seated at the high bench. Diego and Saif are standing side by side in front of Kianga's spot on the bench at a wide podium that faces the crowd. Diego is hunched over it, his forearms resting on the chestnut wood. Saif is drawn up to his full height, his hand gripping one side of the podium fiercely.

More than a hundred Fabled, Mages, and Shifters fill every seat. Every pair of eyes is on me. Sweat breaks out on the back of my neck. I take a few tentative steps toward the bench, and no one stops me, so it must be what I'm supposed to do. I spot both Ousmane and Himesh in the crowd of bodies. Hyun-Joo is seated in the back row.

Diego smirks and raises his chin at me as I approach stiffly. As he takes in my outfit, and the blades at my hip, his expression blazes with pride.

I step with a bit more confidence.

Saif's eyes widen and his lips part slightly as he looks at me. He glances at Excalibur on my hip, in the scabbard he had gotten for me, and his tender smile as he grabs the hilt of *Dhabiha* warms the chill of my blood.

I pull my shoulder blades together slightly, and take a deep breath as I reach the podium.

I put both of my hands on the wood, and they each reach out and clasp one. I squeeze their hands hard and look between them, gathering strength before I raise my eyes to Kianga.

She radiates power. "Eilidh," she says loudly, and I blink, but manage not to flinch. "We've gathered everyone here so that we can hear your report, and make the plans to act on it. What did you discover from King Auberon?"

She gestures for me to turn and face the crowded room. I walk around the podium and stand between Saif and Diego. Saif places his right hand on the small of my back. Diego puts his left hand on my right thigh. I take a steadying breath, and raise my voice to the crowd.

"King Auberon - my father - is Arthur Pendragon." More whispers and gasps as the crowd looks at one another.

"Show them." Kianga's voice rings from behind me.

How do I — oh.

I unsheathe Excalibur slowly, careful not to slice Saif in half with the blade. My right arm vibrates as I hold it aloft. Sunlight glints off the blade, sending a million lights into the crowd.

The front row of spectators lean forward, and I hold the pommel out for them to see. Several of them reel back when they read the name. Soon, the entire crowd is buzzing.

"This is my father's sword. As you can see, this . . . is Excalibur."

It's the first time I've said its name aloud. Suddenly, my hand blazes with rust-colored light, and there's the familiar buzzing in my navel. *Oh, god, what —?*

The light travels up the hilt and explodes out of the tip of the blade in a shower of sparks that dissipate before they touch anyone.

I bring the sword down in front of me, staring in awe.

"Holy *shit*," Diego breathes. Saif just stares.

I sheath the sword again, shakily. Every eye in the room is widened at me. If anyone had doubted my story at first, Excalibur had just made sure they no longer do.

Or, so I think.

Mòrag speaks behind me. "Arthur Pendragon lived more than a thousand years ago, if he even lived at all. This may be a powerful sword, may even be Excalibur itself. But why do you think that Auberon Danodraic is really Arthur Pendragon? How would he even be alive? He isn't a Fabled or a Shifter with that ability."

I grit my teeth. "He has the Holy Grail," I say over my shoulder, so everyone can hear me.

Saif stiffens beside me. "His goblet."

I snort. "I always thought of it as a chalice," I say quietly.

"Fucking synonyms," Diego murmurs.

Indeed.

The centaur, Lycysius, speaks next. "What of his magic? Arthur wasn't a Mage in the legends. Merlin was."

I wrack my brain for a moment, then nearly fall to my knees. I brace myself on the podium. "Merlin." I turn to Kianga. "I need to go back to the bedroom. The book —" She holds up a hand to cut me off, and picks something up off a shelf below my view, built into the bench. She tosses the book on Arthur Pendragon at me, and I catch it.

"I thought we might need that." I don't even know when she would have grabbed it from my bag, but there's no time to ask.

I flip through it until I find the picture of the cloaked figure casting a spell. Diego and Saif lean in to look at the page. I point to the end of Merlin's staff, and the reddish-brown glow emanating from a large gem on the top of it.

"Jasper," Diego says hoarsely.

"What?" I ask, as I hand the book to Kianga, and she passes it around the bench for the Council members to look at.

"That gem. It's a huge hunk of Jasper," Diego says.

I stare at him.

He shrugs, looking out over the crowd. "I like crystals."

"The stained glass window," Saif says, his brow wrinkled in thought, and I hiss through my teeth. The red rock, swirled with black and gray.

"It was right in front of us the whole time." I shake my head. "All of it."

"The bastard was practically begging for someone to put the pieces together," Diego growls.

"And who knows when they would have, if not for her," Kianga says. "Eilidh. Tell everyone what happened last night."

I gaze out at the crowd, and inhale deeply.

I recount every detail I can remember. What Auberon's - *Arthur's* - living quarters look like, how Excalibur had been on a stone plaque, how it had called to me for weeks. I tell them how my father had previously ranted about Earth being ravaged, and how he was going to save it.

My stomach churns as the room erupts in chatter again, and the Council members lean together to discuss. I take the opportunity to speak quietly with Saif and Diego. "He mentioned that my kids would inherit the Danodraic magic, too."

Saif frowns. "But you can't even have kids."

"And I don't *want* to," I whisper fiercely. "I never did. Not my own, anyway. With my family's mental health history?" I put a hand to my temple, feeling a headache brewing. "And that was just my mom's side, for fuck's sake. But my father doesn't know that."

He holds up his hands placatingly. "I'm sorry," he says, sincerely.

I sigh. "No, it's okay. Besides, Diego's already got one."

Saif's jaw drops open in the same instant that Diego's claws extend and dig into the podium. "What?" He hisses in horror.

I smirk and put my hand over his. "I'm kidding. Hyun-Joo assured me Colby's baby isn't yours. As if that was necessary. Can't exactly picture you changing a diaper."

He winces, but the tension goes out of his shoulders.

"Who's Colby?" Saif asks.

"Brunette," Diego chokes out.

"Everyone," Kianga says suddenly, and then every eye in the courtroom snaps to her.

"We all need to prepare. We don't know what Auberon —" She pauses, and scoffs. "We don't know what *Arthur* is going to do next. He may simply think his daughter ran off with her lover. Or he may be marching toward our doorstep as we speak."

I expect panic to sweep through the crowd, but there's only grim determination. They've known this day was coming for a long time.

"Reach out to your contacts. Warn them. Spread the word of who we're really dealing with. Tell them to prepare for a battle. But let them know." She looks down at me, and I hold her gaze. "We've got a new weapon."

Secrets

The courtroom slowly clears out. Finally, Hyun-Joo is the only one left in the audience. The four of us approach her, and Kianga opens her arms silently. Hyun-Joo rises, wraps her arms around Kianga, and is instantly wracked with sobs.

"I missed you," she sniffles into Kianga's shirt as she cries.

Kianga squeezes her tightly, eyes glistening. "I missed you, too."

Hyun-Joo releases her, wiping her eyes, and abruptly turns to Diego, who winces. "How could you not tell me?"

"Please, *mi vida*. I'm so sorry." Diego's voice wavers.

Hyun-Joo throws herself back into her seat with a huff, then sniffs and looks away from him. I've never seen her like this. I can't stand it. I nudge Saif and tilt my head at Diego. Saif puts a hand on this arm, and Diego looks at him, stricken.

"Let's go," Saif says gently. He guides Diego out of the room. I throw my leg over the chair in front of Hyun-Joo and sit down, my arms and chin resting on the back. Kianga crosses her arms and sighs.

Hyun-Joo tucks a strand of hair behind her ear. "If you're going to tell me I should forgive him, save your breath."

I look pointedly at the ground and twirl a piece of hair around one finger. "I was actually going to tell you that you should punch him in the face."

She laughs out loud. "Well, I didn't expect that." She turns toward me, her defenses lowered just a fraction.

"It's cathartic, trust me." I smile at her, and one corner of her mouth lifts back at me. "Although, I got a very different result than what you will."

She shakes her head amusedly. "I don't even want to know."

I snort. "No, you don't."

Kianga crouches down and puts a hand on her knee. "For what it's worth, I know it killed him to not be able to tell you. But it was to make sure Arthur couldn't get any information out of you."

Hyun-Joo swallows. "I know. But . . . we've told each other *everything* for more than a decade," she says sadly. "And of all the things to keep from me." She shakes her head. "I know it was necessary. But it still hurts."

I smile sadly. "I know exactly what you mean."

She sighs. "You do, don't you?"

I stand and reach for her hand. She looks at my palm for a moment, but then lets me pull her to her feet. Then she moves in closer, and wraps her arms around my torso. I freeze for a moment, then hug her back.

"I hope you know how much he loves you," I say to the top of her head. She makes a strangled noise, and when she backs away, she swipes a hand across her eyes quickly.

I keep my arm around her shoulder as the three of us exit the room. Diego is hunched over against a wall not far away, and Saif is leaning in close to him, speaking softly, one hand rubbing up and down Diego's arm comfortingly.

"Diego," I say firmly as we approach. He turns to Hyun-Joo. Saif takes one look at her expression, and takes a step away from Diego.

"Just know that I told her to do this," I say. I release her from my grasp.

He raises an eyebrow at me as she closes the distance between them. "Told her to do wh —"

Hyun-Joo slaps him full across the face. The *crack* reverberates against the wall. Saif winces at the sound. Diego brings a hand to his cheek and stares at her incredulously. Then he turns to me. "What the *fuck*?"

I shrug. "I told her it would make her feel better."

"And she was right," Hyun-Joo says, shaking her hand idly. "We promised not to keep secrets from each other. No matter what." She glares at him.

"*¡Ay, coño!* It was to keep you safe!" Diego throws his hands into the air, exasperated.

"You don't get to make that choice for me!" She says vehemently.

I cross my arms. "Hmm. He really likes making decisions for people, huh?"

He looks at me, his mouth working. He turns to Saif for help, but Saif glances at us and shakes his head. "Nope. You're on your own with this one."

Diego begins muttering in Spanish, then turns and stalks in the direction of the bedroom. Hyun-Joo runs and falls into step beside him, shoving into him gently.

"I know you can hit harder than that." He wraps an arm around her.

She flips her hair off her shoulder. "Next time, I will."

When we get to our room, I lean Excalibur against the wall by the shoe rack, but Saif snatches it up, scandalized.

"*Eilidh!*"

I raise my palms to the ceiling. "What?"

He prowls to the second wardrobe, wiping imaginary dust from the scabbard. I roll my eyes. He opens one the of doors and shows me hooks that have been installed on the inside. Once Excalibur is hanging safely in the wardrobe, he heads straight to the beverage cart.

At first, I think he's pouring drinks, but instead, he grabs a jar of coffee beans. I make my way over and wrap my arms around him. "So . . ."

He smirks and glances at me. "I'm making enough for everyone."

I lean up and kiss him on the cheek. "You're too good to me."

He shakes his head idly, still smiling.

I meander over to Kianga, who is sitting at her desk, tapping rapid-fire messages into her phone.

Diego and Hyun-Joo are bent together in quiet conversation near the door. Hyun-Joo looks alarmed, and Diego is shaking his head. "I can't," he whispers. She frowns at him reproachfully.

I turn to Kianga, not wanting to eavesdrop. "I'm sorry I didn't complete the mission."

She sighs, but doesn't sound angry. "We'll figure it out. There has to be a way to find them. At least we know what we're actually dealing with now. Besides, I don't want you near him if he's the one who tried to kill you. I just wish we knew *why*."

I nod slowly. "Me too. But I think he's changed his mind about it. He seems to want to keep me around now. He said he 'acted too soon.'" I shudder. "I think he wants me to want me to pop out some kids."

"Which is ridiculous," Saif says, walking over to us with two mugs, grimacing. "And impossible. But he doesn't know that." He hands us the mugs as Kianga looks back at me, questioningly.

"Hysterectomy," I say simply, and sip the steaming hot coffee. It's absolutely delicious. Saif sits down on the floor to my left, opposite Kianga.

She nods thoughtfully. "You always said you didn't want kids. Finally find a doctor to do it?"

Hyun-Joo holds her hand out to Diego, jerking her head toward us. He stares at the floor the whole way as they make their way to us.

"After battling with them for years, yeah, finally," I say as they sit opposite me, completing our circle. I smile.

"Just curious. Why didn't you want kids?" Hyun-Joo asks.

I take a deep breath, gathering the energy to explain. "My mom was - well, *is*, I guess - an alcoholic. So was my grandmother, though she had been sober for decades by the time I came along. I drank for a couple years, but then stopped. I . . . felt myself slipping. Didn't want to risk it."

Saif puts a hand on my knee. "Were you . . . when you almost . . . were you dr—?"

"Yes." I swallow hard. "I poured it all out when I got home that morning." Silence stretches as I pick at the fabric of my shorts. "Besides, with all the other mental health issues we Shaws collect? I didn't want to pass all that on." I sip more of the coffee.

Hyun-Joo puts a hand on Diego's knee and nods at me. "That was a very responsible decision."

I drain my mug and nod gratefully. "Thanks." I've gotten some very mixed reactions through the years from people when it comes to this topic. Some from total strangers.

Diego emits a drawn-out sigh. "Eilidh," he says quietly. "I have something to tell you." He briefly glances at Kianga and Saif. "*All* of you." He looks back at the ground.

"Oh god, you're pregnant," I say, trying to make him laugh. He hasn't even smiled since he saw me walking down the aisle in the courtroom. "Well, better you than me."

He grimaces and looks up from the floor; his eyes are glistening.

I stretch my leg out and put a foot against his shin. "Hey, what's wrong?" I ask gently.

He takes a deep breath and looks me in the eye. "You joked earlier that I had a child."

I nod, my brow furrowed. "I'm sorry. Was that offensive? Do you not want kids more than *I* don't want kids?"

He shakes his head. "No, it's not that. It's that . . . I do. I have a daughter."

Seaside

No one says anything for several long moments.

I burst into laughter. "You do not."

He doesn't smile. Neither does Hyun-Joo.

My smile slowly dies. "You're serious."

He nods. I draw my foot back toward myself, and he winces. Saif and Kianga are both wide-eyed. I look at the floor in front of Diego. "How?"

"Her mom and I — we were young and stupid. She was born when we were sixteen."

I shake myself slightly. "So she's . . ."

"Nineteen."

My whole body is trembling, and I'm suddenly freezing. I pull my emerald cloak around myself tightly.

"Is she . . . here?" I whisper.

"Absolutely not," he says fiercely. "She lives in Tucson, with her mom." Hyun-Joo nudges him. He sighs. "And . . . my brother. They've been married for fifteen years now."

I shake my head.

"What's her name?" Saif asks gently.

Diego is still staring at me. I am still staring at the floor.

"Daniela," he says. His voice takes on a protective quality that I've never heard before. "She's named after my brother. Daniel's a couple years younger than me, but we were close as kids. It just happened to work out that Estelle - Daniela's mom - fell for him."

Kianga finally speaks. "Why didn't you ever tell me? We talked about . . . you knew I always wanted kids." She sounds as hurt as I feel.

He looks at her guiltily. "I just didn't know how. Besides, she lives on Earth. She wouldn't be *ours*."

She raises her brows and blinks several times. "Ouch."

I push myself up the wall and stride away from everyone.

"Eilidh." Diego says behind me, but I'm already zipping my boots back up next to the door.

I slam it behind me as I exit. I walk blindly through the halls of Tal Basta, my mind racing. I reach for Excalibur, but realize with a jolt that I left it in the wardrobe. *Fuck.* I grip the hilt of my dagger instead.

He's a father. *To a whole person. Nineteen?*

Thoughts swirl through my head too quickly for me to catch. I clutch my pendant until I find myself at the exit. I push the door and stride into the sunlight. The grass outside is as brown and dead as ever. It crunches as I shift into my wolf form and run across the field.

Eventually, I hear waves crashing. After a few more minutes, I crest a hill, and then all I can see ahead of me is deep blue water.

Now *that* is an ocean. If the waves of Nabeyha Lake are large, these are monstrous. I sit down on a cliff side and look at the water numbly. I don't know how long I sit for, my thoughts raging along with the tide.

~~~~~~~~~~

Steps crunch the grass behind me. I can tell who it is from the footfalls.
~~~~~~~~~~

"I don't think I want to talk to you right now."

Diego sits beside me, and looks out at the waves. "You don't have to talk. But can I explain?"

I shrug.

He sighs. "Eilidh, I love you. I'm sorry I kept something so big from you." He places a hand on my knee, and I flinch. He removes his hand and puts it on the ground between us.

I take a shaky breath. "That's not it," I whisper. It's not like I hadn't kept things from him before. I had figured out a little while ago what had been bothering me the most. "It's just that . . . I don't even know you."

"Yes, you do," he protests, but I turn to him fiercely.

"No, Diego, I *don't*. Not really." Tears sting the corners of my eyes. "How . . . how can I love you so much when I know almost *nothing* about you?" I turn back toward the water, trembling. "About who you used to be?"

A corner of his mouth lifts. "Eilidh," he says quietly. "I don't even know your favorite color. But I don't need to know every little thing about you to know that I love you. To know how big your heart is. How smart and strong and fierce you are. I do want to learn the little things, eventually, but I'm looking forward to doing that over time. For the rest of forever."

I pick at some grass, trying to sort through my tumultuous emotions. Maybe I'm more angry with myself than anything. I've never asked him about his family — not once. Not only am I awful at sharing my own past, I also block out everyone else's.

"So, what is it?" He bumps his shoulder into me. "Your favorite color?"

"Blue, green, and purple," I mumble.

He blinks. "I'm not the *best* at math, but that's more than one."

I lift my chin. "They're the colors of the aurora. They belong together."

His eyes twinkle. "You can only have one favorite."

I tilt my head at him and give him a long look. "Well, I have three favorites. Who decided we always have to choose just one?"

He huffs a laugh, shaking his head at the ground. "Point taken. But you're forgetting one of the colors. Your aurora isn't complete."

I furrow my brow. "What am I missing?"

He runs his hand through my hair. "Red. It isn't complete without the red."

I swallow hard.

He smirks. "So. What do you want to know about me?"

I shrug. "Everything," I whisper. "I want to know everything about you. But there's just so much that I didn't. That I don't. You're a *father*, Diego." The words sound completely absurd.

He sighs. When he speaks, there's more pain in his voice than I've ever heard before. "I'm not a father, Daniel is. *He* raised my daughter for me. I couldn't . . . I *wasn't* there for her. I've missed so much."

My heart aches for him. I place a hand on his thigh.

"Investigating that gang . . . that was my last article for that paper. I was going to move back home after that, and be a better dad." His voice breaks, and when he looks up at the sky, the sunlight glints off the unshed tears in his eyes.

"I'm so sorry," I whisper.

He grabs my hand and squeezes tightly. "But even before I got bitten, it was hard. I fucked everything up. I broke Estelle's heart because I wasn't ready to be a father. She wasn't ready to be a mother, either, but she did it anyway."

His lip curls in an infinitesimal smile. "She was always stronger than me. And then Daniel stepped in, even though he was just a kid himself. We had a fight about it, right before I left for college. He was giving me one more chance to step up, and I didn't."

He shakes his head. "Estelle had to put her dreams on hold, but I was selfish. I got to do what I wanted. She didn't get to go back to school until Daniela went to Kindergarten. She got her GED, then a Bachelor's in Chemistry, and then her Ph.D. She became a pharmacist. She's *brilliant*. And Daniel's the one who was there for her. And for Daniela."

"Does . . . does Daniela know she isn't his?" I ask.

He nods. "Estelle never hid it from her. About a year after Imane . . . disappeared, I had enough control that I finally trusted myself to try to see her, so I went to Tucson. Daniel took one look at me and almost threw me off their front porch, but Estelle stopped him. We sat and talked, then Daniela got home from school, and we all talked some more. She . . . didn't like me. For a long time."

"That's understandable."

He exhales quickly through his nose. "I know. I wouldn't have blamed her if she hated me forever. She doesn't, though; she's too compassionate for that, just like her mom."

"When did you see her last?"

He frowns. "August. When she moved into her dorm."

I recall that he and Hyun-Joo had indeed been gone for a weekend four months ago, right before my second full moon as a werewolf. At the time, I had just assumed they were on a romantic getaway.

He looks out mournfully at the water. "I try to see her every year for Christmas, but obviously I'm not going to make it this year. I missed her graduation in June, too."

Guilt constricts my chest. He had been too busy saving me to be there for his daughter. It's a moment he'll never get back. "Do they know about . . . you?"

His laugh is devoid of humor. "That I'm a blood-sucking monster and attack dog for a deranged king? No. They think I work for a newspaper in Queens."

I wince. "You should tell them, you know. Especially since she's an adult. Finding out about your dad's secret identity *sucks*, trust me. But she deserves to know."

He winces and shakes his head. "She's still a kid to me. I can't do that to her."

I growl, and he looks at me, alarmed. "What did Hyun-Joo and I tell you?"

He looks at me blankly.

"You don't get to make decisions for everyone else. She's your *daughter*, Diego. *Talk* to her. Stop trying to carry the weight of the world on your shoulders when there are *plenty* of people who want to help you hold it. You're not Atlas."

He blinks, and a true smirk crosses his face for the first time in hours. "Look who's talking." A breeze swirls all around us.

"What does that mean?"

He tilts his head at me, like the answer is obvious. "I may try to hold the weight of the world, Eilidh, but *you* would bleed yourself dry for it."

I slap him playfully. "I would not."

He rubs his cheek, still smirking. "I'll *think* about telling her. Okay?"

I nod. "I would love to meet her someday. Whenever you say it's okay." I pick at the grass nervously.

He smiles and cups my cheek. "Of course I want you to meet her, *querida*. Imane already said she'll arrange our flight to Tucson once we're done saving the world."

I laugh loudly, and he pulls me into a kiss. I lean into it with a smile, clutching the back of his neck.

"I hate to interrupt, but I'm afraid I must," says a voice from behind us. We break apart and twist abruptly.

My father is standing about twenty yards behind us, wearing an amused expression.

Valentina and Martín are standing on either side of him, looking murderous.

Fallout

Diego bounds to his feet, his claws lengthening instantly, but I'm frozen in place on the ground. I can't get my legs to move.

No. He can't be here. How *can he be here?*

My father tilts his head at me. "I told you we would chat more, Daughter. I thought you wanted to know more about how we're going to save the world?"

I goggle at him.

"Eilidh, what's going on?" Valentina's voice is icy. "Why did you leave?"

Martín says nothing, but he's glaring so hard that I worry he might actually set me on fire.

They're both wearing their battle suits; Valentina's is once again the color of Merlot. Martín's is a deep, burnt orange.

Diego hisses under his breath. "*Mi sol*, run. Go back to Tal Basta. Tell Imane and Saif."

I stare up at him, wide-eyed, shaking my head. "I'm not leaving you with him."

"Eilidh!" Valentina strides toward me, and I finally regain control of my muscles. I stand just as she comes to a stop, about three feet from me. "Auberon says you're working with the Mongrels. And Saif." She spits his name venomously. "Is that true?"

I hold my hands out placatingly. "Val, it's complicated. Please, just trust me. There's so much you don't know."

Her eyes blaze with fury. "And whose fault is *that*?"

I flinch, and reach a hand out for her to take. "Val, I'm sorry, but please listen —"

"No," she spits. "*You* listen."

I recoil.

"All I ever tried to do was help you, and show you that you weren't alone. I told you *everything* that mattered." Her voice breaks. "Getting you to open up is like trying to bleed a *stone*, Eilidh, but I *tried*. I tried *so hard*. Because I loved you like a sister."

Tears stream down my cheeks. None of the men have moved a muscle since she started yelling at me.

"I thought that maybe for *once* I had found someone who wouldn't push me away. But you're back for a few weeks and then you just *run*? And leave me behind? For what? To be with the man who nearly killed Martín?" She points back at her brother.

I glance at him. He glares back at me. There is no love in his eyes any longer. For the first time, I see a man who has been hardened by life, and hurt over and over by those who were supposed to love him.

My heart splinters.

"We couldn't find you. And Saif didn't mean to; you don't understand," I plead. "Please, Auberon isn't who you think he is, Saif was trying to *save* me. My father is Ar—"

She takes a step forward and slaps me. Diego grabs her by the arms, and flings her away from me.

She lands in a heap on the grass.

Through the stars exploding across my vision, a ball of flame bursting to life in Martín's hand. But just as Diego turns to him and crouches, preparing for a fight, my father reaches out and places a hand across Martín's chest, stopping him in his tracks.

Diego speaks to Valentina, his wary gaze still on Martín. "I'm sorry, kid."

She stands, not bothering to brush herself off. "Fuck you," she croaks.

"Val," I breathe, rubbing the side of my face.

She doesn't look at me again. She walks back to stand behind my father, and takes Martín's hand.

"I hope you see how your choices are affecting us, Eilidh." Mock concern twists Arthur's features.

I clench my teeth and briefly consider transforming and launching myself at him to bite his head off, but if he's half as powerful as Diego and Kianga say, then I have no chance.

"I know it's not your fault. Saif and Diego have poisoned your mind," he says. "They've turned you against me. I wanted to show you what the people who *really* love you think. Please." He reaches a hand out toward me. His voice is sweet and caring. "Come home."

My stomach churns. "The only poison is *you*," I say through my teeth. "You've been poisoning this dimension for a thousand years, *Arthur*."

Valentina shakes her head and scoffs derisively. "He said you would say something like that. I think that wolfsbane knocked something loose in your head, Eilidh. A man can have any name stamped into a sword. It's all a misunderstanding, but you're too selfish to see it."

I shake my head in disbelief. "You didn't see — it *called* to me, it . . . it lit up for me! How am I being *selfish*?"

She rolls her eyes. "All you care about is being with your . . . " She looks at Diego, disgusted. "Playthings."

I gape at her. "That is not . . . Val, you *have* to listen!"

"We're done listening," Martín growls, low and dangerous.

"Eilidh." My father holds his hand out to me again. "This is your last chance to come of your own accord. Do as you're told."

My blood runs cold. I shift into my wolf form and draw myself up to my full height.

My father sighs. "Very well."

He snaps his fingers.

Martín shoots a bolt of fire at Diego, and Valentina whips a lasso of water at my front ankles, dragging me to the ground, and across the grass toward her.

I snap at them, but my teeth pass through the streams harmlessly. Diego, who had rolled away from me to avoid Martín's flames, yells with wordless rage.

His anger stokes my own. I look at Valentina as my vision flashes red, and a burst of my magic flies at her, knocking her back through the air.

It's Martín's turn to bellow with rage. He turns his attention from Diego to me. He twirls his hand in a wide circle above his head, and a ring of fire bursts to life around me.

I start sweating instantly as primal fear shoots through me. I jump over the flames toward Martín, and hit him square in the chest with my paws. His cry of pain as his head collides with the ground digs into my heart.

I transform back with a sob and cradle his head. "I'm so sorry."

My father has been watching the fray with a small, amused smile on his face. He chuckles as I weep over Martín. Valentina hasn't gotten up either, but I see her chest rising and falling.

Diego steps between my father and I.

"No!" *Not again.* I drag myself to my feet and pull him back. "This is my fight," I hiss.

"It's mine, too," he growls back at me. I glare at him, and my father laughs in earnest. We both turn to him.

"Actually," he says, wiping a tear of mirth from his eye, "It's everyone's."

He twirls a hand, and more than a hundred small, reddish-brown cyclones crackling with lightning appear in the brown field behind him.

When the cyclones disappear, they leave behind a field full of The Fabled, as well as other non-humanoid magical creatures. But something is wrong with them; they're completely still, and their expressions are utterly blank.

All their eyes are glowing with a rust-colored light.

War

"Afraid to fight me yourself, coward?" I hiss.

He chuckles. "I *can't* fight you myself, Eilidh. Our magic cannot be used against itself. I told you. We are bound by ancient blood."

My jaw drops open. *I can't hurt him with my magic? Then how —?*

"Bring her to me at the pyramid. Him, you can kill." My father disappears in a crackling cyclone of his own, and then I see him, a hundred yards away, striding toward Tal Basta.

"He can teleport," I breathe in horror.

Every Fabled in the field starts walking toward us. Ogres, Fae, centaurs, and every other manner of magical creature have their attention focused solely on us. The closest ones are only about thirty yards away. They don't seem to be in a hurry.

Diego grabs my hand. "Can you take us to Tal Basta? We have to warn them."

"I have no idea." My eyes go immediately to Martín and Valentina.

"You have to try, Eilidh."

"Grab Val." I kneel, and grab Martín. Diego runs to Valentina, picks her up, and runs back toward me.

"Okay. Hold on tight." I clutch his hand, and hold tight to Martín's shirt with my other. I squeeze my eyes shut, feeling the rage pulsing through me. In the next second, we're caught up in a cyclone, and crash to the ground in our bedroom.

It's empty.

I pant as I stand, swaying. "Fuck. That took a lot of energy."

Valentina and Martín lie silently, but they're both breathing. We'll have to leave them here.

Excalibur is no longer in the wardrobe when I fling it open. *Did I seriously manage to lose a legendary fucking sword?* I collapse to my knees. Diego scoops me up and runs out of the room.

"Where's Bastet?" He screams.

Every eye turns to him, and to me in his arms. "Dining hall," says a Fae woman nearby.

Diego takes off at a run. "Prepare for war," he calls to everyone within earshot. "Arthur is on the island. He's coming."

A flurry of motion erupts around us.

When he bursts through the door of the dining hall, he spots Kianga, Saif, and Hyun-Joo immediately, and runs to their table.

Kianga rises to her feet in horror at the sight of us. "Diego, what —"

"Arthur." He deposits me in Saif's lap. Saif pulls me against his chest, holding me upright. He cups my cheek, examining me for a wound. "He's on the island. He's coming. And he has an army."

Saif's arms tighten around me. "We have to get her out of here."

Diego blinks at him in confusion. "Who?"

Saif scrunches his nose at him with equal confusion. "What do you mean, 'who?' Eilidh!"

I shake my head against him. "I have to fight him."

Saif looks at me like I've lost my mind. "You can't fight him. He's too strong. Look at you!"

Diego bristles. "Really? You *still* don't believe in her?"

Saif's eyes blaze with fury. "I'm not going to let her kill herself just to prove a point. And if he doesn't kill her, he's going to keep her in a cage until she cooperates with him — or possibly forever. I can't live with that. Can you?"

Diego holds a palm up at Saif. "I can't do this with you anymore," he bites. "We don't have time." He turns to Kianga and they start making plans.

Saif turns to me. "*Please*, my love. Get out of here."

I shake my head at him fiercely. "I'm not running. I'm *done* running."

He closes his eyes and sets his jaw in grim determination. "Okay. Then we'll fight. Take this." He taps something metal. I twist in his lap, and breathe a sigh of relief.

Excalibur is strapped to his hip. "*Dhabiha* is in the bedroom. I just didn't want to let this out of my sight."

"You're more responsible than I am," I say flatly.

He begins to unbuckle it, but I put my hand over his. "Keep it for now. It will do more good in your hands, anyway."

"But —"

"Saif, *please*."

He sighs. "Okay."

Five minutes later, every Fabled, Shifter, and Mage in Tal Basta is outside, prepared for battle. Kianga, Diego, Hyun-Joo, Saif, and I make up the front line.

The Order members are all in their battle suits; Hyun-Joo's is the color of obsidian. Diego's is navy, and he has donned his red vambraces; the blades glint in the sunlight. Saif's suit is a brilliant ivory; Excalibur gleams in his hand. It looks like it was made for him. Kianga is in full goddess regalia, cat mask included, her crochet braids tied back firmly. She runs a nail along her ax blade as we wait.

Some of the Fae had put magical barriers around all our blades so that we don't mortally wound any of the enemies. The blades would only go so deep; any fatal wounds will glance off the enemy unless our own lives are in danger. The plan is to incapacitate whenever possible, slay as a last resort only. We don't know if we can break the spell my father's army is under, but we have to try.

One Fae had said, as she ran her hands over my dagger, that the magic would know when we needed to strike to kill, and the barrier would dissolve.

Magic, I had thought in awe.

I'm still wearing the outfit that Zaehora had all but shoved me into this morning, though I've abandoned the cape by the entrance to the pyramid. The last thing I need is getting snagged on something, and dying because of a fucking cape.

The Council stands behind us, their expressions severe, their weapons at the ready. We stand for several minutes in tense silence.

Then I see my father over the hill, more than two hundred yards away. He stands still for a moment, then raises one hand. It's as if he flips a switch; massive, gray clouds erupt across the sky, blocking out the sun, and turning the brilliant day to an instant dusk.

Then his army crests the hill behind him, and pours across the field.

We rush at them. As we run, Hyun-Joo and Diego run to the left, Kianga forges straight ahead with the Council on her tail, and Saif and I veer right.

Diego looses a few arrows from his vambraces at my father, if only to distract him. He can't focus on everything at once. The arrows stop in midair, and turn back around, streaking toward one of our centaurs. He falls as the arrows pierce his abdomen.

Or maybe he can.

Our armies collide in a cataclysmic explosion of teeth, blades, and magic. Bolts of fire and lightning, swirling shadow creatures, water, ice, and energy all ricochet around the field. The earth quakes and trembles below us intermittently, and rocks and boulders are flung through the air. Wyverns, succubi, and incubi soar through the sky, their fangs and talons flashing even in the dusky light.

I lose sight of the others in the fray, but Saif and I fight back-to-back. He alternates throwing seeds to tangle enemies in vines, and wielding Excalibur with ethereal grace and ferocity. Many of my father's Fabled are knocked to the ground, unconscious, and will likely wake with concussions. But at least they'll be alive.

We make our way slowly through the press of bodies toward my father, cutting a path as we go.

I fight mostly in my wolf form. I'm faster and stronger this way, and I can hold my own, so Saif doesn't need to worry about me. He had insisted that he stay by my side, but I can at least make sure he focuses on protecting himself before me. Not to mention, I have far more endurance in this form.

I see flashes of my father's magic throughout the battlefield. Unlike Kianga and her army, my father has no compunction for the preservation of life. Bodies fly wherever his magic explodes, his soldiers and ours alike.

I growl and bare my teeth as I knock an incubus to the ground, and one of our Mages traps him under a barrier of small lightning bolts. It gives me an idea.

My father isn't the only one with Merlin's magic.

I transform back, and wave my hand at my next opponent, an ogre. My magic snakes around them in ropes, and they crash to the ground, immobilized. I look at my hand in awe.

Adrenaline surges through me.

The next Fabled to charge at me is a satyr. She puts her horns down as she rushes me, but I wave my hand at her, and she freezes, then collapses to the ground, as if asleep.

Holy shit.

For several more minutes, we fight. Around us, the tide seems to turn. More of my father's army falls, and ours surges forward. We get closer and closer to my father.

We can do this, I think. I let out a single, triumphant laugh.

And then a huge wall of flame explodes in the center of the battlefield.

No.

Saif and I turn back toward Tal Basta just as a giant tidal wave knocks into us, and begins sucking us back toward the pyramid.

The Peñas have joined the battle.

Broken Bonds

The wave drags Saif and I back to where we had started. I sputter as we finally come to a stop, and grab Saif frantically as he sits up and begins coughing up water. He's still got Excalibur in one hand.

"Finally. Justice." I look up, and Valentina is standing above us, perched on a boulder. Martín is standing not far away, orchestrating his flames like a maestro, ravaging the battlefield. Screams erupt everywhere they touch.

"Are you seriously going to kill me, Val?" I ask incredulously.

She twists her mouth in disgust. "Not *you*."

She pulls a small knife from her belt, tosses it in the air, and hits it with a blast of water toward Saif. He just manages to parry it from one knee, and he clambers to his feet, breathing heavily.

I realize with a terrified jolt that he has a long gash in his thigh, and blood is pouring down his leg. Excalibur must have cut him in the tidal wave. Apparently the barrier around the blade had considered the water an enemy. *Not technically wrong.*

I forget about Valentina totally for a moment, and reach out a hand to his leg, intent on healing him.

"I don't think so," she spits. She flings dozens of needles of water at me, and I have to jump back from him. Just as I do, Martín turns his attention to Saif, and hurls a ball of flame at him. Saif dives to his right, farther away from me.

"No!" I scream.

Martín looks at me for just a moment, his expression full of disappointment, then reaches into his pocket, and throws some kind of powdery substance at me. A vortex of flame flares up, and then I'm encased in a jagged bubble of thick glass. There are small holes in various spots where sharp pieces of glass overlap, but none of them are large enough for me to even get a hand through.

Sand. He threw sand at me. The glass warps the image in front of me, but I can see Saif, hunched over, as blood streams from his thigh down into the grass. I pound on the glass bubble and scream as I search for a weak point.

There isn't one.

Valentina hurls another knife at Saif, and he just barely turns in time to avoid it piercing his heart, but it slices across his left arm. He drops Excalibur, and reaches to apply pressure to the wound.

"No!" I scream again. I slash desperately against the glass with my dagger, but it barely leaves a mark. Panic grips my chest as I watch Saif crawl backward across the grass. I shift into my wolf form and claw at the bubble, but it still doesn't give. I rip at jagged pieces with my teeth, but all I manage to do is cut my mouth. Blood pours down my chin and into my fur.

Diego! I scream in my mind. I don't know if he's close enough to hear me, but I don't know what else to do.

Kianga! Please come back! They're going to kill him!

They advance on Saif as he collapses into the grass, red pooling around him.

"You idiot!" I hiss at myself. I shift back quickly and press both hands to the glass. It explodes outward in an instant, and I begin to run toward Saif, but then something stops me in my tracks. I am suddenly frozen in midair, unable to move any of my limbs.

What the fuck? My eyes land on Valentina, and fear twists my stomach. She's got one hand held out toward me, and I can see her arm shaking with the effort of wielding her magic.

She's controlling my blood. I had no idea she could even do that. By her wide eyes, I'm not sure she knew she could, either.

"It's okay," Saif rasps. "I understand." The Peñas both halt in their tracks and look at one another.

"Val," I choke out, barely able to move my lips. "Please."

Valentina's voice is icy as she turns to me. "He . . . he has to pay."

"Why?" I sob, fighting her for control of my mouth. "Is that what this battlefield needs? More bloodshed? Don't you see what Auberon has done to us? To everyone?"

She doesn't answer, but her eyes flick out over the field and widen, as if she hadn't really processed what was happening before now.

Her hold on me wavers for just a split second, and I make it a step closer to him. "Saif was *protecting* me. He fucked up, but he only ever wanted to get me away from my father, because he's a monster. He didn't mean for anyone to get hurt. He loves you both."

I look at Martín, though he doesn't quite meet my gaze. "Martín, you should have seen the way Saif cried when he heard you were alive. He was prepared to live with the guilt of what he did forever. He even said that you should never forgive him. But *please.*"

I can't wipe the tears away from my cheeks as they stream down from my eyes in rivers. "Please don't hurt him. Don't do anything you can't take back."

Neither of them move other than to look at one another once again. Then Martín turns back to Saif, and his shoulders rise and fall heavily. Saif makes no move to protect himself. He won't hurt his brother again, even if it means laying down his own life.

None of us say anything for several agonizing seconds.

Martín raises a hand, and terror shoots through me. I open my mouth to scream, but he just puts that hand on Valentina's shoulder.

The fight goes out of her; she drops to her knees, and her hold on me releases instantaneously.

I don't hesitate. I rush to Saif and drop to his side. His eyes are sliding in and out of focus, and I grit my teeth at the pallor of his face.

The roar of a jaguar from behind me makes me jump.

"Eilidh!" Diego and Kianga rush to my side. She rumbles deep in her chest, prowling toward the Peñas, teeth bared.

Flames explode in Martín's hands as he steps in front of Valentina.

"Get back!" Diego snarls, his fangs and claws extended.

"Stop!" I scream, pressing my hand to Saif's thigh. The wound on his arm will have to wait. I grit my teeth, looking out over the battlefield. Rage burns inside me. Saif emits a pained grunt as his skin begins to knit itself together.

"Hey," I say, cupping his cheek with my free hand. "It's okay. You'll be fine. I've got you." Color begins to return to his cheeks.

His eyes slide back into focus a few seconds later, and he smiles at me. I smile back, then lean down and give him a tender kiss.

"Thank you, my love," he says quietly when we pull apart. He runs a hand over my hair.

I chuckle. "You aren't dying on me that easily. You're stuck with me forever."

He smiles sideways as he sits up. "I can think of worse places to be."

And then magic explodes around us, surrounding Saif and I in a towering wall of rust-colored fire.

A Shadow Falls

The Peñas, Diego, and Kianga all go flying backward through the air. Saif snatches Excalibur from the ground and steps in front of me, looking for the threat, but nothing is near us. My father is still standing on the hill at the opposite end of the battlefield. I grip Saif's arm.

"Do you think he missed us?" I ask, breathless.

"Not for a second," he growls, and wipes sweat from his brow.

I frown. The flames don't affect me at all, but Saif is going to overheat before long.

I look back to where my father had been, but he's gone. "What the f—"

"Get back!" Saif snarls.

I look around him, and my breath catches.

"I just want my sword," Arthur says with a smile, holding out his hand. He's all of three paces away from us; his flames are reflected in his eyes.

Saif's grip on Excalibur tightens as he stands up to his full height. "It isn't yours anymore. You're no longer worthy of it."

Arthur's calm facade drops immediately; he snarls and raises a hand toward Saif, who brings Excalibur up on instinct to parry the blow. But I have no idea if that will work, and if the lightning bolt my father shot isn't stopped by the blade, it will go right into Saif's heart.

Like hell. I grab Saif's wrist with both hands. *"Excalibur!"* My power surges through him and into the sword, which explodes into thousands of sparks, just like it had in the courtroom earlier today. *Please keep him safe.* I really hope this telepathic connection goes both ways.

My father's lightning bounces off the wall of sparks, and all our magic fizzles out with a violent electric hiss. He growls, and with a sweeping motion of both his hands, the flames around us widen into a larger circle. Then he opens his palms to the sky, and the clouds above dissipate in an instant.

Neither army seems to notice the return of the sun — the bloodshed continues.

"What the fuck was the point of that?" I ask him scathingly.

He smirks. "You'll see. In the meantime." A rust-colored sword forms in his left hand, undulating like a live current. He whirls it around, as if trying to get the weight just right.

Saif does the same with Excalibur, which is still glowing with my magic. *Safe,* the sword whispers. I sigh with relief.

I step back as the two of them begin prowling around each other.

"You can't beat me, boy. You never could," Arthur sneers.

Saif looks at me with a small smile and flourishes Excalibur behind his back the same way he always did with *Dhabiha* in the training yard before his duels with Diego. "I never had a reason to before."

My father chuckles, and the sound makes my skin crawl. "How touching. But what about this: Drop my sword right now, and we can forget any of this happened. You two can come home. I would be happy to call you my son, and your progeny will be forces to be reckoned with. It will more than make up for the headache caused here today."

Saif and I exchange a glance, and, despite myself, I bark a humorless laugh. He winks at me, and turns back to my father. "Sorry, Your Majesty, but I just can't accept those terms."

My father tilts his head to the sky and smiles. "So be it."

A screeching roar from high above us makes me grit my teeth. Saif and I both look up. There's a huge black wyvern circling high above our heads. "That's gonna be a problem, isn't it?" I murmur.

He nods solemnly. "Hopefully the others can handle it."

"A shame you'll never find out if they do." My father lunges at Saif, and a scream rips from my throat as their swords collide.

I back away toward the flames, trembling and helpless. I don't want to distract Saif, and I can't do anything to my father.

They clash like Titans.

Sparks fly from Arthur's sword with each blow. I can barely track their movements. They're both so *fast*. I realize with a jolt that Saif had been holding back when he sparred with Diego. If he had moved like this, Diego would never have won a single match.

Suddenly, something moves under my feet, and I right myself at the last second. "What the fuck?"

The grass is writhing back and forth like a living thing, growing sporadically. It takes me a moment to realize what's happening. I look to Saif in awe. As he does battle with my father, he controls the grass around him, trying to snatch at the King's feet and throw him off balance.

But Arthur has no trouble shooting blasts to block the grass with one hand while he wields the magic sword with the other. Saif hadn't been lying when he said my father was terrifying with a blade.

Eilidh! Kianga's voice rings in my mind. I whip around to see her prowling in her jaguar form on the other side of the flames. Diego is beside her, his eyes wide, flicking between me and Saif.

"Are you okay?" I ask him, but he points to his ear and the wall of flames between us, shaking his head. He can't hear me.

I shift. *Are you okay?* I cast the thought toward both of them.

He mouths a vehement, *No!*

No, we aren't fucking okay! Kianga snarls. *This fire is some kind of force field. We can't get through, and neither can any of the Mages.*

Fantastic. I turn back to make sure Saif is still on his feet. I can smell his sweat in my wolf form — it's pouring down him now. I've got to douse these fucking flames. I concentrate for a moment, rage pooling in my stomach.

Saif bellows in fury. I whip toward him just as he executes a maneuver with Excalibur that results in Arthur's sword flying from his hands. It fizzles into nothingness before it hits the ground.

My father stands utterly still as Saif puts Excalibur's blade to his neck.

A beat passes where nothing moves, save the flames around us and the sweat running down Saif's brow.

Do it.

He doesn't. They stare at one another.

Saif, do it!

He swallows hard, then finally brings the blade back to deal the killing blow.

Arthur smirks and disappears in a whirlwind.

My snarl of rage is drowned out by another roar from above that makes us all look up. The beast above is diving toward us like a meteor.

What the fuck is that? Kianga asks, panic causing her words to bounce around my head.

Wyvern, I reply, looking back at the flames. I can solve that problem, at least. They flicker for a moment, but burn back brighter, like a trick birthday candle. *Fuck!*

Eilidh, that's not a wyvern, that's a fucking —

A dragon crashes to the ground in front of me just as I manage to douse the flames. The earth quakes, and the vicious gale from its wings whips my fur. I lose my hold on my wolf form — in the blink of an eye, I'm scrambling back away from mountainous creature on two legs.

I bump directly into Saif, and he clutches my upper arms. *"Ya rab,"* he breathes.

It's not a wyvern; it's at least twice the size of a wyvern. It's got four legs, and long, thick wings sprout from its back, each section tipped with deadly spikes. Its eyes are glowing with my father's magic just like his army.

The dragon is the color of coal; it sucks the sunshine into it like a black hole. It might as well be a living, breathing shadow. My skin crawls at the sight of its undulating muscles as it takes a step toward us.

The roar that erupts from its mouth rends my mind in half. I collapse to my knees, holding my ears. Saif holds his as well, but with his normal hearing, he stays upright.

The roar stops, and Saif screams. "No!"

He throws himself at me, and we tumble across the grass. Wind swirls around us — the dragon's front claws missed us by inches.

Saif lands on top of me, and I see stars as my head slams into the earth.

"Run!" He drags me to my feet, and I sway slightly before getting my bearings.

"No!" I put my hand on my dagger, debating whether it will do any good against the monster in front of me.

"Eilidh, *please!"* He tosses seeds at the dragon. Wicked-looking vines erupt from them, with thorns at least four inches long. They wrap around its legs, and it hisses like a snake, but keeps moving, snapping the vines, heedless of the purple blood that leaks from its wounds.

We can hurt it. I shift back into my wolf form and lunge.

"Eilidh!" He yells, but then he's forced to dive to the side as the dragon opens its maw and purple fire erupts from it.

I launch myself into the air and sink my teeth into its side. The scales are sharp as knives, but they're not impenetrable. Its purple blood and mine cascade down my chin and the dragon's flank, coalescing into a magenta that would be beautiful under any other circumstances.

The dragon twists its long neck in fury and snaps at me.

I dodge, and run behind it. As I reach the other side, I see Saif wielding Excalibur, fighting the dragon from the front. It slashes at him, but he parries, throwing all his strength back against the dragon's leg to keep from being crushed.

I howl in fury, wishing I could claw my way up to the dragon's flank and rip its throat out. Just then, an arrow flies past the dragon's head, missing by inches. Another one lands in its flank a second later, and the dragon flinches away from the pain.

I look around wildly to see Diego firing arrows from his vambraces, running to Saif's side. Kianga heads toward me in her jaguar form. Relief floods through me. This dragon can't take all four of us. Together, we're unstoppable.

Kianga jumps at the dragon, digging her claws into its side. The dragon rears back, but she clutches in deep, ripping into it with her teeth. She comes away just as bloody as I had, but she doesn't stop.

I can't climb like she can with my canine claws, but I bite into the dragon's haunches high and low, dodging its back legs when it kicks at me, and its long tail, which is thrashing viciously back and forth. It could easily impale me on one of the long, glinting spikes, and it probably wouldn't even notice.

I run toward its head. *Kianga's got that side, you go up its other!* Diego slashes its leg once more with his vambrace, then nods, and leaps at the dragon, his claws extended.

I run to Saif's side just as he lands a blow to its chin with Excalibur, which is coated in purple blood. The dragon roars in fury, and I drop to the ground in pain as it rears back, its neck and front limbs thrashing through the air with deadly speed. I lose my grip on my wolf form, and slip back into my skin, clutching desperately at my ears. At the edge of my vision, I see Diego drop to the ground clutching his ears as well.

The screams of the most terrifying fictional dinosaur have absolutely nothing on the unearthly sound that rips from the dragon's mouth. It rattles my very bones. I look up to see its foot-long teeth coming toward me, and time freezes.

The world stands still for one agonizing, eternal moment.

I am going to die. It's not the first time the thought has crossed my mind.

But it will be the last.

I raise my chin.

And then Saif throws himself at me, shoving me out of the dragon's trajectory. Its roar cuts off as its jaw closes around his torso.

I let out a bloodcurdling scream. My vision goes completely red, and magic explodes out from me like a nuclear bomb.

Everything within thirty yards of me is flung wildly into the air, grass and earth included. Everything except Saif; the dragon releases him as it's thrown through the air, and he drops to the ground in a heap several yards away from me.

I stand in one smooth motion in the middle of a crater as the dragon comes crashing back down to earth, far away. Diego and Kianga land far off as well, but right now, I only have eyes for Saif.

He writhes in agony on the ground.

I sprint to him in an instant, and when I drop to his side, I land in a puddle of slick blood.

"Saif," I rasp. I run my hands all over him, pressing against the deep gashes in his torso from the dragon's fangs to staunch the bleeding.

He coughs up blood, and there's purple mixed with the red.

"What's happening?" I breathe.

I look closer at his wounds, and the blood that gushes from them. A viscous purple liquid seeps out of them, mixing with his blood. The resulting magenta concoction seeps into his ivory suit.

"Saif, what —"

He groans and rolls to his back, clutching his abdomen. "Burning," he manages through his teeth, before coughing up more blood.

I gape at him in horror as I clutch his torso. "What's burning? It didn't breathe fire on you." My magic flares around my hand, but it seeps into his skin uselessly. It has no effect.

No.

He convulses. "Venom," he growls.

I shake my head rapidly. *Oh, please, no.*

I shoot another wave of magic into him. It has no effect .

"No," I whisper. Tears blur my vision. "I'll fix you," I sob, clutching his face with one hand as I pulse wave after wave of magic into his torso.

His convulsing slows, but he's sweating more profusely now, and his teeth begin chattering. He reaches up a shaky hand and tugs my hair. "Eilidh," he gasps, and closes his eyes.

"Saif, *no*, stay with me!" I smack his cheek rapidly, and his eyes flutter half open. I hold his hand tightly to the side of my face, and rock back and forth. His fingers are still tangled in my hair, though his strength is gone.

"You can." He takes a rattling breath. "Win."

I press my forehead to his. "Saif!" I sob again, as he closes his eyes once more. "*Please!*"

"*Lahabi,*" he whispers faintly. I wouldn't hear him without my lupine abilities.

His head lolls to the side, and I scream his name again as he stops moving.

He doesn't hear me.

Diego tugs at me from behind, ripping Saif's hand out of my grasp. I have no idea when he got up from being thrown. "Eilidh," he chokes out.

"No!" I thrash wildly and twist out of his grasp. I fall back to the ground next to Saif and shake him vigorously. "Saif. Wake up. *Please.*"

He doesn't move.

I look to where the dragon landed. It's gone. I see a small body nearby, probably a fallen Mage, but the dragon must have flown off.

Blind rage explodes in my chest, causing red sparks to shoot around me wildly. I look down again at Saif. He is utterly, unnervingly still.

I stand slowly and back away from him.

Diego pulls me back, farther away from Saif. I hear him, but his voice is muffled, as if we're underwater. "You have to get out of here. Anywhere. I'll find you. Just *run.*" He pleads with me desperately.

I turn to stare at him, wide-eyed. "What?" I can barely even hear him over the one thought screaming in my mind.

Saif is dead.

Those three words ring through my head over and over, and each syllable is agony, like a knife is being driven into my heart over and over.

Saif is *dead.*

"*Run!*" Diego begs me again.

Something deep within me snaps, and the agony stops. I feel nothing at all.

Nothing, that is, other than rage.

I turn to my father across the battlefield, at least two hundred yards away. I can't see the details of his face, but I know for certain that if I could, it'd be twisted in a sadistic grin.

I start running.

Invincible

I shift mid-stride. Each time my paws hit the ground, lightning explodes around them, propelling each step faster than the last. Both armies jump out of my way as I approach, creating a path for me. Our soldiers look at me with a mixture of awe, confusion, and fear. They don't even know that the entire world has turned upside down yet.

I howl in fury as I get closer to Arthur. I'll be plunging my dagger into his chest in just a few seconds. I'll rip his heart out with my teeth and claws. I'll destroy it, just as he has done to mine.

I'm ten yards away when I shift back, and five when I leap at my father, and bring my dagger down directly above his heart.

At least, I try to.

I hit my target, but it's like his skin is made of diamonds. The blade shatters into pieces.

My wrist follows suit. I scream in agony and clutch it as I land on the ground in a heap at my father's feet.

I suck in a breath and kick at my father's legs, trying desperately to knock him to the ground. I connect with his knees and shins over and over, but he doesn't budge an inch. It's like I'm fighting with a mountain, and screaming for it to bow to me.

Finally, I stop kicking, and lie at my father's feet, screaming wordlessly. The pain from my shattered wrist is nothing compared to the pain from my shattered heart.

He crouches down, propping his elbows on his knees. His mouth is twisted into a cruel smile. He lifts his eye patch, and a rust-colored glow blazes from his eye. He doesn't have a left eye; Merlin's jasper gemstone is lodged in his empty socket.

I gag and dry heave into the grass, but then he stands and curls his fingers, and I float up, suspended by an invisible chain around my neck. I rake my nails into my throat and kick wildly, but he holds me steady. He's going to strangle me.

For a split second the thought gives me peace, and I stop kicking. I'll either see Saif again, or I'll no longer be living to feel the pain.

But then Diego and Kianga's faces flash before me, and I kick out again, panicking.

"You can't harm me, Daughter. No one can. I'm invincible."

My vision dims at the edges as I continue to struggle.

"I have more magic than you can ever hope to imagine. The Grail and Merlin's gemstone have gotten me through the last thousand years, helped me dispose of all your siblings that have caused me grief. You will be no different if you cross me again. But you've proven that you can be useful to me, so I will give you one more chance."

The invisible chain around my neck disappears, and I crash to the ground, gasping for air against the dead grass. He puts the toe of his boot under my chin, lifting my gaze to his, and sneers.

"Bury your lover. Mourn him, and think hard about whether you want to keep fighting me. When you're ready, come to me alone, and pledge your fealty. But don't take too long; even I have limited patience. Once you have joined me, we will use the Mongrels to save the world, and put the remaining humans in their proper place under our boots."

He tilts his head in contemplation. "And maybe, eventually, *if* you prove yourself loyal, I will bring him back for you."

I gape at him. Bring him back? *No, that's impossible. Don't trust a desperate foe.*

My father swirls his hand in the air, and he and his army disappear in whirlwinds of rust-colored cyclones.

Shattered

Kianga lands in front of me as a jaguar. Diego drops to my side, and when he sees me cradling my right arm, grabs my shattered wrist, and examines it.

Kianga shifts back and picks up the hilt of my dagger. The blade itself is in a million tiny pieces, scattered through the grass; there is no recovering it, but at least the hilt can be saved.

I scream again as Diego holds my wrist fast and pulls medical tape from one of his pouches. I groan in agony as he wraps my wrist, but he doesn't stop.

Kianga holds my forehead to hers as he wraps me from palm to elbow, and I scream in rage. "I know it hurts. I know."

But that's not what hurts. My soul hurts. A piece of me has been ripped away, just as if I've lost a limb.

When Diego is done wrapping my wrist, he hugs me to his chest, and I sob against him. Kianga places a hand on my back, and I hear her crying too.

I suddenly feel like I'm being suffocated. I push against Diego and he lets me go immediately. I press my forehead into the grass and scream.

They don't move. They just stay with me as I shatter.

When I can't produce any more sounds through my raw throat, I stand and begin walking silently back toward Saif's body. Diego and

Kianga follow.

As we approach, he looks like he could be sleeping. Except he's lying on his back in the grass, and he doesn't sleep on his back. He sleeps on his stomach. Sometimes his side, but only when he's pressed against me.

I'll have to roll him so he doesn't get uncomfortable, I think distantly.

But as I get closer to him, he looks less and less like he's sleeping. His glasses are askew. One leg is twisted oddly. I collapse to my knees and have to crawl the last few feet to him through the magenta-stained grass.

I reach up and fix his glasses with a hand that shakes so badly I fear I may snap them.

He needs those, I can't break them.

But he doesn't need them. Not anymore.

His eyes are shut tightly. I shake him gently, whimpering. He needs to snap out of it. We have to regroup. We need to prepare for the next fight. I need to tell him how much I love him again. For the rest of his life.

I shake him harder. He doesn't shove me back playfully, or smile sideways at me. He doesn't do anything. I pull his head into my lap.

I just need to tell him one more time that I love him. That's all. Just one more time. I didn't get to say it enough. We were supposed to say it to each other for however many years he had left. But I didn't even get him for *one*.

Just one more time, I beg the Universe silently as I rock him back and forth. *Just wake him up for me so I can tell him one more time, and then you can have him back.*

Objectively, I understand why the Universe wants to take him for itself. He's fierce. He's loving. He's perfect.

He's a martyr.

But the Universe has to understand that it's not its turn yet. He's still *mine*. It can't have him. Not yet. I need him. He holds me together. He makes sure I'm safe.

"Take me instead," I whisper. If it just lets me tell him one more time how much I love him, how he is one of the pieces that complete me, how I can't possibly function without him, it can have me.

They need him, I think dully. Diego is the warrior. Kianga is the leader. Saif is the heart. I am the wreck that they all got stuck with; that they get dragged down by. Without our heart, how can we go on?

Yes, the Universe can have me instead. They'll be fine without me, but they need him. Our lifeblood beats through him. Without him, we will fail. Without him, the world is doomed.

My infinite lifespan in exchange for his human one? That's more than fair.

"Give him back," I hiss.

Saif doesn't move. He doesn't sit up, cup a hand to my cheek, and kiss me tenderly. He doesn't push his glasses up the bridge of his nose. He doesn't brew me a cup of tea or ask me if my bandages need changed.

I run my hands through his dark curls. Tears drip from my face onto his. I wipe them away furiously.

"Give him *back!*" I try to scream it, but my throat is already raw. It comes out as a croak. I collapse down onto him, sobbing into his chest. Every time I've laid my head on his chest before, he's been warm, and his heart would beat just below my ear.

Now there is nothing but cold and silence.

"I love you," I rasp.

He doesn't tell me he loves me too. He doesn't kiss me with his soft lips and hold me tightly. He doesn't take my hand and rub his thumb back and forth over my palm.

He just lies there, the late afternoon sunlight turning him into a statuesque picture of perfection. I look up, enraged. The sky is beautiful, just like it always is here in this cursed place. A piece of my heart is gone. My soul has been irreparably fractured, and the sun has the audacity to shine down on me like it's any other day.

Shouldn't it have fallen out of the sky already?

"Please. I can't lose you too. Please don't leave me," I look down at Saif's face, still in my hands. "You never told me about the lava monsters."

And he never will. *How many more stories have died with him?*

I lay his head down on the grass, suddenly feeling like if I touch his cooling skin another moment, my mind will shatter into fragments that I will never be able to put back together.

I trip over my hands and fall as I try to back up, forgetting that my right wrist is currently in many more pieces than it should be. Even with my healing factor, it will be some time before I can put any weight on it.

My head smacks into the ground, and the jolt acts as a shock to my system. I feel myself transform, and a moment later, I throw back my head and howl. It reverberates through the field, and over the hills. The other werewolves are the only ones who don't cover their ears in pain.

I hope my father can still hear me, wherever he is. I hope he hears the pain he has caused me. I hope he hears how he has shattered my soul.

That way, when I kill him, there will be no doubt in his mind as to why.

Laid to Rest

We bury Saif that night under the stars.

Martín and the other Fire Mages light hundreds of torches that are driven into the ground throughout the field outside Tal Basta, lighting up the night.

Several long rows of graves are dug for the day's fallen, but I can only look at his. Diego and Martín dig it themselves, with shovels, at the foot of the boulder. It takes them several hours.

Kianga carries on with her duties, leading her people. They need her, and she is there for them. She doesn't get to have human emotions right now; goddesses do not have human emotions.

Hyun-Joo and Valentina follow behind her, helping with whatever they can.

I sit with Saif's body the entire time, numb to the world. I can't touch him, even through the shroud Mòrag placed over him; if I touch him, I won't be able to let go of him, and they will have to put me in the ground, too. But I sit with him. I'm not leaving him alone.

Valentina approaches me at one point, and says that I should go inside, find something to eat, or get some sleep.

"How am I supposed to do that without him?" I ask her quietly, not tearing my gaze from Diego and Martín as they sink further into the earth.

She doesn't have an answer for me. She walks away.

Finally, Diego and Martín crawl out of the pit. They're covered in dirt and sweat; the sweat on their faces is mixed with tears.

Diego walks over, slowly, and kneels in front of me. He is silent for a long moment. I stare at him, my eyes unfocused. I'm looking right through him. I hear Kianga and the others walk up behind me.

"It's time, Eilidh," Diego whispers.

I shake my head silently. Tears stream down my cheeks in an instant. "No. I can fix him. I'll figure it out."

Diego grits his teeth as fresh tears slide down his cheeks. "He's *gone.*"

I move to slap him across the face, but he catches my wrist, and clutches it tightly as I try to yank it away.

Kianga puts a hand on my shoulder. "Lee. We need to say goodbye."

"*No!*" I scream, and several people near us jump. "I can't say any more *fucking* goodbyes. I won't!"

Diego finally releases me; I put a hand on Saif's shoulder, and magic blazes around my fingers. *Live.*

Nothing happens.

Kianga touches my shoulder again, and pulls me back from him. I try to fight, but her grip is like iron.

Diego picks Saif's body up off the ground, and turns toward the grave.

"Please don't take him away!" I sob, collapsing to the ground. Kianga folds herself over me, shaking with tears as well. Someone drops to my other side, and I faintly register that it's Valentina. She grips my thigh tightly as I sob into the grass.

Kianga pulls me to my feet. She and Valentina prop me up as we walk to the side of the grave.

Hyun-Joo creates a horizontal force field. Diego lays Saif gently upon it, and removes the shroud. He runs a finger over Saif's cheek and plants a kiss on his forehead before he takes a step back. Martín picks a blade up from the ground, lays it on top of Saif, and folds his hands over the hilt. It's *Dhabiha*.

"Get that off of him," I whisper furiously. Everyone looks at me. "He was a *healer*," I hiss.

I won't force him to hold that scimitar in death, just as he had been forced to in life. He was a healer by nature; he had no choice but to become a soldier.

Diego shakes his head at me firmly. "He was a warrior, too. He *chose* to hold that blade to protect people."

I glare at him furiously.

Hyun-Joo waves her hand, and Saif moves away from them. He hovers above the opening in the ground for an eternity.

Then she makes another motion, and lowers Saif gently into the cold, dark, earth. It embraces him easily.

Despite their best efforts, Kianga and Valentina can no longer hold me up. I fall to my knees at the graveside. Diego takes Val's place at my side. Martín picks up a shovel, like he's about to start filling in the grave.

"Wait!" I shriek, and everyone jumps again.

I teleport effortlessly to Kianga's room and dig through my pack furiously for a moment. *He can't go without this.* I teleport back in an instant.

I kneel on the ground, the flower journal in my lap, and open it to the first page.

The very first green dahlia Saif had given me stares back at me from the page. I gently remove the thin layer used to press it, and grab it delicately by the stem. I set the journal down on the ground, and cradle the dahlia for a moment. I kiss its delicate petals, and drop it into the grave. It lands on Saif's sternum.

"I love you." I rip a clod of dirt from the ground, and sprinkle it onto him. The dirt runs through my fingers, taking a piece of myself with it.

Kianga and Diego each do the same. Then the three of us sit back as Hyun-Joo, Martín, and Valentina pick up the shovels and begin tossing the dirt on top of him.

I look up at the moon. She's in her Waning Gibbous form tonight; if she has any words of comfort for me, I can't hear them.

She silently travels across the sky as they cover him, laying him to rest. Throughout the field, our army extinguishes the torches as they finish burying their dead, and head inside. Eventually, there is only the Order members, Kianga, and myself. A handful of torches surround us.

Finally, all the dirt has been placed back in the grave. The earth has reclaimed him.

He's gone.

Diego moves for the first time since they started. He walks to the boulder and kneels, then extends a claw and begins to scratch into it.

Blood drips down his fingers as he rips his claws and skin against the rough boulder, but he doesn't stop. When he stands and backs away, Kianga lets out a sob.

Saif Rahim. A warrior. A healer. A good man.

Dreams Part 1

M*y house is on fire.*

    A dragon descended from the sky and set it ablaze. Or was it a bomb?

And is there even a difference?

My house is on fire, and I must have been inside. I didn't think I was. I thought I had been at school when the dragon was dropped on us with the press of a button from thousands of miles away.

But I must have been inside. I must have died with my family.

Because I am on fire, too.

Flashback

Saif opens his door, and I step inside for the first time. We're just leaving the solarium, and his room is deliciously cool in comparison. A heavenly floral scent hits me as I cross the threshold. I take in the explosion of color around me. On a shelf next to his desk, a giant pothos plant cascades down to the ground, and up the wall, supported by tiny hooks. It takes up the majority of two walls.

The spaces between the leaves are taken up by small beakers of water that are held to the wall with metal coils. He's got orchids, zinnias, pansies, and numerous flowers I don't know the names of propagating in the beakers.

A vase of dahlias sits on his nightstand, but none of them are green; they're various shades of pink, purple, and orange.

He closes his door gently and leans back against it as I walk to the plants, smelling them, and running my fingers delicately over the leaves and petals.

"You're incredible," I say as I look at the tiny root system jutting out of a ZZ plant cutting. "Everything you do is so . . . beautiful."

He moves away from the door, and wraps his arms around me from behind. He runs his fingers across the exposed skin between the high waist of my long black skirt and my white cropped shirt. Goosebumps erupt on my skin as he leans in and kisses the crook of my neck.

"I've had a beautiful muse lately," he rumbles in my ear. His beard tickles the delicate skin of my neck. Butterflies explode in my stomach, and I reach up and run my fingers through his hair. He had cut it a bit after he returned from his mission to get intel on Bleddyn, but that had been several weeks ago, and he hasn't cut it again since. I love it.

I moan deeply as he presses himself to my back, runs a hand down over my curves, and grips my hip. He pulses behind the zipper of his jeans, and starts to grow.

"Come here," he whispers. He pulls me with him as he steps toward his desk. He turns the chair around so that its back is against the desk, sits down, and pulls me onto his lap. My skirt billows around our legs.

I brace myself against the desk with one hand and hold his neck with the other, running my thumb along his jaw as our kisses deepen. He grips my soft waist and pulls me down harder onto him.

I gasp softly as his erection rubs between my legs, against the thin fabric of the cotton shorts I have on under my skirt, and he chuckles against my mouth. "Do you see what you do to me?" He teases.

I bite his bottom lip softly. "I certainly feel what I do to you."

He looks up at me, his eyes lidded heavily, his lips parted. He licks his bottom lip where I had bitten him, and I lean into his neck, moaning as I kiss him there as well.

He runs his fingers up my back, and pulls the scrunchie out of the bun at the nape of my neck. My hair cascades down my back in frizzy waves. He tangles his fingers through them, then tugs at the strands, and I shiver with pleasure.

He pulls me into another deep kiss, and slips his hands under my skirt. He takes his time running his hands up my legs and pulling the waistband of my shorts down. I prop myself up slightly as he slips them down my legs and tosses them to the floor.

He digs his fingers deliciously into my thighs, and I whimper against his lips.

"Your turn." He winks at me.

I unbutton his jeans and he lifts himself off the chair so I can pull them *down. I leave his boxer briefs on, but reach through the hole, and pull his erection free.*

He exhales heavily as I stroke him up and down. I rub his tip back and forth along my clit a few times, and soon, we're both wet from my excitement.

"Fuck, Eilidh," he groans. "I need to be inside you."

"Mmm," I throw my head back and moan as I adjust myself slightly, and slide down around his thick shaft. He echoes me as he raises his hips up to thrust deeper inside me.

I start agonizingly slow, teasing him and myself, then steadily increase my pace. He runs his hands all along my body, pulls me down onto his mouth for tender kisses, and shoves my bra up to suck on my nipples. He grips my ass, pulls my hair, and curses under his breath as I ride him.

Suddenly, he wraps his arms around me tightly and stands. I yelp in delight as I come down hard onto him in midair. He turns and sets me down on the edge of his desk, then reaches around me and swipes his arm across the surface, knocking stacks of books and papers to the ground.

He shoves me over lightly, then kneels, and puts his head between my legs. I put a hand over my mouth and moan loudly into my palm as his tongue circles my clit, then slips inside me.

I reach up above my head, dig my nails into the edge of the desk, and push harder into his mouth. He moans against me, shooting tiny lightning bolts up my center.

"Oh fuck, Saif, I'm close," I pant not long after.

He stands quickly, pulls me to my feet, and kisses me softly. I moan into his mouth.

Then he twists me around and bends me over his desk. He hitches my skirt up above my hips, kicks my feet close together, and thrusts himself into me, splitting me in two with his girth.

I whimper loudly against the desk as he drives himself deep into my pussy. Soon, his movements become jerky, and his thrusting erratic. "Oh, fuck," he moans. "You're incredible, Eilidh."

It tips me over the edge. I dig my nails into the edge of the desk as my orgasm wracks my muscles with pleasure. He continues thrusting even after his own orgasm stops, keeping mine going.

Finally, though, I stop quivering, and he pulls out of me. He leans over me and plants kisses up my spine, then a final one on the back of my head, into my disheveled hair.

He pulls me to the bed with him after that, and we snuggle together until sleep overtakes us, blanketed in a heavenly floral scent.

Grief

When I open my eyes, they're wet with tears.

That dream.

It had been a perfectly preserved memory, like a video projector had been installed in my brain and rolled the film across the back of my eyelids. Seeing him again, so crystal clear, so happy, was wonderful.

But now I'm awake, and my body knows instinctively that he's gone. I will never again wake up in a world with him in it, and that realization is more than I can take.

So I don't.

I feel the pieces of myself shift apart. It feels like I'm hovering, separated from my body. It's like looking at a 3D image without the special glasses on. My layers overlap, but don't fully coalesce. I no longer feel my aching heart, or the pain threatening to rip me to shreds. That's happening to my body, but not to *me*.

The tears dry up.

I realize distantly that I'm in Kianga's bed, though I don't remember coming here. I don't remember anything after reading the epitaph Diego had scratched into the boulder.

I drag myself out of bed and look around numbly. No one else is in the room. I spot the mug that Saif had put my coffee in yesterday on Kianga's desk, and walk over to it. A brown ring is dried on the bottom. I pick the mug up, and press my lips to the handle, where he had last touched it.

I walk into the bathroom. His charcoal soap is lying on a shelf in the shower. I sit in the tub and hold the bar to my nose. An ache spreads through my chest, and I clutch it to my heart. I lean back against the tub and let his scent wash over me.

My father's words echo over and over in my head. *I will bring him back for you.*

But that's impossible . . . isn't it?

Take 'impossible' out of your goddamn vocabulary. I had sneered those words at Saif myself not so long ago.

I don't know how long I sit in the tub, motionless. Finally, I hear the door to the bedroom open, and Kianga whispering. Diego answers her quietly, but then he must spot the empty bed. "Eilidh?" He calls sharply.

I don't have the energy to reply. I knock on the side of the tub instead.

Kianga opens the door to the bathroom, and her mouth twists in pity when she spots me. She looks exhausted, like she hasn't slept in days.

I must look pathetic. I just don't care.

"Lee," she says, entering the room. Diego enters behind her. His eyes are dull, and he, too, looks like he's running on no sleep.

I say nothing. I just stare at them, clutching Saif's soap in my hands.

She walks over and reaches for it, but I jerk away. She recoils slightly, clearly stung.

It's all I have left.

That's not fair. I know that, far in the back of my mind. She loved him too. But I don't care about that right now, either.

I am being selfish.

She holds her palm out. I look at it blankly.

"Come on, *Lobita*," Diego says. "You can't spend the rest of your life in here."

I can fucking try. But I blink a few times, and take her hand. She pulls me to my feet, and I step out of the tub. I don't let go of the soap as we walk back into the bedroom.

Hyun-Joo and the Peñas are present as well; for the first time, it's feeling cramped in here. I slump to the glass wall and slide to the floor silently.

Diego grabs something off Kianga's desk, and brings it to me. He kneels in front of me and holds it out.

It's Saif's diary.

I snatch it from his grasp. He grabs the soap from mine. I glare at him for a moment, but he puts my hand on the cover of the diary, and I clutch that to me instead. He takes the soap back to the bathroom, then closes the door firmly behind him when he reemerges.

Hyun-Joo breaks the silence. "Eilidh." Her tone is softer than I've ever heard it before.

I don't look at her.

"We need to know what happened."

I shake my head once. They saw what happened. Saif is dead. What else matters?

"She means with your father," Diego says.

I shrug.

He takes a step like he wants to come over to me, but he slumps to the ground against the door instead. Hyun-Joo rushes to his side, and tilts his face to her, seeing for the first time how dull his eyes are.

She doesn't bother taking him to another room. She holds her arm out wordlessly, and he takes it. His fangs slide into the vein on the inside of her elbow easily, and he drinks.

Her breath catches as she shuts her eyes. He can't release his venom to give her any relief from the pain like he can with me. She's feeling the full effect of his razor-sharp fangs digging into her, draining her of her strength.

She doesn't make a sound.

Everyone else looks away, but I just stare at them. He was right; it *is* clinical. When he's done, he pulls her into his lap, and lays her head against his shoulder. He holds her arm tightly to staunch the bleeding.

Kianga kneels in front of me. "Eilidh."

I tear my gaze from Diego and look into her eyes, which are ringed by dark circles. She puts both her hands on my shoulders and squeezes. "I need you to come back to me. We all need you."

I try to respond to her — I even manage to part my lips, but I can't speak.

She sighs. "Come on, Lee, please. I lost you for months after your grandparents' accident, and that was okay back then, but we don't have that luxury this time. It's shitty, and it's not fair, and we should be allowed the time to grieve. Saif deserves to be grieved. But right now, we have a world to save."

My blood turns to ice, and I instantly begin trembling.

"Fuck the world," I rasp.

She blinks at me in shock. "What?"

I stare at her, shaking with cold fury. Saif had given everything to the world, had dedicated his life to saving everyone in it, and look how it had repaid him.

In blood.

I lean forward and hiss at her like a feral animal. "Fuck it. Arthur won. Let it burn."

She gapes at me like she's never seen me before. "What are you *talking* about? He didn't *win*!" She spreads her arms wide. "*We* are all still here. And so are hundreds of thousands of others who are counting on us."

I'm standing over her before I even realize that I have moved a muscle.

"I don't *care!*" I scream. No one else moves. "We can't win, Kianga! I can't beat him! I can't use my magic against him, and he's fucking indestructible! Didn't you see how my dagger shattered on his *skin?*"

I kick viciously at her desk chair, and send it flying into the wall. I get a sickening rush of satisfaction at the dent it leaves behind.

"It's all been for *nothing!* If I can't kill him, then what is the *point* of all this?" I throw one arm out, still clutching Saif's diary with the other. "We *lost,* Kianga. He's going to use The Fabled to subjugate humanity! It's what he's been planning all along. He said he's going to save the world, but he's going to decimate its inhabitants to do it."

I drop to my knees, suddenly drained. My voice comes out as a harsh whisper. "And I can't stop him. I *lost.* I lost my dagger. And I lost Saif. For *nothing.*" My voice breaks and I curl over into a ball, sobbing into the floor, the diary clutched painfully hard to my chest. The corners dig into my skin, but I don't loosen my grip.

"I should have just done what he wanted. At least then Saif would be alive. He killed him to punish me. It's all my fault."

I will bring him back for you.

"Look at me," she commands in her most domineering Bastet voice.

Despite myself, I do. I sit up and turn to her, glaring.

She slaps me across the face, and everyone else in the room flinches at the *crack.* "Get ahold of yourself, Shaw," she says through her teeth.

As the stars fade from my vision, I gape at her in fury.

She rips the diary from my grasp.

"No!" I shriek, but she thrusts it back at me a moment later, pointing at a line. I snatch the book back, and look at it.

She's so incredibly strong.

I don't know how I have any more tears to cry, but they fall down my cheeks. "*He* made me strong," I whine.

Kianga's eyes blaze with fury. We've had our spats over the years, but she's never been quite as incensed with me as she is now. I flinch back from her, just a fraction.

"The fuck he did," she snarls. "You're the strongest person I know, Eilidh. You always were. So fucking act like it."

No one else in the room moves. She gestures at Diego, whose eyes are glistening as he watches us. *"Tesoro."*

But she doesn't stop. *"He* didn't make you strong, either. *You* made you strong. Diego made you realize how far you could fly. Saif was a soft spot for you to land when you fell. But *neither* of them put that strength and determination into your heart. *That* has always been there. You were born with it." Tears run down her cheeks as she speaks. Kianga, who almost never cries.

I can't even blink.

"Look at your ankle," she commands, and I do. The semicolon tattoo with the black cat's head on top stands out against my skin. "You did *that* all by yourself. *Without* any magic or supernatural abilities. You were a regular human who kept going, despite everything life threw at you. *That* is strength."

I shake my head. "But the cat —"

"A fucking cat didn't stop you from jumping off a bridge, you *idiot.* You stopped yourself. The cat just made you stop and think, and that's what I'm doing now. So *think.*"

I clamp my mouth shut.

"What would Saif tell you right now?" She asks.

I'm silent for a long moment, almost afraid to answer her. "He'd tell me that it's too dangerous," I say quietly.

She presses her lips into a tight line. "Because he would be worried about you. But then you would argue with him, and he would give in to you. And *then* what would he say?"

I let out a strangled sob. "He would say, 'I've got you, *Lahabi.* I believe in you.'"

Kianga drops to her knees and clutches my shoulders fiercely. "I've got you, Eilidh. I believe in you."

She cups my cheek. "We've *all* got you. You're not alone anymore. We're here. And *he's* here." She touches my chest, just above my heart. "He'll always be here."

I collapse into her and sob.

A second later, Diego drops next to us, and wraps us both in his arms. The three of us cry together.

Ink

Later that afternoon, I find myself lying outside on the ground next to the boulder. My father's words echo in my head over and over, like a chant.

I will bring him back for you.

When the sun sets, I head back inside. I ask Kianga if she has anyone who can give me a tattoo, and she doesn't question me. She brings me to a young Mage whose door is covered in beautiful drawings.

"Her name is Brooke. She ran a tattoo studio in LA until she got her magic a year ago," Kianga explains as we walk to the Mage's door. "She's one of our best healers."

I exhale through my nose. Every tattoo artist becomes a healer at some point in their careers, even if they don't know it.

Brooke's eyes go wide when she opens her door to Kianga and I. She's a white woman with a jet-black pixie cut and striking blue eyes; she's lucky if she's five feet tall. Every inch of her neck, arms, and legs that I can see is covered in gorgeous tattoos.

When I explain to her what I want, I see her soul light up in her eyes. This is what she was born for.

Healing.

She makes a quick sketch. It's perfect. She lays the stencil on me and begins.

She works through the night. Kianga shifts into her jaguar

form and sleeps on the floor while Brooke turns my skin into a masterpiece.

~~~~~~~~~

As sunlight begins to stream through the glass wall, Kianga stirs. Brooke is just finishing up using her magic to heal me — no need for peeling and plastic wrap this time.

Kianga stretches and walks over to me as I look in a mirror. She whistles. "That's amazing."

"Brooke, you're the eighth wonder of the world." I frown at my reflection. "Or however many wonders this fucking place has. Thank you."

She laughs. "You're welcome. I'm glad you like it."

I look back in the mirror, and take in the sight.

My entire left arm, from shoulder to wrist, is wrapped in green vines. As we exit Brooke's room, she's already collapsing onto her bed. I nearly trip over Diego, who is sprawled on the floor outside Brooke's door.

"Have you been out here all night?" I ask, as Kianga pulls him to his feet.

He tilts his head side-to-side, cracking his neck. "I just wanted to keep watch for you. Be here if either of you needed me."

He reaches for my hand, and I take it for a moment, but then step back from them. "Oh," I murmur at the floor. I turn quickly and walk away from them both without another word.

Eventually, I try to figure out where my feet are carrying me, and I realize that they're heading for the dining hall to get some breakfast. I haven't eaten since . . . when *had* I last eaten?

My healing factor can only keep my stomach from grumbling for so long, and it had started shortly after Brooke had begun pumping
~~~~~~~~~

ink into me. It's practically screaming at me now; I'm famished. I expect that once I get some food in me, I'll be able to sort through my swirling thoughts.

What I don't expect is that, in the middle of the line, while piling food onto my tray, I will begin crying when I see a jar of peanut butter next to a plate piled high with toast.

The poor Fae woman standing behind the glass divider stares at me with her wide, black eyes as tears begin to stream down my face. "I'm sorry," I whisper hoarsely.

I leave my tray and walk outside, wandering aimlessly. Finally, I come to a tree, and slide to the ground, savoring the feel of the rough bark against my skin. I lean my head back against it, and grip my left forearm with my right hand as tightly as I can.

I dig my nails into the fresh ivy, and shatter into pieces as birds sing and fly overhead, like it's any other day.

I hear them both approach and sit down, and I take a steadying breath. When I open my eyes again, Kianga and Diego are sitting on the ground a few feet away from me. She sets my tray of food on the ground roughly and slides it at me, but though my stomach growls loudly, I just look at it.

"Eat, or I'll get someone to hook you to an IV. You're not going to waste away on me, Eilidh. That's not what he would want." Kianga's eyes blaze with anger.

I pull my legs up on either side of my stomach. I know, in the back of my mind, that she has every right to be angry with me. She and Diego are hurting too, yet here they are, taking care of me. *They shouldn't bother.*

I reach for a granola bar on the tray and take a bite. It tastes like ash in my mouth, but I don't spit it out.

Kianga continues glaring at me as I eat. When she speaks, her words are clipped. "You're allowed to be sad. You're allowed to feel broken. We *all* do. But you don't get to isolate and withdraw. You don't get to shut down this time. We aren't going to let you."

Anger flares up in my stomach out of nowhere. I don't know why; it's not logical. But grief is never logical. I set down the remainder of the bar before it explodes in my hand.

I will bring him back for you.

There is too much pain inside me. I can't keep it contained; it's seeping out through my pores. I stand and kick the tray as I stride away.

"Eilidh, stop! This isn't you!" She stands, and reaches for me. Her fingers grip hard into my left arm, warping the vines.

I rip my arm out of her grasp. "How would you know?" I hiss.

She recoils. "What?"

"How would you *know?*" I yell.

"Eilidh." Diego stands and steps toward me, holding out a hand. Extending an olive branch.

I think of the times I had done the same for him, and he had walked away from me. Slammed literal doors in my face.

"How would *either* of you know?" I blink away angry tears. "*You* never came back for me." I jab my finger at Kianga. "You let me think you were dead, Kianga. For *eleven* years."

She looks like I slapped her across the face.

I turn to Diego, who has lowered his hand. He wears the same expression that he did in the kitchen at Arkenvale when I was biting into a bloody steak. Like he's readying himself for the monster inside me to go for his jugular.

It does.

"And *you* pushed me away from the day we met. You can try to justify it all you want, say you were trying to protect me. But that's bullshit, and you know it. You never once asked me how *I* felt. What decision *I* would have made. Because you were *scared.*" His shoulders rise and fall heavily, but he doesn't respond.

"So don't either of you *dare* talk to me about isolating. Saif —" My voice breaks. I let out a cry of frustration, and rake my nails across my scalp. Angry tears prick the corners of my eyes, threatening to finally spill out.

"Saif was the *only* one who was there for me."

"That is not fair," Kianga breathes. She looks like she's about to cry as well.

Good, the monster sneers.

"Fair?" I take a step toward her. She doesn't back away, but Diego puts a protective hand on her shoulder, and narrows his eyes at me, just one, infinitesimal bit.

I stop in my tracks and look at them for a moment, then purse my lips.

Okay then. I exhale quickly through my nose. "Nothing is fair." I turn on my heel and leave them outside with the singing birds.

They don't follow me.

Kindred Spirits

I wander through Tal Basta, my mind swirling. Cats hiss and scatter away from me, but I pay them no mind.

I will bring him back for you.

But how? I had resurrected Martín, but he had only just died; his body was still warm. Is my father really strong enough to bring someone back who had been long dead? Who had been killed by a dragon's venom that had been resistant to the magic we both share?

Unless it isn't his magic that can do it.

I return to the bedroom around midday just long enough to grab my bag. I make sure that my flower journal, Saif's diary, and the book on Arthur Pendragon are all there, then throw it over my shoulder.

When I open the wardrobe, Excalibur is hanging on the door once again, in the scabbard Saif had given me. I swallow the lump in my throat as I strap it around my hip.

Then I see the hilt of my dagger lying at the bottom of the wardrobe, and pick it up tenderly. The sapphire eyes of the wolves gleam up at me accusingly. "I'm sorry," I whisper, running a finger over the fangs of one of the wolves that form the crossguard.

"You headed somewhere, Doll?"

I don't jump. I just turn to see Zaehora leaning against the door frame, her tail flicking back and forth behind her.

I look her up and down once, trying to figure out if she'll stop me if I say yes, but there's a mischievous glint in her eye, like always.

"Yeah," I say simply. "But I need something first. Where's the armory?"

She grins.

~~~~~~~~~

Five minutes later, she's showing me around a large room on the third floor of the west side of the pyramid.

I run my hands over the blades of dozens of weapons from all over the world. Well, all over *my* world. Every culture's blade seems to be represented here.

"Do you know if any of these are pure silver?" I ask as I look around for someone, as if there will be a store associate nearby just waiting to look in the back for me. I don't feel the familiar zapping of energy when I touch any of them. "This place needs a weapons master," I mumble.

Zaehora snorts. "If only there was a sexy Fabled from Hell who knew everything about every weapon in here." She sighs in mock despair.

I turn to her, one brow raised. I'm not in the mood for sarcasm. "Okay, I get it. Sorry for assuming you're just a pretty face."

She raises an eyebrow back at me. "You think I'm pretty, Red?"

I blink at her. A beat passes in silence.

"I know that I'm the one who's *literally* red, Doll. You can laugh." She winks.

I shake myself. "So. Silver. Any?" I clear my throat.

She pulls a box off the top shelf of a metal rack and sets it on a work bench. When she opens it, my eyes widen. Bars of silver, each about the size of a tube of lip balm, fill the box.

I whistle softly. "This is all pure?"
~~~~~~~~~

"As a bride on her wedding day," she says, running her hand through them.

I grimace. "Ew."

She chuckles. "Sorry. When you've been around as long as I have, old phrases slip out now and then."

I pick up a bar to examine it. The faintest trickle of my energy seeps through my skin into the silver. It's like the hug of an old friend. I drop it back in the box, and it lands with a *clink*.

"How long *have* you been around?" I ask.

She taps a nail to her plump lip. I inhale evenly. "One of the first things I remember is some Macedon running around conquering everything. Named a city after his horse. Olivander or something."

My eyes bulge. "Alexander the Great?" One of my undergrad professors had liked to refer to him as "Alexander the Bastard," but that's less recognizable.

She snaps her fingers. "That's the one."

I blink. "He lived more than two thousand years ago."

She shrugs. "That sounds right."

I rub a hand over my face, shaking my head slightly. "Okay." I puff out my cheeks and exhale. "Anyway. Where's your smith? I need to make this into a blade for my dagger." I look at my hand, wondering if I can do it with my magic.

She leans down on the table, her chin in one hand. I very pointedly look her in the eye, and not down the front of her shirt. "What, you do that, too?"

"I have many talents." Her eyes rove down my body. "Some are more fun than others."

"I — here." I pull my dagger hilt out of my bag and place it quickly on the table. *What the fuck is wrong with you?* I berate myself internally. And then I remind myself that it's not me. It's her. I look at the succubus again. "Can you meet me outside in an hour with my dagger?"

She sighs and rises to her full, considerable height. She's definitely got a few inches on Diego. "For you, Doll, I'll make it work." She grabs my hilt and a few bars of silver.

"Thank you." I turn on my heel and leave the armory so she can't see my burning cheeks.

~~~~~~~~~~

It takes me nearly twenty minutes to find the Mage I'm looking for. I'm dubious as the ogre I ask points toward the door, but I open it and walk into the large kitchen, and find the door to the walk-in pantry that he had described to me.

I hear him talking as I walk toward it.

"Ousmane?" I call, and put my hand on the knob.

"Oi!" He replies from inside. "Come in!" I open the door and see him crouched in a corner, holding out a handful of peanuts.

He's talking to a brown rat the size of a chihuahua.

I take a step back. "What . . . are you doing?"

He smiles. "Just gossiping."

I look at the rat. Its beady eyes look back at me evenly as it plucks a peanut from Ousmane's palm. "Cluny was just giving me his scouting report."

I blink. "Oh. Sorry to . . . interrupt."

The rat continues looking at me. I have no idea what rat decorum is, but I give it a nod. It nods back, and scampers off through a miniature archway in the wall. I had seen several of them throughout Tal Basta, but had assumed they were for the cats.

I run a hand over my face.

Ousmane glances at my left arm. "Love the new ink. Did you need me for something?" He asks brightly.
~~~~~~~~~~

I shake myself, and push the image of the rat from my mind. "Yeah. I actually wanted to ask you if you have any reference books on ancient Britain at your store? Encyclopedias, historical texts, anything like that?" I lean against the wall.

"Maybe even a book of fairy tales or something? If not, could you maybe you connect me with your contacts from Earth?"

He strokes his curly beard thoughtfully. "I got good news and bad news, love."

I sigh. "Bad."

"I don't have any books like that in my store, and I'm afraid I won't be going back there again anyway, now that the rebellion is out in the open. Good news is that I don't have to hook you up with anyone else to find one. *I* am my contact on Earth."

I blink at him. "Oh. But, when I asked you before —"

"Yeah, that was a lie. Sorry." He shrugs sheepishly. "Didn't want the King's dog knowing about my comings and goings. Don't need to draw suspicion to the innocent bookseller."

I frown down at him. "I'm a wolf, not a dog," I snip. "Shouldn't someone who talks to animals know that?"

He raises a brow at me in confusion, then laughs again. "Not *you!* Your vampire." He reaches up as high as he can, trying to estimate Diego's height.

I wince. "Oh. Sorry. I'm . . . I guess I'm on edge." I grab my left arm.

He makes a thoughtful noise. "I understand. I'm . . . really sorry for your loss. Saif always seemed like a good chap."

I bite down hard on the inside of my cheek, and feel myself slide apart before I can stop it. *Oh well.*

"Yeah," I say dully. "Well, I don't want to take you away from your duties here. I'll find something myself. Sorry I bothered you."

I turn and walk out of the pantry, gripping Excalibur's hilt.

Ousmane follows me, his short legs pumping hard to keep up with my stride. "Does your research have to do with him?"

"Mm-hmm." I keep walking. I don't know why I don't lie.

"Then, I want to help. I can leave the rats with instructions in my absence."

I think distantly of a comedy special I had watched once where the comedian spouted off sentences that had never before been spoken. *He missed one.*

"Okay, sure."

He's silent for a moment. "Not to mansplain research to a librarian, but . . . wouldn't it be easier to just look on the internet?"

I stop in my tracks, and shake myself. "What? How did you know —"

He huffs a bit as he stops beside me. "Heard Saif tell Bastet at lunch a few weeks ago. That man never stopped talking about you for long."

I grip Excalibur's hilt tightly and clear my throat. "The internet?" I whisper, as if the word is foreign to me.

He nods. "Yeah. Would that help, rather than looking through who knows how many books? We can't do it here in Tenazeryth, all we have is comm lines, but —"

I cut him off with a cackle. "Oh my *god*, I've been stuck in a fairy tale for too long. *Yes.* That would absolutely be easier." I wipe a tear of mirth from my eye. "Holy shit."

He smiles. "I get it. It's easy for the everyday things from our dimension to slip away the longer you're here. That's partly why I started going back more myself. For as wonderful as New Camlann is in some ways, there's still a lot that's missing." He sighs. "Like good coffee. I'd kill for just one place that has a good iced macchiato."

I smile wide as I start walking once more toward the exit. "Ousmane, do you believe in kindred spirits?"

Prisoner

I'm sitting with my back against the boulder, my fingers gliding idly through the grass between it and the freshly churned dirt, when Zaehora exits Tal Basta.

Ousmane is nearby, talking to some birds that have perched on his shoulder. Apparently, they're great conversationalists. I told Saif all about my plan while we waited for her. I could hear him, clear as day, telling me not to do it. *Ever the martyr.*

I ignore his warnings.

"So what's the plan, Doll?" Zaehora asks as she approaches.

I nod at Ousmane. "We're going to Earth to do some research. I have questions about my father's past that I need answers to, and it's not like there's anyone around who can tell me. So, research it is. I'm not sure how long we'll be gone."

She looks at the ground, a smile playing at her lips. Before I can ask her what's funny, she tosses my dagger at me. "Here you go. Fresh new blade."

I snatch the hilt out of midair. The jolt that rushes up my arm makes me gasp. More energy than usual seeps down out my fingertips.

Ousmane walks over to us as I turn it over a few times, examining it. The blade looks somehow sharper than ever, even though the old one never dulled. *Oh, shit.*

"Will this blade dull?" I ask her, sliding it into the holster on my right thigh. I stand, bracing myself against the boulder. I've never had to sharpen it before. I never even sharpened my kitchen knives back home.

"Nope." She puts her hands on her hips and looks down her nose at me severely. "Ask me why."

I roll my eyes. "Why?"

"That hilt is cursed."

I look down at it, alarmed, like the wolves are going to come to life and bite me. "What do you mean?"

"I mean, the hilt of that dagger has been embedded with some seriously evil and twisted magic. It also had a tracking spell on it. I found a very helpful Mage to break that. But the curse is stuck."

I stare at her in horror as realization sets in. *A tracking spell?* I slide back down the boulder. "He knew I was here the whole time."

She doesn't remove her hands from her hips. "It would seem so."

I put my head in my hands. "Oh god," I groan. All the effort we went to to throw him off the trail. The web of lies Diego wove. All for nothing. He was toying with us, waiting to see what we would reveal. To see where our loyalties lied.

I look up at the rows of graves around the field. At the dirt directly in front of me, separating me from Saif by what might as well be a million miles.

"It's all my fault," I whisper. "I led him straight to you."

He doesn't answer.

"What Mage did you find?" Ousmane asks Zaehora. "I don't know of anyone who could do something like that. How did they know the hilt is cursed?"

"Because she put it there."

I look up sharply. "Who?"

"Our prisoner," she says simply. That mischievous glint in her eye is practically a conflagration.

"Our . . . what?"

She flashes a dazzling smile. "Come on. Let me introduce you."

~~~~~~~~~~

Zaehora leads us to the dungeon, where three ogres stand guarding the door. The one in the middle just nods as she passes.

We descend the stone steps, and she walks to a cell near the back, on the left. She kicks the bars, and the prisoner stirs as Ousmane and I take in the sight before us.

A petite white woman is lying on the ground at the back of the cell. She's got thick, wavy hair the color of raven feathers, and she's wearing a deep violet dress straight out of the Middle Ages. It's a sturdy material with sleeves that brush against the floor as she stands.

Her collarbones stand out starkly just above the embroidered neckline, and her lilac eyes bore into me as she approaches the bars. Her deep, matte plum lips are curled into a sinister sneer.

Ousmane backs up, and Zaehora steps to the side, but I can't move. I'm rooted to the floor. My lip trembles as she reaches her side of the bars.

She looks up at me like she's sizing me up for slaughter. It's probably not far from the truth. Her face is free of blemishes, but strangely ageless, as if she could be anywhere between twenty and sixty.

"So you're the one who burned Arthur's curse out of me." Her alto voice reverberates around the dungeon and snaps me from my trance.

I shrug helplessly. "Am I?" I croak.

"Mmm. Do you know who I am, girl?"

I blink and inhale slowly. "Morgan Le Fay," I whisper.

She barks a harsh laugh. "That's one of my names, yes. But that's
~~~~~~~~~~

not what I meant. Do you know who I *am?*"

I don't understand. "No," I squeak.

"Your father never told you?"

"He's not the most open person."

She grins at me, nodding slowly. "Now *there* is an understatement."

"Who . . . who are you then?" I ask shakily. I can't believe she hasn't struck me with a bolt of lightning yet, or brought Tal Basta down on my head.

Her silken chuckle is rich. "*I*, Little One, am your stepmother. And I'm going to help you kill your father."

Breakout

I sway on my feet. "My . . ." I grip the bars to steady myself. "What?"

"Repeating myself is not something I enjoy."

"Sorry," I whisper. She frowns. "How . . . are you here?" I ask slowly.

"Does it matter?" She asks scathingly. "Do you have time to listen to my life story? I should warn you, it's rather long. Or do you want my help to bring Arthur to his knees?"

"I." My mouth works silently, searching for a response. I look at Ousmane, who is sitting with his back against the bars of a cell opposite us, his eyes wide. Zaehora is standing as still as a statue at my right, her arms crossed. Her black eyes look at me appraisingly. She raises her brows at me. *Come on, Red,* she mouths.

"I at least need to know what I'm dealing with here," I say, some strength finally returning to my voice. I look at Morgana, and a small smirk is lifting one corner of her dark lips.

"I don't care how you're here, in the cosmic sense. I care what you're doing *here*, in a cell. How long were you under my father's control? If you want him dead, why haven't you broken out and gone after him yourself?"

This could be some kind of elaborate hoax. She might still be under his control, or at least working with him.

I look at her hands, and her long nails, which are painted the same color as her lips. I see, for the first time, that all her fingertips are covered in black tendrils, just like I had seen in the book. *Tattoos*, I realize. "What happened to your magic?"

She looks at me amusedly for a moment, then lifts her right hand toward the wall, and one of the stones in the center explodes into a million pebbles that cascade to the ground. Her gaze doesn't leave mine.

"My magic is perfectly intact, girl. I am only in this cell as a show of good faith." Her voice lowers to a venomous whisper. "I don't make enemies if I don't have to. I'm too old for pointless squabbles. You and I want the same thing, so let's work together to get it. I have been under your father's control for the last five *hundred* years. I *promise* you that I want him dead more than you do."

I feel the weight of Saif's head cradled in my arms, picture him writhing in pain as he bleeds out, using his final words to make *me* feel better. To tell me I can win.

"I'm not so sure that's true," I hiss through my teeth. I grip Excalibur's hilt so hard that the sword vibrates in its scabbard.

She looks down at it, and her eyebrows shoot up at the center. "Oh good, you've inherited the blade. That will help."

"I stole it, actually," I say.

She grins. "Even better."

I see why Zaehora likes her. I turn to the succubus and Ousmane. "Can you give us a minute?"

Ousmane looks at Zaehora for direction. She nods at him, and saunters behind me on her way down the hall. "Make good choices," she teases.

I wait until I hear the door to the dungeon close before I look at Morgana again. She's moved away from me, and is leaning against the back wall of the cell, her arms crossed.

"Do you remember the fight?" I ask quietly.

She doesn't move, but her eyes narrow just slightly. "Mm-hmm."

"The man." I swallow. "The man you killed."

A beat passes. "He was important to you." It isn't a question.

I blink rapidly. "Very," I whisper.

"I'm sorry," she says quietly.

I lift my chin. "My father said he could bring him back."

She closes her eyes and exhales slowly, but she doesn't answer.

"So it's possible." My voice shakes.

She opens her lilac eyes again; they're deep pools of sorrow. "Possible, yes. Advisable? Ethical? No."

Adrenaline pulses through me. "How?"

"What do you know of the legends of Arthur Pendragon?"

I glare at her. "Depends on the version, but enough. What does it matter?"

"How did he die?" She tilts her head at me.

I blink. "He didn't. Obviously."

She looks up at the ceiling. "Yes, he did."

I stare at her. "You brought him back."

She slides to the ground and brings her knees to her chest. She looks — ashamed? "Yes." She stares hard at the ground.

"Why?" I ask, incredulously.

She looks up at me, her eyes as hard as diamonds. "Because I loved him."

"How could you love *him*?" I ask her sharply.

She leans her head back against the wall. "It's a long story."

I grind my teeth. "What's the short version?"

She sighs. "Your father was once the most valiant and powerful man in the Western *world*, Little One. He was . . . legendary." She shrugs, and her eyes swirl with memories.

I slide down to my knees, gripping the bars. Part of me had been hoping he had always been evil. Knowing he truly had been good at one time only makes it worse. "What happened to him?"

She twists her mouth ruefully. "Life."

My shoulders sag.

"Your father once loved with reckless abandon. He cared so deeply about everything. His kingdom. His people." Her jaw tenses, and fire blazes in her eyes. "His Queen." She spits the word.

I can't even blink.

"He loved *her* most of all. And she betrayed him."

I wince. "But . . . she couldn't help who she fell in love with. She wanted Lancelot —"

"She *chose* Lancelot," Morgana hisses. "She didn't have to, but she did it anyway. Arthur *told* her she didn't have to choose. He wanted her to be happy, and he loved Lancelot, too. Not as much as he loved her, but enough. He was willing to *try*. And Guinevere walked away from him without so much as a backward glance."

My mind whirs dizzyingly. I press my forehead to the bars.

She continues, biting every word out like poison. "Then Lancelot went and got himself killed, and she died of a 'broken heart.'" Her fingers curl like talons with her air quotes. "But not before Arthur offered himself to her, *again*. Despite everything, he still loved her. But he was never enough for her, because she was selfish."

I balk. "A breakup doesn't excuse his actions. He doesn't get a free pass for eternal war crimes just because he was *sad*. You can't put any of that on her."

She gives me a curious look. "In any case, something broke in him after that. He was never the same. It was like he had buried his soul with her, and his body just kept going."

My lip trembles. *That*, I understand.

"I tried to help him, and so did Merlin. I loved him . . . so much," she says shakily. "I tried to show him that he was enough, at least for me. He gave himself to me in every way after that. Every way but one." She swipes at her eyes. "Because no matter how warm his bed was, his heart was still cold."

I grimace. "How did he die?"

She scoffs softly. "At the hands of his nephew, Mordred. A pointless squabble over the throne. Mordred thought your father was no longer serving his people. Utterly false. His kingdom was the only thing Arthur cared about by then." She looks away and swallows hard.

"But your father was old, and slow, and Mordred was in his prime. Arthur stood no chance. Merlin and I didn't arrive until it was too late. We buried him with Excalibur. And then . . ." She looks at me, as if she's prepared for me to judge her very harshly for whatever comes next.

"Then about a century later, I found the Grail."

"You?" I ask breathlessly. "*You* found it?"

She nods. Her eyes unfocus once more as she watches her past play out in her mind. "I thought it would be enough. The Grail is imbued with ancient magic, beyond what even I possessed. I exhumed his bones, and poured The Enchantress' lake water over them. But it didn't work."

She grits her teeth angrily. "It should have worked. And then Merlin tried to stop me. He said that I was meddling in things I couldn't control. Things that were too powerful for me. But he didn't understand. I would have burned down the world and everyone in it, if only I could tell Arthur I loved him one more time."

My heart hammers at the echoes of my thoughts as I had cradled Saif's body.

"So I killed him," she says simply. "Merlin fell, and I took his gemstone. I threw everything I had at your father's bones. My magic. Merlin's. The Grail's. And finally, Excalibur began to glow, and the water that covered his bones began to boil. I'll spare you the gruesome reanimation process, but then, he was back, young once more, and stronger than ever."

If I wasn't gripping the iron bars so tightly, I would collapse. "So, you brought my father back from the dead all by yourself?" I try to keep the admiration out of my voice, but some creeps in just the same.

She frowns. "Yes. But I no longer have access to Merlin's magic, so I need your help to undo it."

My jaw quivers. "Can you . . . can you do it again?"

She glares at me. "I probably could, with your help, or the Jasper."

Relief washes over me, and a sob escapes my throat. "Thank y—"

"But I won't."

My stomach drops, and my teeth click loudly with the force of me snapping my mouth shut. "What?" I whisper, when I regain control of my jaw muscles. "Why?"

She rises to her feet and steps toward me slowly. "Your father had been distant before his death, but when I brought him back, he was something else entirely. He was a *monster*. And for a *very* long time, I didn't care."

She shakes her head and shrugs helplessly. "I was in love. And he was finally loving me back. I didn't care that he began slaughtering anyone who got in his way on his quest to regain power."

She shudders at what are likely very bloody memories. "He took back his throne, but under a new name. Obviously, for the average citizen of Camelot, seeing King Arthur reclaim the throne several generations after his death would have been . . . disconcerting."

She grimaces. "So he posed as a new king, with a new name. I don't even remember all the identities he's used over the years. The Danodraic name he's using now is only about ten generations deep, if I recall correctly."

"Twelve, including me," I whisper.

Sympathy flashes across her face for a brief moment. "Yes. He's managed to do something similar over and over again. If anyone ever suspected anything, they never did anything about it. They had peace and prosperity. Why should they care?"

"You said he was controlling you the last five hundred years. What happened?"

She shakes her head ruefully. "I finally realized how much devastation I had caused. I tried to put him down, tried to atone for my sins, but by then, he was too powerful. He didn't want *me*, but he wasn't going to give up my magic. So he used me."

Her jaw clenches. "I was fully aware of *everything*, but I couldn't break free of his spell." She clenches her fist, and purple blood seeps out around her dark nails. Her eyes bore into me, ablaze with fury. "I'll spare you the details. But just know, girl, that there are more ways to break a person than you could *ever* imagine."

I swallow the bile rising in my throat. Maybe she *does* want him dead more than me. But then I shake my head. "But . . . he was already broken *before* you brought him back. Saif was - he *is* - a hero." I choke on unshed tears.

Her gaze is thick with pity. "Your father was a hero once too, Little One."

I look at the ground and continue shaking my head. "Saif is different."

She scoffs. "They're all *different*. That's why they're all the same."

I rise furiously. "You don't understand —" My next word sticks in my throat, and I let out a strangled noise.

Morgana's eyes begin to glow purple, and she raises a hand to me, her fingers curled into several different positions. The black tendrils around her fingertips undulate sickeningly, elongating up her limbs, and her hair begins to float around her, writhing like black snakes.

Her power radiates over me in waves. It feels like every cell in my body is being pulled in opposite directions, but I can't move a muscle. I can't even scream.

"*You* don't understand, girl." Her voice reverberates around the dungeon, alto, soprano, and baritone layers clashing against one another, all at once. "I will *not* be made into a weapon by anyone, *ever* again. I'll die before I watch another Pendragon descend into madness over their grief. I will put you down like a dog before I let you repeat the sins of your father. Before you repeat *my* sins."

She flicks her wrist, and I crash to the ground, gasping and clutching my throat. My mouth fills with a warm, coppery taste, like I'm kissing Diego; I bit my tongue when I hit the stone floor. Her hair falls back down, and her eyes return to normal, though her gaze is glacial. "Do I make myself clear?"

I grit my teeth. She didn't know Saif. She doesn't know how special he was. *Is.* But she's not going to help me if I piss her off again. I spit blood onto the floor and nod. "Yes," I bite out.

"Splendid. Now, stand back."

I scramble away from the bars just as she blasts them across the hall, and they crash into the cell opposite hers. She walks to me and holds out a hand. "Let's go, Little One. I do believe the 'goddess' that runs this place will be wondering what that noise was, and it won't take her long to figure it out. She seems sharp."

I take her hand, and she hauls me to my feet easily, despite being half a foot shorter than me. "Wait, she knows you're here?" I follow her quickly as she strides to the stairs.

She doesn't slow as she turns to look at me over her shoulder. "Who do you think ordered me to be locked up? She and that mountainous bat of hers interrogated me that entire first night. Or rather, they tried to. Not much you can get out of someone who has nothing to lose. When I asked to see the Witch who had freed me, all they would say was that she was unavailable."

"He's not a bat," I mutter, then scurry up the stairs after her. "And I was asleep."

She snorts. "And no wonder. The power it took to do what you did would have been enough to drain an army."

"I'm also not a Wi—" I nearly trip up the stairs as she blasts the door open. I see the ogres scatter as the door falls to the ground.

"What the hell are you *doing?*" I screech at her. Ousmane runs for cover, but Zaehora stands a few feet away, grinning brilliantly.

Morgana turns and holds out her hand to me, and I take it automatically. *What the hell am I doing?*

"Making an impression," Morgana says with an innocent shrug.

"Eilidh!" I look up to see Kianga leaning over the railing of the second floor, gawking at me.

Diego rushes to her side, and stares down at me in horror. "Eilidh, *no!*"

I clench my jaw. "Good."

Morgana smiles devilishly as her eyes begin to glow again. Purple flames erupt around us, and I immediately begin sweating.

Diego leaps over the railing and lands a few feet away. *"Eilidh!"*

My eyes widen as he reaches for me. "Get back!" I scream.

Zaehora snatches him by the back of his shirt and tosses him bodily to the ground, shielding him just as Tal Basta explodes.

Regroup

The flames that had exploded throughout the pyramid shatter the glass above, and everything hangs suspended, as if time has stopped, for several heartbeats. Then the glass repairs itself, and the fire comes rushing back toward us.

I collapse in a heap as it winks out at our feet. "Diego." I roll slowly, and try to rise, but immediately pitch sideways. The world spins around me.

Morgana falls to her knees beside me, panting and clutching her chest. "He's fine, Little One."

I lift my head with a groan, and see that she's right. Zaehora is taking her time crawling off of him, but he's at least unburnt.

I press my forehead to the cool marble floor and breathe deep.

"What the fuck did you do to her, you *witch*?" Diego asks as he crawls toward me.

"I'm fine," I say into the marble.

He rolls me over. "The fuck you are," he spits through his bared fangs.

I put a hand to his cheek. "Are you okay?"

He frowns. "I'm fine. You're the one that went up in flames."

My lower lip trembles as I clutch the front of his shirt. *You almost got him killed, too.*

Morgana leans back on an elbow. "She's fine, bat. Give her a minute to breathe and a snack, and she'll be right as rain."

"Why does she keep calling you a bat?" I ask him languidly.

He just shakes his head. "I don't know. I'm ignoring it. Not the worst thing I've been called by a white woman."

I grimace; I'm sure it isn't.

Morgana stands shakily and dusts off her dress. "You're a vampire," she says simply, as if that provides an explanation.

Diego rolls his eyes. "Actually, these fangs are from the costume shop. Easy mistake."

"Well, your behavior is more befitting of a jester. Go with that next time."

Kianga crashes to the ground in her jaguar form, then shifts, and snatches Morgana by the front of her dress. "Answer the fucking question. What. Did you. *Do?*"

Morgana just frowns at her. "I fixed your wards."

Kianga blinks several times. "You." She releases the front of Morgana's dress. "You what?"

Morgana straightens her bodice. "Arthur broke your wards while he was here. I fixed them. But I couldn't do it with my power alone, so I channeled some of hers." She nods at me.

Kianga looks back and forth between us for a moment, clearly trying to decide if she should thank Morgana or strangle her for draining me.

I make the decision for her. "Thank you for doing that." I look pointedly at Kianga and Diego.

They exchange a look, and finally, Kianga crosses her arms. "Okay, fine. Thank you. But next time, don't just fucking drain someone. Ask first."

Morgana is unperturbed. "I had to see for myself how much raw power she has. If I had given her a warning, I wouldn't have gotten an accurate measurement."

I can't help but bark a laugh as Diego hauls me to my feet. "And what's the magical barometer say, Ms. Fey?"

Morgana smiles at me, and several crows feet reveal themselves at the corners of her lilac eyes. "You're going to save the world."

~~~~~~~~~~

"Power isn't the issue — you have plenty of that. What you lack is control."

I stare at Morgana from my spot on the floor. The Council, the Order, the ancient Witch, and myself have taken up residence in the courtroom. I notice that Hyun-Joo, Diego, Val, and Martín all sit in the same circle formation they would around my father's round table, albeit more spread out.

The only one missing is Saif.

I clutch my left forearm tightly. "So what? If you can just use me like a battery, why do I need control?"

"Because you're a ticking time bomb. You're a danger to everyone."

Half the people in the room start talking at once. I close my eyes and take a calming breath.

"Quiet!" Kianga slams a fist against the bench, and everyone in the room freezes, Morgana included, though she's looking at Kianga with an approving smirk. "Let the Witch talk," Kianga growls, leaning back, and crossing her arms.

I roll my eyes. "*Now* you want to listen to her," I mutter.

Kianga tilts her head sharply and narrows her eyes at me. "I already *tried* to listen to her."

"You didn't try to *listen* to her, you tried to get her to *talk*. That's something else entirely!"

"*Thalla 's cagainn bruis*," Mòrag mutters to herself.

"*Falbh dàirich fhèin!*" I snap.
~~~~~~~~~~

Her mouth literally falls open. "How . . . ?"

"My grandfather grew up in the Highlands, you bitch." I stand, and everyone in the room tenses. Hyun-Joo is looking with concern at Diego, whose face is completely blank. Val's expression is pinched, and wary; Martín clutches her shoulder protectively. Kianga's expression is thick with disappointment.

I turn and stride from the room.

"Eilidh we don't have time for —" Kianga begins, but I slam the door shut, and hear her spouting curses behind it as I walk away.

~~~~~~~~~~

Of all the people I don't want approaching me as I lie beside Saif's grave with my head on my paws, it's Mòrag. And yet, she strides over and sits down beside me without a care. I sigh through my nose as she settles herself.

"Where did your *seanair* grow up?" She asks, as if there had been no break in our conversation.

Inverness, I finally reply grudgingly.

"Hmm. I was there once. Grew up in Shetland, though."

One of my ears perks up before I can stop it. *You grew up in Scotland?*

"Some hundred or so years ago, aye, did you think I put on the accent for fun?"

I put my ear back down.

She huffs. "*Tha cianalas orm*," she says softly.

I wince. I had heard my grandfather say that a million times, too. There's no direct translation for the deep yearning, the all-consuming longing for home, but the way his eyes had misted over every time he said it had always made my heart ache for him.

It's a feeling I've never been able to relate to. I've never had a real home, no four walls that I've been able to call my own for long
~~~~~~~~~~

enough to grow attached. Only people.

And the Universe always rips those away from me, too.

We sit in silence for a moment as I brood.

"I'm sorry about him, you know," she finally says, nodding to the dirt in front of us.

My hackles rise. *Don't.*

"I mean it. I wouldn't have been a few weeks ago. He did get Callum killed, after all. But . . ." She trails off.

It's been a long few weeks, I finish.

She huffs air through her nose. "Aye."

I hadn't spared a single thought for the wulver Martín had incinerated the night Saif gave me the wolfsbane tea. *Was he part of your pack? Callum?*

She closes her eyes. "Not originally. He was an orphan. Had barely lost his milk teeth when your father killed his pack, and kidnapped one of his cousins. He was only spared because he had wandered off by himself, and wasn't there."

She sighs. "He was always so hot-headed. So ready to jump into battle and get his revenge. I told him to stay behind, but he followed anyway. And it cost him his life."

I swallow. *I'm sorry.*

"Thanks."

Another long silence. *Is that why you hate me? Callum?*

She looks down at me evenly. "Not just that. I hate you for a lot of reasons."

A growl rumbles deep in my throat. *Oh, good.*

She smiles humorlessly. "You remind me of him, you know. Callum. You're going to get yourself killed," she says matter-of-factly.

Well, then all your problems will be solved, won't they?

Her smile drops. "My concern is that you're going to get Bastet killed with you."

I bare my teeth and rise to sit on my haunches. *I would never put her in danger.*

"She's already *in* danger, pup. She's been leading a rebellion against a tyrant for the last decade. But things were going well until you showed up. We were making progress. We had a plan. And then you come along, and now look."

She gestures toward the rows of graves.

"Chaos and blood. That's what you are. Just like your father."

I jump to my feet, glaring at her, trembling violently. *You don't fucking know me.*

She returns my gaze evenly. There's no hostility in her words, just cold hard fact. "All I need to know is that you're a danger to my daughter, just like you were to him."

I look at Saif's grave, and something within me breaks.

I turn and run back into the pyramid.

Dreams Part 2

I am on fire.

The new vampire I saved last night just smiled at me, and my cheeks are flaming, just like his eyes.

My chest burns from the claw marks he left when he first woke up, but they'll heal. He made it. That's what matters.

Now every time he smiles at me, my blood runs hot — too hot.

Everything is burning.

Patience

Ten minutes later, I'm striding through the halls of Tal Basta, my cloak billowing behind me. I grip Excalibur's hilt with one hand, and the strap of my pack with the other.

I raise my hand to pound a fist on the door that a centaur had pointed me to, but a velvety chuckle behind me causes me to halt.

"What's so funny?" I snip, not bothering to look at Zaehora.

"I was wondering how long it would take you. Finally running away?"

I bite the inside of my lip. "I'm not running away."

The door in front of me opens, and Morgana gazes up at me with a bored expression. Her lilac eyes flit between me and Zaehora. "Well, come on." She turns and walks to the desk on the other side of the bedroom. I sigh heavily and follow, leaning into one corner as Zaehora closes the door and perches on the edge of the bed.

Morgana leans back in her chair and examines her plum nails. "So," she says simply.

"Take me to him." I ignore the way Zaehora's black lips curl into a smirk.

"No." She doesn't even need to ask who I mean.

"I'm going to kill him once and for all and be done with this."

She throws her head back, and her long, raven-colored waves nearly brush the ground. "Think, Little One."

"I *think* that you'd better take me to him yourself, or I'm going alone, and then you'll never get your chance for revenge."

She makes a thoughtful noise. "How are you going to do it?"

I gesture vaguely at myself and begin counting on my fingers. "I've got a legendary sword, a cursed dagger, werewolf powers, and the magic of Merlin him-fucking-self. One of those will kill him."

She counts on her own fingers. "The sword does you no good unless you can break his wards and get to his skin, which would take your magic, which he is immune to. The curse on the dagger does nothing but protect the hilt, and is specifically designed to work against anyone *save* a Pendragon if an attempt to break it is made. And your werewolf powers."

She looks me up and down appraisingly. "Well I suppose you could yell at him telepathically, but I'm afraid not even your tongue is sharp enough to kill him. Unless you can convince the moon to drop on his head, they'll do you no good."

I rake my hands through my hair. "Then what the fuck am I supposed to *do*, Morgana?" I slump to the floor, lean against the wall, and bring my legs up on either side of my stomach. "I'm completely fucking useless."

She sighs. "You're failing your first lesson."

I glare at her. "And what's that?"

She looks back at me evenly. "Patience."

I snort.

She doesn't smile.

"Wait, seriously?"

"I am not an *unserious* woman, Little One." She blinks at me slowly.

I throw my hands in the air. "How long am I supposed to wait? Until my father wipes out half of humanity?"

"Until you have even a *scintilla* of patience."

"You don't even know me. I could be the *most* patient person ever."

I raise my chin at her.

She tilts her head forward and looks at me through her long, dark eyelashes. "There is *so* much of your father in you, girl."

"Fuck you." But I look at the ivy twisted around my left forearm and bite down hard on the inside of my lip to keep the tears at bay. *Chaos and blood.*

"Don't take it personally. You're right. I *don't* know you. But I can tell already that you are your father's daughter."

"Tch."

She raises an eyebrow in irritation. "You broke one of the most powerful Witches in history out of jail and grabbed her hand blindly for a chance at revenge."

Zaehora snickers.

"I — you weren't going anywhere!"

She smirks. "You didn't know that."

I think back to what I had told Diego when he was on the other side of the bars a few weeks ago. *Afraid I'll incite a prison break, I think.*

I fucking hate when she's right.

"So what?"

She rolls her eyes. "So I know for a fact that didn't come from your mother; she was a coward. She would never have reached for a chance to get anywhere."

I blanch. "You knew my mother?"

"Of course I did. I knew all your father's . . . dalliances." She twists her mouth. "Honestly, I was grateful to all of them. They were a nice distraction for him, whenever they would catch his eye."

My stomach churns. "How?"

"He always kept me close, for when he needed my magic. And to keep the curse firmly intact if it began to slip."

"Then why haven't I seen you?" I ask. "Why haven't any of the

Order members *ever* seen you?"

She shrugs. "You never went into his room."

I clutch my knees. "How haven't you snapped? I would be burning the world down if I were you."

She smirks. "*Patience.* I know he'll get what's coming to him. I will get my justice." Her smirk turns bloodthirsty. "And a small amount of spite doesn't hurt."

I run a hand through my hair. "I'm . . . I'm so sorry. I could have rescued you sooner if only —"

"Don't apologize. He would have just killed you," she says simply. "He's done it before."

Zaehora makes a thoughtful noise from her place on the bed. "Maybe your dad *is* worse than mine, Red."

"Lucky me," I rasp, then run a hand over my face. "Okay, fine. I'll be patient. But what do we do while we wait?"

She glances around the room. "How about a change of scenery?"

Temporary Home

"Right here is perfect." Morgana halts about a hundred yards to the north of Tal Basta, at the edge of a dying pine forest. I halt. Zaehora descends from the sky with a *whoosh*.

I give her a withering look. "You don't have to chaperone me, you know."

"Who said it was you I was watching?" She asks as she tucks her wings into their neutral position on her back. The triangular tip of her tail flits with amusement.

I glance at Morgana, who is walking in a straight line, measuring out her steps. "It's pretty obvious. You're always looming over me. Tell *Bastet* that if she wants me watched, she should do it her fucking self."

She smirks, her black eyes twinkling in the sunlight. "I don't get in the middle of lover's quarrels. That's above my pay grade."

Morgana stops dead in her tracks, and her head whips up. "Lover's quarrel?" She raises a brow at me. "You and the goddess? But I thought —"

"And the vampire," Zaehora supplies, bouncing onto her tiptoes, clearly enjoying this far too much. Understanding dawns in Morgana's eyes.

I look away, rubbing my left forearm. "Yeah. Except they both think I'm a fucking monster now, and they're right, so." I clutch my pendant until the corners of the crescent moon leave indentations in my flesh. "They're better off without me."

Zaehora's smirk slides off her face as I speak. "You're an idiot if you think that's true, Red."

I bristle. "That's actually one of the nicer things that I've been called today, so thanks."

Morgana sighs heavily and begins counting off her steps once more, turning at a ninety-degree angle. "Like father," she mutters.

I throw my hands into the air. "What did I say *now*?"

"Face it, Doll," Zaehora says with a snicker, crossing her arms as she watches Morgana. "Your story is a *lot* like your dad's. Even down to the love . . . square?" She raises a thoughtful brow and taps her lip. "Rectangle?"

"Perhaps a rhombus," Morgana remarks lightly.

"All that's left is for you to die." Zaehora shrugs.

"I'll get right on that," I say scathingly. "What are you doing?" I finally ask Morgana.

She steps back from the square she had walked and closes her eyes. The tattoos around her fingers begin to undulate and extend up her arm. "Making myself at home."

With a flick of both wrists, purple flames erupt from the ground along the path she had walked.

A small cottage slowly forms from the ground up as the flames rise. Thick squares of multicolored stone, a black wooden door with a small window on either side, topped off with a sloping slate roof, stand in front of us as the flames fizzle into the sky.

Zaehora emits a low whistle.

Morgana ascends the three steps leading to the front door and beckons us to follow her inside.

Zaehora dips into a low bow, sweeping one arm toward the door. "Your Grace."

I scowl and walk inside. "I want lesson two to be hexes," I say to Morgana as I instinctively kick my shoes off by the door. "Or how to banish a succubus back to H— holy shit!"

I look around the cottage. Except that isn't what it is at all — I've stepped into a fucking *mansion*. It's surprisingly modern, with light gray walls, and a dark, hardwood floor that reflects the lights of several chandeliers. A white couch takes up one side of the room. Morgana throws herself down on it, sighing contentedly, and Zaehora follows suit, draping her wings over the back of it. There's a purple fire roaring in the hearth that casts a faint glow across both women. A black and white map of Tenazeryth hangs above the mantle.

A high bar with stools on this side of it separates the living room and the spacious kitchen. Stainless steel appliances shine, and the granite counter tops are spotless. I gasp, and run to a giant silver machine on one counter.

"You okay, Doll?" Zaehora calls out, alarmed.

I wrap my arms around the espresso machine. "No, but I will be."

Ten minutes later, I sit on the couch and sip on my iced latte; when I had opened the fridge, it was stuffed full of produce and a pitcher of oat milk, of all things. "I never would have pegged an ancient Witch to go for this style of interior design."

Morgana shifts against the plush cushions. "I needed a change of pace. This is sterile. Devoid of history."

I make a thoughtful noise at the back of my throat. "Yeah, that makes sense."

"And bigger on the inside," Zaehora remarks.

I gape at her. "How do you . . . ?"

She grins. "What? I've spent plenty of time on Earth. For all their faults, and their blip of a lifespan, humans tell wonderful stories."

Morgana runs her fingers through her hair. "Their blip of a lifespan is the *reason* mortals tell such wonderful stories."

I tuck my feet under myself and look into the flames, frowning. Zaehora pokes my knee with the tip of her tail, and I turn my frown on her. "What?"

She smirks. "Every time you get that look on your face, something ends up exploding. Just trying to head it off at the pass. Penny for your thoughts?"

My eyes flick to Morgana, who is looking at me intently. "I just . . . mortal lifespans are a bitch."

"Your goddess," Morgana says.

I blink back tears. *If only she really was one.* "I already got Saif killed," I whisper. "If I don't get her killed, too, I'll have to watch her die one day. I don't think I can do that again."

Morgana sits up straighter. "Again?"

"It's . . . it's a long story."

She and Zaehora exchange a look. "Well," she says. "Then it's a good thing you're working on your first lesson."

I sigh heavily, take another sip of coffee, and begin. I tell them everything. How Kianga and I had grown up together. How I had always loved her, even though I thought she could never love me the same way. How she died, but . . . didn't. How I had been bitten by Bleddyn, and saved by the Order.

I tell them about Saif, how he had cared for me, and how we had fallen in love. I tell them about Diego, and how I had hated him passionately, until I had realized that I didn't.

Remarkable, how love and hate are two sides of the same fiery coin.

I recount how he and I were captured by the rebellion, and the revelations that had followed. I even tell them that the four of us had found our own form of happiness, if only for a moment, before it had been stolen from us. I keep the details to myself, obviously, but I can tell they understand.

I tell them how I had raged at Kianga and Diego this morning. How Diego had looked ready to fight me, had put his hand on Kianga's shoulder to shield her from the likes of me. "Because that's what I've become, isn't it? Chaos and blood." I look at my hands, which spark briefly, before I take a steadying breath. "It's what everyone has said all day. I'm a monster."

When I'm done, twilight has blanketed the world outside. Zaehora's face is grave. Morgana looks at me with an expression I can't quite read. It seems to be a mixture of amusement and pity. And, maybe, just a shred of understanding. She shakes her head slowly.

"Like daughter."

Calling

After saying goodnight to Morgana, Zaehora and I exit her cottage. I sit down on the stone steps and prop my chin in my hands, my elbows digging into my thighs. The light from Tal Basta casts long shadows from the various stones and fallen trees around us.

Zaehora notices that I'm not following her, and turns partially around. I stare at her for a moment, allowing my eyes to rove down her form. Half of her is illuminated in the soft purple glow of the fire inside; the other half is shrouded in darkness.

Both sides of her are beautiful.

"Now what are you thinking, Red?" She asks quietly.

I drag my eyes up to meet hers. "I think . . . that you should go," I say shakily.

She tilts her head gently to one side, and her silky bob brushes against her jawline. "I understand how it feels, you know."

I swallow hard. "How what feels?"

Her eyes are lidded heavily. "How it feels for everyone to see you as a monster. How the only thing you can ever be in their eyes is what they already think you are." She sits down slowly at my side, her long, muscular legs stretched over the steps. "I understand how the desire —" Her eyes dart to my mouth and back up. "To be understood can wreck a person."

She leans into me.

I retreat backward, pressing myself into the stone archway that frames the front door. "Stop," I rasp.

She licks her lips. "Stop what?"

I rip my eyes from her lips. "Using your powers on me."

She chuckles. "See?" She leans back. "Only ever what they think you are. I've never once used my powers on you, Eilidh. I don't need to. Whatever you feel when you're near me is all natural."

I swallow.

"And if you were wondering, I know *exactly* what you feel. When you were on trial, standing between your men, and facing down Bastet, I could barely concentrate with all the energy crackling between the four of you. That sustained me for *days*."

"I'm sorry," I whisper. "For assuming."

"Hmm." She looks me up and down. "So? What do you say?"

I shudder. "I can't. I have . . . them." *All three of them.*

She puts her lips to my ear. She smells like amber and sandalwood. "I'm not trying to steal you from anyone, and I'm not trying to replace *him*. I know I never could." She moves one hand to my jaw, and my breath catches. "And your vampire already said it was okay, if that helps."

I flinch. "Is *he* the one who sent you?"

Her mouth twists in amusement. "No one *sent* me. Believe it or not, no one has to be forced into being around you. Some people just *like* you. He just said that he doesn't mind if I . . . help you relax."

My mind reels, trying to process that while I shake my head. "Still I . . . I can't."

She sighs and leans back slowly. "Fine. But if you change your mind, call me." She pulls a cell phone from a pocket of her pants and lays it on the ground between us.

She stands and jumps into the air without another word, her wings flapping silently as she heads toward the pyramid.

~~~~~~~~~

I open the door to the cottage slowly, and Morgana looks up from her mug of tea.

"Can I stay here tonight?" I ask in a small voice. "Please?"

A second mug flames to existence, hanging in midair in front of my face. I take it wordlessly as I kick off my shoes, and sit on the opposite side of the couch with my feet tucked under me. My taste buds sing at the taste of the chamomile, but my heart aches painfully in my chest. How many days ago had Saif made me that last mug of coffee? Two? A million?

She watches me as she sips her own tea. I watch the fire and pick at the fabric of the couch. "What if I'm not strong enough to beat him?" I whisper.

She considers her answer carefully. "You aren't. Not alone. But neither am I. That's why we need each other." She turns to the fire, and the purple flames reflect off her pupils.

I chew on my lip, unsure if that made me feel any better. "Are you . . . a Shifter?" I ask quietly. "Or . . . something else? How did you become a dragon? We all thought dragons weren't even *real*."

She sighs. "I have been able to take the form of a dragon for as long as I can remember. I don't know if I'm considered a Shifter or not. I suppose, maybe I am. But, as far as I know, I'm the only one."

I stare at her for a moment. "That sounds . . . lonely."

Her mouth tightens at the corners. "I suppose it is," she says quietly.

"How did you meet my father? Some of the legends say you were lovers, others say you were siblings." I cringe at the thought. "What's the truth?"

She leans back heavily into the couch, and looks up at the ceiling.
~~~~~~~~~

"We were raised together, but we aren't related. I was a ward of his father's."

"Uther," I say.

She nods. "My father was a Lord who got a bit too spirited for Uther's liking. He demanded me as a ward to ensure my father's cooperation. I was just a baby when I was taken from my parents. I don't remember them at all; they were killed when I was a child." Her mouth twists. "Uther had them murdered."

I clutch my pendant and swallow the lump in my throat.

Morgana rises abruptly. "I'm going to bed, Little One. It has been a *very* long time since I slept comfortably, and I'm rather looking forward to it. If I sleep through tomorrow as well, don't be surprised."

"Wait."

She pauses.

"Um . . . thank you." She looks at me curiously over her shoulder. I clarify. "For letting me stay." I look hard at the floor. "Kianga and Diego . . . I don't know what's happening with us, so. Thank you. And I'm sorry they locked you up."

She whirls around, steps toward me, and kneels to my level. Her eyes blaze with passion. "Stop apologizing on behalf of other people. You cannot control what they do."

I lean back at the venom in her tone.

She bares her teeth. "Their decisions are not yours, and neither are their mistakes. No matter how much you think your minds are one. They never are."

As she ascends the black floating staircase to the second floor, I squeeze my pendant, relishing the way the points of the crescent moon dig into my skin.

The only thing worth fighting for.

~~~~~~~~~~
~~~~~~~~~~

I brew a cup of coffee and head upstairs. The first door on the left has an "M" written in elegant script etched into the dark wood. The door at the far end of the hallway has an "E."

Either Morgana conjured this room for me while we were speaking on the couch, or she had made sure to include a room for me here when she built the cottage. My stomach twists strangely at that thought.

I enter the bedroom suite and take it in. It looks rather like a hotel that I would never have been able to afford in my previous life without dipping into my retirement funds. A plush, king-sized, four-poster bed with sheer, pistachio-colored curtains and satin sheets occupies most of the main area. A sleek white vanity sits in one corner, and there's an open door to a walk-in closet in the other. I peek into the bathroom and see a deep tub with jets, as well as a shower, both of which I'm desperate to get into.

I wander over to the walk-in closet, and see that it's full of clothing. Though, I think with a small smile, it still doesn't seem as packed as the wardrobe Valentina filled for me at Arkenvale. I take my pendant off and lay it on the vanity.

I toss my dirty clothes onto the bathroom floor and take a long, scalding shower. Once I've scrubbed every inch of myself several times over, I begin to fill up the tub, and sit on the edge to examine the phone.

The design is unremarkable; it's a basic, rectangular brick, about the size of my hand. But when I flip it over, I notice that the rebellion's symbol - my pendant - has been carved into it with either lasers, or the magic equivalent. I hit the button at the bottom, and the screen lights up. The interface is similar to Kianga's computer — sleek and clean.

I turn on the jets and slide down into the water — my muscles sing with satisfaction.

I thumb through the phone, find the settings, and change the color scheme to a soft brown. Then I find the contact page, and scroll through the list. I don't know most of the names, but some of them jump out at me.

Ousmane, Himesh, and, to my surprise, even Hyun-Joo and the Peñas have been added, so they must have been given phones at some point within the last few days. I scroll past Mòrag's name with a huff. I eye Zaehora's name near the bottom of the list, and chew the inside of my cheek.

I notice a tab labeled "Favorites," and tap it. My breath catches as I read the names.

Bastet.

Rahim, Saif.

Vidales, Diego.

I set the phone on the floor and plunge under the water, holding my breath for as long as I can. I come up only long enough to gulp more air, then submerge myself again, and scream.

The sound is not the least bit muffled by the jets.

Eventually, I drain the tub, and pad over to the linen closet. I'm pleasantly surprised when the bath towel is actually large enough to wrap around myself, and even has some extra material to spare. I throw another one around my hair, pick up the phone, and go lie in bed.

I lie tucked under the sheets for some time, staring at the dark screen of the phone, my mind churning with the day's events. Just this morning, I had been clutching my new tattoo and crying over peanut butter and toast.

Now, I'm in a magical cottage with a stepmother I never knew I had, who also happens to be one of the most powerful Witches in history.

I think of Zaehora's words, and think about what others see me as.

Chaos and blood, Mòrag had called me.

A ticking time bomb, according to Morgana. Though, admittedly, she had also said I was going to save the world.

But can I do that before I hurt everyone I love?

"So many people have labels for me," I mutter to myself.

Brighter than the sun.

The only thing worth the fight.

My flame.

"But a label isn't who you *are*. Who *am* I?" I whisper.

The only thing you can ever be in their eyes is what they already think you are.

Everyone thinks I'm a monster, and so far, I've agreed with them.

I pick up the phone, willing my hands not to tremble, and type out the message.

Please come.

Not even five minutes later, sitting on the stone steps of the cottage, I see her shadowy figure crossing the field, and even catch her tail flitting back and forth. I inhale shakily, praying to every force in the Universe that I'm doing the right thing. That for once, a decision I make won't end in chaos and blood.

Her face finally comes into the halo of purple light cast by the fire blazing inside, and my heart beats faster at the sight of her. "You came," I say quietly as I stand.

Kianga shifts back to her human form and searches my eyes as she steps closer. "Of course I did," she whispers. "You asked me to."

I clutch my left forearm and take a deep breath. "I don't know if what I'm doing is right, Kianga. I don't know if I'm going to be strong enough to beat Arthur. I don't know how I'm going to get up every day for the rest of my eternal fucking life, and remember that Saif is gone, and carry on."

She puts a hand on my cheek and wipes away a tear.

"All I know is that I can't wake up every day, and have you gone too, and it be because I pushed you away just because I was scared. If you want to go, you can, and I'll understand. I know you'd be perfectly happy without me. And safer."

Her glistening eyes reflect the purple fire that burns through the window.

"But I promise, if you stay, that I won't ever let you go. I don't want to push you away anymore. I don't want to be a monster." I put my hand over hers. "I just want to be yours, Kianga."

She pulls me into a slow kiss. When we part, she holds our foreheads together. "You're not a monster, Eilidh," she whispers. "And I'm not going anywhere. Ever again."

Together

I lay her down softly on the bed, climb on top of her, and straddle her hips. "I love you." I kiss her neck. "I'm sorry," I whisper.

"I'm sorry, too," she breathes.

I kiss down over her chest, pull her tunic up to expose her stomach, and kiss down that as well. When I get to her black leggings, I pull at them with my teeth. She leans her head back and moans, arching her hips into me.

I grab the waistband from my teeth and pull it down quickly, tossing her pants to my floor. I'm running my tongue over her clit by the time they hit the floor. She moans loudly, and I gesture at the door. *Quiet.* I feel my magic form a barrier and tie itself off.

I reach under her tunic as I move my tongue up and down over her, and lightly pinch her nipples. She moans again, and pushes into my face. I don't mind; I need her far more than I need air. She *is* my air. I moan against her clit, and she shivers.

I move my hands down her curves, gripping into her waist, her hips, her thighs. She twists her fingers into my hair, and pulls me away from her. "Wh — what?" I gasp. She gazes down at me, her eyes lidded heavily. "Take your fucking pants off," she commands.

My eyes widen of their own volition, but I comply immediately. As my linen pants hit the floor, she motions for me to straddle her. I wipe my chin and hook one leg around her hips.

She moans desperately as I start grinding our pussies together.

I could listen to this woman moan for the rest of my life, and it would never be enough. I lift one of her legs into the air and plant haphazard kisses all over it.

"Fuck, Eilidh." She grips the headboard. "Right there. Don't stop."

I don't change a thing. I keep moving my hips in a steady, circular motion, and she begins to shake and gasp underneath me.

"Fuck!" She gasps, and bites her lips. The sight of her coming undone under me sends me over the edge.

"Oh, my *god*," I moan, and then I'm wracked with waves of pleasure. I collapse down onto her, and kiss her neck as I continue moving my hips, keeping both our orgasms going.

She pulls my hair and scratches down my back, hard, just how I like it. I moan into her neck, and finally, we both slow. I throw myself down dramatically, and she bounces with the mattress, laughing.

"Was that a tub with jets I spied in your bathroom?" She asks innocently, running an almond-shaped nail down my thigh. I cock an eyebrow.

Ten minutes later, we've found a band for her to keep her braids up, and have filled the tub.

She slides down into the tub, moaning as the jets hit her back. She leans back with a satisfied sigh and looks me up and down. I will myself not to shuffle. "Get in."

<div style="text-align:center">~~~~~~~~~~</div>

I wake up to Diego sliding into the bed behind me as the first rays of dawn are just beginning to light the sky outside.

"Shh, go back to sleep, *amor*," he says under his breath. He curls around me and lays an arm across us, resting his hand on Kianga's hip. She nuzzles against me in her sleep, and I plant a soft kiss on her bonnet.

"Who let you in?" I whisper.

He shrugs. "The door opened for me. Now sleep."

But I won't be able to sleep if I don't say this to him now. "I'm sorry."

He's silent for a moment, as if contemplating if he really wants to know the answer to his next question. "For what?"

So many things. But, for now, all I say is, "I get it now. Wanting to distance yourself to keep someone safe." I hold Kianga tighter, and she sighs contentedly in my arms.

He plants a long kiss on my neck, then whispers in my ear, tickling the sensitive skin delightfully. "We'll keep her safe together."

If only that were possible.

Reflections

L̲ater that morning, Kianga and Diego leave for a Council meeting, so I take another bath before wandering downstairs. Morgana is meditating on the couch, her legs crossed underneath her.

After I make myself a coffee, I wander over to the fireplace and study the map. As my eyes rove over it idly, something catches my attention. "Mordrenian Forest?" I whisper.

"Named after the nephew who slew him."

I turn to Morgana, whose eyes are now open, and fixed on the map. "But why —"

"Your father is a deeply sentimental man, in his own twisted way," she says tightly. "And he appreciates power, no matter the circumstances." She nods at the map. "Almost everything is named after something or someone from his past."

I turn to the map again, but nothing jumps out at me. She appears at my side, and points at a few cities. "Sagramore was one of his knights. Taliesin was a bard who sang of Arthur's triumphs far and wide. Eigyr is named for his mother."

I frown. "He said his mother's name was Egwene."

"He says a lot of things, Little One."

I make a small sound of understanding. He had said his father's name was Adelbern, after all. "That story about meeting my mother in college was all bullshit, wasn't it?"

She just nods.

I sigh. "So when he got to Tenazeryth, how did he take power and rename everything? Or wasn't there a ruler before?" I furrow my brow. "When *did* he get here, anyway?"

She pinches the bridge of her nose. "He didn't *get* here. He *created* here after he came to the so-called 'New World' to find a new home. He couldn't hold Camelot together forever; the world had changed around him, and he was searching for a new place to put down his roots. But once he got to North America, he realized there was nothing *new* about the place. There was nowhere on Earth left for him to go, unless he wanted to live with the penguins. So he created Tenazeryth. That was shortly after he possessed me, and of course he botched it. He didn't know how to do it properly, and he wasn't patient enough to research the correct way."

"So, wait. *Is* Tenazeryth its own dimension?" I ask for clarification.

She shakes her head ruefully. "He just created a faulty reflection and tethered it to Earth instead of creating a new pocket dimension, which would have been self-sustaining and stable."

I look out the window for a moment in thought. "That's why there's no cyclical climate here. It's not *real*. It's like a . . . mirror."

She nods and sits at the bar. "The metaphor isn't perfect, but more or less, you're right. It was summer when he created Tenazeryth, and it's been summer ever since. It's also why this place is dying at a faster rate. That 'mirror' intensifies everything. He's right about one thing: Earth is dying, and the effects of the changing climate are magnified here. Everything that happens to that Earth happens tenfold here. Tenazeryth's time is running out."

I frown. "But the effects of Earth's changing climate *is* the weather. Crazier storms, higher temperatures. Tenazeryth doesn't have weather to affect."

She nods patiently. "But that's not all that's happening. Humans don't have the ability to sense - or the technology to measure - what *else* they're doing, but it's happening all the same. And that's what is hurting Tenazeryth. Why it's withering away."

I cock an eyebrow at her. "What else are they doing?"

"Ripping holes in the fabric of their dimension," she says matter-of-factly.

I gape at her in horror, then shake my head. "So, what do we do? What do we *actually* do? How can we save it all?"

She looks back at me evenly for a moment. "I have no idea," she finally says.

I blanch. "If - when - we kill my father, what happens to Tenazeryth?"

She shrugs. "Hopefully nothing."

"*Hopefully?* If his magic is what's holding this place together —"

Her jaw is set. "Listen, Little One. Arthur has to die. That's all there is to it. If that means Tenazeryth dies with him, then so be it. That is not my main concern. My main concern is making him pay for the horrors he has wrought upon countless lives. Not least of all, mine." Her last sentence is low and venomous.

I shake my head in horror. "There are countless lives *here*. We can't just doom them so we can get our revenge. How does that make us better than him?"

She twists her mouth, and she suddenly seems very tired. "There are yet more lives on Earth that will be extinguished if we fail. Dooming them *all* would make us infinitely *worse* than him."

She conjures herself a plate of food. There are bits of bacon, onions, cockles, and fried green cakes.

"What is *that?*"

"Swansea," she says, before taking a bite. "Would you like a plate?"

I grimace. "I'm full, thanks."

She shrugs.

"Maybe . . . with our combined magic, we can save Tenazeryth. Maybe we can hold it together if we need to, and then, after he's dead, we can create a new dimension. A stable one."

Morgana doesn't look convinced, but she doesn't argue. "Perhaps, Little One. Perhaps."

I sigh and sip my coffee in silence. Five minutes go by in silence. Finally, I look back at Morgana, who is grinning at me. "What?"

"Congratulations, young Pendragon. You've passed Lesson One."

I tilt my head at her, then remember. *Patience.*

I smirk at her and push my stool away from the bar. "I'm a Shaw. What's Lesson Two?"

Lesson Two

"Bring your awareness to your navel. Feel your magic?" Morgana is perched on the log, cross-legged, with her eyes shut softly. She looks completely serene.

I shift against the bark of the log, poke the soft skin at my center, and try to focus on it. "I don't feel anything."

"It's there. You just have to find it."

I open my eyes. "Does it feel like a buzzing for you, too?"

She shakes her head gently, not opening her eyes. "Mine is a fire. It burns."

"Does it . . . hurt?"

"Yes, but no."

I make a thoughtful noise.

"Now focus. Activate your magic, and try to keep it on a low simmer."

"I . . . I can't activate it very easily. Only when I'm angry." I pick at the bark on the log some more. I'm quickly stripping it bare.

She opens her eyes at that. "Angry?"

I nod. "My father said that's how it activates. It's how it happened on its own, before I even knew I had magic."

She's silent for a long moment. "You're held captive by your emotions," she says. "They rule you."

I squint at her quizzically. "What else is there to be ruled by?"

She shakes her head at me, a small smile on her face. "So like your father."

I grit my teeth. "I wish you would stop saying that."

She chuckles. "Think of your goddess, Little One. Is *she* ruled by her emotions?"

"Of course she is," I reply automatically, but then I frown in thought. "Well, I mean . . . no. I guess not," I finish quietly. Kianga has a firm hold on her emotions; she always has. She's analytical, and cool-headed. She's never the one who needs held together as she sobs. She steps up and gets shit done.

"And your vampire?"

I scoff. "I didn't even know he *had* emotions for a long time." I cross my arms. "He pushed me away for months. Buried his emotions because he didn't want me to get hurt."

She nods. "Precisely. I could tell almost immediately that those two use their heads to get them through life. Not their hearts." She gestures at me. "You don't think. You feel. You feel *everything*. Too much. Your heart is forever on your sleeve, which is why it keeps getting hurt. Just like your father."

I huff. "I didn't know I was signing up to be psychoanalyzed."

"Well, you were," Morgana replies. "Your magic will never be under your control if you can only activate it based on feelings, especially *anger*. It will fester. You'll poison yourself from the inside out, just like him. You need balance. Use your *head*."

I grumble and shift again on the log. "I know how to use my head. I have a fucking Master's Degree."

She pinches the bridge of her nose. "Just because you have knowledge, doesn't mean you have any sense."

My jaw hangs open at that.

~~~~~~~~~~
~~~~~~~~~~

By midday, I have a massive headache. Funnily enough, changing the very way you operate is a taxing endeavor.

Morgana, to her credit, is endlessly patient with me. Far more patient, in fact, than I am with myself. Whenever I snap, she reassures me calmly.

"It's difficult work. If introspection was easy, the world would be a utopia. You don't have to be perfect at it immediately."

I grit my teeth as I shoot an angry blast at a dead tree. "I don't have a thousand years to hone my skills," I shout. "If I can't figure out how to control my magic, my father is going to win."

She walks up behind me and places her hands on my upper arms. "Breathe."

"If I breathe, I'm going to *feel*," I bite out.

"Eilidh, I didn't say to shut down *all* your emotions. I said you need *balance*."

"And I don't know what that *means*!" I cry out. "How can I pick and choose when to think and when to feel?"

She reaches up, and I flinch, thinking she's going to strike me, but she lays a warm hand on my cheek. I close my eyes.

"Breathe," she commands quietly.

I inhale shakily.

"Again." We go through this process several times.

"Now tell me what you're feeling."

"Angry," I bite out.

"Clearly. But with who?" She presses.

"Myself." I whisper.

She brings her other hand to my face. "Why? Because you're struggling today?"

I nod.

"And?" She probes. Her lilac gaze is knowing; it strips me bare. There's no hiding the truth from this woman.

So I don't.

"Because I couldn't save him." Tears instantly stream down over her hands, but she doesn't move away from me. "I wasn't strong enough."

Her eyes are full of pity. I shut mine again. I don't want her pity.

"When did you start feeling like you had to be the one to fix everyone around you?"

"I don't. I just wanted to save *him*."

"*Just* him?" She asks.

"Yes." I say firmly. "Just him."

She releases me, and takes a step back. "Alright. Then run back to your goddess."

I blink. "I — what?"

"Well, he's gone," she says simply. My eye twitches. "So, if that's all you wanted to do, then there's no point in continuing. We can just let your father do as he pleases."

She strides away from me. "Run along."

"Morgana, *stop*."

She halts in her tracks.

"I get it." She turns back toward me, and I spread my arms wide. "Everyone, okay? Everyone."

She tilts her head at me. "When?"

I look away from her, shaking my head slowly, and swallow hard. "I was four."

She crosses her arms.

"I . . . I hid my mom's liquor bottles in my bed, underneath my stuffed animals. I didn't even know what the bottles were, but I knew when she drank from them, that she . . . she would get sad." I wipe away a tear viciously. "And then when she got sad, she would cry, and then she'd go to bed, and I wouldn't see her until the next day."

I sniff. "She got mad instead, but that was okay. I could handle a few slaps. Because at least she was *there*."

A look I can't interpret flashes across Morgana's face, but then it's replaced with neutral curiosity once more. "And then?"

I grit my teeth. "And then I was six, and the most recent piece of trash she brought home hit her, so I grabbed a kitchen knife." I look up at the sky. "He . . . he just laughed at me, and locked me in a closet. Then he got bored and left, but not before busting out our fucking window."

It had been the middle of winter, and in New York, that's no fucking joke. At least, it hadn't been back then, back when several feet of snow was typical. I take a shuddering breath. "And then she drank herself into a stupor, and forgot to let me out until the next day."

Morgana takes a few steps toward me. "And then?" She asks quietly.

I rake my nails into my hair, and hold my head in my hands. "And then I was eight, and she was dropping me off with my grandparents. She told me that she needed to get better, that she'd come back for me when she did. And I never saw her again."

Morgana puts her hands on my shoulders.

"I wasn't strong enough. I couldn't fix her. I couldn't make her *want* to stay for me. I wasn't enough for her to want to get better. And then over and over again, I lost the people I loved. I was *never* strong enough."

Morgana looks up into my eyes sadly and presses a finger to my forehead. "You've gotten your feelings out. Now what is your head telling you?"

"That it wasn't my fault," I recite quietly.

"And your heart is still telling you it was."

I nod against her finger.

She sighs.

Conduits

The next day, after I try several more unsuccessful attempts to spark my magic while calm, Morgana stalks into the cottage, and I kick a log in anger. When she reemerges, she's carrying Excalibur and my dagger. *Holy shit, is she going to stab me?*

But she just tosses Excalibur on the ground at my feet. I yelp and pick it up, brushing the dirt from the scabbard. "What the fuck?"

"Draw your blade."

I loop the belt around my hips and roll my eyes at her. "You have my blade," I say, nodding at the dagger in her hands.

She puts her hands on her hips. "This is *my* dagger, actually," she says in a clipped voice.

I nearly cut my own thigh as I unsheathe Excalibur. "*Yours?*"

She nods. "Your father gave it to me. Before he . . . changed." She caresses the wolf on the pommel. "It used to be dragons," she says quietly.

"I'm so—" She give me a sharp look, and I clamp my mouth shut. She looks at me for another moment, then gestures at Excalibur. "For training, *that* is your blade. It's yours anyway, if it called to you as you say."

I glance at the legendary sword in my right hand. It suddenly feels significantly heavier. "But I'm not good with a sword," I mumble.

"You don't have to be. It's more than just a blade; it's a conduit."

I breathe deeply as my energy saps out of my right hand into the hilt. "A conduit?"

"For your magic." She holds my - *her* - dagger in the air. "Agrona." Morgana's voice rings through the trees.

The dagger lights up, purple flames licking all around the blade, burning far above her head.

I gasp and take a single step back. "What in the *world?*"

"That's her name," Morgana says, and the flames disappear in an instant. She slides the dagger into the holster and wraps it around her thigh; she has to wind the belt around twice to get it to fit her slim leg.

"I . . . I didn't know that. I never got it to do *that.*" I pat Excalibur's hilt. "But . . . *this* does something similar when I say its name."

She nods. "When a Witch holds an instrument that is theirs - *truly* theirs - they can use it as a conduit for their magic. Saying the name isn't necessary all the time, but it can help focus the power."

I frown. "Saif's blade never did anything like that." He had held *Dhabiha* and said her name plenty of times, but no greenery had ever sprung up around the curved blade.

"He was a Mage, not a Warlock." She says this as if it's obvious.

I squint at her. "Is there a difference?"

She puffs out her cheeks and exhales loudly. "He only had one type of power?"

"Yes, he could control plants, but I don't —"

"That's the difference." She stops pacing. "Merlin was a Warlock; his power came from his gemstone, and he could do . . . just about anything. You'll be able to, as well, eventually. You could even heal those scars of yours."

She gestures at my left shoulder, which I grab protectively. "No," I blurt.

When she just raises a brow at me, I struggle to find the right words. "They're . . . part of me." How many hours had Saif spent tending to them? How many times had he kissed them? He had loved me despite my scars — all of them.

She shrugs. "Fine. Anyway, your father, when he fused the stone with himself, became a Warlock as well. But he's the only one left."

She grins wickedly. "And now, he's outnumbered by Witches."

I make a mental note to discuss the illusion of the gender binary with her later as I look at her tattooed fingertips. "So what about you? Where does your power come from?"

She places one hand gently on her abdomen, and examines the tattoos on the other. "I've made countless sacrifices in my long life, Little One. I gave up something I had always wanted for the power I could not otherwise have. It was . . . just another sacrifice."

A beat passes. "Okay," I say quietly, not wanting to press the issue.

She nods. "Now, unsheathe your blade, and hold it tightly. Focus all your energy into it."

I do.

"Now, release your magic into it. Be angry if you need to at first, but then, see if you can calm yourself, and maintain your hold on the magic."

I try to calmly reach into myself and coax my magic out, like the scared kitten I had lured out from under the bleachers in the gymnasium at school last year. Some first-grader had hidden her new companion in her backpack, and had promptly lost it.

Focus, Shaw. I shake the memory away, and take a deep breath, trying to activate the buzzing in my navel.

Nothing happens. I clench my jaw. *This is never going to fucking work.*

The buzzing kick-starts, travels up my torso, and down my arm. Excalibur begins glowing.

"Perfect," Morgana encourages me. "Now calm yourself, but hold the magic. Sink your claws into it."

What the fuck does that mean?

I breathe deeply. The magic falters for a moment, and my heart sinks. But then, it's as if Excalibur and I share a feedback loop; the energy that had drained away from me into the blade suddenly rushes back into me, and I in turn pump more into the blade. Sparks erupt from the tip, and I hold it aloft.

Morgana cries out triumphantly. "Yes! Exactly like that!" She points to a log about twenty yards away. "Slice the air toward that log. Break it!"

Wielding a sword after six months of getting used to a dagger is proving impossible, at least for me.

I do the only thing I can think of to get a good swipe with the sword — I swing it like a bat at the log. A blast of magic shoots out from Excalibur's sharp edge as I slice the air, and the log splits cleanly in two.

I scream in shock, and Morgana clenches her fists in excitement. "Yes!" She turns to me, and pulls Agrona from the holster on her thigh. "Now, fight!"

"Wha—" She leaps, bringing the dagger at my chest. I yelp and bring Excalibur up instinctively with two hands, just managing to parry her blow. "What the *fuck*?" I yell.

But she pays me no mind; she moves in a flurry of motion, her long hair and sleeves whipping around her. She comes at me again, poised to slash me across the face. I once again act on pure instinct; my self-preservation alone prevents me from getting another scar. Although, with being so off-balance, I fall with the force of blocking her blow.

"Don't worry about being a master swordswoman," she commands, pacing around me like a lion about to pounce on a downed gazelle.

I stand and shake myself out.

"You aren't going to beat anyone with your blade skills alone; least of all your father. He's cut through platoons single-handedly, and that was before he had Merlin's magic. Remember: Excalibur is a conduit, not just a blade. Use it to its full potential."

She lunges at me again. This time, I don't try to maneuver around her or get my foot placement just right. I simply raise the blade toward her, and snarl, *"Back!"*

A blast of my magic shoots out of the end of the blade, and crashes into Morgana. She flies through the air, dropping Agrona, and lands in a heap next to the cottage.

"Shit!" I drop Excalibur in the dirt and rush to her side. I roll her onto her back as soon as I drop to her side. "Morgana, are you —?"

She's smiling up at me brilliantly.

I stare down at her in shock. "What?" I sit back on my heels, panting.

She sits up, grabs both of my cheeks, and brings our foreheads together. "I'm so proud of you."

Secret's Out

That night, I curl up in my bed with Saif's diary for the first time since his death. It takes me a considerable amount of time to build up the courage to put it on my lap, and even longer to actually open it. The entry I flip to is the night of my second full moon as a werewolf.

Well, the secret's out, although I'm not sure it was ever really a secret — it's only been a few days, after all, since we . . .

And anyway, the Peñas already knew how I feel. Martín has been teasing me for weeks, and elbows me every time he catches me staring at Eilidh when she isn't looking.

Like I can help it. How could I not stare? Watching the way she takes every challenge head-on, no matter what. She's like a wildfire that refuses to be put out; she just burns every hurdle down on her way to victory. She's unstoppable. She's glorious. It makes Diego furious.

It makes me love her even more.

I wasn't sure she would want anyone to know about us, but she held my hand today like she was proud to be doing so. We had a wonderful day at the beach, and she never once seemed embarrassed or shy. In fact, she was quite the opposite at one point. I could have taken her clothes off and made love to her there on that boulder. Truthfully, Val did me a favor when she doused us — I was in desperate need of a cold shower.

There are a few lines of Arabic after that which I skip, making a mental note to find someone soon who can translate it for me. He continues in English on the next page.

I miss her. She's only been gone for an hour, and I miss her like I haven't seen her in weeks. It's like my heart doesn't function correctly when she isn't around. Like she's the flame that keeps it beating.

She's out in the greenhouse with Diego now. She wanted me to be with her tonight, and he was only too happy to explain why I'm not able to be. Cocky bastard.

I wish I could have taken a picture of the look on his face when Martin made the scimitar joke, or when Eilidh kissed me goodbye. He can try to mask his emotions on his face all he wants; those ruby eyes of his scream all his thoughts loud and clear. They always have.

I emit a small laugh as I wipe my tears. *You idiot. If you had just let go of your anger, you'd have realized what you really felt for him.*

Two sides of the same fiery coin.

Staring that deeply into someone's eyes is not exactly annoying coworker behavior. Much more rivals to lovers. Maybe they could have had a few years of happiness together, if they had just had a single honest conversation with one another.

I close the book gently and hug it to my chest as I roll onto my side. I want to read more, but I also don't want to get through it too quickly. There's an entry for every day, but that still isn't enough.

He won't get to write any more entries. Once I'm done with it, it will truly feel like he's gone. I'm not ready for that.

I won't ever be ready for that.

I set my jaw firmly. *And I won't ever have to be.*

He'll be back.

Dreams Part 3

I am on fire.

The tears that stream down my cheeks after she tells me she loves him burn my skin like lava. Her smile dampens the flames, but only just. She's happy, and for that, at least, I am grateful.

But then, he tells me that she's gone, and every time I look at him, I burn with rage.

The conflagration wants to consume him, and I desperately want to let it.

Just as it's consuming me.

~ Third Quarter ~

Whatever it Takes

"Focus," Morgana instructs as she shoots a fireball at me.

I attempt to sink my claws into it, as she has been telling me to do for the last few days. I slice Excalibur at the burst of purple flame like a butterfly net. The flame extinguishes entirely.

I groan. "I'm trying."

"Try harder." She flings a larger flame at me. "Sink your claws in and redirect the energy back at me."

I tense my jaw and try to snare the fire with my magic. For one second, it feels like I did it. I can feel my magic close around something tangible inside the flame. But then an explosion of magenta lights up the air around us.

My feedback loop with Excalibur shuts off like a switch has been thrown, and I collapse to my knees. *"Fuck!"*

Morgana pads over and drops to the ground beside me. "You did it, Little One. You're almost ready."

I shake my head and pant; I'm utterly drained. "I thought I did, but apparently not." I wipe sweat from my brow.

She puts a hand on my shoulder. "You *did* do it. It was only a moment, but you managed. You'll get better."

I throw myself back on the ground, and glare up at the sky.

"What's troubling you?" Morgana lies down beside me, folding her hands on her stomach.

I snort. "What *isn't* troubling me?" I bite.

She makes a thoughtful noise. "If it makes you feel better, your father isn't on the move. I'd be able to sense if he were."

I look at her from the corner of my eye. "That does make me feel a little better, I guess. But if you can sense him, can he sense you? Does he know we're working together?" Worry grips my stomach.

"No," she says quickly. "Your father's magic is much stronger. It creates ripples in the world that are impossible to ignore. You'll feel them too, after you're close enough to sense them for the first time. The small amounts of power I'm using aren't enough to sense more than a few dozen miles away. "

She calls what she's doing small? A shiver runs through me. "Can you sense me?"

She nods. "Of course I can. You're stronger than me."

I grimace at that. "How is he so much more powerful than you? How the hell am I?"

She frowns. "Your father siphoned my magic from me constantly through the last five centuries. What he couldn't use for himself, he dampened. I'm still working on digging it back up."

I scratch into the dirt for a moment. "Is that what you're doing when you're meditating? Trying to . . . dig up your magic?"

She nods. "I'm recovering it bit by bit, but it would be a long time before I could get it all back."

I frown. "'Would?'"

She blinks. "Will," she says quickly. "It *will* be a long time."

I sit straight up. "Morgana."

One corner of her mouth lifts. "Yes, Little One?"

"What does that mean?"

She doesn't look at me.

I shake my head. "Your magic *will* come back eventually. You *will* be here to get it back. *Right?*" My voice crackles.

She sits up and sighs. "Eilidh. I'm prepared to do whatever it takes to beat your father. No matter what."

"What are you *talking* about?" I hiss.

"He's the most powerful Warlock in the world, but he's not invincible. You have raw power, and I'm trying to help you mold it. Your power, combined with my experience and ability, will be able to reverse the resurrection spell."

"Yes, that was always the plan. For us to win. Together."

She nods. "And the power that will take, the power that you have, that I will have to channel . . . is probably going to kill me."

I shake my head. "Then I'm not doing it."

Her eyes narrow. "Yes, you will," she says icily. "We're going to win, and you're going to live happily ever after."

"Morgana," I whisper. "We . . . we'll figure something out. Another way."

She stands. "Stop. There *is* no other way."

I look up at her, stricken.

She takes a deep breath, and places a hand on my shoulder. "I'll do what I must, Little One. Your father will be defeated. Don't worry about anything other than that."

For what seems like an eternity after she goes back into the cottage, I lie on the ground, silently staring at the darkening sky. The moon is mostly dark tonight; I'll be getting no advice from her.

Grim determination fills me. If Morgana thinks I'm going to let another person sacrifice themselves for me, she's out of her fucking mind.

No, when the time comes, I'll make sure she lives, one way or another. Whatever it takes.

And after my father is dead, she's going to help me bring Saif back.

Crush (Diego)

Valentina's doe eyes are the first things I see when I open the bedroom door. "Hey, Boss," she says in a small voice.

"Hey, kid. How are you doing?" I step back and gesture for her to come in. Imane spins around from her computer, her expression severe with concentration.

Val hesitates. "I can come back later if it's a bad time."

Imane realizes she's glaring, and plasters a smile on her face. "No, you're fine. Valentina, right?" She stands and crosses the room to us. She knows Val's name, but she's trying to put her at ease.

Val glances up at me, and I smile reassuringly. She squares her shoulders as Imane reaches us. "Yes ma'am."

Imane looks her up and down. "How are my Water Mages behaving for you? Not giving you any grief, I hope?"

Val shakes her head. "No, they're all great. And the Fire Mages have all taken to Martín, too."

Imane nods. "Good, I'm glad to hear it."

A beat passes. Imane blinks a few times, clearly anxious to get back to the computer, where she's been corresponding with a dozen different rebels, and overseeing the transport of the army to New Camlann on wyvernback.

Tempest had sent word a few days ago that Balin has finally defected — with the promise of Eilidh taking the throne once Arthur is dead.

That will be a fight for another day.

Imane has been in overdrive since then, her body taught with stress. In two days, under the light of the full moon, we're making our move.

"What did you need, Val?" I ask gently.

She clears her throat. "I just wanted to ask about Eilidh. How she's doing with . . . everything. She hasn't spoken to me since —" She glances at a pothos that Saif had hung from the ceiling, and swallows hard. "Since the battle," she finishes in a whisper.

Imane winces, and we exchange a look.

I've got this. You go back to work.

"I'll let you two talk." She squeezes Val's shoulder firmly, and goes back to the desk.

I nod toward the door. "Let's take a walk."

Valentina and I wander around the top floor of the pyramid as we talk. "How's she doing with that Le Fey woman?" She asks, hugging herself as we stroll.

"Well, nothing else has exploded yet, so I think she's getting a handle on her magic, at least."

She chuckles weakly. "That's good. And that succubus . . ." She taps her fingers on her arm nervously.

I raise an eyebrow. *I think Valentina might have a crush.* "Zaehora. What about her?"

Val clears her throat. "She seems . . . nice. For watching out for Eilidh."

I snort. "Yeah, she is." A pain in the ass, certainly, but nice, nonetheless.

She shakes herself. "Anyway, that's all. I just wanted to ask how she's doing."

I furrow my brow. "Why didn't you just ask her yourself?"

At that, she stops and leans heavily on the barrier, looking down at the ground floor. "We got him killed," she rasps. Tears spring to her eyes instantly, and I put a hand on her back.

My heart aches in my chest, and it takes me a moment to keep my own tears at bay. "You didn't, Val. Arthur's the only one to blame."

She just shakes her head.

I take a deep breath. I don't know if there's technically an Order anymore, but she's still my responsibility nonetheless. "Valentina."

She inhales shakily, but meets my stern gaze.

"You and Martín are *not* responsible for what happened to him. *¿Tu me entiendes?* Arthur came here for blood. S—" My voice cracks. I can't even say his name, or I'll break. I clear my throat. "He knew the risks. We all did." She nods, though I can tell she isn't fully convinced.

My phone makes a screeching noise in my pocket. "*¿Qué carajo?*" I pull it out and read the text from Hyun-Joo that she got held up with the archers, but that she'd meet me in the cafeteria for lunch later. "Wish this thing would stop yelling at me," I mutter.

Valentina's mouth tilts in a small smile. "Put it on silent."

I examine the cold brick in my hand. "How?"

"Here." She flips a small switch on one side of it and hands it back just as another text comes through, and it buzzes in my palm.

"You're a lifesaver, Val."

She sighs. "Maybe I *should* just go talk to Eilidh myself."

I pull her into a hug, and she clings to me tightly. "I think that would be a good idea. She's at the Witch's cottage right now. And Zaehora is with her," I say teasingly.

I feel her heartbeat quicken against me, and she pulls back, bouncing on her toes. "Oh. Good. I mean, whatever, that's fine."

I send her on her way with a small smile, then head back into the bedroom, where Imane is knocking back a mug of coffee.

"*Tesoro,* you need some water."

"There's water in coffee," she responds without looking at me, typing furiously.

I grab a glass and pour her a water from the cold pitcher on the beverage cart that always magically fills itself back up. "Drink." I set the glass on her desk and pop a metal straw into it.

She growls, but does as she's told. When she sets the glass back down, I begin rubbing her tense shoulders. "How's it going?"

She rattles off which squads have checked in at their various destinations around New Camlann, and which have yet to.

"When's the next Council check-in?"

She glances at the clock. "In forty minutes."

"Hmm." I lean down and plant a long kiss in the crook of her neck. "Long time."

She purrs against me. "Is it?" She puts her hand into my hair and tugs gently.

"Let's find out." I scoop her up from the chair, but not before she snatches something out of a drawer. I carry her to the bed and lay her down. "What's that?"

She hesitates a moment, then opens her palm. The birth control device glints up at me, and I pause. "Oh. *Oh*, of course."

"Just to be safe," she says quietly.

I nod, and take it from her. I don't mean to clutch it so tightly that the edges dig into my skin, but when my hand begins to ache, I realize that I am.

She's searching my gaze, and I refuse to look away, as much as I want to. "I know we . . . before, we said we would. . . but now . . ."

Now, it's years later, and the entire world is in chaos, and we might not even make it to see tomorrow, let alone nine months from now. Now, we can't try for a child like we had decided we would do once the werecat was dead.

How many times had we planned everything out, all those years ago? A thousand times, at least. We would finish the mission, then come home, and get married. We would start trying.

We were going to live happily ever after.

"It's okay, *mi amor*," I whisper, kissing her tenderly. "We'll have time."

She swallows hard, but nods. I lean in and kiss her deeply, trying to convey how much I love her, how much she means to me. I'll never be able to, not for as long as she lives. But I'll keep trying, as long as she draws breath.

I remove her clothes slowly, planting long kisses up and down her body until she's writhing underneath me. She moans my name, and my cock throbs. I take my own clothes off, and she licks her lips as she watches. I pull her into another kiss while I apply the magical barrier to myself.

She clutches my neck, gasping softly as I enter her. I move my hips in a circular motion, making sure I slide against her clit with each long thrust. She alternates moaning my name, and whispering curses as I keep my pace steady for her.

I could make love to this woman for the rest of my life, if only I could. "I love you so much," I rumble in her ear, and she makes a delighted noise.

"I love you too, *corazón*."

I glance at the clock. She's got thirty minutes left until her meeting.

I pull out slowly, with a groan, and kiss my way down her body. When my tongue hits her clit, she gasps and grabs a handful of my hair. I moan against her, and she trembles. I lose myself in her, listen to her moaning as her pleasure mounts, then finally crests. She squeezes my head with her thighs, and I have to fight for control of myself before I come as well.

I don't make my way back up her body until she's come another time. By the time I slide my cock in her again, she's completely unraveled, and I'm not far behind.

She's five minutes late to her meeting.

~ Full Moon ~

Rebellion

Kianga and I embrace tightly. "I love you," she whispers.

I inhale shakily. "I love you, too."

She presses her forehead to mine. "Be careful. I believe in you."

"You too," I murmur. "Command the hell out of that army."

She emits a laugh that turns into a sob. "I will. Kick your dad's ass."

I chuckle silently against her. She kisses my forehead and takes a step back.

Diego pulls me into his arms, lifting me off the ground. I wrap my arms around his neck and clutch him tightly.

"I love you, *mi sol*. I know can do this. Come back to me."

I squeeze my eyes shut as tightly as I can to hold the tears back. "I love you, too. Be careful."

He sets me back on the ground and smirks. "When have I ever not been careful?"

I chuckle and wipe my eyes. He and Kianga walk toward the Council and the Order, who are dressed in their battle suits like Diego. Kianga is once again in full goddess regalia, and I am in the outfit she had given me to wow the rebellion — except for the cape.

I turn to Morgana, and she stares back at me intensely. Her jaw is set, and she looks as flawless as ever. "Are you ready, Little One?"

My stomach clenches, and my heart beats like a wild animal against my rib cage. I take a deep breath and dig my heels into the grass. "Yes," I say finally.

She nods. "Good. You can do this. We will win. I promise." She takes my hand and I squeeze it tightly.

We crest the hill together, and I look up at the moon. Her beams cup my cheeks, energizing me. *Victory awaits you, Daughter.*

"I sure hope you're right," I whisper.

A Storm Mage shoots a blast of lightning high into the sky above Arkenvale. An earth-shaking roar of thunder follows almost instantaneously.

Chaos ensues.

Our army pours from every direction over the hills surrounding the castle and rushes toward it. Kianga, Diego, the Council, and the Order lead the charge. For one fleeting second, I think perhaps we really have taken him by surprise, and we can storm the castle easily.

But my father was ready for us. Of course he was. Whether he was prepared to bring them himself, or if we had sprung some kind of trap, cyclones appear everywhere between us and the castle, depositing hundreds of Fabled and other magical creatures. There are more than there had been before.

The armies clash like Titans.

"Draw him out," Morgana says.

I nod, lift Excalibur into the air, and cry its name. Lightning surges from the end and crashes into the east tower. The glass shatters and cascades to the ground, glittering like a waterfall in the moonlight.

"Very good. I imagine it won't be long now. Keep your eyes open." She turns in a circle and glances up at the sky for good measure.

The seconds crawl by. The battle rages in front of us as we wait for my father to appear.

He doesn't.

Before a minute passes, I start fidgeting. "Where is he?" I hiss.

"Patience," she soothes me. "He knows you're eager for the fight. He wants you to come to him."

I grit my teeth as I watch soldiers laying their life on the line on the field in front of me. "We can't wait forever," I growl.

"And we won't. Breathe. Remember where your impatience comes from. He won't resist us long."

The battle rages before us. I pick out the ones I love in the crowd. Diego and Kianga fight back to back, him paralyzing The Fabled with his bite, and her shifting back and forth to alternate between her ax and her claws to deal her blows.

To my left, a towering vortex of combined flame and water rips across the field — Valentina and Martín.

I spot Hyun-Joo in the midst of other Mages who can create force fields. She molds one of hers into a bow and arrow, and shoots at an ogre, knocking them out cold.

Another agonizing minute passes. Our army is holding fast, and doing their best not to use lethal force, but they can't stop everything. Blood begins to seep into the ground.

I clench my fist, digging my nails deeply into my palm.

"Morgana we have to —"

She collapses to the ground.

"Morgana!" I drop to my knees beside her, and shake her.

She groans and opens her eyes. "He's here."

Then I feel him, too. The hairs on my arms stand on end. Electricity crackles through the air. I look at the sky and back to her, panicked. "Are you okay?"

"I'm fine." She grits her teeth and pulls herself up by clutching at my corset. "He's trying to get into my head."

My eyes widen farther than I thought possible. "You can hold him off, right?"

She rakes her long nails into her hair. "Yes," she finally pants.

I pull her to her feet, but I'm afraid to let go of her once she's standing. "Are you sure?"

"She's not. I can hear her doubt."

I whip around to see my father grinning at us. I open my mouth to retort, but Morgana isn't wasting time on mind games and petty quips. Still holding me tightly with one hand, fire suddenly explodes from her other, and flies toward my father like a meteor.

He disappears in a whirlwind a split second before her flames engulf the spot where he stood. He appears twenty feet to the side, looking, for the first time since I've known him, *rattled*. But it only lasts a moment before his face twists in rage.

"You're letting her siphon your strength?" He spits at me.

I sneer. "It's over, Arthur. You can't beat us both."

She shoots another blast at him, somehow faster than the last. He throws up a shield at the last moment, but it explodes with the force of our combined power.

"Eilidh, don't hold back," Morgana hisses. "Let go."

Like hell.

There is true fear in his eye when the magic dissipates.

I bark a laugh. Maybe Morgana won't be in danger, after all, if he's already frightened. With the work we've been doing for the last few weeks, combined with moon radiating above, I haven't even broken a sweat yet.

His eye narrows. "I wasn't going to stoop to this. I have standards, after all. But you leave me no choice."

"What are you talk— *fuck*!" He's already teleported. "Where did he go?" I growl.

"There!" Morgana points toward the castle, where he has just appeared on the front steps. "Let's end this," she says grimly.

I search her lilac eyes once more then nod. "Okay."

We rush together toward the castle. I create a barrier around us, and she blasts The Fabled with weak stunning spells. We're both doing the minimum to conserve as much energy as possible.

We're about halfway to the front door of the castle when my father's voice booms throughout the field. "You know, a father's love is a very precious thing."

Every one of his soldiers stops moving instantly, mid-motion. It takes a beat, but then ours halt as well, glancing around warily.

"What?" I murmur. *What the fuck is he talking about?*

"It is something that no one who does not have children could ever possibly understand. What a father wouldn't do for his child."

"How do I yell like that?" I ask Morgana. She raises her palm to me, taps my throat, and takes a step back, covering her ears.

"You're not exactly Father of the Year." My voice echoes across the field as well, as if I'm holding an invisible megaphone. "You tried to have me murdered. Twice!"

"We all make mistakes, my dear," he replies with a wave of his hand. "Parents included. Although you know that better than most, don't you?"

I clench my jaw. "What are you wasting your breath for? I'm not going to forgive you for everything you've done. Nothing you say can make me stop."

His chuckle reverberates throughout the field, and I shiver. "Perhaps not, Daughter. But you're not the only one who's here to kill me, are you?"

I glance at Morgana, but he continues before I can reply.

"No, my First Paladin is here to kill me as well."

I furrow my brow. *Diego?* "And we're going to succeed," I bite out.

"What price would you be willing to pay to see me defeated?"

"Anything," I snap.

He cackles madly. "That may be, but what price do you think *he* would be willing to pay?"

I growl, and it rumbles over the hills. "Anything!" I yell, beginning to stalk toward him once more. *Fuck this.*

"I'm afraid, my dear, that you're mistaken. There are a few things that I know he would be unwilling to sacrifice to beat me today."

Morgana shakes her head at me as we walk, but I can't resist. "And what would those be?"

"One of them is you, dear girl, since he's been smitten with you since you first arrived here. Lucky for him, I wouldn't dream of disposing of you at this point. I've invested far too much in you. You've proven that you will be useful, once you figure out it's not worth fighting me."

"A shame you've never heard of the sunk-cost fallacy," I sneer. "What would the other thing be?"

I'm close enough now to see his face twist in a sadistic sneer as he waves a hand. A whirlwind appears beside him and dissipates, leaving behind something that takes me a second to process.

He's holding a young woman aloft, suspended in a cage of magic that undulates with rippling energy.

She's got deep tan skin, and glossy chestnut hair tied back in a long ponytail, secured by a white headband. She's wearing an oversized blue shirt and gray athletic shorts, like she had been plucked from the gym.

I can see, even from this distance, that her narrowed eyes are filled with fury; she glares at my father like she would strangle him if she were free. There is not a trace of fear in her expression. Her face, though, gives me pause. There's something about her that looks familiar, but I've certainly never seen her before.

I tilt my head at the absurd scene in front of me. *Who the fuck is that?* I shake myself. "Do you really think a damsel in distress is going to make me stop?"

He throws back his head and laughs. "No, my dear, it won't stop you. But it will stop *him*."

I cross my arms at him defiantly. "And how —"

"Daniela!" Diego's scream echoes across the field without any magical enhancement.

My blood freezes. *Oh, no.*

Exchange

"Who is that?" Morgana asks quietly. She raises a palm to my throat again and removes the volume-enhancing spell.

"Diego's daughter," I rasp.

Morgana's eyes widen and she turns back toward the scene unfolding in front of us. "Oh, dear," she murmurs.

I see Diego emerge from a line of Fabled and run toward my father. "Let her go!" He snarls.

Electricity explodes throughout the cage. Daniela's piercing scream breaks me out of my frozen stupor.

I begin sprinting as Diego screeches to a halt. He snatches the back of my suit as I try to run past him. *"Stop!"*

I stare at him, wide-eyed as the electricity coursing through the cage finally stops. Daniela's scream cuts off instantly as she collapses.

"You see, my dear?" My father's voice is no longer magically enhanced, but we're close enough, and the field is silent enough, that we can hear him perfectly fine. "A father's love is a very precious thing."

I've never seen Diego look the way he does right now. Fear, hatred, rage, helplessness, and nausea all flash across his face as he stares at me, still holding me tightly. "You can't," he rasps.

I shake my head at him. "I can save her —"

"You can't, you naive child. If either of you - or anyone else - take another step toward me, the girl dies. And I promise, it will not be quick."

Daniela rises slowly to her elbows. "Fuck you," she spits.

My father eyes her with a chuckle. "I see she has your fighting spirit, Diego. She would make a wonderful addition to the Order. Perhaps you ought to turn her."

Daniela scrunches her nose. "Turn me to wh—"

"*¡Daniela, cállate!*" Diego yells, his voice cracking with fear.

She yells back at him in Spanish, and he shakes his head silently. She turns to me, and repeats herself in English. "Tell me what's happening!"

I open my mouth, but Arthur doesn't give me the chance to speak. "What's happening, Miss Vidales, is that your father has been selfish. I took him in when he had no one else. He would have died alone in the desert if not for me. I gave him a new life, and a purpose, and he betrayed me."

Daniela looks back and forth between Diego, Arthur, and me. I shake my head at her, hoping she understands. What she says, however, nearly knocks me off my feet. It does, in fact, send Diego to his knees. "Being selfish is what he's best at."

Arthur makes a sadistically delighted noise. He's enjoying himself, getting off on the pain he's causing.

"Let the girl go, Arthur." Morgana says calmly as she steps up beside me.

He sneers. "No, I don't think I will, my love."

She bares her teeth. "I am *not* —"

"Take me instead."

I shake myself. Surely, I had not just heard Diego say that. But he's slowly climbing to his feet, his face grim and determined. "Let my daughter go, unharmed, and take me instead."

I gape at him, but he doesn't look at me. "Diego, you can't —"

"Deal." Arthur waves a hand, and the cage around Daniela dissolves immediately. With another swift gesture, he flings her toward us. Diego catches her easily, then squeezes her tightly, and sets her on the ground beside me.

She tries to pull away, but he plants a firm kiss on her head. "This is Eilidh. Go with her. She'll keep you safe."

Daniela looks at me, anger blazing in her deep brown eyes. She's a few inches taller than me, and the way she looks down her nose at me makes me feel even shorter.

I look from her to Diego, blinking back tears. "No, *please*," I step toward him, and he steps back.

"I'm sorry, *mi sol*." His jaw is set.

"Come, Diego. Now." My father gestures, and Diego is pulled by an invisible chain. He flies through the air and crashes to my father's feet, and I scream.

"*No!*"

Morgana clutches my arm; I hadn't even realized that I had begun to run for them.

"I can't force you to stand with me, Daughter." My father sneers at me cruelly. "But I can make sure you won't stop me. If you make one more move, he will be joining Saif."

My vision flashes red, and I tremble with rage as sparks explode around me. Morgana hisses in pain, but she doesn't release me. My nails begin to elongate into claws, digging into the flesh of my palms. Warm blood drips from my hands into the grass. Diego can't move; he just kneels at my father's feet. Morgana's grip tightens on my left arm, warping the ivy leaves around her fingers.

Suddenly, I hear Kianga behind me. "Eilidh."

I turn to her. Her mask has been discarded, and she's staring at me. *Everyone* is staring at me. The Council is not far behind Kianga; all their gazes bore into me as well.

Behind them, the Peñas are gaping in horror between me and Diego. Several of the other Mages have put Hyun-Joo in a literal bubble of magic to keep her back. She slams a shoulder against it, and though it flickers, it doesn't break.

Zaehora has one arm around Tempest, whose face is streaked with tears as she thrashes ferociously against the succubus, to no avail. Zaehora's other hand is clamped firmly over Tempest's mouth, muffling her screams.

My eyes widen. I realize that everyone is waiting for me to make a decision.

The world stops spinning.

I look to Kianga once more. "What do we do?"

Daniela takes a menacing step toward me. "You can start by getting my dad away from that motherfu—"

Suddenly, a purple strip of magic covers her mouth, and though she tries to claw it off, her fingers pass right through it. I turn to Morgana, who is lowering her hand; she's finally released me. "Where should I send her? Tell me, and then we'll finish this."

I gape at her. "We can't finish anything — he'll kill Diego."

Mòrag scoffs. "What will it be, pup? Will you help us save the world? Or will you throw away everything this rebellion has worked toward for years for one man? Surely even you cannot be so selfish."

Her words from what feels like a lifetime ago echo through my head. *Chaos and blood.*

I glare at her for a moment, then turn back to Kianga. She looks, for the first time ever, at a loss, like she doesn't know what to do. Her eyes dart back and forth between the army she built over the last decade of her life, and Diego. Her wide eyes hold no answer for me. Suddenly, I know exactly what she'll choose if I let her think about it too long.

And then I will have lost all three of them.

Like hell.

I look at Morgana, who takes a step back. The Witch purses her lips and raises her chin at me. Her jaw is set; she knows what I chose. "Don't make me take the magic from you unwillingly, Eilidh."

I shake my head at her faintly.

My father chuckles behind me. "Oh dear, it seems you two are not on the same page."

Morgana closes her eyes in consternation and sighs heavily.

"No." My voice is steady. "I won't let you. I've lost too much already."

When she opens her eyes again, they're glowing. "I'm sorry, Little O—"

She doesn't get the chance to finish her sentence. I don't have to think about what to do; my heart controls my actions. I twirl my hand in the air, and the entirety of both armies disappears in whirling cyclones, along with her and Daniela. They will all be back at Tal Basta in another moment.

I raise Excalibur with my right hand and cry its name. Lightning explodes from the tip, and a rust-colored bubble expands all around Arkenvale. Nothing, and no one, is getting in or out of here. Not while I'm alive.

I collapse to the ground, utterly drained, and only then do I register that Kianga is clutching my left arm. "No," I hiss at her as my vision flickers. "You were supposed to go with them. You aren't supposed to be here."

She pulls me tight. "I'm not leaving you again."

"How touching." Arthur shoots a blast of magic at Kianga.

She collapses, and I scream.

Legendary

"*K*ianga!" I shake her vigorously. For a split-second, it's Saif's body in my arms again. I can practically feel his blood caking under my fingernails. Adrenaline pulses through me. *"Please!"*

"Really, Eilidh, calm yourself." Arthur almost sounds bored.

"I'll fucking kill you!" I'm just about to shift when Kianga grabs my wrist.

"Eilidh, what's wrong?"

I spin toward her, and inhale sharply. "No."

Her eyes are glowing red. "Eilidh." She sounds so *normal*. My skin crawls. "Everything's okay! Let us show you."

My stomach churns. This may look and sound like Kianga, but her personality is all wrong. "What —"

Cyclones catch us all up, and in the next moment, I crash to a cool tiled floor. I sit up gingerly, clutching my head, and look around.

Now this *is a fucking castle.*

The throne room is long and wide. Thick stones make up the entirety of the walls and floor. A long red carpet runs all the way to a dais at the far end of the room.

It looks just as I had always pictured the throne room of the legendary King Arthur would.

On top of the dais, up three large steps, sits an ornate golden throne.

My father sits upon it, staring back at me evenly. His gold and red gaze fills me with dread.

"Come on!" Kianga says cheerily as she pulls me to my feet. We walk past at least a dozen suits of armor as I gaze around the long room. Moonlight beams in through the windows, just barely outshone by the light from torches along the wall.

Tapestries hang on the walls between each of the windows. Golden bears and dragons dance on red backgrounds, snarling at unseen enemies.

My father spreads his arms wide as we approach. "Welcome to Castle Camelot, Eilidh."

I frown. *No wonder they never found it.* "How?" I breathe.

He smirks. "I brought my castle with me when I built Tenazeryth. I couldn't just leave it behind on Earth. I just tucked it into my chambers at Arkenvale."

I narrow my eyes at him. "So you've finally decided to tell the truth?"

He shrugs. "I assume my wife revealed all my secrets anyway."

I purse my lips and continue to walk alongside Kianga. When we're about halfway to my father, she halts silently. He raises one hand, and I tense.

"Relax," he says. I bite my cheek to stifle a retort. He waves a palm, and a small cyclone appears in front of him, depositing Diego on the floor in its wake. He isn't being controlled, though; he's chained to the ground. He takes one look at me and hangs his head.

I glare at my father. "Let them go. I'm the one you want."

He rolls his eyes. "How very noble of you. But you know I can't do that." He grabs his chalice - the Grail - from the thick armrest of the throne and takes a long swig of wine.

I raise my chin at him. "If you let them go, I'll do whatever you want."

He sets the Grail down with a *clunk*. "Don't insult my intelligence, girl. We both know you're lying. If I send them away, you'll just get yourself killed trying to stop me. No, I think I'll keep them close, and keep you compliant."

We stare at one another for a long moment. "Why are you doing this?" I finally ask.

He raises a brow at me. "You know why," he replies. "To save the world."

I scoff. "Do you honestly believe that you're the hero of this story? You want to wipe out half of humanity and subjugate the rest!"

He shrugs, completely unbothered. "Of course I'm the hero of this story. What hero is more legendary than I?"

"Robin Hood," I spit.

He doesn't indulge me. "If humanity continues on as it has, unchecked and unrestrained, they'll kill themselves soon anyway, and Tenazeryth with them. Think about it."

He stands and takes a step down the dais. "If I can make Earth *half* as sustainable as Tenazeryth, I save not only the remaining humans, but also every life here. Isn't that worth it?"

I grind my teeth together. "No," I bite out.

He smirks. "You know that isn't true." He takes another step down.

"What are you going to do?" I sneer. "How exactly are you going to *save* the world?"

He snorts. "I'm not going to monologue and give you a chance to squirm your way out of this, Daughter. You're either with me or against me, so make your choice. I would *like* to have you by my side. I would *like* to see you leading with me."

He glances at my stomach, and I cross my arms in disgust. "I would *like* for you to carry on the Pendragon bloodline. For so long I was content being the last. But, truth be told, I have grown lonely." His tone softens. "You've shown me what it's truly like to have a family."

I try to keep my mouth shut as fury chills my stomach, I really do. I do not succeed.

"You kept Morgana caged by your side for five hundred years. You had plenty of flings. How could you have been *lonely*?" I ask, scornfully.

He chuckles. "Having my physical needs met is not the same thing as having a familial bond." He raises a brow at me. "You know that well, I hear. From Diego's research on you, you take after me more than you ever knew."

I flush. "I am *nothing* like you."

His grin grows wider. "Keep telling yourself that, my dear. But you're certainly not like your mother. She hadn't changed at all in over thirty years."

My heart drops into my stomach. "When did you see my mother?"

He taps a finger to his mouth, as if he actually has to think about it. "Early last year, actually. Shortly after Diego found her for me."

I gape at Diego, whose head snaps up as he looks at my father in utter confusion. "I did no such thing," he rasps.

Arthur chuckles. "Oh, but you did. Don't you remember, my boy? The woman I had you track down while you were on your leave last winter?"

Diego's eyes widen in horror, but then he shakes his head. "No, that wasn't her. Her last name wasn't Shaw."

My lip quivers. "Hayden," I whisper.

Diego turns green.

I drop to my knees.

Kianga giggles at my side. "Remember when you found out she had gotten married, Eilidh? How upset you were?" She sounds far too excited at the memory. Her glowing red eyes don't blink.

I curl in on myself as the memory hits me like a truck. It's not a day I will ever be able to forget. Not for the rest of my immortal days.

"Remember how she just wrote it in a card for you like she was chatting about the weather?" She cackles, deranged. "'By the way, wanted to let you know I got married last year. His name is Max Hayden. Happy twentieth birthday!'"

I press my hands to my ears, but I can't block out her laughter.

Ancient Blood

Diego's eyes are filled with tears as he shakes his head. "I'm so sorry, Eilidh."

I hang my head for several long moments. "What did you do to her?" I hiss.

"Nothing she didn't deserve," Arthur growls cruelly.

I glare up at him from under my eyelashes, but he isn't looking at me. His gaze is unfocused, and he's staring far above my head. "I was just tying up some lose ends. I really *had* thought that she had terminated the pregnancy, you know. But it's always best to confirm in person."

Bile rises in my throat.

"And then, as soon as I asked her about you, she told me everything. How *powerful* you were. She didn't even try to lie to protect you, as other women have in the past when I've had to iron out a wrinkle." His grin widens sadistically. "No, Amelia Shaw was many things, but brave was certainly not one."

I realize that tears are flowing down my cheeks. "Did you kill her?" I whisper. His gold and red gaze snaps back to me. The way the jasper moves like an eyeball makes my stomach roil.

"She had been working on killing herself for thirty years. I merely put an end to her suffering."

Diego thrashes uselessly against his chains. "Eilidh, I'm sorry! I swear, I didn't know!"

I don't look at him.

I stand slowly, drawing myself up to my full height. Arthur watches me with mild curiosity. I take a deep breath and reach for Excalibur's hilt, but my hand passes through air. "Where is my sword?" I ask calmly.

His demeanor changes in a flash. "*Your* sword?" He roars. I don't flinch. "You *stole* Excalibur from me! It is *mine*! I *earned* it." His face is twisted with rage as he flings his cloak to the side, and I see Excalibur strapped to his hip, still in my scabbard.

I smirk at him. "Sure, more than a thousand years ago maybe, but even that hunk of metal knows you aren't worthy anymore. That's why it called to *me*."

His eyes narrow dangerously. "Watch your tongue, girl."

I snort and hold my palms out at him in mock placation. "Sorry, didn't realize you were so possessive over your toys."

He sneers, then looks at Kianga and flicks his wrist as if he's shooing away a bug. She's blasted with a huge ball of Merlin's magic, which flings her sideways, and she crashes into a suit of armor.

"No!" I yell over the din. I lower my left hand slowly, which I had flung toward her at the same moment my father had shot her with his spell.

I hope with all my heart that he didn't see my magic fly toward her at the same time as his. I have no idea what I had done to free Morgana from his spell, but I know what I was feeling at the time. It's the same thing I'm feeling now. *Make it stop.*

I just hope it worked.

He sneers. "I am not the only one who is possessive over my *toys*, am I?"

Kianga crawls away from the armor, closer toward the dais, and collapses. I don't look at her again. I turn and walk idly to the opposite side of the room, and his gaze follows me.

If I draw too much attention to her, he'll notice that as she rises to her elbows, she's inching closer and closer toward the dais.

Diego glances at her once from the corner of his eye, then looks only at me.

I clear my throat. "So what's the plan? I drink from the Grail to make myself impervious to injury and rule by your side forever? While you keep the people I love under your boot?"

He puts his arms behind his back and shakes his head amusedly. "If you both prove yourselves loyal, then he will be perfectly free. I don't care what you do with him, as long as you continue my line with someone who has magic."

I twist my mouth in annoyance despite myself. "*I* have magic," I snip.

He rolls his eyes. "And if you have a child with a Mage, that child will probably inherit *both* your abilities."

I clamp my mouth shut and shake myself. *It doesn't matter. Focus, Shaw.*

"So I drink from the Grail and become indestructible," I press.

He scoffs. "That's not what the Grail does. It keeps me alive. Merlin's magic makes me indestructible. I will show you how to do it as well."

Just wanted to confirm, I think smugly. I nod as if considering his offer, as my mind whirls.

Maybe I don't need Morgana to undo the resurrection spell after all. Maybe I don't need her to kill him. I just need the Grail. But how does it *work*?

I swallow. "What about Saif? You said you would bring him back."

Kianga freezes for a moment, but then keeps crawling.

Diego makes an incredulous noise from the ground. "*What?*"

I ignore him. "If you bring him back and I . . . continue your line.

How would you keep him alive for me? Would he drink from the Grail, too?"

My father's mouth twists in disgust. "Absolutely not. The Grail can only keep one person alive at a time. He'd have to drink my blood from it. No, you will just have to make due with whatever time together I decide to grant you."

I blink rapidly. *Drink his blood?* How the hell do I get his blood when he can't be hurt?

Kianga is inching closer and closer to the dais. I can't exactly change shift to speak with her telepathically, but I scream my thoughts at her nonetheless.

Get me the Grail.

Maybe somehow she can sense my thoughts. We may not be connected through our supernatural abilities or magic right now, but we're still connected by our hearts. Just as we have been our whole lives.

Arthur crosses his arms. "Besides, I said *maybe*, if you prove yourself loyal, I would bring him back. But that will be very far in the future. I'm sure you can find another paramour in the meantime."

I bite the inside of my cheeks to prevent myself from gagging. "How would you bring him back?"

His condescending smile returns. "You'll just have to wait and see, my dear." He sneers. "But would you really want him back before your own mother? I could bring *her* back, you know. I could make her stay with you this time."

I lean my head back and look up at the vaulted stone ceiling, a twisted smile forming on my lips. "Why would I choose the woman who abandoned me over the man I love?"

His approving chuckle turns my stomach. "You're just like me, Eilidh. You make me so proud."

He begins to turn back toward Kianga, and I say the first thing that pops into my head out of sheer desperation. "You're right. I am like you."

He halts and raises his eyebrows.

Kianga is still a few feet away from the throne. I spread my arms wide. "I am. Morgana said it over and over, and I denied it every time. But she was right." I inhale shakily. "Because I don't care that she's gone. My mother's been dead to me since I was eight years old."

He grins at me like I'm the best thing he's ever seen. "That's my girl."

I blink back tears.

Finally, Kianga reaches the back of the dais. She stands upright, slinks quietly up to the throne, and grabs the Grail, as silent as a cat. She raises the Grail into the air, waiting for a signal.

I can't help it; my eyes flick to her. Arthur sees this and whirls just as she launches the Grail at me. He snarls as it flies through the air. I jump and catch it as he grips Kianga's shirt and blasts her with magic; she flies toward me and crashes to the ground a few feet away.

Like Daughter

Fear paralyzes me for a full second, but then she rolls and groans, and I rush to her side. She clutches my arm as Arthur suddenly bursts into cruel laughter.

"Give the Grail back, you little fool. Don't make me take it from you. It does you no good unless you have my blood anyway, and you can't make me bleed."

I stare at the Grail in my hand. It's just a simple fucking cup, but the destruction that it has caused is unfathomable. The destruction that it has *yet* to cause will be even worse.

If I can't stop my father, then the world is doomed. *Both* worlds. He'll crush anyone who gets in his way.

Like hell.

But to kill him, someone has to drink his blood from the Grail, and he's completely impervious to injury. How the fuck am I supposed to kill him when I don't have his blood?

All at once, realization hits me.

Could it actually be so simple?

There's only one way to find out. But how to do it? I'm going to need a lot to make sure it works. Only half of it comes from him, after all.

A mad smile creeps across my face. Kianga and Diego are both looking at me, waiting for me to make a move. I have to do this. For them. Grim determination fills me.

My father's patience has run out. "Eilidh!" He barks. "Do as I say! I am your *father*!"

I throw my head back and cackle madly.

"I have waited my *whole life* to hear those words." I shake my head, wiping tears of mirth from my eyes. I smirk at my father as I help Kianga sit up. "You say I need your blood to take the power of the Grail?"

He snarls. "Yes, you idiot! Which you don't have, and cannot get. So hand it back before I take it from you, and make you regret it." He stalks down the steps of the dais menacingly.

I laugh again, and I sound unhinged, even to my own ears. "*I'm* the idiot? Sorry *Dad*, but if I am, it's your fault. After all, I'm just. Like. You."

I grab my dagger from its holster and hold both it and the Grail in my right hand. My father's eye flashes with confusion, and he frowns.

"You say I can't get your blood." I wince as I push the tip of my dagger into the crook of my elbow, in the center of an ivy leaf, and a speck of crimson blooms around it.

Kianga hisses, "Eilidh, no!"

"But I already have it." His face twists in horror and realization, and he sends a blast of magic at me, but I throw up a shield, and it explodes in a useless shower of sparks. We're bound by the same ancient, magical blood after all.

I smile brilliantly at him as a single tear streams down my cheek. "This is for Saif."

I slash viciously at my arm, dragging the point of the dagger from my elbow to my wrist, and hot blood spurts from the gash. The pain is momentarily blinding. I drop the dagger and hold the Grail to the wound.

A moment later, the grail is full, and I hold it out to Kianga.

"Drink," I command. She doesn't hesitate; she puts the cup to her lips and tilts her head back, gulping.

I hope it's enough.

It will have to be enough.

My father screams in fury, but then it cuts off, strangled. I fall to my knees, already lightheaded, and Kianga drops the Grail as she reaches for me. It clatters to the floor, the last drops of blood splashing everywhere. My father is only steps away, but something is wrong with him. His movements are erratic. I watch him dizzily.

Cracks spider wildly across his skin, and a golden glow seeps out of them. As I watch, taking shallow breaths, he begins convulsing, and pieces of his body fall away, shattering on the stone floor like glass.

A mad thought crosses my mind, and I try to laugh, but my energy has fled from my body; it's running out all over the floor.

He looks like a stained glass window.

He looks at me one last time, his one eye wide with terror, but it's no longer gold.

It's a blazing emerald green.

All at once, all the pieces of him rip apart from each other and crash to the ground. The pile of glass shards that was once my father glows golden, and then it's gone. Excalibur clatters to the ground, as does Merlin's jasper gemstone. The golden light swirls across the ground and circles Kianga.

"What —"

The light races up over her, setting her aglow. It seeps into her skin, and she clutches her temples, groaning.

Diego scrambles toward us; his chains had dissolved when my father did. He crashes to the ground beside us as she opens her eyes again with a gasp. Her brown irises have turned golden; Kianga

Nabil now holds the power of the Holy Grail.

I giggle weakly, and they both look at me like I've gone mad. "You're immortal now," I breathe. "You're a goddess." I slump to the ground.

How nice. The thought brings me peace. She and Diego will be together forever, just as they should be.

Diego rolls me flat on my back against the stone floor, and the hot, sticky blood from my arm quickly pools around me, soaking into my clothes and hair.

My healing factor won't kick in for a few minutes. By then it will be too late. But that's okay.

They both hover over me, and I reach up the hand on my non-ravaged arm. They each grab it, and I smile faintly as my eyes flutter shut.

"I love you," I whisper. *Utterly. Irrevocably.*

I see Saif when I close my eyes, and he reaches out for me. "I've got you, my love."

Eternally.

The four of us have our hands clasped together as I die.

Sunset (Diego)

There's *so much* blood. It looks like she's swimming in it. It fills my nostrils and the scent of her intoxicates me, just like it always has, ever since that night in the clearing, when she took one look at me and ran. But I can't lose myself in it right now.

"No no no *mi alma* please!"

Her eyes flutter shut, and she smiles faintly. "There you are," she whispers, her lips barely moving, before she goes still.

I drag her into my arms.

I don't know what to do. Imane rips off her gold tunic and wraps it around Eilidh's bleeding arm, pulling it as tightly as she can. It's soaked in seconds. Her golden eyes are filled with tears.

My head is reeling with the scent of Eilidh's magical blood.

I kiss her desperately, over and over. That works in all the stories, doesn't it?

But I'm no Prince Charming.

She's completely limp. She looks like a broken doll in my arms. I bite her neck, hoping the venom will shock her system, will slow her bleeding, will do *something*. The blood from her neck covers my lips.

Nothing happens.

I twist my hands into her soaked waves. I've always loved the color of her hair; it has always reminded me of a sunset. But now that red is much darker, and sticky, and it's seeping under my nails. I move my fingers to her neck, looking desperately for a pulse. There isn't one.

"Imane!"

Dawn (Kianga)

We're losing her.

I just got her back, and I'm losing her.

I can't do this again. I won't.

"No no no *mi alma* please!" In all the time I knew Diego, in all the time I've gotten to re-know him since he came back to me, I have never heard him sound as broken as he does now. He's holding Eilidh's limp form like she's a life preserver keeping him afloat in a hurricane.

She whispers something that I can't make out. I want to curl up in a ball and never get up again.

But I have to do something.

I rip my tunic over my head and wrap it around her arm. *Eilidh, you bitch, why did you have to cut so* deep? I tie the tunic as tightly as I can.

It had been effective. And sure, she had saved the world. Had saved *two*, in fact. But had she stopped to think for one second about *my* world? About what losing her would do to me? I already lost Saif. I can't lose her too.

I refuse.

I'll fight Death itself if I fucking have to.

Diego kisses her frantically like he thinks she's under an evil queen's sleeping spell. When nothing happens, he bites her, his fangs sinking into her flesh. She doesn't move. The only thing he's managing to do is smear her blood all over himself.

As he takes her pulse, I reach for the Grail and spin it around in my hand, as if directions for use will be stamped somewhere on it.

"Imane!"

In my entire life, I have always known what to do, what steps to take next to get what I wanted. The first time I hadn't was when Arthur had Diego kneeling at his feet earlier tonight, forcing Eilidh to choose between him and the world.

The second time is right now.

Diego is muttering in Spanish to Eilidh, his forehead pressed against hers, his eyes clamped shut. Her arms hang like she's a marionette whose strings have been cut. She is paler than she usually is — deathly pale.

I look around frantically. There has to be an answer, something to use to save her. The first rays of dawn are just beginning to beam through the windows. Something red glints nearby, where Arthur had stood as he had shattered, lying on the floor next to Excalibur. I crawl toward it and snatch it up, only faintly registering what it is before it's in my hand.

Merlin's jasper gemstone. *Of course.* I let out a sob, and Diego turns to me, tears streaming down his cheeks.

I scramble back to Diego and Eilidh's body. *Now what?* I have no idea.

I show him the stone. "How do we work this thing?" I ask desperately.

His breath catches. "I don't know. But put your hand on her arm," he says, suddenly frantic. I rip the shirt off her arm - it's soaked through anyway - and press the stone against her tattered skin. The ivy has been shredded. My stomach churns at the sight, but I hold steady.

"Now what, Diego?"

He leaves one arm wrapped around Eilidh's shoulders, puts his free hand over mine, and we push the stone against her wound together.

"What do you want more than anything else in the world right now?" His crimson eyes are glistening.

I let out another sob and lean my forehead against his.

"I want her back." I look at the stone in my hand. *Please.*

A tiny vibration buzzes to life in my navel. I can see from Diego's widened eyes that he feels it in himself too. The vibration travels up from my center and shoots down my arm. Pools of reddish-brown light form around our overlapping hands and shoot into Eilidh's arm.

As I watch with a mixture of horror and fascination, her ghostly skin begins to ripple of its own accord, and reaches to itself, stitching itself together. Suddenly, once her skin is back together and no more blood is dripping from her, the light flares up, blinding us momentarily.

Eilidh gasps.

Diego screams her name.

I clutch her tightly, sobbing.

Recovery

It has been six weeks since we defeated Arthur Pendragon.

For the first week, I mostly slept. Though Merlin's jasper had healed my physical wound, my mind still needed time to recover. Morgana had conjured up a second bed in my room and stayed with me, after thoroughly reaming me out for sending her and everyone else away and literally getting myself killed.

"Imprudent! Reckless! Foolhardy!" Her lexicon of insults had been quite impressive. When English was no longer adequate, she had insulted me in Welsh, and even, I think, Latin, though I could only imagine what she was saying to me. Probably more of the same.

When she was done, she had glared at me and crossed her arms. "I'm so proud of you," she had whispered.

Daniela, to her credit, took everything incredibly well. We had all sat at the round table in the east tower while Diego told her everything that he had been through since she had been born. All of his triumphs, and all of his mistakes.

Both lists were long.

She apologized for what she had said on the battlefield. "I thought he would let me go if I made it seem like we aren't close."

Diego had hugged her fiercely, and cried into her silky, chestnut brown hair. "I'm so sorry, *mijita*. You were so brave."

She and Kianga became instant best friends, and Kianga had

promised that we would visit as soon as we could. Then Morgana had sent Daniela back to her college dorm.

During the second week, Morgana and I poured over what felt like every book in Arkenvale, starting with the ones in my father's living quarters. My head pounded every evening from squinting over my father's cramped handwriting all day, and Diego brewed me strong cups of hibiscus tea.

Finally, two weeks exactly after Arthur's demise, we came across a journal that he had written while he was creating Tenazeryth.

In the journal, he detailed the exact spells he used to create the reflection that is Tenazeryth. Morgana scoffed at it over and over, muttering insults. I suppressed my laughter every time.

That night, the two of us stood hand in hand on the cliff side, looking across Nabeyha Lake. Arthur had started at the center when creating the continent; he started with a lake that would provide life to his new world, had made up a name based on *beatha*, the Scottish Gaelic word for life, and then named the closest city after the place where he had died centuries before.

Sentimental in his own twisted way.

We each sent our magic into the water, and anchored the lake, the life force of Tenazeryth, to a brand new dimension.

The third week we spent going around to the major cities in Tenazeryth, doing the same thing. We will need to anchor the entire continent eventually, but we start where the most people have settled.

The fourth week we took to rest once more, and readjust to our new home in Arkenvale.

Morgana razed Arthur's living quarters to the ground, her purple flames blazing, then reassembled new quarters for Diego, Kianga, and myself. She took an empty room along the south wall of the castle.

We decide to leave the rest of Castle Camelot alone for now.

Eventually, we will try to pull it from the pocket dimension, but not just yet.

We've got other things to expend our energy on right now.

The fifth and sixth weeks had been a blur; we would spend our mornings teleporting around the continent to anchor various areas, such as the forests, which were were the most in need of revitalization. Most evenings I spent trying to organize the library, desperate for something menial and familiar to pass the time.

For a few days, I vehemently opposed moving any of Saif's things, but then Kianga won the argument once and for all, and we moved his journals and everything we had left of him into our new quarters.

Now, it's Saif's birthday, and I'm sitting on top of Arkenvale in a tree I had transported up here. I can't grow things from seeds like he could, but I've gotten very good at levitation and object manipulation.

I stare at the sunset, wearing the outfit he had helped me pick out for our day in New Camlann. The only difference is that I have my emerald cloak on now instead of the brown one that still hangs in my wardrobe. I run my fingers over the gold and silver stitching around the hem absently.

Well, technically, it's the day *before* Saif's birthday. But there is no February 29th this year, and he said he celebrated a day early. That's good enough for me.

I read the last few lines of the final entry in his journal for the hundredth time.

She brings out a side of me that I never knew was there. She makes me feel secure. She makes me feel accepted. She feels like . . . home.

I shut the book and focus for a moment, until a small cyclone sends it back to my desk. That word echoes through my head over and over until it blends with itself and swirls into a meaningless hum.

Home.

The others are giving me my space, against their better judgment, but I had insisted that I was okay. Kianga had given me a long golden look before she and Diego went back inside, but now, finally, I am alone.

Once the sun goes down, and everyone is asleep, I'm leaving.

I am going home.

In our search for answers on how to anchor Tenazeryth in its own dimension, I had come across another journal of my father's, which I had promptly hidden from Morgana.

In it, he recounts how he transported many things from his past to his new world, just like Castle Camelot.

Nabeyha Lake, it turns out, is more than just the lake he started with when he created his own world; he had transported it to Tenazeryth from Earth. It's *the* lake. The Enchantress' Lake.

But the Lady hadn't given him a sword like many of the legends say; Excalibur had indeed been pulled from a magical stone, back when my father had been worthy.

No, she had given him a dagger. A dagger with dragons on the hilt, in honor of his name. The dagger's hilt held water with the gift of life inside it, for those who knew how to unlock its true power. Luckily, my father detailed exactly how.

All I have to do is undo the curse he made Morgana put on it; she had, under his control, wrapped the hilt in layers of twisted magic to preserve it, and curse anyone but a Pendragon if they tried to open it. Once I undo them, and say the Welsh phrase he wrote in the diary, the hilt will open, and water from the lake will stream from it. There is enough magic contained in the hilt to power exactly one life.

I don't know why he never used it to bring Guinevere back; that is one thing he doesn't recount in his diaries. Maybe he was afraid she still wouldn't love him enough. Maybe he was afraid that she wouldn't love him at *all* after seeing what he had become.

But I already know Saif loved me.

Agrona is strapped tightly to my right thigh. I have Excalibur - glamoured, so as not to call attention to it - on my left hip. I will use it to enhance my power, and make myself strong enough to do what I need to.

I don't need Morgana to bring Saif back, just like I didn't need her to defeat Arthur.

I just need my blades.

Finally - *finally* - Arkenvale falls silent. I no longer hear the others talking, laughing, and going about their nightly routines.

I take a deep breath, then press my forehead to the bark of the tree. *I'll see you soon, love.* My cyclone catches me up, and I land in a dark field on a small island, far to the west.

I stride purposefully toward Saif's grave, my eyes locked on the boulder.

"Are we really going to have to do this, Eilidh?" A ringing alto voice asks from behind me.

Fuck. I turn and look into Morgana's eyes as the last of her flames burn out.

We stare at one another for two long heartbeats.

Then I shoot a blast of magic at her, just to hold her until I'm done. *Freeze.*

Metamorphosis

Morgana blocks my blast easily, and her eyes begin to glow. Her power radiates over me, trying to stop me in my tracks.

"You can't win, girl. I won't let you. I told you, I will die before I watch you repeat my sins. You *cannot* do this."

"Just *listen* to me!" I bellow as I fling her spell back at her. She screams in rage as she deflects it.

"Saif is *not* my father! I am not *you*, Morgana!" I try to snare her ankles with a crackling spell, but she throws up a force field of flame at the last second, and my spell ricochets away.

"You're right!" She spits as she sends a ball of flame at me, which I catch and fire up into the air. "At least *I* had the excuse of ignorance. Your mistake will be *much* worse."

"He is not a *mistake!*" My scream echoes across the open field, and reverberates against the walls of Tal Basta. My vision turns red, and fury chills my blood.

"The only way you'll get me to help you raise him is if you control me just as your father did." Morgana's magic arches up into the sky, and forms a smoky purple dragon, which dives at me.

I glare at it as it barrels toward me, too furious to be impressed. *Fuck this.*

"I don't need your help anymore!" I reach out to snag the dragon's heart, even though I know it doesn't technically *have* a heart; it's just magic, twisted into a zoomorphic shape.

But by reaching toward what I picture as its heart, I snare its essence. Whatever gives it power and form is suddenly ripped free of the creature, and I'm holding it in my mind's eye. I sink my magic's claws into it. The dragon's eyes glow red.

Got you.

I open my arms wide as the dragon hits me with the force of a meteorite, and magic explodes around me. A buzzing begins in my navel, which turns to a sizzle, and then, to a roaring inferno. As the fire burns through my veins, my vision pulses back and forth from rust to purple, then finally, as I collapse to the ground, the world goes magenta.

I breathe deeply against the dead grass for a moment, catching my breath. At least, I begin to. But by the time I take my second breath, I realize that I am not winded at all. In fact, I feel more power rippling through my mind and body than I've ever felt before. More power than I've ever *imagined*.

I stand easily, and hold up my hands. They look normal.

I pinch my thumbs and pointer fingers together. *Testing, testing.*

Morgana, who has been frozen since the dragon hit me, suddenly moves toward me. "No!"

I snap my fingers.

A magenta bonfire explodes around me. My ears begin ringing violently, but the painful thrumming on my eardrums fills me with euphoria.

Everything within ten feet of me sizzles. The flames begin consuming the brown grass like a ravenous monster.

I watch with morbid curiosity, the way one watches a spider twirling a fly in its web. If the fire keeps going, the entire sky will be lit up with a reddish-purple hue as the world burns down.

How beautiful that will be.

Morgana waves her hands desperately at the flames. Her magic ricochets off them harmlessly.

I stare at the spreading fire, and I'm hit with a wave of emotion. For a split second, I think it's regret. It *should* be regret, right?

It isn't.

It's excitement.

A smile spreads slowly across my face as power ripples through me. I'm *invincible.*

Morgana turns to me, her eyes wide with something I have never seen on her face before. Fear. She's *terrified* of me.

I begin cackling madly. I just absorbed the magic of one of the most powerful Witches in history, and melded it with my own. She can't stop me now.

No one can stop me.

I can do anything. I can fix it *all.*

I turn toward Saif's grave and read the epitaph Diego had scratched into the boulder, bleeding profusely as he did so, and I scoff derisively.

A good man.

He was the *best* man.

He *is* the best man. He still can be.

I can fix him.

I raise my left hand toward the boulder just as Morgana throws herself into me.

Or, rather, she tries to.

She hits a barrier a centimeter away from my skin, and a ripple of the magenta force field follows her to the ground as she lands in a heap.

I look down at her calmly. She glares up at me, her lilac irises still bright with fear, but her face is set in determination. I raise an eyebrow at her.

"I'm not going to hurt you, you know." My voice echoes with layers of tenor and soprano. "I never wanted to hurt you. I just want him back." I turn back toward the boulder.

"And then what?" She spits.

I halt. "And then I have him again, obviously."

"You won't." She shakes her head as she stands, trembling.

I twist my mouth in annoyance. "I told you, he isn't like my fa—"

"You're right." She throws her hands up. "Is that what you want to hear? You're *right*. He wasn't like your father. He was a great man. Maybe even a *good* man. He wasn't a monster hellbent on burning the world down just to get what he wanted."

She raises her chin at me, as if she's preparing for her next words to be her last. "*You* are that monster, Eilidh. You're *literally* burning everything down. You're being a selfish *child*." She gestures behind us, where the magenta flames are rapidly spreading over the field.

My eye twitches.

She flinches, but doesn't move. "Do you think he's going to want to be with you once he sees what you've done? What you've *become*?" She looks me up and down, disgusted.

"I haven't *done* anything wrong!" I say petulantly. "And what I've *become*, is powerful!" I snarl. My left arm trembles slightly; the vines seem to come to life for a moment, undulating like the black tendrils around Morgana's fingertips.

"Did he love you for your power?" She asks quietly.

Tears spring to my eyes. "He loved my strength," I hiss.

She gazes at me sadly. "That's not the same thing."

I look away. I have no interest in her pity. I'm too angry for her pity. "And maybe I *am* being a child. But so what? It's about time, since I never got to *be* a child! I've had everything and everyone I loved ripped away from me over and over. I am done letting the Universe give me happiness just to tear me apart when it takes it away. I finally have the chance to take something *back*. Why shouldn't I?"

She closes her eyes and shakes her head softly.

I continue. "And *selfish*? What would be selfish would be marching to that cemetery and bringing my grandparents back, too. What would be selfish would be finding that trucker, and burning him alive, or taking his family from him, like he did to me. What would be *selfish* would be ripping a hole in time, and going back to force my mother to *stay*. To *care*."

The tears escape my eyes and flow down my cheeks. "I *could* be selfish, Morgana. I could make her love me with this power. I could fix all her mistakes. I could make her be a mom. I could *give myself* a mom."

Morgana opens her eyes again. They are full of tears as well.

My voice breaks and trembles just like my outstretched arm. "Because I *never* had one. Because *she* was selfish," I sob.

Morgana raises a hand slowly, and places it on my outstretched arm, her fingers resting gently on the ivy. She doesn't hit a barrier this time.

I'm trembling like mad; I'm too full of pain and anger. It's going to rip me apart from the inside. I'm going to explode like a supernova.

"Your life has not been easy, and it has certainly not been fair. I know you never had a mother, Eilidh, and I'm so sorry."

She reaches her other hand up to my face, wipes my tears, and cups my cheek. Her voice is steady. "But you have one now."

I shatter.

My knees hit the ground with a hard thud, and my energy seeps down into it. Morgana lowers herself to the ground gently, and wraps her arms around me. I sob into her chest, and she rocks me back and forth.

"I miss him so much," I gasp.

"I know, Little One. I know. You're allowed to. Some things just can't be fixed; they just have to hurt for awhile. But I'm here. I'll always be here." She plants a kiss into my hair, and I clutch her dress.

"I'm sorry. I'm so sorry," I sob into her.

"I know," she says again. "You're still growing. We both are. But now we can grow together."

The flames spreading across the field die as my energy escapes me, leaving behind acres of white ash, like a field of freshly fallen snow.

Dreams Part 4

Emerald flames consume me.

The inferno roars through my blood, causing chemical reactions, and rearranging my cells; I undergo a total metamorphosis.

She creates a new universe each time she touches my skin.

With every brush of her hand, she remakes me.

I am born anew in her flames.

Born Anew

We gather at Saif's grave on the day of the winter solstice. It's been exactly one year since we lost him, nearly to the hour. I lift my face to the sky, and a flake alights upon my nose. I smile.

Hello, love.

The last ten months have been a blur; we've all been working to restore balance to Tenazeryth. Together, Morgana and I have worked to sever its ties to Earth, and anchor it more firmly in its own new dimension, but it's been slow and draining work.

A pleasant side effect, though, has been the weather. With each square mile we tie off from the tenuous hold on Earth and anchor to this new dimension, the weather has begun to cycle. A few months ago, Tenazeryth saw the changing of leaves for the first time in its history.

"Do you ever find it ironic that we're literally instigating climate change?" I ask Morgana as we stand under an awning and watch rain fall not more than a few minutes after we had secured the area. A giggle escapes me as the thunder rolls above us.

She rolls her eyes, but her mouth is turned up at one corner.

While she and I have been busy with this, the rest of the Order, and the remnants of Kianga's army, have taken to helping citizens acclimate to their changing world. With weather that has never been experienced before, and the very land springing back to life, growing pains are popping up everywhere.

Kianga and Diego have been organizing the building of dams and dikes for rivers that have begun to flood, as well as the distribution of food and supplies for Fabled, Shifters, and Mages alike who are trying to find new lives after the war. They've also been handling every other squabble that comes up while running a nation.

There have been several hiccups. My father had been loved far and wide, after all. The Lords have been working with us to convince the masses of his evil deeds, but not everyone seems to care what he did. To them, Auberon Danodraic had been usurped by his power-hungry bastard daughter. It will be some time before we have the majority of the country on our side, but we'll get there eventually.

Not to mention, Kianga has been in meetings with Balin more and more frequently, which are apparently not going well. Yesterday, she had come home in a particularly foul mood, and asked me to go with her to the next one, which will be held after the New Year.

I don't know what Balin would want to see me for, but I agreed anyway. I'll be by her side for whatever is to come. And since I could see that she was still too tense, I crawled under her desk and distracted her for a bit. It's a lot, being a queen and a goddess, and I was more than happy to help her relieve some stress.

As the flurries whirl around us like a snow globe, we all take turns telling Saif about what we've been up to. Martín gets a bit too detailed when he describes his new boyfriend, and Val throws a snowball at him.

Hyun-Joo lets Saif know that Morgana and I have commandeered his solarium, and that I have managed to not kill everything in it. She doesn't tell him, though, that I am *absolutely* cheating, and using my upgraded magic much of the time. Except for on the fig tree. I'm learning how to care for that the old-fashioned way.

He was right, though. The food just isn't the same.

Diego tells Saif about how Daniela is doing at college; she's now halfway through her sophomore year, and she's top of her class. She's also captain of the soccer team; she's a natural leader, just like her dad.

She's going to be a botanist. "She would have loved to meet you." Diego's voice breaks, and Kianga holds him close.

When we had visited Diego's family over the summer, Daniela had told me all about how she wants to solve world hunger by engineering food plants to be resistant to extreme temperatures, common diseases, and drought. Much of it had gone over my head, but she seemed to know what she was talking about. She's got a mind for science, just like her mom.

Her other favorite topic of conversation during that visit had been that she desperately wants to be a big sister, since Estelle and Daniel had never had any biological kids of their own.

Diego had blushed as red as his eyes when she mentioned it the first time. I collapsed in a fit of laughter against Kianga, who reassured Daniela that she would try her best. Diego left the room after that, and went to cook a full three-course meal in the kitchen.

Last week, on one of our rare free days, Kianga and I were doing some shopping when she suddenly had to run into the closest bathroom and vomit. After some quick math, we rushed to an apothecary, and then, a couple minutes later, kissed and cried happy tears together when they told us the results of the test.

She's got the tiniest pair of shoes I've ever seen in a gift-wrapped box that she's giving to Diego tonight when we get back to Arkenvale.

What she doesn't know is that he's got a surprise gift for her, too. He and I spent all our spare time during the summer and fall designing it, and Zaehora had worked on it for weeks to get the placement of the gemstones just right.

It turns out that when there's no war going on that requires her to forge weapons, the succubus loves creating jewelry and accessories of all kinds, and she's damn good at it. She had even mentioned - with a mischievous twinkle in her eye - that she could make me a collar for Diego.

I'm considering taking her up on the offer.

Diego and I had discussed our future at length the night he told me he wanted to ask Kianga to marry him. I had reassured him, both before and after our kisses had grown intense, and we took some time to be selfish, that I was okay with it, and that I wasn't ready to take that step myself just yet. They will enjoy a few years together as newlyweds - and parents - before I might be.

I feel a headache brewing, and put a hand to my temple. They've been plaguing me more and more lately. My healing factor doesn't seem to be doing me much good, but the headaches are more of a nuisance than anything. I'm sure they'll get better once I have some down time. Whenever that will be.

Morgana rubs my back a few times through my cloak, her hand bumping lightly over the stitching of the sun and moon.

When we've all finished our stories for Saif, the Peñas and Hyun-Joo head into Tal Basta to help where they can in the kitchen before we head home. It's late afternoon, and dinner is being prepared.

Tal Basta has transformed from the epicenter of a rebellion to a shelter for all manner of lost beings. The feast that the Council - now led by Mòrag - is making is supposedly big enough to feed a dozen wyverns.

After the four of us are alone, Kianga and Diego stand together on one side of the grave. She leans her head on Diego's shoulder and sniffles. He rubs his hand up and down her other side. "I know, *cariño*. I miss him, too."

I stand on the opposite side of the grave next to Morgana. She puts a hand on my shoulder, and pulls something large out from under her cloak. It's a gift-wrapped box. She must have magicked it small to hide it on her person.

"What's this?" I ask, a small smile on my lips.

She bites her lip nervously, which throws me off. She's *never* nervous. I look down at the box warily. *Is this thing going to bite me?* "Mom, what —"

"Just open it!" She puts her hands over her mouth and bounces on her toes. I look over at Diego and Kianga to see if they had anything to do with this, but their ruby and golden gazes are blank; they look as clueless as I feel.

I shake the box; it's got a familiar weight to it. I rip at the paper, which I set aflame in one hand, then pull the lid off the box.

It's a huge book, and it looks brand new. I run my hand over the gorgeous embossed cover. Finally, I take in the title.

A Comprehensive Guide to Magical Beings.

"What in the world?" I breathe.

"There are actually a few books," she says quickly beside me. "This is just the first one in the set. There's a lot more information in this than in that tripe your father wrote. And this time, it's accurate."

I gape at her. "How did you do this?"

"I've been spending all my free time in the library, going through a thousand years of documents," she says. "And I've been interviewing The Fabled." She taps the book. "Ousmane helped."

"Wow, keep busy for once, why don't you?" I chuckle.

"Look at the bookmarked page." She's practically vibrating with excitement.

"Okay, okay, don't spontaneously combust." I find the page with a beautiful black satin bookmark. I flip the book open, and gasp.

The page is dedicated to dragons. The picture to the left is a gorgeous and incredibly lifelike drawing depicting a sky blue dragon with gleaming scales.

"Read it," she breathes.

I glance at her, and read aloud so Diego and Kianga can hear as well.

"Dragons, long thought to be extinct, were rediscovered after the fall of Arthur Pendragon." I look up at her, alarmed.

She's got both her fists clenched, and is on her tiptoes so she can see the page that I'm holding close to my face.

"A colony was discovered deep in the Marchog Du Mountains just months after Pendragon's fall, leading to the knowledge found in this guide."

My heart is pounding against my ribs. Kianga and Diego have both walked around to lean over my shoulder and read the page as well. I scan further down.

Unlike their Fabled cousin the wyvern, dragons are Shifters, like werecats, vampires, and werewolves. In contrast to many other Shifters, who can only increase their numbers through a bite, dragons are also able to reproduce through conventional means. Any resulting offspring will also be a dragon.

I gasp. "Your parents?"

She nods. "Were Shifters. Uther took me when he found out. Then he had them killed."

I look at her sadly for another moment, then turn back to the page.

While the venom of a dragon's bite will indeed turn a victim, it is not an immediate process, such as for vampires, or even a short one, such as for werewolves, which only lasts two weeks. Due to the intensity of the transformation, the body must undergo a long and total change before it can be turned.

A dragon's metamorphosis takes precisely one year, down to the hour. Once the dragon rises from its slumber, it will, for all intents and purposes, be immortal, just as vampires and werewolves are known to be.

I read the final paragraph over and over again.

"Metamorphosis," I rasp. I look up at the Witch. Tears are streaming down her cheeks in earnest.

Kianga sways, and Diego catches her. "*Tesoro,* are you okay? Have you eaten today?"

I hear him as if from underwater. I fall to my knees, clutching the book to my chest. "One year?" I whisper, looking up at my mother from the snow.

She drops to her knees in front of me, and cups my cheeks. "To the hour, Little One. To the hour."

The earth rumbles below us. I stop breathing, and my vision flashes magenta with an aching pulse in my temples. There is utter stillness for four heartbeats.

And then something huge explodes out of the ground in front of us. The boulder flies backward, and I instinctively put up a magenta barrier between my family and the flying dirt and snow.

We all look up into the sky just as something huge drops to the ground, shaking the earth.

It's an enormous dragon; bigger than my mother's dragon form by far. Its pearly scales are so brilliantly bright that it looks like a living star. I stare at it, unmoving, just willing the light to burn into my retinas forever.

The dragon's gleaming black eyes land on me, then it tosses its head back, and brilliant emerald flames erupt from its mouth, streaming high into the sky.

I continue staring as I hand the book to my mother and stand. My family stays crouched on the ground behind me as I walk toward the dragon. My boots crunch in the snow with each steady step.

The dragon's flames stop, and it brings its head back down. I reach up and put a hand on its nose, and then its cheek. Its scales are as sharp as knives, but I don't even register the magenta blood that runs down my palm.

The dragon breathes out heavily, its breath swirling my cloak, then disappears.

And then he stands in front of me, my bloody hand on his cheek, soaking his velvety beard. He presses his forehead to mine, and his warm brown eyes fill my vision. He wraps his arms around my waist, and I wrap mine around the back of his neck.

I refuse to blink, just in case he disappears. In case this is all a dream. If it is, I never want to wake up.

He lets out a warm, booming laugh that quickly turns into a sob. *"Lahabi."*

Translation Table

Chapter	Original Text	English Translation
Civilization	Habibti	My dear
Trial	Lobita	Little Wolf
Impossible	Habibi	My dear
	Qamar	Moon
Lost Treasure	Lahabi	My flame
Immense Power	Querido	Darling
	Dhabiha	Offering/Sacrifice
Reconciliation	Querida	Darling
Drinking	Mil gracias	Thank you very much
	Et tu	And you?
	Cariño	Dear/sweetheart
	Si, amor?	Yes, love?
	Tu es muy caliente	You are very hot
Dreaming	Hayati	My life
Invisible Connections	Corazón	Heart
	Pendejo	Asshole/Idiot
Worship	Tesoro	Treasure
Into the Woods	Coño	Fuck
	Obstinada	Stubborn

Chapter	Original Text	English Translation
Homecoming	Vamos	Come on
Useful (Kianga)	Ya rab	Oh, Lord
	Rohi	My soulmate
	Albi	My heart
	Ana uhibbuki	I love you
Succession (Diego)	Mi diosa	My goddess
Hidden Talents	Exquisito	Exquisite
Selfish	Mi sol	My sun
	Impaciente	Impatient
Old Friend	Jeogiyo?	Excuse me?
	Mi vida	My life
Regroup	Thalla 's cagainn bruis	(Expression) Go and chew a brush
	Falbh dàirich fhèin	Go fuck yourself
	Seanair	Grandfather
	Tha cianalas orm	I have a deep homesickness
Crush (Diego)	¿Tu me entiendes?	You understand me?
	¿Qué carajo?	What the fuck?
Exchange	¡Cállate!	Shut up!
Sunset (Diego)	Mi alma	My soul

Acknowledgments

To the Universe. A worthy adversary if there ever was one.

To my characters. Thank you for letting me tell your stories. Don't worry — we aren't done yet.

And to you, dear readers. May you always know that you are enough.

About the Author

Maria J. Hart was born and grew up in Pennsylvania, but she was raised in hundreds of different fantastical worlds that she found through books, movies, and video games. She is the author of The Blood of Tenazeryth, a collection of paranormal romance duologies and related works. She still resides in Pennsylvania, but now works in fantastical worlds of her own creation. Her hobbies include collecting books and comics (she sometimes even reads them), bothering her political representatives to be better humans (they are not generally receptive), and attempting to befriend the squirrels in her backyard (who are marginally more receptive than the politicians).

You can connect with me on:

- https://linktr.ee/MariaJHart
- https://x.com/mariajhart
- https://www.facebook.com/profile.php?id=61561681965678
- https://bsky.app/profile/mariajhart.bsky.social

Subscribe to my newsletter:

- https://substack.com/@mariajhart

Also by Maria J. Hart

BORN ANEW IN BLOOD

Eilidh is a loner who is perfectly happy to spend her days curled up with a good book rather than another human. That is, until one day when an otherworldly stranger asks her out on a date, and she ends up tied to a stone slab as a sacrifice to a fairy tale monster. After a botched rescue leaves her mutilated and cursed, she has to learn how to adjust to her magical new home, her new abilities, and the Mages who take her in.